Memoirs of an
Accidental Hustler

Memoirs of an Accidental Hustler

J. M. Benjamin

URBAN
BOOKS

www.urbanbooks.net

Urban Books, LLC
300 Farmingdale Road, NY-Route 109
Farmingdale, NY 11735

Memoirs of an Accidental Hustler
Copyright © 2017 J. M. Benjamin

ISBN 13: 978-1-62286-694-6
ISBN 10: 1-62286-694-0

First Mass Market Printing June 2018
First Trade Paperback Printing March 2017
Printed in the United States of America

10 9 8 7 6 5 4 3 2 1

*This is a work of fiction. Any references or similarities
to actual events, real people, living or dead, or to real
locales are intended to give the novel a sense of reality. Any similarity in other names, characters, places,
and incidents is entirely coincidental.*

Distributed by Kensington Publishing Corp.
Submit Orders to:
Customer Service
400 Hahn Road
Westminster, MD 21157-4627
Phone: 1-800-733-3000
Fax: 1-800-659-2436

This book is dedicated to all of
those who aspired to be one thing in life but
became another for whatever reason.

To you I say, it's not always about
how you start but often how you finish.

Life is about 90 percent of what happens to you
and
10 percent how you react to it.

Never give up; finish the race and finish strong!

Acknowledgments

As always, I'd like to thank Allah for the strength and endurance He continues to grant me to do what I do. Without His Guidance and Protection, none of this could be possible. Allah Is Akbar (The Greatest)!

To my family, thank you for being patient, understanding, and supportive throughout my career as well as personally. It is you all who keep me grounded and focused on what's most important: Mom, Stacey, Yaseena, Jamillah, Jameel, Bro (As Salaamu Alaikum), Kima, and Sham. I love you all!

To my A New Quality Family: J-Rod Nider, over the years I've watched you grow like a proud Big Bro, but it is still a work in progress. Let's get that "Breaking London" (July 2011) out so your success story can be seen and heard and everybody will stop blaming me for it not being out (Ha!). Nyema, three years later and

Acknowledgments

A New Quality is still standing. You were there to see its birth, became the First Lady, and gave us *Back Stabbers I*. You know what we did with that; now let's take it to another level with *Back Stabbers II* (March 2011). FiFi Cureton, ANQP diva, you believed I could make it happen with "Have You Ever . . . ?" And I did. You showed them what you could do; now prove that you're here to stay with the sequel "Would You Ever . . . Again?" (May 2011). Randy "Ski" Thompson, what can I say, pure talent, my dude. "Ski Mask Way I" was serious but "Ski Mask Way II" was the truth. You got 'em on edge waiting for Part III. Cherie Johnson, you could've gone to any publishing house you wanted with your status and connections and you chose ANQP. I enjoyed working with you and Kat on "Around The World Twice," but your joint "Peaches N Cream" (June 2011) is going to be the one to gain you the recognition you deserve as an author. Kevin "Glorious" Gause, I know it got rough for you along the way but you were patient, my dude, and didn't give up; because of that *The Robbery Report* is available wherever books are sold. We going right back in with "The Robbery Report II" (October 2011). Erica K. Barnes, being the newest member of the family, I'd like to welcome you. They say "three's a charm" so I expect "Allure" (May 2011) to be your best book yet. You all have become and are a part of my family, and a family who grinds together eats together!

A special acknowledgment goes out to Locksie "The Queen of Book Reviews" of ARC Book Club Inc. for her contribution and advice with this story. Her piranha constructive criticism was what I needed to complete this book. To her I say, thanks!

And to all of my book clubs, bookstores, and booksellers, Sugar & Spice (my first book club), Hakeem & Tyson of Black N Noble, Maxwell, all Urban Knowledge, Horizon Books, etc. Without you guys where would I be? Thank you all!

Although I did not use either title, I would like to give a special thanks to all of my Facebook friends who voted on the title for this book. Your support was and is greatly appreciated. Facebook/Jm Benjamin.

Thank you to:

Bernice Dickey, Natasha Hawkins, Imani True, Sekenia Lewis, Sabrina Brooks, Yvette Sparrow, 21st St Urban Pub, Tamikka Simmons, Patrica Barksdale, Theresa Baines, Traci Di, Angela Concepcion-Butler, Tra Curry, Kevin Glorious Gause, Nancy Broughton, Cherie Johnson,

Acknowledgments

Esther Reyes, Kisha Green, Raymond Francis, Jessica Ann Robinson, Alicia Evans, RaJohn Mann, Leah Dudley, Latanya Norris, Tricia Brent, Markesha Nairn, Sharresa Simmons, Anna Black, Sylrenzo Bennett, Charaine Drayton, Ali Abdul-Raheem, Tameka Yolanda Bethea, Love is me Love, Deborah Cardona, Tammy Rosa, Shirley Gordon, Sharon Walker, Ada LocQueen Don Martin, Aaron Bebo, Kim Knight, and Carla Pennington.

Prologue

I can't believe this! I'm back in this hellhole again. Caged like a fuckin' animal; helpless. All alone in this cold and desolate place they call a jail holding cell. I never thought it would turn out like this, that I would turn out like this. I never thought I'd have to feel the tight grip of these metal bracelets around my wrists again, digging into my flesh to the point of nearly cutting through my skin like a razor blade. I never thought I'd be sitting on this silver metal bench, staring at these gray paint-chipped walls, absorbing the toxic smell of stale urine from the urinal or feeling the chill from the coldness of this cell and air conditioning combined ever again.

I never thought these butterflies fluttering in my stomach would ever have to return or that life as I once knew it would be flashing before my eyes again. I never thought I'd be wrapping my hands around these bars and clenching them tightly until my palms begin to sweat profusely, fingers begin to cramp, and knuckles turn white; or that I'd be banging my head in between the six inches that separated them, cursing myself until my head began to pulsate from the pain again.

I never thought I'd have to see the look on my girl's face when they came for me. I never thought my mom would have to get that phone call telling her she had lost another child. Damn! I promised them. What was I thinking? I just never really thought it could happen, never thought about it period.

But then again, that's a lie, because I actually did. I was reminded all the time that it could, but I just kept right on doing me and disregarded the signs. I knew there was a strong possibility! I knew. And I knew better. The signs were right there in front of my damn face, everywhere I looked, but I pretended not to see them and I just ignored them. I knew this shit was lurking around the corner, just waiting for me to turn and run right into it. I knew the clock was ticking and it was just a matter of time before it stopped. I knew time waited for no one and it wasn't on my side. I knew better, because I sat and watched those before me and closest to me run out of time, and I saw what happened to them.

I knew better because it was up, under, and all around me despite my being sheltered from it in the beginning. They tried to warn me, but I didn't listen, and they tried to show me, but I didn't want to learn. Now, because of that, I've lost everything: my family, my freedom and, yes, even my life. And this is how it happened. This is my story.

The Beginning

August 3, 1982. It was Saturday morning and I was extremely happy, because today I got to see my father. It was his birthday. Any normal eight-year-old kid would be overwhelmed by their dad's birthday, but I was more than that because I didn't get to see my dad every day since he didn't live with us anymore. The Bad People had him.

That's what my mom said. The Bad People came to our home in Brooklyn, New York, and took him away from us when I was six. Since then, he'd been with them in New Jersey. I only got to see him on the weekends for a couple of hours, which was not a very long time, especially when I had to split it with my brother, two sisters, and my moms. Even though I didn't like the place my dad lived, I looked forward to taking the trip each weekend to see him. I liked to look out the window at the stores while we rode down Canal Street and see all the different colors of people shopping and walking. I also liked going through the Holland Tunnel because my mom told us it was built underwater; so I imagined us in a special type of submarine car floating to New Jersey.

The place where my dad lived was huge. It was kind of shaped like and looked like the White House where the president lives; but it was light green and brick, and there was a pond in front of it with ducks and geese. A few times, I saw some rabbits hopping around and, on Thanksgiving, I saw wild turkeys walking around. I knew my mother felt the same way I did about where my dad lived because the words, "I hate this place," were mumbled under her breath every time we pulled up.

I could tell my mother missed my dad because she was always crying, kissing, and hugging him the whole time she spent with him, and then when we'd get home she'd cry some more. I missed him too, but I cried when I was in my bed, while it was dark so no one could see me. I knew my brother could hear me, though, because I could hear him too. We shared a room together.

I thought my dad would be disappointed if he knew that my brother and I were crying, because he always told us how we had to be strong, and that we were the men of the house now that he was gone.

My brother Kamal was a year older than I was, but you'd have thought we were twins. Not just because we looked alike only he was darker, but because we acted and thought alike, too; plus, we liked the same things, which was why we did everything together. I also had two sisters. My oldest sister's name was Monique and she was ten. Jasmine, who was only five, was my little sister; and I—my name is Kamil—was the next to the youngest.

"Everybody better be getting dressed," my mother shouted from her bedroom. "You know today's your father's birthday and I want to get there early."

"I'm all ready, Ma," I yelled back.

"I'm all ready, Ma!" my brother mocked me sarcastically.

I started to rush him because he knew I didn't like to be teased, but I knew it would end up in a wrestling match and I didn't want to get in trouble for messing up my clothes.

My mother continued with her yelling. "Monique, do you have your sister dressed yet?"

"Yes, Mom, I'm finishing up with her hair now, and I just have to put my shoes on."

"Okay. I expect everyone to be in the car within the next ten minutes, and make sure you get your daddy's food package from out the kitchen."

"Kamil, you bet' not try to get in the front seat either, boy!" Monique popped her head in my room and threatened, reading me like a book. She knew how much I liked to ride in the front seat of my dad's 1980 Cadillac. I knew if he weren't away he'd have had a 1982 model like my uncle Jerry did, because he used to trade his in for a new one every year. His '80 still looked just as good as the '82s though. It was cream with a white leather top and the seats to match, and it had shiny spokes with the best tires that money could buy. At least that's what I used to hear my dad say. All the other kids in the neighborhood admired my dad's and uncle's cars. When he was home, he and my uncle Jerry were inseparable. I guessed that was where Kamal and I got our closeness from.

Although I was a boy and boys were supposed to be tougher than girls, I wasn't taking any chances going up against my sister, because I had seen her in action plenty of times before to know better. One time, at the private school we go to, she was in a fight with this bully who was much older and bigger than I was, and I remembered what she did to him. For him to be at least fifty pounds heavier and four inches taller then her, she managed to fracture his nose, bust his lip, and give him a black eye. That alone was enough for me to know not to mess with her, so I let her have the front seat.

Ever since my dad had been gone, though, Kamal and I had become overprotective of our sisters, especially Jasmine, because she was the youngest and was at the age where she would get into any- and everything within reaching distance anyway. She and Monique were so pretty that my brother and I knew we were going to have to beat a bunch of boys up for trying to talk to them when they got a little older. Even though we were younger than Monique was, we had already chased a few guys away and they began getting the hint that our sister was off-limits. Monique would be mad at us for doing it but "that's what brothers are for," my dad told us.

"Monique, give me your sister's hand and get your daddy's package out the back seat. Kamal and Kamil, go get in line while I take your father's bag over to the desk so we don't have to wait too long to get in," my mom told us, as we did what she said.

As usual, after she sent Kamal and me to the grocery store to get everything she had written down, my moms slaved over the stove nearly all night to make sure my dad would have all of his favorite dishes when we visited him. He didn't eat meat, red or white, so everything really consisted of vegetables. He was something called a vegan. We were not vegans, but my mother and father only allowed us to eat certain meats and forbade us from eating pork.

"I hope Dad got some junk food or something set up for us in there like he usually does, 'cause I'm getting tired of eating all that healthy stuff Ma be feeding us. She be buggin' with all of that," Kamal complained.

"For real she be trippin', but you know Dad is gonna hook us up. Knowing him, he probably even got a cake with candles up in here for his birthday," I said.

"Yeah, you right. Knowing Dad he probably does. I know he gonna be surprised that we came early today."

"I was thinking the same thing," I agreed with my brother. Normally my mother would bring us to the afternoon visit, but today she wanted us to spend the entire morning and some of the afternoon with my father on his birthday.

"Numbers sixty through ninety-five," the dark-skinned Bad Guy called out.

He's almost as big as my dad, I thought as I stared at him. I wondered what it was my father had done so bad that it would make this man not like him so much that he'd want to keep him away from us. I wished that he knew my dad the way that we did; then maybe he would let him come home with us. I wasn't used to seeing the Bad Guy because this was the first time we had come to see my dad so early, but he looked no different from the ones I was used to seeing in the gray and blue Bad Guy uniforms.

As our number was called, we all trailed behind my mother as she casually made her way toward the front part of the area where you had to be searched and scanned by the black thing that beeped and looked like something from *Star Wars.* Countless of different fragrances people wore tickled my nostrils as we crammed together with other visitors the way sardines were bunched together in a can.

"Key up!" That's what the Bad Guy always yelled right before the huge, rusted metal doors opened just enough for us to walk through to get to where they were holding my dad. My mother always took her time, keeping us close to her and all the while careful not to bump anyone or step on anyone's toes. I was sure she moved this way due to the many fights that broke out between women for those very same reasons. One time I saw a woman actually trampled over after falling down from being forcefully pushed through the cracked door.

As I walked through my heart started racing with excitement like it was when I first woke up that morning. I knew that in just a few moments my dad would be wrapping me up in one of his famous bear hugs, and then he'd toss me up in the air as if I were lighter than a feather. Then he'd do the same to my brother and sisters.

When we stepped into the visiting area, as usual the place was crowded. People were everywhere, men, women, and children. I was looking all around trying to spot my dad, but I was so short that I couldn't locate him in the crowd. I couldn't see a thing. Apparently, my moms must've spotted him, because she began pushing her way through the crowded room of visitors as we followed. Then, all of a sudden, she just stopped.

I immediately began looking around for my dad. I was sure that any minute now he would be busting through the crowd. To my surprise, as the crowd parted, I looked up and there was my dad sitting right there in front of us. He was smiling and looking as if he was having a good time. His muscles were bulging through his shirt, and his afro was all neat the way it always was. Everything looked to be normal, except for the fact that he was being fed cake by some pretty, light-skinned girl; not prettier than my moms, but a lot younger. He was enjoying himself so much that he didn't even see us standing there. It wasn't until my moms called his name that he noticed us. With record-breaking speed, my dad had made it from where he was sitting to directly in front of my mom and us.

I could see the tears beginning to roll down my mother's face as she tried to find the words to say to my father. And then they just spilled out. "I hope that tramp was worth your family, because you just lost it!" Her words started out weak but ended strong.

None of us knew what was really going on, but I knew that something was wrong; and seeing the unfamiliar look on my mom's face confirmed it all as she turned to us and said, "Kids, let's go!"

Just as we were about to exit the room, my father came up behind my mom and grabbed her by the arm. He began to try to explain whatever it was that needed explaining. "Wait a minute, hold up!" he yelled. "That broad back there don't mean nothing to me. You're the only woman I love and I'm not tryin' to lose you over some nonsense. How you think I've been makin' all that money I've been sending home for you and the kids?" he asked; and then answered his own question. "Because that broad been bringing me stuff up here that I would never ask you to bring 'cause I love you and care about you and the kids too much to disrespect you like that," he said, looking around as he lowered his voice.

I could tell whatever he was talking about he didn't want the Bad People to hear him. But not only did the Bad People not hear him, neither did my moms. It was as though his words had fallen on deaf ears.

Wiping her face, my mother calmly spoke. "I won't play this game with you anymore. I love my children and myself too much to throw my life, time, and love away on someone who only cares about himself, who thinks he can buy everything and that fast money is the best money. Money isn't everything. You can't buy love and happiness, and the fast way isn't always the best way, Jay. How can you say you love me and you'd never disrespect me? What do you call having another woman up here when you have a wife and kids?" my mother stated.

My father started to answer, but my moms cut him off. "Save it, Jay. I don't even want to hear what you have to say. I'm tired of all of your lies. I can't take it anymore. It's over!" she cried out.

Since I was the closest to her, my mother took hold of my hand and she began walking away, with my brother and sisters trailing along, leaving my dad standing there. Hearing my mother's words and not knowing the next time I'd see him, I couldn't help but take one last look back at my dad as I walked alongside my mom. As long as I lived, I'd never forget the expression on his face as he watched us leave. As he stood there, shaking his head, he had the look of someone who had just lost something very valuable and didn't know where to find it. I didn't fully understand at the time but that day marked the first day of a new life for all of us; and that was the last time I ever saw my dad while he was away.

Chapter One

Twenty Months Later

"Grandma, I finished my homework. Can I go outside now?"

"Okay, but if you go on the other side don't cross those train tracks. Walk your tail around and stay away from that handball court. Don't let me catch or hear your butt was over there, Kamil, you hear me?" my grandmother warned. The handball court was where all the older people hung out doing illegal things. I knew better than to defy her. She didn't play when it came to following the rules or, rather, her rules. Besides, I knew it was because she was concerned about my safety.

"Yes," I answered without hesitation.

"Can I go too, Grams? I'm done," Mal asked, straightening up his books.

"Yeah, you can go too; but what I tell you about calling me Grams like I'm some old woman or something? I told you before about picking up that street talk and bringing it up in this house with you, boy."

"Excuse me, Grandma," Mal corrected himself.

With the exception of her long silver hair, nothing about my grandmother indicated that she was an old woman. She had smooth almond-colored skin and a perfectly round face. Even though she had given birth to my moms and six uncles, she wasn't a big lady and stood only five feet tall. I had seen pictures of her when she was a teenager and she still looked the same. She was small in size but huge in heart and was full of life and full of energy. She always said, "You're only as old as you feel, and I'll be twenty-one years young on my next birthday."

After the last time we saw my dad, things began to change. Actually, everything began to change. We moved out of our neighborhood in Brooklyn and moved in with my grandmother in the projects. She lived out in New Jersey, where my parents were originally from.

We started seeing less of my moms because she was now working two jobs. When my dad had been there, he did all the working. Even when the Bad People took him away from us he used to send money to my moms, but then he just stopped. I never really knew what type of job he had, but I knew that it had to be a good one because we never wanted for anything, and never had to struggle—up until now, anyway. All I knew about my dad's job was that he used to travel a lot and would sometimes be gone for days, even weeks, at a time. I guessed he was some type of traveling salesman, so when I was asked what my father did for a living I just used to say he was a businessman.

In spite of my moms working, there were a lot of strangers coming to the house demanding money when we still lived in Brooklyn. At first, I used to think that they were Jehovah's Witnesses, but then I knew that it couldn't have been them because she wouldn't have opened the door. I didn't figure out that all the strangers were bill collectors until the gas and electric got turned off, and we had to move from our brownstone because my mom couldn't maintain the rent while raising four kids on her income.

Don't get me wrong, Jersey was okay, but still it wasn't New York, so like anything else that's new or different you had to get used to it. I knew a lot of the kids out here in the projects though, because every summer my moms used to send Mal and me to my grandmother's to spend time with her, not knowing that my brother and I had to fight the whole time we were out there just to prove that we were tough New Yorkers. Jersey kids thought New York kids couldn't fight. They thought that we only knew how to rob and steal or, in our case, they thought we were too uppity to know how to defend ourselves. But my dad and uncle used to box and they taught us. After all the fights we had, we were finally accepted in the Jersey ghetto as two of the boys; and we looked forward to our summer trips to Plainfield.

"Yo, Ant, what up?" My brother spotted one of our homeboys from building 532.

"Chillin', chillin', what up with you?" They gave each other a pound and embraced one another.

"We tryin' to see what's goin' on out here in the hood," said Mal jokingly.

Ant was twelve years old, two years older than me and one year older than Kamal; but he treated us as if we were all the same age. We learned a lot from Ant, because he grew up in the streets so he was more hip to how things were running out there.

His father was where we used to go visit my dad; but he told us that his dad was away for selling drugs. It was Ant who broke me out of saying that the Bad People had my dad and started me saying he was "away." The more he began to educate us about where we now lived, the more Mal and I began to question what it was our father was really away for.

Ant also had a brother who sold drugs. He was only seventeen, but he already had a 1980 Caddy, similar to the one my dad used to drive. Ant told us how his brother always bought him the freshest clothes. They were fly, too, and Mal and I were envious, especially since we were still wearing some of the same gear we had since we moved from New York, and now we had to share our clothes and wear hand-me-downs from the Salvation Army.

"Let's go over Trev's crib and see what's up, see if we can put together a free-for-all or something," Ant said.

"Bet," Mal and I agreed.

Trevor lived in building 120 on the Elmwood side of the projects, and he was Ant's best friend. Their families were actually two of the first to move into the Elmwood Gardens housing projects back in the sixties and they were close, so it was only right that when they were born and grew up they became close themselves. I found out my grandmother was one of the first to move around here after my grandfather had died from a heart attack, and she couldn't afford to pay the mortgage on the house they had lived in for four years until his death.

"Who is it?" we heard Trevor asking from the other side of the door.

"It's the police. Open up before I kick it in!" yelled Ant, trying to disguise his voice.

"Kick it in and you're gonna pay for it, nigga," Trevor yelled back as he opened the door and embraced his best friend, recognizing Ant's voice.

"Trev, what it is?" said Ant.

"You know, maxin' and relaxin', that's all. Mal, Mil, what up? We got muthafuckin' New York in the house!" he shouted, and laughter began to fill the little apartment.

"Forget you," said Mal, laughing along with them. It was something we were used to, not being from Jersey. It was our own little joke.

Once Trevor closed the door behind us, the rest of the crew began pulling their beers, cigarettes, and weed back out. Everyone had hidden whatever they were doing when Ant pretended to be the police. All of our boys hung out over at Trevor's crib doing the things they knew they couldn't get caught doing at home, except for Ant, unless they wanted to die at a young age; but Trevor's crib was cool because his moms worked mostly all day, so he practically had the house to himself Monday through Friday.

"Nigga, why you gotta play so muthafuckin' much?" Shareef asked Ant.

"Man, cool out. Trev knew it was me."

Outside of Trevor and Shareef, the rest of the gang consisted of Quadir, Shawn, Mark, and Black. Everybody was pretty much around the same age, between the ages of eleven and fourteen. In fact, I was really the youngest out of the bunch and the littlest, too; but I was accepted just the same, because I had heart and wasn't afraid to fight.

"Yo, Mil, come hit this spliff, nigga. This that shit right here," said Black, coughing from the smoke. Black was the oldest and had the most experience around the projects. His real name was Bernard, but he earned the name Black from the darkness of his complexion.

"Nah, man, you know I don't smoke, kid. I don't even know how to," I answered, shaking my head. I knew he was trying to be funny because he knew my brother and I didn't smoke or drink.

"Oh, that's right. I forgot you a young whippersnapper," Black joked. "But you still my nigga, even if you don't get any bigga," he added in a laughing manner, while taking another pull of the joint. "This is for you, baby boy!" He held the weed wrapped in white paper in my direction before passing it to Quadir, who gladly accepted it.

"Yo, Trev, we was comin' over here to see if we could get a football game goin' on the other side, but you niggas up in here getting all high and shit, so that cancels that," Ant said disappointedly.

"Maaaan, ain't nobody all high and drunk up in here, nigga," Trevor said defensively. "You always comin' at us sideways every time we tryin'a have a good time, actin' like we some of them junky and whino muthafuckas out there on the block. We just havin' a little fun, know what I'm sayin'?" Trev stated. "Besides, the alcohol and weed make me play better and harder anyway, so let's rock. You ain't sayin' nothing!" he concluded with a smile before Ant had a chance to rebut.

We were all used to them going at it like brothers. It was comical to us and we knew it was all in love. At some point, we all had gotten into it with one another, but the next day we would be right back to kicking it again like the boys we were.

Everyone jumped up hearing Trevor's words and one by one we began spilling out of his apartment, headed over to the field on the other side of the tracks.

"We ain't got all day, momma's boys," Black was the first to yell as we approached the field.

"Word up," Shareef followed up.

While everybody else crossed the train tracks to get to the other side of the projects, Mal and I walked around, remembering what our grandmother had told us, so they all had to wait for us. Kamal stuck up his middle finger at Black's comment while I stuck mine up at Shareef. Before it could escalate to anything else, Trevor started picking teams.

"Me, Quadir, Shawn, and Mark, against you, Mil, Mal, and Black," he said to Ant. "Reef, you ref the game."

"Why the fuck I gotta ref the game?" Shareef questioned.

"Nigga, you know why you gotta ref the game. 'Cause ya ass is wack and you don't know how to play," Trev said, as we all burst into laughter. Everybody around the projects, with the exception of Shareef, was good in everything we played, from football to basketball down to baseball. Although we weren't originally from the projects, Mal and I loved playing sports just as much as we did watching them, but when it came to God handing down skills and talents in the athletic departments Shareef was standing in the wrong line. He couldn't catch a football even if it landed in his hands; he couldn't swing a bat if his life depended on it; and he couldn't dribble a basketball unless he used two hands, no matter how many times we tried to teach him.

"But I can fight," Reef spat back. That was his response every time.

"I bet you won't win if we jump ya punk ass, nigga," was Ant's comeback each time, as we laughed even harder.

Up ahead of the field was the handball court. All of the older teenagers and old heads hung out up there, either hustling, getting high and drinking, shooting dice, shining up their rides, kicking it to girls, playing ball, or just coolin' out.

I was always good with remembering faces and names, so I knew all the hustlers and the cars they drove, too, and they knew who Mal and I were, through my dad and Uncle Jerry. It wasn't until Ant's brother told him that my dad was a street legend out there that I began to realize my father wasn't any type of traveling salesman.

The more we hung around Ant and the rest of our friends the more Mal and I learned. I didn't want to at first, but as time went on I had no choice but to believe what they were saying about my father. In passing, my brother and I would hear some of the hustlers saying things like, "Their dad was clockin' major dough," or "Their dad was paid." Because of who he was in the streets, we received a lot of respect from the people who hung out by the handball court.

While we were out there playing football, we noticed that guys were beginning to scatter, running all over the place; and then we saw the police jump out of their unmarked and patrol cars from everywhere, both in plain clothes and uniforms. Some guys sprinted into the housing projects complex while others made a mad dash for the bridge and the train tracks. Just as I was about to move out of the way, one of the fleeing runners seemed as if he was about to hit me with a football tackle. I tried to maneuver out of his way but it was too late; he was already up on me. I braced myself for the hit.

"Li'l Mil, hold this," he said as he continued to fly right past me, headed in the direction of the train tracks.

I knew who the guy was. Everybody knew. His name was Mustafa. He was a nineteen-year-old hustler from the projects who was known for being thorough, a ladies' man, and one of the best dressers in the hood. Ant told us how he was well respected by all in the streets, young and old, and didn't take any junk from nobody. Without giving it a second thought, I took what Mustafa had handed me and shoved it into my left sweatpants pocket. A few seconds later, one policeman, who was out of breath from giving chase, came to a complete stop in front of all of us.

"Hey, you kids, did you see anybody drop anything by you?" the plainclothes officer asked us.

"No, sir," we all answered in unison, knowing that even if we had we still wouldn't have answered him truthfully.

"All right, well, we need you to clear this area so we can search it," he said.

We were used to one of our playing sessions being broken up because of something that had happened up by the handball court. There was always something going on in the West End Gardens housing projects known as the Bricks. Because the ones we lived in were newer, they called the Bricks the Old Projects and ours the New Projects. Hustlers from both sides would go back and forth over the train tracks hanging out and hustling unless they were beefing with each other. When that happened, we weren't allowed to play on the other side. But for the most part everyone got along.

As we were leaving, Ant saw his brother hemmed up against the police car with handcuffs on, along with a few of the other local hustlers from our side of the projects.

"Man, my mom is gonna kill Terrance when she finds out they caught him again," Ant cried. "This is the second time this month he's been in the youth house."

That's what they called the juvenile detention center for anybody under the age of eighteen years. It was a type of jail for young people that held you until you were released to the custody of your parents by the judge. All the guys Kamal and I hung with, except for Ant, had already been there at least once, and they bragged about it as if were a fun place to be or it made you cool.

Speaking of the youth house, if the plain-clothes officer knew what I had in my pocket, I would've been right alongside Terrance and the rest of them, handcuffed and on my way to the detention center. My mother would've killed me if that had happened. She wouldn't have understood the position I was in at the time. I knew my dad would have, though. It was either take what Mustafa handed me and do exactly what I did with it, drop it and let the cops find it, or hand it to them. If I didn't take it then I would've been looked at as a sucka by my friends; if I would've dropped it and somebody saw me I would've been looked at as a coward; and if I would've given it to the police then I would've been looked at as a snitch. Even though I knew I had no business accepting what Mustafa had given me to hold, I knew I didn't want to be labeled as a sucka, coward, or snitch.

We all went our separate ways, slapping one another five. I couldn't wait to tell Kamal what Mustafa had given me back there. No one had seen him give it to me. I really didn't know what it was myself, but I was curious to find out.

I took a glance back to make sure our boys were out of range before I spoke. They were already up the rocks and on the tracks, crossing back over. "Mal, guess what?" I said, looking around to see if anyone else could hear me.

"What up, Mil?"

"Yo, when Mu ran past us in the field he tossed me something and told me to hold it," I said, waiting for his reaction.

"What? What is you talkin' about?"

"You heard me. Mu tossed me something to hold when we were back there in the field playing football."

"And you took it?"

"What was I supposed to do? He was runnin'. I couldn't catch up to him and say, 'No, I can't hold this, take it back.' And I couldn't turn it over to the cops 'cause that would've been snitchin', and I don't want no rep like that 'cause nobody respects a snitch or rat."

"Where you learn that at?" Mal asked.

"I heard Dad say it one time when him and Uncle Jerry was in the living room talking. Trev and them said it a few times too when they be talking about the youth house."

"Yeah, you right. I remember. And, plus, Mom and Dad taught us to always mind our business. We don't see nothin', we don't hear nothin', and we don't know nothin'. Yo, whatever you got don't pull it out here, though. Wait until we get in the house; and make sure you act normal when we get in there 'cause Grandma ain't slow. She's from the old school and she'll know somethin's up."

My brother had said a mouthful. My grandmother was as sharp as they came. For someone who never really left the house she always knew everything about everything. Whenever she would be talking to my mom, or one of her friends who came over or called on the phone, she would always start out by saying, "It's not any of my business, but you know so-and-so did this," or "Such-and-such happened to so-and-so." There wasn't anything that you could do or say without my grandmother not catching wind of it.

"I'm not, and I know Grandma be on point," I agreed with my brother.

"You boys are back early. Is everything all right?" my grandmother greeted us as soon as we walked through the door and passed the kitchen. We could smell what she was cooking the moment we entered the building. No one's fried chicken smelled better than my grandmother's.

"Some boys got chased and the police broke up the game," Kamal answered for us.

My grandmother just shook her head. We prepared for the "I told you" speech but surprisingly it didn't come. I made my way to our room as Mal followed.

"Did you lock the door behind you?" I asked Mal as I pulled the plastic sandwich bag out of my pocket.

"Yeah, it's locked, boy. Stop being so paranoid like you used some of that stuff already," Kamal whispered back.

I shot him a look that made him know that I thought he was talking out of the side of his neck, saying something like that.

When I opened the plastic bag, I saw it contained a bunch of tiny little balloons, some red and some blue. Thirty-five reds and fifteen blues, to be exact. "What the heck is this?" I said aloud, surprised to be seeing balloons instead of drugs.

"Don't be stupid," said Kamal. "It's drugs. The drugs are in the balloons, goofy."

"How do you know?" I asked curiously.

"Because I used to hear the guys out there hustling, yellin', 'I got that Boy and Girl,' and then I'd see the fiends lined up to spend their money in exchange for the balloons. I asked Ant what were Boy and Girl, and he told me that his brother told him that Boy, in the blue balloons, was dope, and Girl, in the red ones, was coke, and that the Boys go for five dollars and the Girls go for ten."

"So you mean to tell me that these little balloons are worth four hundred twenty-five dollars?" I asked my brother as I calculated the value in my head, which was easy to do because math was my strongest subject in school, as well as my favorite.

"Yep," Mal replied.

"Dag! Mu must be rich if he got it like that."

"Man, that ain't nothing. They be out there with more than that on 'em. Put all that stuff back in the bag and tie it back the way it was before you opened it," Mal told me. "Tomorrow, as soon as you see Mustafa, we gonna give him that stuff back; and I don't want to hear about it again," Kamal demanded.

"I'm with you on that, bro. I don't want no part of this either," I agreed.

The next morning, before Kamal and I went off to school, we looked for Mustafa, but he was nowhere to be found. Out of fear of Moms or Grandmother finding the package in the house, I took it to school with me. Here I was, just turned ten years old last month, in school with over $400 worth of drugs in my pocket, not able to do any schoolwork, waiting for class to let out so I could get back around the projects and give Mustafa his stuff.

At 2:45 school let out and I waited for Mal out front.

"Yo, you a'ight, bro? You look like you about to pass out," Mal said to me.

"Man, this stuff been drivin' me crazy all day being in my pocket. I don't know how they do it, standin' out there like that around the way, 'cause I feel like Five-O gonna run down on me any minute now. I wonder if Dad had to go through this when he was our age," I stated to my brother.

"I wish he were here. Then we could've gone to him for help, 'cause if Moms found out she'd flip out and probably try to keep us in the house until we turned twenty-one."

"You got that right," said Mal.

As we turned the corner, approaching the projects, I heard my name. "Ay yo, li'l Mil!"

When I turned around to look, I saw Mustafa rolling down the black-tinted window of a pearl black BMW 318i with gold rims, and a gold front grill to match. You could tell it was brand new, because it still had the dealer temp tags in the back window.

"Yo, get in," he leaned over toward the passenger's side and shouted. "I wanna talk to you for a minute. Li'l Mal, you too." He gestured to him.

Mal and I both knew what he wanted to talk about, but we still were a little nervous about getting in the car with him. We knew if our moms, our grandmother, or someone who knew them saw us getting in this car we'd be in serious trouble. I looked both ways to make sure the coast was clear then walked over to the passenger's front door and hesitantly opened it to get in the front seat, as Kamal opened the back door and hopped in.

When we closed the doors, Mustafa drove off to the sounds of the latest Run-D.M.C. cut, "Here We Go," rolling the tinted window back up. This was the first time I'd actually ever been in a drug dealer's car, but being in the car with Mustafa felt like being in any other, ordinary person's ride, with the exception of his appearance.

When we got in, the inside of the Beemer smelled like Mu had just come from the barbershop. His sharp chin-strapped line and goatee confirmed it. As he drove, I tried not to stare, but I couldn't help it. He was sharp from head to toe. On his left hand, he had a two-finger gold ring with a dollar sign on it that covered his pinky and ring fingers. He had two separate rings on his middle and pointer fingers; one had an M and the other had a U. On his right hand, he had a four-finger ring on, with lion heads on both sides, with red rubies in their eyes. I could see the name MUSTAFA in between them, on the plate of the ring. Around his neck, he had three different sizes of gold rope chains, with medallions on them. He wore a pair of silk pants with a silk shirt to match, only the shirt was yellow, and the pants were black. To top it off, he rocked a yellow and black beanie with a tassel dangling from it and he had on the black and yellow British Walkers. Everything he had on matched and coincided with his ride. I was in awe.

The sound of his voice snapped me out of my daze. "Yo, remember yesterday when I ran past you?" he stated rather than asked as he lowered the volume of his music.

I tried to answer, but instead I was only able to nod. I wasn't afraid, but I was nervous. I had never been so nervous in my life. Maybe because

I knew what I had done was wrong and I knew the consequences behind my actions. I just wanted it all to be over.

"What did you do with that?" Mustafa asked in a cool tone.

"I got it right here, just the way you gave it to me, Mu. And I didn't tell anybody. Well, except for my brother, but he didn't tell anybody," I rambled.

"Relax, Mil. I believe you, and I'm not gonna hurt you, either, so chill," he said with a grin on his face.

"Okay." It wasn't so much what he said, but how he looked when he said it that put me at ease.

"Yo, Big Jay ya pops, right?" he asked.

"Yeah," I answered, never hearing anyone refer to my dad as "Big Jay" before; but I knew they called him Jay, which was short for Jayson.

"Your pops is a good man, so I knew the apple didn't fall far from the tree," Mu said. I was too young to understand what he meant by the statement. He must've remembered that he was talking to a couple of kids, because he broke it down so Mal and I could understand. "What I mean is, I figured you were just like your pops," he rephrased his comment. "That's why I trusted you like that with my stash."

All I could say was, "Thanks," not really knowing whether what he had just said required a response. But out of politeness I responded to what I believed was a compliment.

"Li'l Mil, stay the way you are and you'll go far in this world," he told me. "'Cause a man is measured by three things in life." His tone changed. It became smoother, but serious. "And that's his loyalty, respect and, most importantly, his money," he quoted as if he read the lines straight out of some philosophical book.

Then he pulled out a knot of money filled with nothing but hundreds, bigger than both of my hands put together. My eyes grew wide. It looked as if it could've been over $10,000. I noticed that he didn't have any twenties, tens, fives, or singles in his bankroll, as he peeled off two hundred-dollar bills and gave one to me and one to Kamal, saying, "This is for you, for holding it down, and this one is for you, Kamal, for havin' your brother's back. Always hold each other down, no matter what," he told us as he took the sandwich bag from me. "And stay away from this," he said in a much sterner tone, holding the bag in the air. "'Cause this shit will kill you! You understand?"

Mal and I both nodded yes.

Mustafa pulled over, up the street from the projects, and let us out by the vegetable garden on the corner of West Second and Liberty Street.

Just as he was about to pull off, he rolled down his window. "If either one of you ever needs anything, just let me know."

Then the words of Whodini's latest cut, "Friends," flowed out of his sunroof and filled the air as he pulled off. From that day on, I had a different outlook on drug dealers.

Chapter Two

Two Years Later

"Hey, Kamil."

I heard my name sung in unison as I unchained my bike from the bike rack while waiting for my brother to come and do the same. For getting good grades last year, Mustafa bought Mal and me matching Diamondback bikes. Mine was light blue, because blue was my favorite color, and Kamal's was light green. They both came with the white pegs on the front and back. The only thing wrong with the bikes was that we couldn't keep them at home because we'd get questioned and then killed by both our moms and our grandmother, so we had to leave them over at Ant's crib because his moms was cool.

After that day in the car, Mustafa had been making sure Mal and I always had a couple of dollars in our pockets. He always asked us how we were doing in school and rewarded us when we got good grades on tests and report cards. When some of our boys passed to go on to the seventh grade, the middle school they would have normally attended was changed. The city decided to send the kids from the Elmwood Gardens housing projects to Maxson Middle School on the east end, which was on the opposite side of the town, and let the kids from the West End Gardens housing projects to stay at Hubbard, due to all neighborhood rivalry fights that took place on school property. I guessed they didn't think about the saying, "You can take the person out of the projects, but you can't take the projects out of the person," because while the beefs decreased at the west end middle school, they increased on the east end.

Before school even started my boys were already saying how they didn't like the kids up there and how they were punks because they lived on the east end and the kids up there were either intimidated, afraid, or just didn't like us just because we lived in the projects. The east end was considered to be the better and quieter part of town while the west end was referred to as the bad and ghetto part of town. I had heard enough stories from my friends to know that once I got there I'd be considered just another kid from the projects.

I turned around to see who was speaking to me. I was greeted with three bright smiles. I recognized them, but one stood out above all.

"Hey, what up?" I responded, as the darkest one of the three girls and I made eye contact.

Lisa was her name. Lisa Goodman. She was in a few of my classes. All three girls were from the east end of town. Because they lived borderline, they attended the elementary we did.

"Go ahead. Ask him." The lighter of the three, named Felicia, nudged Lisa with her shoulder as they giggled.

"Okay!" Lisa exclaimed.

"Ask me what?" I was curious.

"We're having a pool party after graduation is over and school lets out, and we wanted to know if you and your brother would like to come, seeing as how today is the last day of school and we might not see each other again until the summer's over."

Today was the last day of school until September, and tonight was graduation for those who were moving on from elementary school to junior high; and Mal and I were among the graduates. Kamal was supposed to have graduated the year before, but he was left back a grade. Everyone thought he let his grades drop just to stay another year with me, because of how close we were, but I knew the real reason was that he had gotten lazy and slacked off on his studying. He knew too, and he was reminded of it every time he looked in the mirror and saw the welts on his back from the extension cord my moms had nearly beaten him half to death with.

"I don't know, shorty, I gotta check with my brother and see what he thinks," I told her.

"Does everybody from New York use the word 'shorty'?" asked Felicia.

All I could do was laugh because all of the girls in the neighborhood had been asking me that. I had recently started using it since going back to Brooklyn to visit some of my cousins. They were all saying it so I brought it back to Jersey with me.

"Okay, kid, I see you surrounded by three of the finest shorties in the school," shouted Kamal as he walked up on us.

"What's up, Kamal?" Felicia flashed the same smile at my brother that she had at me when they first walked up. "We were just inviting you and Kamil to a pool party that we are having to celebrate the end of the school year, and graduation from elementary school to junior high, since we're going to Maxson in September."

"Shorty, no offense, but you know we don't hang on the east like that," Mal said as nice as possible.

"Technically you're not from the east or the west end," Lisa spoke up.

"You're from another state, so why should it matter what part of town it's on, as long as you're enjoying yourself and having a good time?" Felicia stated.

"Right, right, true, true," was all Mal said. That was his way of trying to be funny, so I stepped up and said something.

"Give us the time, place, and date, and if we can, we'll try to make it, but if we can't then we apologize for not being able to." I directed my words to Lisa.

She smiled. It didn't take a genius to figure out she liked me. She kept staring at me before taking out a pen and a piece of paper and writing everything down, including her phone number. "Please call if you can't make it," she said.

"I will."

All three of them waved as they walked off; but as they got a few feet up, Lisa turned around and flashed one last smile. And I smiled back.

Chapter Three

To see the look on my mom's and grand-mother's faces when they called my and Kamal's names back to back for our diplomas made keeping my grades up all the more worth it. My mother looked as if she were the happi-est woman on the planet to have her two sons graduate. I hadn't seen her that happy in a long time. Between her being stressed over work and school, and still hurt from the situation with my dad, she hardly ever smiled anymore. Today, her grin was from ear to ear, though, and she had a lot to be proud of.

The Benson family had had a good school year. Monique was exceptionally smart, so instead of her becoming a freshman in high school they skipped her from eighth grade to tenth. Not only was it a good year for my family, but also for the Robertsons and Thompsons, because Shareef and Black had graduated with us, so nearly the entire projects were in the house. Even some of the local hustlers were in attendance, including Mustafa, who I saw standing all the way in the back posted up.

After the ceremony, we were met with cries and hugs. "Look at my babies." My moms embraced Mal and me. "I am so proud of you and I love you both," she went on.

"We know, Ma," Mal and I both offered.

"Let me get my hugs in, Sister. They're my babies too, and I helped raise 'em and change their diapers," my grandmother chimed in, calling my moms by her childhood nickname. "They wouldn't have made it this far if I hadn't stayed on their behinds," my grandmother added. "Isn't that right, you two?"

"Yes, Grandma," Mal and I answered. Our replies earned us huge bear hugs.

Both Monique and Jasmine gave us hugs too. Monique hugged us up top while Jasmine wrapped her arms around our waists and congratulated us.

"I told all the girls up in Maxson to watch out because my two little brothers were coming up there in September to break some hearts," Monique leaned over and whispered into my and Mal's ears. The three of us shared a laugh the way only siblings could together, as Jasmine stared at us wondering what she had missed.

"Sister, take a picture of me and my two handsome young men," my grandmother told my moms.

I could almost detect some hurt in my mom's eyes, as she envied the relationship that Mal and I had with our grandmother. I believed at that moment she thought about how she'd been missing out on all of our lives while she worked and went to school to further her education, in order to get a better paying job. If she only knew that I understood. We all did. We knew that she was just trying to make a better life for us in the absence of our father.

The flash went off and nearly blinded me, snapping me out of my daze. "Ma, come over here," I said, "and take this picture with us. You know without you there'd be no us."

"I couldn't have said it any better myself," Kamal followed up with.

"We love you, Ma," we both said as she got in between the two of us; and then we kissed her on opposite cheeks just as the flash was going off for a second time. I could taste the salt from my mother's tears on the side of her face, but this time I knew they were tears of joy and not of pain, because today was a happy day for her, for all of us.

"Ma, we're gonna go say congratulations to Black and Shareef. We'll be right back," Mal told her.

"Okay, but if you take any pictures tell Teresa and Tim I said I want copies."

"Reef, Black, what it is?" Mal shouted, as we all slapped five.

"With grammar like that I don't know how you graduated, kid," Black said jokingly.

"We did it, man!" Black boasted. "On to the next phase. You think we gonna make it another six years of this school shit?" he asked.

"I don't know about you two, but Mal and I owe it to our moms and grandmother, and to ourselves too, because we ain't tryin' to turn out like our dad; and you should be thinking the same way, 'cause your fathers ain't no different," I pointed out.

"Yeah, I'm wit' you on that, kid," Black said, agreeing with me.

"Yo, here comes Mustafa," Reef interrupted.

When we turned to look, Mu was standing there smiling. "Yeah, that's what I'm talking about! Getting that education and takin' some of these high-power jobs away from these white folks. You little brothers are the future," Mu bellowed. "You young brothers have to break the cycle and show them that you're not products of your environment. Just because you're from the hood doesn't mean that you have to be involved in what goes on in the hood. You brothers are the next presidents, senators, governors, mayors, lawyers, doctors, and teachers of the future. I'm proud of all four of you. It's too late for me, but it's not too late for you, so make it count."

Mu had been coming at Mal and me like that ever since that day we were in his car. He had become a father figure to us. We were already respected because of who our dad was, but we started receiving a different type of love from the hood once they saw that Mu took a liking to us.

"Pardon me, little homies, while I rap with your boys right quick," Mu said to Shareef and Black.

"Yeah, Mu, no problem." Both Black and Shareef nodded, before giving us pounds and hugs.

"See y'all back in the hood," Black said.

"Bet," Mal answered.

Mu waited until they were gone before he spoke. "I hope you were listening to everything I was just sayin' 'cause that was real. If I had the chance to get my education I would, but I'm too deep in the game now and ain't no turning back for me. I quit school when I was younger than the two of you and since then I've been getting my education in the streets, the education of survival, that is. Nothing you can ever learn in any books you read will ever prepare you for the streets. You can only learn what I know by experience.

"But this shit is not for y'all. Let's hope that you don't have to go through what me and your pops had to. I know if he were here he would be schoolin' you the same way, and I got respect for him; that's why I'm comin' at you like this. Stay in school," he ended as he handed us each envelopes; and then he walked off.

Mal and I opened them at the same time. Inside were crisp hundred-dollar bills in each one, along with a key that was too small to belong to a car with a note that read:

Meet me in the field tomorrow morning.

The morning couldn't come soon enough, as I tossed and turned in my bed, thinking about so many things. Kamal was sound asleep. I could hear him snoring from his bed. Flashes of the last time I had seen my dad flooded my thoughts. I could still see images of the pretty, light-skinned girl who changed my family's life as we once knew it. I could see the tears that rolled down my mother's face and I could still remember the words that my father said to her that were unconvincing, and the words that she said to him in return that convinced him that it was really over. I knew that I didn't want to ever turn out like my dad and put my family through what he had put us through when I got older. That's why I was determined to stay in school and do the right thing like Mustafa had said.

"Kamal, wake up. It's nine o'clock. Mu's probably out there waiting for us."

"Oh, word. I almost forgot about that," Mal said as he jumped out of the bed and went to the bathroom.

"Hurry up, kid. I'm tryin' to get down to the field," I yelled. For as long as I could remember, Kamal had been slower than a turtle when it came to doing anything or going anywhere. He always moved as if time waited for him or something.

"Yo, I was beginning to think y'all ain't want these damn things," Mu said, standing in between two mopeds with ribbons on them.

"Oh, snap! These joints are slammin'!" we both yelled as we ran over to the mopeds and hopped on them. We'd had an idea what the keys were for but to see them was another story.

Hooked on the sides were helmets with our names written in cursive. "Mu, man, this is the best, kid," I said to him, reaching my hand out to shake his.

Instead, he grabbed it and pulled me off the bike, wrapped his arms around me, and said, "I got love for you little brothers. Y'all my hearts!"

Something inside of me was triggered and I felt the love. No other man had made me feel that safe and loved since my dad. From that day on, I no longer looked at Mustafa as a drug dealer, but as a father figure and male role model instead, and I thought that Kamal felt the same way.

"We got love for you too," I said, speaking for the both of us.

Mustafa stood there just staring at us strangely for a moment. "Y'all gonna be good for life," he then said, wrapping his arms around the both of us. "I got y'all," he added, before releasing us. I thought that day he had officially adopted us as his sons or little brothers.

There was nothing else to be said. Mu hopped in his car, blew the horn at us, threw the peace sign out the window, and then he was gone.

"Dag, Mu got a lot of love for us," I said to my brother.

"I was thinking the same thing."

"Yo, where we gonna keep these at?" I asked Kamal when Mu left.

"Where else? At Ant's crib," he replied.

"Oh, shit, where you get these from?" Ant blurted out with an envious expression on his face.

"Mu got them for us for graduation," Mal answered.

"Yo, that nigga Mu love you niggas. Either that or he groomin' you to put you on the payroll," Ant stated.

"Man, like you said, he got a lot of love for us," I snapped back, taking offense to what Ant had said. "He don't even be comin' at us like that on some hustlin' for him stuff."

"I'm just sayin'." Ant threw his hands up. "Mu got niggas our age now pumpin' for him, so you never know, but if you say so then I'm wit' you on that," Ant responded, cleaning up what he had said, sensing that he had crossed the line with his last remark.

"Yo, Ant, we need to stash these here until we find a place to put 'em. You know you can ride 'em whenever you want," Mal told him.

"You know you can leave 'em here, and I appreciate you telling me I can ride whenever I want, but I'm cool 'cause Terrance supposed to get me one as soon as he sells his old Caddy and get a new one, which should probably be this week. So this summer we should be ridin' three the hard way through the hood on the west end and the east end, too."

Ant's mentioning of the east end reminded me of what I had promised to do. I said peace to Ant, told my brother I'd see him when he got in, and then I headed home to make a phone call.

Chapter Four

"Hello? May I speak to Lisa please?"

"This is she, who's calling?"

"This is Kamil, from the projects."

"I know who you are Kamil, you don't have to say where you're from," she said laughing.

"Oh, pardon me, it's a habit. I guess a bad habit I picked up from being around my boys. And I'm not used to calling anybody's house asking for a girl, either."

She laughed again. "Excuse me; I'm not laughing at you, only at what you said."

"I'm being honest, though. You're the first girl I ever called."

"Really?" she asked, sounding surprised.

"Yeah, I'm not playing."

"Well, then, I'm glad that I'm the first."

I didn't know what to say, so I went into the reason why I really called. "I just wanted to let you know that my brother and I are coming to your pool party, but I was wondering if we could bring a friend?"

"Yeah, that's not a problem," she quickly replied. "I'm just glad you decided to come."

I believed her because I could hear the excitement in her voice.

"Can I say something without you taking it the wrong way?" she asked.

"Sure, what's up?"

"You don't sound like you're from the projects."

Now it was my turn to laugh. "What does somebody from the projects sound like?"

"I don't know, it's just that most of the guys in our school from there or from the west end period talk like they're all big, bad, and too cool; but not you. You sound so calm and nice, even though you look cool and bad, but not big because you're short." I could tell that she was smiling through the phone when she made her last comment.

"I understand what you mean," I said to her. "My moms and my grandmother don't tolerate any street talk, or any street anything for that matter in the house, so since I'm in the house more than I am in the streets, I focus on talking properly. When I'm around my boys, we all talk alike. I don't really curse. My grandmother says people curse to substitute for words they don't know, so she makes me and my brother and sisters study the dictionary. Besides, if she caught me swearing, she would wash my mouth out with soap, and I'm not joking, either."

Lisa chuckled. "Sounds like you have some good women raising you."

"Yeah, they're the best."

"What about your dad?"

"He's locked up. I haven't seen him since I was eight years old."

"Wow, that's a long time."

"Yeah, but I have my moms and grandmother. Listen, I gotta go, but I'll see you this weekend," I said, in a hurry to get off the phone.

"Okay, see you then. Nice talking to you."

"You too," I ended. I didn't understand why it bothered me so much to talk about my father or for someone to question me about him. I hated that my dad made me feel this way.

"Mal, I spoke to those shorties from the east end who are giving the pool party—well, one of them anyway—and I told her we were comin' through, and we were bringin' a friend. I thought, you, Ant, and me could roll up there on our bikes since Ant is gonna have his this weekend too. You wit' it?"

"Yeah, you know I'm down. I heard there's some nice shorties up there we ain't even seen yet."

Lately Kamal had been talking about girls, which was cool, but I had my mind on more important things, like a summer job so I could make some extra money to get me some fresh gear for the next school year. From the hundred dollars Mu gave me for graduation, I only spent ten of that, and that was because I was real hungry one day, so I still had ninety dollars of it saved up. Kamal said that he still had eighty of his. To be so young, we both knew how to manage money. I wondered if we had gotten that from our dad.

The pool party was on Saturday, and Ant got his bike on Friday. He zoomed past us showing off, beeping the horn. He made a U-turn, stopped in front of us, and jumped off his new bike.

"It's on now!" Ant bellowed, rolling up on us.

"Yo, I just rode through downtown and I saw these fly-ass Hawaiian suits up in Jay Cee's, in all flavors, for twenty-five bucks. If we get those we'll be the flyest niggas at the party, what's up?" Ant asked.

"Man, I'm not tryin' to waste no twenty-five dollars on no outfit to try to impress the east end heads," I told him. I wasn't trying to spend twenty-five dollars out of the ninety I had, leaving me with only sixty-five, for an outfit that would be out of style by the time I went back to school. Mu taught me that something like that would be hustling backward.

Ant must've read my mind. "Yo, Mil, that's nothing. There goes Mu right over there; ask him for fifty bucks for you and Mal. You know he'll give it to you if you tell him what it's for."

As much as I hated to admit it, Ant was right, but I didn't want to look like I was begging or looking for some type of handout. I had never asked Mu for anything. He had always given without Mal or I having to ask.

Mu was leaning on the front hood of his car talking to one of the older project chicks I had seen all the other hustlers trying to get with. "He's over there busy anyway. I don't wanna bust his groove," I said to Ant, making an excuse so I didn't have to ask.

"Man, he ain't never too busy for you and Mal. Let's go over there and see." Ant was already making his way over to where Mu was posted up and Mal and I followed.

When Mu saw us, he called for us to come over to where he and the chick he was talking to were. "Yo, young bloods, what it be like?" He gave us daps.

"What up, Mu?" we all said.

"Ay yo, Reece, these are my two hearts right here, Kamil and Kamal. They brothers, and this their partner Ant," he introduced us.

"I know Ant already; that's Terrance li'l brother. I don't know these two, though, but nice to meet you anyway," she said. "Mu, they're cute."

"Nice to meet you too and thank you," we both said.

"Hey, Reece," Ant said.

You could tell that she was older than Mu, but you still knew that he was in control.

"You probably heard of their pops, Big Jay from New York," Mu said proudly as if it were his own father he was speaking about. "Remember he used to be around here?"

"Oh, yeah, that's why they look familiar, and so cute. Their father was a handsome man and he had all the girls around here goin' crazy," she said, and then stopped as if she had said too much already. "How is Big Jay doin' anyway?" She addressed me, trying to change the subject.

"I don't know. He locked up," I said, no longer using the term "away."

"Tell him Reecie said hi when you speak to him."

"Yeah, okay," I said, brushing her off.

Mu sensed that I was bothered by what Reece had said about my dad, and he jumped in. "What's up, kid?"

"Nah, we ain't mean to bother you, Mu, but me, Mal, and Ant are goin' to this pool party tomorrow on the east and we—"

I didn't get to finish what I saying because he cut me off. "Say no more. How much you need?"

"They got these Hawaiian suits downtown for twenty-five dollars and we wanted to bust them out at the party."

Mu smiled, pulled out his stack, gave me fifty dollars, gave Kamal fifty, and told us to buy two different flavors.

"Thanks, Mu," Mal and I said.

"Don't worry about that. What I told you before? If you need anything just ask, and anything means just that: anything! Consider that dough early school shoppin' money. You know my boys gotta be the sharpest li'l niggas in the building. I got y'all before school start back, a'ight?"

"Yeah, Mu," was our only response.

I was really speechless because I had no idea Mu even had that on his mind. Here I was trying to figure out how I was going to find some type of job to save up some money for my gear, but Mu made sure I'd be able to enjoy my summer after all.

Chapter Five

623 West Eighth Street was the address we were looking for. We pulled onto the sidewalk one by one in front of the house. Other kids were walking up in their bathing suits and swimming trunks, slowing down to see whose faces would appear from under the helmets. Somebody must've told Lisa about the three of us pulling up out front, because I saw her coming from the backyard with a black-and-white two-piece bathing suit on, fitting her perfectly. Her hair was pulled back. It made her look more mature then she already was, like a younger version of the model Naomi Campbell. Surprisingly, I could tell that she knew who we were, and which helmet I was under, because she walked right over to my bike just as I was pulling it off.

"Nice bike," she said.

"Thanks."

"Nice outfit, too. All three of you," she complimented us, not wanting to leave Mal and Ant out.

"This is my friend Ant."

She cut me off. "From the projects," she said, making a joke that flew over both Mal's and Ant's heads.

We both laughed. "I'll explain later," I told them.

"Nice to meet you, Ant."

"The same," he answered, trying to look and sound all hard, like Lisa said most guys from the west end did.

Lisa just smiled. "We got food and stuff in the back. Follow me." I watched as she sashayed up her driveway.

We got off our bikes and started toward the backyard. "Ant, chill out, man," I whispered to him as we walked to the backyard. "This ain't that type of party, kid. We out the hood now." Ant was my boy, and I loved him to death, but I didn't want him to embarrass us and make people think that because we were from the projects we didn't know how to act.

"I got you, man," he said, putting me at ease.

"I know you do." I put my hand on my boy's shoulder to let him know I meant no harm.

I must admit, when we stepped in the back, all eyes were on us. If a prize were being given out for best dressed, it would have been a three-way tie among me, Mal, and Ant. I had on the royal blue Hawaiian set, with the red and yellow print,

Kamal had on the green one, with red and blue print, and Ant had on the red, with green and blue print on it; all similar, yet different.

Shorties outnumbered the guys three to one, and they were definitely clocking us, but Lisa had my undivided attention. She made me a plate of food while we talked for a while. Although I didn't get in the pool, Mal and Ant did. At first, the east end guys were standing off to the sides staring and whispering among themselves about us; but once they saw the girls were all in the pool with Mal and Ant, they all hopped in and joined in the water games that my brother and my boy had started up. Everyone looked like they were enjoying themselves.

That day it wasn't about east end or west end, who was smarter or who was tougher; it was about guys and girls having fun. I was glad that I had gone, and I was even more glad that I had made a new friend.

Chapter Six

It was the Fourth of July, and it was just as hot out as the fireworks that would be shooting off all day. Most parents took their kids to the parade downtown and then to Green Brook Park in town or Green Acres in North Plainfield later on that night to see the fireworks show. But not us. After the parade, we'd hang out and go back and forth from our projects to across the tracks in the field, while the whole hood would be cooking out. It was like one big family reunion. Mothers, fathers, sisters, brothers, cousins, nieces, nephews, and friends, you name it, they'd be there. But if you weren't from either side of the projects or knew somebody from around there, then it would be in your best interest not to come around because you'd be asking for trouble.

When the sun went down, the hustlers put on their own fireworks show for all of us, with the works that they brought from either Canal Street in Manhattan or South of the Border, in the middle of North Carolina and South Carolina, for those guys who traveled. I invited Lisa, but her parents wouldn't let her come because they said it was too dangerous for her around here. Since the pool party, we had been talking on the phone on a regular basis.

It was almost time for the parade to start and the projects were definitely going to be out there deep. By now, all of us had mopeds, and everybody agreed to ride downtown together. Out of all of us, Mark and Shawn had the flyest ones because theirs were hooked up. They had gotten theirs from selling packages for an old head name Clyde, who was originally from the South but was an OG around the way, which was an old-school gangster.

"Where these niggas at?" questioned Ant, referring to Trevor and the rest of them.

As soon as he said it, Trevor and them came bucking under the bridge, rolling up in the field.

"We was about to leave your punk asses, takin' all long and shit," Ant said to Trevor.

"Man, shut the fuck up, you wasn't about to leave nobody. That's like Voltron forming without the head," Trevor said, as we all started cracking up.

"Mal, Mil, what up?"

"Same stuff, different day," Mal answered.

"I hear that."

"What up, Trev?" I replied.

"Yo, we can kick it later. Let's get up outta here and bounce to this parade, and stop bullshittin'," Ant hollered, before peeling off.

We all looked at each other and laughed, as we followed suit.

The parade was wack, like it always was every year, but toward the end it turned out to be kind of fly because everybody thought that we were a part of it when we were riding behind the firetrucks, which was usually the last thing you saw at the end of every parade. Little kids were waving and clapping, and wanting us to beep our horns. Some of them even wanted us to give them a ride. That was the only fun part of the day, but the real fun wouldn't really start until we got back around the way and chilled in the field, watching the fireworks go off.

Just as I figured, everybody and their mother was at the cookout in the field, and as night fell people began to thin out, because although it was supposed to be a celebration, some of the elderly people didn't trust being outside in the projects after dark. It was just like that.

Mal and I had to practically beg our moms to let us stay out, even though my grandmother disapproved of it. Monique and Jasmine couldn't be in the field at night, though. They had to watch from the window. Being boys allowed us to get away with a lot more than the girls could, regardless of the fact that Monique was older than Kamal and me.

Me, Mal, Ant, Trevor, and the rest of my boys were leaning up against the fence waiting for the show to kick off. The only two who weren't there with us were Mark and Shawn. They were up at the handball court with all the other hustlers who were letting off the fireworks. I knew if I would've asked Mu he would've let Mal and me chill up there with him too, but I didn't want to leave Ant and them hanging like that.

Boom! Boom! Crack! Crack! Pop! Pop! The fireworks were sounding off.

"Yo, that shit look dope!" Ant shouted.

"Word! Them niggas went all out this year on that shit," Trevor added.

"One day I'm gonna cop me a whole bunch of shit like that and light the projects up with some shit that spell my name. Trev!" He illustrated this, waving his hand across the air as if his name was actually being spelled.

Ba-Boom! Ba-Boom! Crack! Crr-ack!

Bop! Bop! Bop! Pap! Pap!

"Yo, you hear that?" I asked, thinking I had heard something other than fireworks.

"Hear what?" Mal asked.

No sooner had I asked the question than I could hear screaming coming from the handball court's direction, and saw everyone beginning to scatter.

"Oh, shit! Somebody shootin'!" yelled Ant, as we all started ducking, running for cover along with the crowd.

Bop! Bop! Bop! Buck! Buck! Buck!

You could hear more shots being fired simultaneously. From where I was crouched down, I could see a blue station wagon driving slowly down the West Third Street side of the Bricks, with one masked man leaning out of the back window, another out of the front passenger's side, and a third one through the sunroof, all dressed in black and armed with weapons in their hands pointed in the direction of the handball court. The next thing I heard was screeching tires and then the station wagon was gone.

We all made it to safety out of the field and broke to our cribs. This time Mal and I went over the tracks rather than around. As Mal and I got to the door of our building, I could see both my mom and my grandmother in their nightgowns, with tearful eyes and worried looks on their faces as we walked in the building. Although we had gotten used to the shootouts and hearing gunfire, this was one Fourth of July that Mal and I would never forget.

Chapter Seven

Last night's entertainment turned into an unforgettable tragedy. The front page of the *Courier News*, which was a local newspaper that covered the surrounding area, caught my attention. It read, FOURTH OF JULY MASSACRE, 3 DEAD 4 WOUNDED. When I opened the newspaper to see the article on what happened, it read the following:

Last night, July 4, 1986, witnesses say that two unidentified gunmen opened fire on a crowd of spectators at a Fourth of July fireworks gathering at a local park on the 400 block of West End Avenue located in the Liberty Elm Garden.

The death total of this incident is three and the total injuries sustained were four. Three are stable and one is in critical condition.

The deceased victims have been identified as nineteen-year-old Terrance Smalls, eighteen-year-old Trina Smith, and a fifteen-year-old boy whose name was not released to the press due to his being a minor. Among the victims wounded is another minor, a fourteen-year-old who is in critical condition. Sources say that the boy may be paralyzed from the waist down.

Eighteen-year-old Michael Harvey was treated and released for a gunshot wound in the leg. Twenty-year-old William Thomas was also treated and released for a graze by a 9 mm bullet to the arm. Twenty-one-year-old Mustafa Ali received treatment for a graze to the arm.

Although only two gunmen were reported, police say that they've found at least four different calibers of shell casings, and sources say this was most likely a drug-related incident.

I couldn't believe what my eyes had just read. I wanted to believe that the newspaper had made some type of mistake or I was reading a misprint of the event, but my gut told me that there was no mistake about what I read and my eyes were not deceiving me.

The only names I recognized were Mustafa's and Terrance's. I couldn't believe Terrance got killed. I knew Mal and I needed to go check on Ant and his moms, because I knew they were going crazy right about now. The paper also said that two minors got hit, one dead and the other in critical condition. I hoped that it wasn't our boys, 'cause I knew that Mark and Shawn were up there last night too, but I didn't think they'd be a part of all that.

"Mal, read this." I handed the newspaper to my brother as he came out of the bathroom.

As Kamal read what I had just finished reading, he blurted out what I had already thought. "Yo, I think them two minors might be Mark and Shawn, bro. Damn! We gots to shoot over to Ant's crib and check on him and Ms. Smalls." We wasted no time throwing something on and we bolted out the door.

By the time we had walked from our crib to Ant's all had been confirmed. According to the word on the street, Mark had caught a bullet in the back of the head and one in the neck as he was running, trying to get away. He died instantly. Shawn got shot in the groin and in the chest and was in critical condition. Terrance was hit twice in the face and three times in the stomach. The shorty, Tina, was Terrance's girlfriend.

She caught a bullet to the heart and one in the stomach, killing both her and the baby she was carrying. She was seven months pregnant.

Ant was flipping out when Ms. Smalls opened the door for us. "Oh, thank God. Kamal and Kamil, I'm glad you're here," Ms. Smalls cried out when she saw that it was us. "They took one of my babies last night; please don't let them take my other one from me. Anthony is talking crazy. I don't want him going out there killing nobody or getting himself killed. My heart couldn't take it," she said, exhausted, as she fell into my arms.

"Don't worry about it, ma, we not gonna let Ant do anything to get himself hurt or in trouble," I tried to assure her, wondering myself if I could be calmed down if it were Mal who had gotten killed.

"Fuck that! I'm gonna get them muthafuckas," Ant screamed, punching the wall and knocking things over. Kamal tried to grab him, but Ant was so out of control that he punched him in the mouth. Mal knew he didn't mean it, so he just backed up and waited for Ant to tire himself out and cool off.

"Why, man?" Ant kept asking over and over, with uncontrollable tears running down his face. He stopped fighting and let Kamal wrap his arms around him.

"I know it hurts, man. Let it out, bro, let it out," Mal said to him. "I'm here for you, kid."

I could see in Kamal's face that he felt Ant's pain, and the tears began to fall from his own eyes. Knowing my brother, I knew Ant's loss made him think about if it had been me, just as I did when I was holding Ms. Smalls in my arms.

I fought back my tears, but I was hurting inside. Although they may have been hurting the most, it wasn't just Ant and Ms. Smalls's loss. It was a loss for all of us. Ant was like a brother to us and we were family. Not only had we lost Terrance, we had also lost one of our boys, Mark.

"Let's take him outside to get some air," I suggested to Mal, seeing that Ant was beginning to calm down.

"I wanna go on the other side," Ant requested. We didn't question Ant. Instead, we followed as he ran up the tracks headed for the field.

When we got to the other side, I looked across the field where everything had jumped off the previous night. There was no one in sight. The only thing that you could see was the yellow police tape and the blue wooden horses blocking off the area. You could see the cops had chalked an outline of the dead bodies where they had lain, and chalked circles around the places where they had found bullet shells, so we took

Ant to the back so he didn't have to see any of that.

By then, Trev, Black, Reef, and Quadir had rolled up on the mopeds. No one said a word. They all just took turns hugging Ant. It was a real emotional and sentimental moment among us, for this was the first time tragedy had actually struck so close to home and brought all of us together like this to show just how close we really were.

Quadir broke the silence. "This is for the niggas who can't be here," he said as he cracked open a forty ounce of Olde English 800, took a sip, passed it, and then began cracking open another one. Trevor pulled out a fat joint and lit it up. The smell of weed clogged the air, as he took a few pulls and inhaled, and then passed it to Ant.

"Here, baby boy, this'll help ease the pain," Trevor said to him.

Ant grabbed the spliff and took a long and hard pull, and began to choke from the smoke. I was surprised to see Ant take the joint because he didn't smoke, but I understood it was about anything that could help to escape the reality of what had happened last night.

"Mal, hit this," Black said, passing my brother the forty of Olde E.

Without hesitation, Mal took the forty ounce and began gulping the alcohol, just as I had seen Quadir do. I couldn't believe Mal was drinking, because we had made a pact that we would never drink or do any type of drugs, ever, but here was my brother drinking beer.

"Mil, take this," Mal said, putting the bottle in my face.

I stared at it as if it were the plague.

"Man, I said take this shit!" my brother based at me. "Two of our boys just got smoked and another one is lyin' up in the hospital fucked up and might not make it either, and you bullshittin' like you can't pay them no respect," he yelled.

I never heard my brother talk like that, let alone to me, but I knew what had happened last night was the cause of both his and Ant's behavior. I took the bottle of beer and started to drink. I held my breath to avoid the stale smell. The taste was kind of bitter and I didn't like it, but I continued drinking because it wasn't about whether I liked it. It was about paying my respects.

That day was a sad day. I took a drink for the first time that day; and I knew I had allowed peer pressure to persuade me to do something I knew I had no business doing.

Chapter Eight

It was ten days until school started back up, and I hadn't seen Mustafa since the Fourth of July incident. Shawn was out of the hospital, but he didn't want any visitors. I heard he had taken Mark's death real hard and felt somewhat to blame. He said he was the one who encouraged Mark to drop out of school so they both could hustle full time.

They were both in high school so I didn't know they had dropped out. Mark was in the tenth grade and Shawn was in the ninth grade when they quit.

Everything was back to normal around the projects. Over a month had gone by and it was business as usual with the addicts and the dealers. Word on the street was that the project guys retaliated on the block that the shooters were supposed to have been from, which was another known drug block on Arlington Avenue, not too far from the high school. It was rumored that the beef started over one of the guys from the projects trying to talk to a girl who was supposed to be dating a guy from Arlington Avenue.

I had been trying to find out about Mu, but nobody seemed to know his whereabouts, so I left it alone, hoping he was okay.

"If y'all want to get these school clothes you better have your behinds at the car by the time I get my pocketbook and car keys," my mom said to us.

My mother had been working really hard these past months to provide for the four of us. Living in the projects with our grandmother allowed her to save money and get an education since public assistance only made my grandmother pay six dollars a month for rent, half of which my mother paid, along with paying for groceries and the phone bill. I had been hearing my mom talk about moving out of the projects and into a bigger place. Although it sounded nice, I had become fine with where I was, and I didn't want to leave the projects. This had become my new home and I had become used to it.

Downtown Newark was the place to shop for black people in Jersey; it was like 125th Street in Harlem, New York. Though downtown looked like a nice place to shop the rest of the city was known to be rough when it came to drugs and violence, worse than where we lived, probably because it was twice as big as my town. The way they described it kind of reminded me of my old neighborhood back in Brooklyn.

"I'm going to tell you right now, Kamil and Kamal. The two of you are only getting five outfits apiece. I don't have a whole lot of money to be spending on y'all clothes just 'cause you trying to keep up with the latest style. And all you getting is one pair of tennis shoes, and one pair of dress shoes, is that understood?" she asked, as if we had a choice.

There were so many stores to choose from, but the ones that we wanted to go into were the ones that my mother was walking right by.

"Ma, can we go in Express?" I asked as we almost passed by the store.

"Kamil, what did I tell you? I'm not out here shopping for any name-brand clothes; I'm out here to get you clothes to put on your back regardless who names are on them. I don't know why you kids go crazy over wearing somebody else name on the back of your behind."

"All right, Ma," I said, blowing hot air.

"I know you didn't just get smart," she shouted "Kamil, don't get cute and make me knock your behind down in front of all these people. You not too big to get your butt whipped."

Embarrassed, I just remained silent. It had been a long time since my moms had talked to me like I was a two-year-old, threatening me with a beating.

The shopping spree ended, and Kamal and I were going back home with nothing we wanted, from shirts all the way down to sneakers. Everything was wack, but there was no way we were going to hurt our mom's feelings, especially knowing how hard she worked just to get us what she had. We both sucked it up and accepted the fact that things were different and we were now among the less fortunate.

Chapter Nine

It was Labor Day weekend, and two days from now would be the first day of school. As usual, the community was cooking out in the field. Kamal was still in bed. He was out front all night kicking it with this sixteen-year-old girl from around back. She was cute, but not cute enough to make me stay up all night talking.

"Kamal?"

"Huh?"

"Mal!"

"What, yo?"

"Yo, I'm going over to Ant's to see what's up."

"Yeah, a'ight, I'll be over there in a couple of hours. What time is it now?"

"A little after ten o'clock."

"I should be up by one. That shorty had me out there talking all night, playing games, beating me in the head about nothin'."

"Yeah, I heard you creeping in early this morning like you were a burglar kid."

On my way to Ant's crib, I heard a horn beep. When I turned around, I saw a candy apple red Benz 190E with deep dish gold hammer rims and a gold grill, with a tan leather rag top and tinted windows. Nobody had to tell me who it was. Even though I had never seen the car before, it only fit one person's style I knew, and that was Mustafa.

"Mil, it's me, Mu. Get in!" he yelled over at me.

I lit up at the sight of Mu. I hadn't been that happy to see another man since the last time I went to see my dad for his birthday. I wasted no time climbing into the Benz.

As soon as I got in Mu drove off. "What up, kid? How you been?"

"I'm a'ight," I replied, revealing how happy I was to see him. "Man, I thought I'd never see you again, Mu. I didn't know what happened to you after I read the papers about the Fourth."

"Nothing ain't happen to me, li'l bro. That was something light. Got a battle scar out the deal," he said nonchalantly, referring to his gunshot wound I had read about in the newspaper. "Other than that, I just been out of town on vacation, layin' low, that's all. Always remember, Mil: when the spot is hot, find somewhere else to chill out until it cools down. That's one of the rules of the game." He dropped one of his many jewels I had become used to him dropping on me. "I bet jokers been getting locked up left and right since I been gone, right?"

"Yup, you right," I responded.

"I just got back from Virginia Beach. My son's mother lives out there, so I went to go chill with them for a little bit," Mu told me.

"How old is your son?" I asked, not knowing that he had any kids.

"He just turned two years old this past August. That's why I was down there so long, celebrating with my li'l man. Where's Mal? This has gotta be the first time I ever seen you without him."

"He's still in the bed, 'sleep, tired from talking to this shorty named Crystal who lives in the back."

"Yeah, I know her," Mu said. "Tell him to watch himself 'cause she plays a lot of games."

"That's what he said too. Why did you come back from Virginia if you were enjoying yourself down there?"

"Because a vacation is just what it's called: a vacation," he started out saying. "You can vacate one area to get away to another to relax, but after you've relaxed you have to return to the reality of your life. Vacations don't last forever." He broke it down to me, then finished up by saying, "Besides I had to get back so I could give you and Mal this trunk full of gear I got for the two of you. What? You thought I forgot, kid?" Mu asked, smiling at me like he just bested me at a game I thought I was going to win.

"Nah, I just thought that you were too busy, but I knew you didn't forget."

"Young buck, let me explain something to you. Never make a promise that you can't keep. Always do what you say you'll do, no matter what."

Now I knew why everybody respected Mustafa: because he not only talked the talk, but he walked the walk. I had already decided that I wanted to be just like him when I got older.

When Mu opened the trunk, I couldn't believe my eyes. All I saw were boxes and boxes of sneakers and bags and bags of clothes piled on top of one another. Nikes, Adidas, and Reeboks were the names on the sneaker boxes, along with the sweat suits to match. In other bags were all the latest jeans, A.J., Cotler, Oslo, Vasco, and the freshest shirts, Le Tigre, the ones that all the known hustlers wore, and underneath all of that were two leather goose-down jackets, one white with black fur and the other black with black fur around the collar.

Mu had gone all out for Kamal and me.

"Oh, junk, Mu, you took care of us on the gear tip," I said excitedly. "Wait until Mal sees this. He's going to flip."

"Didn't I tell you I was gonna have you two lookin' the flyest in school?" he said back with a proud expression on his face, knowing that the mission was accomplished.

"How'd you know our sizes, though?"

"Come on, young buck. I've been shopping for myself for a long time and I was once your age, and your size, so it didn't take a genius to figure it out. But if I was off then let me know and I'll go exchange whatever needs to be exchanged."

I was too busy tripping off all the fly gear that I didn't realize we were in a driveway. "Where are we?" I asked, curious.

"We're at my house."

"I thought you lived in the projects," I said, a little puzzled.

"Mil, you got a lot to learn, young brother. I grew up in the projects, I'm from the projects, and I get money in the projects, but I don't live in the projects anymore. Another rule to live by," he said. "A word to the wise: never lay ya head where you shit at. You wit' me?" Mu asked, making sure I followed.

"Yeah, I'm wit' you," I said, nodding my head.

"Close up the trunk. You might as well come inside while I snatch something up right quick."

When I walked through the door, I was mesmerized. Mu's crib was laid out, looking like something straight out of the TV show *Lifestyles of the Rich and Famous*. He told me to take my shoes off by the door, but I didn't know why until I got past the hall. There was wall-to-wall carpet everywhere.

"Have a seat in the living room," he said, pointing to the right. The living room consisted of a six-piece leather set, with a red calypso carpet, a sixty-inch big-screen TV, with an entertainment system that had a Panasonic stereo system, a Atari 2600 game set, and a bunch of game cartridges, along with a full shelf of cassette tapes. In the middle of the room was a glass table with magazines placed on top, stacked neatly on the left side, and on the other side he had a Quran book. On the walls he had all different types of paintings, and a couple of African-looking masks and statues to match, with spears in the corner. Just from the looks of his living room, you could tell that he was living large, and living single, too.

"You want something to drink?" Mu yelled from the kitchen.

"Nah, I'm good."

"Come here for a minute. I wanna show you something."

I got up and went into the kitchen to see what he wanted to show me, and as I entered the kitchen, it was as though I had just walked into Fort Knox. Mu had dough stacked up on the table so high I couldn't even see his face.

"You see this right here?" he asked, pointing at all the money in front of him. "This is from being smart. This is what's gonna get me outta the streets. I'm about to get out the game, kid, and open up a couple of businesses out here and in VA, so I don't gotta be looking over my shoulder for the rest of my life wonderin' when they comin' to take me down. The name of the game is hit 'em and quit 'em. You gots to make the money and not let the money make you, 'cause ain't no longevity in this game, baby boy."

Mu was always dropping jewels on me and I was always absorbing what he said because he always made sense when he rapped.

"Yeah, I'm going to open up a clothing store right downtown, and a Laundromat, right there in the hood, and a unisex beauty salon/barber shop for my baby moms 'cause she does hair down there in VA. Security! That's what it's all about, security!" he repeated. "Soon as I put this up we outta here. Go back in the living room and wait for me."

***

It was almost one o'clock by the time Mu and I pulled up into the projects. Heads were turning in the field when they saw Mu's Benz roll up.

"Look at everybody sweatin' your ride, Mu," I said to him, glad to be in the passenger's seat.

"Mil, I don't get caught up in all the hype. Those people don't give a fuck about me. If I was pushin' a Gremlin or a Pinto right now, nobody would be lookin' over here. If I got killed today they'd forget my name tomorrow. I'd be just another statistic, that's all, and another brother would be right there to pick up where I left off. The game never changes, only the players, remember that. Yo, I can't stick around, but what are you gonna do with the clothes in the trunk? You know you can't take them home," he said as if reading my mind.

"I'm gonna take everything to Ant's house like me and Mal always do. Let me go get Mal right quick."

"All right, cool. I'm gonna pull around to the side so everybody not in ya business. I wouldn't want ya moms or grams to hear nothin'."

Kamal and Ant were in the field. I could see their mouths open ready to ask a million questions.

"Yo, whose piece is that, Mu's?" Ant asked when I got out of the Benz.

"Yeah."

"I knew it," Mal yelled. "That piece is dope!"

"Yo, I need you to come help me, Mal. Mu got us some gear."

"Word?"

"Ant, we need to keep this stuff in your crib."

"Man, I'm gonna start chargin' you niggas for storage, all that shit you got at my crib," he said, joking. "I knew that anyway. Let's get y'all stuff."

After splitting everything down the middle, Mal and I ended up with three pair of sneakers, three sweat suits, six pair of jeans, six shirts, and a leather goose down jacket apiece. With the gear we had, I knew it was going to be a good school year.

Chapter Ten

It was the first day of school and I had been up since six o'clock that morning, ready. Man, the summer flew by. In spite of all the new gear Mal and I got from Mustafa and my moms, we still decided to do like everybody else when school started back up, which was to rock our old gear, and then bust out with fresh gear the following week.

"Monique, Jasmine, Kamil, Kamal, come eat your breakfast," my grandmother yelled. "I want all of you to be finished eating and out the door by seven thirty. I don't want to find out that any of you were late for your first day at school, you hear me?"

The bell didn't ring until 8:15, and we weren't considered tardy until 8:20. It only took us about twenty-five minutes if we walked, since we lived on the west end and our school was on the east end. What my grandmother didn't know was that with our mopeds it only took us ten minutes to get there, and fifteen if Monique, who knew we had the mopeds and didn't tell, wanted us to drop her off. My grandmother took Jasmine to school, so we didn't have to worry about her.

"We're not going to be late, Grandma," we all promised, smiling at one another.

"Good morning, everybody," my mother said as she came in, buttoning up the top of her blouse.

"Good morning, Ma," we all sang.

"Ma, you're looking good this morning. You sure you're going to work, and not on a hot date?" I asked, sparking a smile out of her.

"Boy, knock it off. You don't get paid to be no comedian," she shot back at me.

To tell the truth, that was the first time that I had seen my moms in the morning since the summer had begun. By the time I woke up, she had already gone to work or, on the weekends, she was always asleep from working so hard. It was definitely good seeing her that particular morning, though it was only for a couple of minutes. My mother kissed all of us, snatched up a piece of toast along with the mug of coffee my grandmother had waiting for her, and then she was out the door.

Everybody was standing outside in front of the building waiting for the bell to ring when we rode up. We knew Black and Shareef were somewhere around because their bikes were already chained to the bike rack.

"NPP in the house!" we heard somebody shout from behind us, knowing that those somebodys had to be Black and Shareef. That was the name we had made up for ourselves in the hood. New Projects Posse was what it stood for, but we weren't a gang. Well, technically we were, because a gang was considered to be two or more people who come together, and we were definitely deeper then that, but we were more of a neighborhood gang who just had each other's backs in and out of school. Every neighborhood had one.

"What it is?" Black said, giving me a pound and a hug.

"It is what it is," Mal answered.

"Chillin'," was all I said.

"Yo, where y'all was at this morning? We waited for y'all in the front for a minute," Black said.

"Probably getting their last kisses and hugs from their moms and grams, like they're going to the army or something," Shareef said, laughing at his own joke.

"I got ya army right here," Mal replied, grabbing the front of his jeans.

"You know I don't play them dick jokes, Mal."

"Both of y'all buggin'," I interrupted. "If you can't take a joke, don't joke."

They both looked at each other, and then turned on me at the same time. "Shut the hell up!" they both said in unison, and we all busted out laughing.

So this is junior high, I remember saying to myself as I took it all in. It looked a lot like elementary school to me, only a little bigger. The card that the guidance counselor gave me said at the top HOMEROOM: ROOM 114. As I walked down the hall, I spotted it. There were about sixteen desks in the class and about twelve people in the class scattered about. I found a desk in the back and grabbed a seat.

"Hello, my name is Ms. Chiles. C-h-i-l-e-s. For those of you who are new here at Maxson, I'd like to welcome you."

Just as Ms. Chiles was about to start her next sentence, she was interrupted by the opening of the classroom door. "Please come in and have a seat." Ms. Chiles gestured. The girl walked in. It was someone I knew. I remember not being able to hold back my smile. It was Lisa Matthews.

"Excuse me," she said. "I had a problem finding the class." She took the first available seat.

"It's all right, Ms. . . . ."

"Matthews. Lisa Matthews," she told the teacher.

"It's all right, Ms. Matthews. You're not the first student to ever do that, and I'm sure that you won't be the last. I'm just glad you could make it. Better late than never," Ms. Chiles teased. "Now, as I was saying," she continued as she repeated her speech.

I didn't get to speak to Lisa in homeroom because she broke out as soon as the bell rang, probably to get a head start on finding her next class, not wanting to be late again. I had hoped that she was in some of my other classes so I could kick it to her. The last few weeks of summer I didn't get to talk to her because so much had happened around my neighborhood.

There were only about six people in my metal shop class when I got there, and neither Mal, Reef, or Black were any of them, but when I took a second glance I saw that there was someone in the class worth seeing. It was Lisa.

I walked up and spoke to her. She looked at me as if I were a stranger or something and was disturbing her from something very important.

"Oh, excuse me, you're speaking now?" she sarcastically remarked.

I was thrown off balance, because she caught me off guard. I wasn't expecting her to respond like that, but I had an idea why.

"I never stopped speaking to you, Lisa. Just because I didn't call doesn't mean that I didn't want to speak to you. A lot has happened down my way in the past few weeks," I began to explain. "And time flew past me. Before I knew it school was starting again." I didn't know why I stood there explaining myself, but for some reason I felt she deserved an explanation. "For what it's worth, I apologize for not calling, and I apologize for bothering you right now," I told her as I turned around to walk off.

"Kamil, wait!" She stopped me. "I'm the one who owes you an apology. I had no right snapping on you like that just now," she said, apologetic.

"Yes, you did. I understand. That was inconsiderate of me. Besides, if the shoe were on the other foot I would've acted like that too, but worse," I added with my signature grin.

She laughed. "Listen to you trying to use big words, 'inconsiderate,'" she mocked me. "And I don't believe you would've acted like I just did, either."

"Maybe not like that, but I would've been mad," I said with a smile on my face.

The teacher cleared his throat. "I don't mean to interrupt your date or anything, but some of us are here to teach and learn about metal shop. This is not the love shop. Do that on your own time."

Everyone in the class began to laugh along with Lisa and me. "Pardon me, Teach," I said as I grabbed a seat.

"It's all right, my brother; and you can call me Mr. Brown," he corrected me. "Although 'Teach' sounds cooler, I don't think my boss would find it appropriate if she heard you saying it," he said.

When class was over, Lisa and I went our separate ways. She told me if we didn't see each other after school to call her later around 5:00 p.m.

The school day was finally winding down. It wasn't so bad, especially since I got to talk to Lisa, but I just had the urge to get out of there. Mal was in my math and social studies classes. Reef was in my science class, along with Lisa, and Black was in my gym class. We all ate lunch together, which was cool because it felt like we were up in the hood chilling.

"Yo, it's a lot of fly honies up in this piece," Black said.

"You ain't lyin'," my brother shouted, giving him a high five.

"I saw that dark brown shorty in science class checkin' you out the whole time we was up in there, Mil. What's up wit' that?" Black said, putting me on the spot.

"Who, Lisa? Yeah, she's cool," I answered. "But why you clockin' me, kid?"

"Nigga, ain't nobody clockin' ya punk ass. I was just sayin' that I peeped her checkin' you out, that's all."

As if Black had conjured her up, Lisa walked right up on our conversation, along with her friends Felicia and Tracy who I remembered from elementary.

"Hey, Kamil. Hey, Kamal. Hey, Black," Lisa said. "I don't know your other friend, but hi anyway."

"What's up?" Shareef said.

"This is my friend Shareef, but everybody calls him Reef."

"What's up, Kamal?" Felicia joined in. "This is like déjà vu," she said.

"Déjà what?" Mal asked.

"You know, like déjà vu, like seeing or doing something twice. Remember last year you two were unchaining your bikes and we invited you to our pool party? Only difference now is that you're unchaining your mopeds and we're asking for rides to Lisa house."

Lisa rolled her eyes at Felicia's boldness. I could tell she had no idea that was the plan.

"Oh, I get it now," Mal said. "I didn't know that's what that was called, though."

"So can we?" Tracy asked.

"Can you what?"

"Can we get a ride to Lisa's?" Tracy followed up with.

"Oh, yeah, that's no problem. Reef, Black, this is Felicia, and Tracy. Tracy, Felicia, these are my boys, Black and Reef," Mal introduced them all.

"Nice to meet you both," Tracy and Felicia said to them.

"The same," they both answered.

"So, who's riding with who?" Kamal asked, looking in Lisa's direction. "Not you, Lisa. We already know the answer to that." He snickered.

Lisa blushed at my brother's comment.

"I'm riding with you, Kamal," Felicia said, approaching his bike.

"Shorty, you can ride with me if you want," Shareef said to Tracy.

"Okay," Tracy replied, giddy.

You could tell this was their first time ever riding on the back of mopeds before by the way they were acting when they got off.

"Thanks for the rides," they all said.

"That was fun as hell," an excited Felicia screamed. "Kamal, you're crazy, swerving through traffic like that; I thought you were going to kill us."

"I'd never do anything to try to hurt you." Mal smiled.

A blind man could see that Felicia was digging my brother.

"Shareef, it was really nice to meet you. I'll see you in school tomorrow. Thanks again for the ride," Tracy said as she ran to Lisa's porch.

"So, Kamil, are you going to call me later?" Lisa asked me.

"I planned on it, unless you don't want me to," I joked.

"Stop playing, boy, you know I want you to call."

"Then I'll call."

Lisa leaned over and kissed me on the cheek. "Thanks for the ride. You better call," she said, smiling.

"I will," I said as cool as I could sound.

They waved good-bye from the porch as we rode off, beeping our horns.

Chapter Eleven

I couldn't believe that it was almost Christmas. Less than two weeks away. It seemed like we were just terrorizing the neighborhood about a week ago on mystery night before Halloween, and celebrating Thanksgiving just the other day. This year was basically over with. Those three months of junior high flew by quickly. I guess time flies when you're having fun, and I was definitely doing that, especially since winter had officially started. Ever since the snow had been on the ground, the projects had been the most fun for us ever. Between having snowball fights, bombing cars, and playing tackle football, I didn't think that it got any better than that in the hood in the wintertime, besides watching the police slip and fall while trying to jump out of their cars chasing the guys around here who were hustling. It was like watching a live cartoon, like the Road Runner or Tom and Jerry.

It was nine days until winter vacation, and school didn't start back up until January 2 of next year. That was eleven days of freedom I was looking forward to. I had been working hard in school to keep up because the work was a little harder than what I was used to. I couldn't believe how much work they had loaded us up with for the Christmas break. I intended to knock all of mine out on the first two days of our vacation and I suggested my brother and boys do the same. But my words fell on deaf ears as they continued to complain.

"Man, I don't know why they gave us all this homework anyway. This supposed to be a vacation," my brother sulked.

"That's what I'm sayin'," Black joined in. "I'm not doin' this shit, kid, unless I can do all of it the night before we have to go back to school. Hell, I might not even go back. My moms don't give a fuck anyway," he added. His words came out of nowhere, surprising us all.

"Don't talk like that, Black," I said, trying to reason with him. "It would make your moms proud to see you bring home your high school diploma," I pointed out. "That piece of paper is going to be your ticket out of the hood, man."

"Mil, check this out, the only paper that's gonna get me and my moms outta the hood is that green paper, you dig what I'm sayin'?"

"Yeah, you right, but you can't get no good-paying job without an education."

"Yo, fuck that! If I can't make it then I'ma take mine in life," Black said angrily.

"Black, you talkin' crazy, man," Reef stepped in. "That's the same attitude your pops had when he was out here. And, no disrespect, but look where it got him. I thought you said you ain't wanna turn out like him when you grew up."

After a short pause Black spoke. He began to shake his head and shift from side to side like a little kid. "You right. I'm buggin' out." He came to his senses. "But school is borin' and wack, and if y'all wasn't up in there I would've been dropped out."

"I hear you, man," Reef replied empathetically. "But remember what we agreed to. We said we were gonna stay in school and gut it out."

We all surrounded Black and gave him a group hug. It was times like this where we really came together. The last thing we wanted was to lose any more of our boys to the streets because of a wrong choice or bad decision.

We were supposed to meet Ant and the rest of them in the field on the other side so we hurried home, dropped off our book bags, and headed for the train tracks. Against our better judgment, every now and again we would defy our grandmother and cross over with our boys. Before anyone who knew our grandmother had a chance to notice us, Mal and I quickly ran up the snow-covered rocks and waited for Black and Shareef to follow.

"Mil." Mal pulled at my coat as he whispered my name. My back was to him so I turned to face him. When I spun around to see what he wanted my eyes widened. A little ways up on the other side of the tracks was one of the hustlers from our side of the projects with his pants down to his ankles, head tilted back, and hands on top of a female's head, who was squatted down in front of him giving him a blowjob.

"Dag!" I said in a low tone. I couldn't believe that we were witnessing the act in person. The closest I had come to ever seeing a female perform oral sex on someone was in a dirty magazine we had found one day by the Dumpster in the back of the projects. Mal and I were mesmerized by the sight. I caught an instant erection just watching.

"Oh, shit! She suckin' the fuck outta his dick!" Shareef bellowed.

"Can I get next?" Black followed up with.

Our trance was broken by the sounds of Black's and Shareef's voices. They had also managed to interrupt the hustler's tricking session. The girl wasted no time. She immediately shot up and tried to hide both her identity and embarrassment by hiding behind the hustler named Rich. Rich, on the other hand, stood there with his exposed manhood still standing at attention.

"What the fuck is wrong with you li'l niggas?' He let out a light chuckle as he reached down for his pants. "You never had your dick sucked before or something?" he asked as if he'd be surprised if our answers were no.

"Our bad, Rich, we were just havin' a li'l fun," Black answered.

"Yeah, well, you just blew my fun," Rich shot back. Rich's next words let us know that the girl hiding behind him had said something in his ear. "Chill the fuck out, Tee. Those are my li'l homies right there; they're not going to say nothin'."

"Nah, we not gonna say nothin'." Shareef assured Rich.

"We appreciate that, li'l homies. I got somethin' for y'all when I catch y'all back in the hood," Rich told us. As we walked off, Rich wasted no time convincing the girl to finish what she had started and we had interrupted.

"Yo, y'all know who that was up there with Rich?" Shareef was the first to ask.

Mal and I were clueless.

"Yeah, that was that chick Tia from building 540," Black replied. "I know that fat ass from anywhere."

When Black said her name and the building she was from it hit me. Tia was considered one of the prettiest girls in the projects. She was also one of if not the youngest mother in our projects. I knew that because my grandmother used to talk about it every time she saw Tia walk past her window with a new outfit while her little two-year-old son always trailed behind her looking like he had just finished playing in the mud. My grandmother would say how she couldn't believe the housing authority allowed a twenty-three-year-old single mother to move into the housing projects. She was old-fashioned when it came to certain things and believed that the projects were for elders and families who were not fortunate to maintain a regular household income. In a conversation, I heard her tell one of our neighbors that she felt Tia was just another young, lazy female who refused to work and used welfare as a crutch to minimize her responsibilities as a woman. If only my grandmother could have seen Tia now. I couldn't understand why she was on the train tracks degrading herself like that until Shareef pointed it out.

"Yo, she must've started getting high," he said.

"I was thinking the same thing," Black chimed in.

"That's messed up." Mal shook his head. "I wonder where her son at while she up there playin' herself," he added.

I was with my brother. That was my thought exactly.

"That trifling bitch probably left him in the crib," Shareef retorted.

I couldn't help but think about Tia's son. I wondered if she'd thought about him while she was on the tracks. In a way, I felt sorry for him because he didn't ask to be here and he had no say on who brought him into the world. I shook my head as I thought about my own family and situation. Even though my dad was locked up at that moment, I was thankful that neither he nor my mom was strung out on drugs and that my moms was able to walk away from the life my dad had introduced her to.

Chapter Twelve

I never believed in Santa Claus, because before my pops went away he and my moms did a poor job of hiding the gifts until Christmas Eve. Plus, we used to peek out the front window while they were taking them out of the trunk of the car, so we always knew what we were getting ahead of time, and that Mr. and Mrs. Claus were none other than Dad and Mom. My mother and grandmother didn't even try to hide the gifts anymore because we were all too big to believe in Santa Claus, even Jasmine. Instead, they just wrapped them up, put them under the tree, and told us we better not touch or open anything until Christmas.

None of us played with toys anymore, besides Jasmine, and she only played with dolls, so we already know that all the gifts were full of clothes. We just hoped they weren't imitations. Mustafa had hooked us up with so much gear that we didn't even have to wear what my moms had bought us for the new school year. Well, we wore it, but only to Ant's house and then we changed over there. It would've broken my mom's heart if she found out what we were doing, and that was the last thing Mal and I wanted to do. She wouldn't understand, though; at least, in our minds that's what we thought.

We didn't think she knew what it was like to go to school and have on low-budget gear while everybody else rocked name brand. We didn't think she knew what it was like to want to be popular rather then being considered a cornball, geek, or nerd. And we didn't think she knew what it was like to be looked down on just because of where you lived.

We all sat around the tree opening up our gifts.

"Thank you, Ma. Thanks, Grandma!" Mal and I kissed them both as we gathered up all the boxes of Christmas clothes we had received.

"You're welcome," my moms said.

"Merry Christmas, babies," was my grandmother's response.

Just as we figured, everything was imitation from the shirts down to the sneakers, but we didn't complain. We knew that we got what our mother and grandmother could afford, and we weren't trying to be ungrateful.

Both Monique and Jasmine seemed happy about what they had received. It didn't matter to Monique what type of clothes my mom brought her because she was going to make them look different anyway. She was into fashion designing and she hooked up every piece of clothing she owned. Jasmine got a bunch of Cabbage Patch Kids, Barbie dolls, and some new dresses. What more could a nine-year-old want?

"Ma, we going outside," Mal and I yelled.

"Okay, but I want you back in time to clean up that mess y'all made in the living room with those wrappers."

Just as we were about to walk out the door the phone rang.

"Kamil, telephone," Monique announced. "It's Liiisssa," my sister said, dragging Lisa's name out trying to be funny.

"Give me the phone, girl." I snatched the phone from my sister. "Hello?"

"Merry Christmas, Kamil," she said.

"Same to you."

"How was your Christmas?" she asked.

"It was good," I answered. "I got bunch of clothes."

"Did you get a hat and gloves?" Lisa asked.

"Nah, why you asked that?"

"I was just asking, that's all. Anyway, I was calling to tell you that when you get a chance, come over to my house 'cause I have a Christmas present for you."

"What?" I said as the guilt hit me, knowing that I didn't even think to get her anything.

"You heard me, I have a Christmas present for you," she repeated.

"Ah, man!" I said, blowing hot air into the phone.

"What, what's wrong?" she asked.

"Nothing."

"No, tell me what's wrong, Kamil," she insisted.

"You got me feeling bad now, because I don't even have a gift for you and you got me something," I admitted.

I could hear her laughing. "Kamil, I didn't get you a present expecting one in return. Besides, your friendship alone is a gift to me, so don't feel bad."

I had never heard anyone refer to me as a gift before, let alone a twelve-year-old girl, but I really believed she meant it.

"All right, since you broke it down like that, I won't feel bad, only if you agree to something," I said.

"What?"

"Let me make it up to you," I asked.

"Make it up how?" she wanted to know.

"Never mind all that, just say yes."

"Okay, Kamil, yes, you can make it up to me," she answered.

"Cool. I'll be over there later to pick up my gift."

After hanging out with Ant and the rest of my boys for a few hours I told Kamal I'd be back in time to go to the Christmas party at the Neighborhood House. The only reason we were going there was because they were having a dance contest for a $100 cash prize and we had to show that the best dancers in the town came from the projects, so we were going to represent. We all agreed that whichever one of us won we'd split the money down the middle. It was like getting paid to go to a party because one of us was guaranteed to win.

Ding dong! The doorbell chimed. It had been awhile since I heard the sound of a doorbell. In the hood, you either knocked on the metal project doors real hard or yelled someone's name real loud, and if nobody answered, they weren't home or just didn't want to be bothered.

"Mommy, I got it," I could hear Lisa saying through the door as she opened it up. "I didn't think you were going to show up," she said.

"I'd never make a promise I couldn't keep," I replied, quoting what I had learned from Mustafa.

"Listen to you, Mr. Responsible," she said teasingly. "You can come in. I have to run upstairs and get your present." She invited me in.

When I stepped in, I was not surprised but impressed. I hadn't gone inside when I came over for the pool party that day, but I knew judging by the outside the inside had to be nice. Their home was neatly furnished. It reminded me of how the inside of our brownstone looked when we were back in Brooklyn.

"Lisa, who's that?" her mother asked from upstairs.

"My friend Kamil from school I told you about. He came to pick up his gift," she said back to her mother.

As I sat there waiting, admiring the family pictures on the wall, a tall, slightly heavyset man came walking down the steps. "How do you do, young man?" He extended his hand. "I'm Lisa's father."

"I'm fine, sir, and yourself?" I shook his hand firmly, which was something my father taught Mal and me to do. I noticed a surprised look on her father's face when I spoke.

"Pretty good," he said back to me in an almost a laughing manner. I guessed he was surprised by the manner in which I had greeted him. "My little girl speaks very highly of you, says you're smarter than her in school," he said matter-of-factly.

"I don't think I am smarter than her, because she's real smart, but I appreciate her saying that about me," I replied.

Just as he was about to say something else both Lisa and her mother came down the stairs, resembling each other almost to the point of being twins, but you could tell who was the mother and who was the daughter.

"So this is Kamil," her mother said, not asking a question but rather making a statement. "Hello, Kamil." Her greeting was short.

"How are you doing, Mrs. Matthews? It's nice to meet you," I politely responded, wanting to make a good impression on her.

"So, you're the one who keeps getting Lisa in trouble for staying on the phone so late at night all the time, huh?" She had a blank stare on her face when she spoke.

I couldn't tell whether she was joking or for real. I just looked at her, puzzled. A sense of nervousness lightly swept through my body and I could feel my palms beginning to moisten.

"Mother!" Lisa exclaimed.

"I'm just messing with the boy," her mother shot back, setting me somewhat at ease, but inside I still felt as though she may have been serious. "You speak very well mannered even when you're on the phone. I can tell your parents raised you respectfully." I wasn't sure if her statement was meant as a compliment because her tone was kind of dry. But I accepted it as one anyway.

"Thank you," was all I said, feeling as though I was on trial for a crime I didn't commit.

She then began her interrogation. "What type of work do your parents do, and have you always attended Plainfield schools?"

Instantly embarrassment filled my gut. I had overheard enough stories from my grandmother and her friends about how the people on the east end thought they were better and more educated than us to understand why I was being asked that question, based on how she had been observing and studying me. Although I was taught to respect my elders, I refused to let Lisa's mother intimidate me. She was literally judging a book by its cover, without knowing what was inside.

"My mother works in customer service for Johnson & Johnson and goes to school at night, while my grandmother watches me and my brother and two sisters. I used to attend a private school in New York, where I am originally from, until we moved out here a few years ago. My father has been in prison for the past four years." I knew I had won her over with the way I had articulated my words and given her my background history. That was, until my very last statement.

As soon as the words rolled off my tongue and out of my mouth, I hated my dad and resented him even more for having to say where he was in front of someone who was judging me without even knowing me. That day I said I would never forgive my father for putting me through this.

"Mary, leave that boy alone," Mr. Matthews came to my defense. "He didn't come here to answer twenty questions; he came for his gift."

I was grateful for Mr. Matthews calling off his wife. He must've seen it in my face how uncomfortable it was for me speaking about my dad, as well as how painful. I could tell Lisa picked up on it too because it looked like she had tears in her eyes and was embarrassed by how her mother had been treating me.

"I didn't mean any harm, Joe," Mrs. Matthews said to her husband. "I was complimenting him on his manners. Kamil, if I said anything to offend you then I apologize. Baby, you have a Merry Christmas and a Happy New Year," she said, and she left and went back upstairs.

"I'm going to let you two talk," Mr. Matthews said. Before he went upstairs he said, "It was nice to meet you, Kamil. I hope you see you again."

"Same to you, sir. Enjoy your holidays," I said.

"Kamil, I am sorry. I did not know my mother was going to question you, but I know she didn't try to disrespect you or anything. That's just how she is with everybody," Lisa said, explaining for her mother.

"That's all right," I said. "I didn't take offense. You're her daughter and she's only making sure you're not interested in a street thug, especially when I'm the Kamil who keeps you in trouble staying on the phone so late all the time," I said jokingly, repeating what her moms had said.

That put a smile on her face. "I knew there was a reason I like you. You can find humor in any situation," she said. "Anybody who can tolerate my mother is worth staying friends with." She smiled. There was a brief pause in her words and a momentary silence. "Anyway, here's your present. Open it," she said all excited.

"There better not be no snake in this box," I said.

"Just open it, boy," she said, punching me in the arm.

"Okay, you don't have to be so violent," I said as I began neatly unwrapping the paper.

"Kamil, you're slow. Let me help you," Lisa said as she started ripping the paper off.

"All right, all right. I get the picture."

Once all the paper was off, I took the top off the box and inside was a new black rabbit fur hat with matching black rabbit gloves with leather in the palms, the same identical fur that was around the collar of my white goose-down jacket.

"Oh, junk! These are fly!" I exclaimed with excitement. "I should've known you got me something like this when you asked me did I get a new hat and gloves. Thank you. I couldn't have asked for a better gift," I genuinely thanked Lisa. "They're gonna be sweatin' me in the hood now, 'cause only the ballers got this hookup," I said, knowing she didn't understand my street lingo.

"Well, I don't know who the ballers are, but I'm glad you like them." Her remark confirmed what I had already thought. "I figured you'd look cute with them on, 'cause ever since the first day of school I seen you with your white goose on and you've been looking cute," she said.

"Come on, don't soup me up like that," I said back to her.

"I'm for real. That white jacket makes you the cutest boy in the whole school."

"Thank you," was all I could think of to say. "I have to go, 'cause me, my brother, and some friends are going to the party at the Neighborhood House; but thank you again for the hat and gloves. They're fly."

"You get to go to real parties?" she asked as if it were a big deal.

"Yeah, they have parties all the time on the west end all over. You've never been to a party before?" I asked.

"No," she answered.

"Not even a house party?" I asked again.

"The only party I've been to besides here is a birthday party for one of my girls, and there's no music or dancing, just games and stuff like that," she said.

"Wow. Well, if you and your girlfriends want to go and you think you can get away, let me know and my brother and I will make sure you have a good time," I offered. I had an idea of how sheltered other kids were on the east end, but after finding out that Lisa had never been to a real party, I realized just how much. I remembered when we had lived liked that back in Brooklyn. "I got to go, but I'll have enough fun for the both of us in case you can't make it," I said as she walked me to the door.

"I wish you could be there," I turned and said. "'Cause I'm in a dance contest tonight for a hundred dollars cash prize."

Her eyes widened and a grin grew across her face. "Get out of here," she exclaimed. "You can't dance."

"What? I can do any dance that's out," I boasted. "You name it, I can do it."

"Like what, Kamil?"

"Anything. The Whop, the Alf, the Cabbage Patch, the Brooklyn Slide, the Biz Mark, Happy Feet; and I can pop, break dance, and I can even do the hustle," I bragged. "My moms taught me that. You want me to keep goin'?"

She stood there laughing. "No, but I still won't believe it until I see you with my own eyes."

"Okay, I'm gonna come over one day and show you and then I want you to apologize."

"That's a deal," she said. We shook on it.

"Tell your parents I said it was nice meeting them."

"I will."

"All right, let me get up outta here. I'll talk to you later."

I could see in her eyes she wished I could stay longer. The word "good-bye" tickled my ears as I made my exit.

Chapter Thirteen

The Neighborhood House was jam-packed. Bodies from all over the west end and some from various parts of the east end, like cliques from Town House and Meadow Brook Village projects heads who were connected either by blood or just being cool with somebody from the west end, were in the house.

"Yo, Ant," Trevor called out. "One of us gonna win that hundred dollars, 'cause I seen most of these niggas at other spots and they are wack. Nobody can fuck with me, you, Mil, and Mal up in here."

Trevor was a club head. He was older than us so he was able to get into more parties than we were. He always hit a spot downtown called the Rendezvous, run by a DJ from Third Street named Cheese, and he came back and shared the night's stories with us. If he learned something new he taught us, and then we would throw our own style into it.

"Trev, you smell like weed. You been smoking?" Ant asked.

"Nigga, you know when I step out I gotta have that Buddha in my system or my dancing is gonna be off," Trevor spat back.

"Man, it's not your dancing I'm worried about; it's your temper," Ant corrected him. "You know when you smoke that shit and drink, you start buggin' out, and we wind up getting into a fight or argument with some niggas."

"Yo, Ant, chill, nigga. I got this. We gonna win this money and be Audi 5000," Trevor said in a cool tone. Whenever he talked like that, we knew he was high from the weed.

"I hope so," my brother added, "because I don't want to have to knock one of these jokers out up in here, BK style with the fifty-two."

"Man, you don't know that shit," Trevor said, running up on Mal with his hands up in combat-ant mode.

"Let something jump off and you'll see," my brother said, instantly catching and blocking Trevor's punch.

"Okay, I see ya work," Trevor spat, impressed. "But save that for them other muthafuckas. Mil, you know that shit too," he said.

I just nodded.

***

Winning the hundred dollars was too easy. Of course, it was me who won, but had Trevor not been high he would have won it because he was a much better dancer than all of us, but me winning it was just like him winning it anyway. At the end of the night, we all had twenty-five more dollars in our pocket than we did when we got there.

"Yo, what up. You wanna walk to the diner and get something to eat before we call it a night?" Ant asked.

Trevor was the first to agree. "Yeah, kid, 'cause that muthafuckin' weed got me hungrier than a hostage."

"Yeah, we wit' that," my brother answered for both of us.

"Let's get up outta here then."

As we were about to leave the Neighborhood House, something caught my attention. I could tell that Mal's attention had also been caught. He must've spotted her right before I did because while I was still trying to adjust my eyes to the sight, he was already making a beeline in that direction.

"What the fuck?" I heard my brother say as he skipped over to what was taking place. It was our older sister Monique. She was trying to get around some guy who wasn't trying to let her pass. He had one hand on the wall while his other hand shifted from her arm to her waist, preventing her from leaving.

Hearing what Kamal said triggered Ant and Trevor off. I had already caught up to Mal, trailing behind him.

"Yo, nigga, get ya muthafuckin' hands off her like that," Mal roared at the kid.

"Kamal?" Monique was surprised to see Mal and me.

"Who the fuck is you and why the fuck you mindin' my business, li'l nigga?" the kid barked back. You could tell he was older than us and he had to be a hustler by the gold in his mouth and the rope chain around his neck.

Not backing down, Mal matched both his stare and tone. "That's my muthafuckin' sister and I ain't your muthafuckin nigga, nigga!" Mal shouted while putting his hands in the kid's face.

I knew it was about to go down 'cause I started getting those butterflies in my stomach like I usually did when I was about to fight or Kamal was about to get into it with somebody, so I positioned myself right on the kid's blind side. He didn't even notice me. He probably thought I was passing through. As soon as he tried to knock Kamal's hand from out his face that's when he became aware of my presence, or at least he felt it. By the time his hand had smacked my brother's, I was catching him with a right hook on the side of his face. For a twelve-year-old, I packed a power punch like a grown man, and I was just as quick. When I landed the punch, I could see the kid going down. Kamal immediately followed with an uppercut to the kid's jaw to ensure that once he went down he stayed there. Nobody really knew what was going on until they heard my sister Monique screaming over the music that was coming out of the Neighborhood House's gymnasium. Trevor and Ant wasted no time stomping homeboy out when he hit the ground.

"Yeah, nigga! NPP in the house," Trevor yelled as he snatched the kid's rope from around his neck.

"You ain't never had a project ass whippin' like this before, punk-ass nigga!" Trevor continued his assault on the hustler, who was unconscious.

"Trev, that's enough," Ant hollered, seeing that the kid on the floor was out, blood all on the ground. "You gonna catch a body, nigga."

"Stop it! Stop, y'all," my sister Monique yelled at us. It was the first time I had actually heard what she had been yelling. We had all blanked out and focused on putting the beat down on the hustler.

By now everyone had gathered to see what was going on, but I guessed the hustler was by himself 'cause ain't nobody show up to help him. Besides, I saw more project heads than anything, so if he had boys so did we. Noticing security headed our way I grabbed my sister by the arm and ran for the exit door.

"Nique, what the fuck you doing up in here anyway?" Mal questioned our sister once we reached the outside. "Does Mommy and Grams know you here? And what the fuck you got on, looking like one of these skeezers?" he said angry.

"Mal, I don't have to answer to you. You ain't my father; you're my little fuckin' brother. You and Mil come in here with your little punk-ass friends like y'all some fuckin' gangsters," she reprimanded him. "I didn't need your help in there. I could handle myself," she said all in one breath.

"Yo! I ain't trying to hear that shit. Take your fuckin' ass home before I drag you there myself."

Growing up, my sister was the toughest out of all of us, but tonight Kamal was in charge and he wasn't playing any games. Just looking at him, you could see that. He looked twice his size, as if he grew in the last half hour. It was true Monique was the oldest but, at that moment, it was as if Mal were the big brother and Monique the little sister.

"Mal, you're overreacting," she tried to explain. "That boy wasn't hurting me; he was about to let me go until you came over there. Do you know who he is and where he's from?" my sister asked, like the hustler was the mayor or somebody important and we were supposed to have known who. "That was Karim from Stebbins."

"I don't care who that nigga was or where he's from; all I know is he shouldn't have had his hands on you like that, or he wouldn't have gotten his ass kicked in there."

I was down with my brother 100 percent just like I knew Ant and Trevor were, but it wasn't no secret. Although we didn't know him by face we all knew of the kid Karim by name and where he was from. He was one of the youngest hustlers from his block who was getting a lot of money and, from what we had heard, when it came to his crew, they were just as deep as the projects. Not only did we jump him and beat him unconscious, Trevor had robbed him of his chain. So, according to the streets, no matter what, that kid's rep was on the line and this thing was far from over. We all knew we had started something and we had no idea how we were going to get out of it or finish it.

We skipped the diner that night and all went home. We had all agreed that the next day we needed to get up early and go to the handball court.

Chapter Fourteen

When we walked up to the handball court nearly everyone you could think of was out there, even the fiends. You would've thought it was a family reunion. There were so many cars out there I was surprised the police didn't show up. I always knew the projects were deep, but to actually see everybody all at one time gave a new meaning to the word "deep." A lot of guys had just come home from doing prison bids that year, so a bunch of them were looking cock diesel, like the Incredible Hulk, over 200 pounds and better. Most of them were posted up by the fence with Mustafa. It looked like he was holding a meeting there while the rest listened. I could tell he spotted me because he waved his hand for me to come over. We all walked over to where the hustlers and gangsters of our hood gathered.

Everybody's face bore different expressions. Most of them possessed smirks while some of them were grilling us hard. I guessed they weren't so happy about us starting a block beef last night. In one of our talks, Mustafa had taught me that beefing and hustling don't mix. He said you couldn't make money if you beefing, because beef drew heat and heat shut the block down.

"Yo, what up, young bucks?" Mu said in a laughing type of way, shaking his head. "What did y'all get us into last night, li'l homies?"

"It wasn't even like that, Mu," Mal spoke up. "That kid Karim had our sister all hemmed up in the corner and wouldn't let her go. I told him to get off of her and he started getting all tough, so I wasn't going to back down 'cause I ain't no coward. I'm from the projects." Kamal's comment got a laugh out of some of the hustlers and gangsters. "I put my hand in his face and he knocked it down," he continued. "That's when Mil caught him with the hook and then we jumped him projects style," Mal finished with.

If they weren't laughing before they were as Mal ended.

"Why'd you have to snatch his chain?" Mu asked. "What, y'all some stick-up kids now?"

"Mu, it just happened like that," Trevor stepped in. "We didn't mean to rob him on purpose. If I wouldn't have taken it somebody else would've 'cause homeboy was out for the count."

The laughter increased at what Trevor said. I thought they all found it hard to believe that a bunch of young teenagers did the kid Karim like that, because he was known for being able to handle himself in battle against two to three street guys at a time on the fighting tip. Because he slept on us because we were young, his reputation had been tarnished.

"Where's the chain at?" Mu asked Trevor.

"At my crib."

"Go get it and bring it here."

Trevor went to go get the chain.

"Listen, we ain't mad at y'all and we ain't gonna let nothing happened to y'all, either, but to dead this y'all gonna have to fight somebody from down there on the one-on-one," Mu told us. "He may be bigger, he may be smaller, he may be younger, or he may be older, but either way y'all gonna have to knuckle up 'cause y'all messin' up our money flow right now and we tryin' to dead this beef as quick as possible, so when Trevor come back we goin' down there," Mu said finally. We had no choice but to agree.

Just as it looked when we walked to the handball court was how it looked when we got down to Third and Stebbins. People were everywhere.

We rode down there twenty cars deep with at least four project heads in each car. Nobody got out. Mu was leading the pack. He rolled down the window and a big, dark-skinned kid sporting a navy blue Kangol, wife beater, and some blue denim jeans, with three fat gold chains draped with medallions around his neck, came over to Mu's BMW.

"Ay yo, Chuck, you get my message?" Mu asked him.

"Yeah, I got it, and Karim agreed to it. Where's the chain, though?"

Mu gave it to him.

"It's too hot around here so we gonna meet y'all in the field and it can jump off over there. I got three of my boys who are going to rock and Karim wants to rock with the li'l nigga he said snuck him."

"Yeah, it's cool, whatever. We'll meet y'all in the field," Mu said as he pulled off followed by the projects convoy.

That day you would've thought that there was a car show the way all the fly cars were lined up from the projects. Benzes, BMs, Jettas, Jags, Volvos, and Jeeps, and every ride in the line was fly.

They were all there, and it was going down. The guys Mal, Ant, and Trevor had to fight were all about their size, maybe a little bigger, but nothing compared to the size of Karim.

That night, the dark must've made him look smaller, because now that I saw him in the daytime he was huge. He looked as if he had been locked up before, a few times to be exact. Words of my father, *"The bigger they are the harder they fall,"* resonated in the back of my mind as I watched my brother prepare to fight first. The kid he had to knuckle up with was no match for him. Mal kept catching him with the okey-doke, faking him with the left and catching him with the right. To finish him off, my brother faked like he was swinging a hook, then dropped down, grabbed him by the calves and earth slammed him like the way they did in WWF. After that, it was over. All the project heads were amped, even the shorties who were out there.

Trevor didn't do as good because the kid had a longer reach and kept popping the jab in his mouth. His lips were all busted, and he couldn't get in, except for one time he caught the kid good in the eye and it turned black and blue on impact. He caught Trevor again and busted his nose. When Trevor felt the blood, out of anger and frustration he rushed the kid and the kid somehow got behind him and put him in a sleeper hold. Mu broke it up before he could put Trevor out, though. When they broke it up, Trevor still wanted to fight, but Mu said it was over.

Ant's fight was a good one to watch. Him and the kid was going blow for blow. At the end, they both had black eyes, bloody noses, and busted lips, but overall I thought Ant took him because he was the smaller guy. The whole time watching the fight I could see the kid Karim over there talking to one of his boys about how he was going to beat me up, but the more I saw my boys fight the more amped I got.

"You ready, kid?" Mu came over and put his hand on my shoulder.

"Yeah," was all I said.

"Yo, you young bucks wanted to see how it feels to be in the game, well, this is a part of the game right here. This is a part of the flipside of the game. You gots to put some work in on the block." Mu addressed all of us, but I knew he was really talking to me.

There was no turning back. By now, more cars had pulled up. All you heard were car doors slamming as we got back to the field. Mu told Mal and them to go wait by the court while he kicked it to me.

"I'm gonna be straight with you, kid," Mu started out saying, "you got the hardest fight out the bunch. Now if you don't want to fight let me know and I'll tell them ain't nothing, and then we'll just get into some gangsta shit after that, know what I'm sayin'?"

I knew Mu wanted me to cop out but, to tell the truth, I wasn't scared. Win, lose, or draw, I was going to fight and I had planned to fight hard. Besides, I felt that if I could knock that kid out with one punch before, I could do it again.

"Nah, Mu, I'm going to fight. Either he's going to beat me up or I'm going to beat him up, right?"

"Right, kid!" Mu answered proudly. "But if you don't want to fight no more just call my name and I'll stop that shit immediately."

"Yo, if he knocks me unconscious then break it up, but other than that I'm not going to give up."

"I always knew you had the heart, kid. I respect you for that and everybody else will too," Mu said. "Now kick that nigga's ass."

Me and Karim squared off. "Knock him out, baby," my brother yelled as I made my way to the center of the circle.

"Yeah, knock me out, li'l nigga," Karim mocked my brother, while flinching, trying to intimidate me.

Instead of jumping, I leaned back just in case he actually tried to throw a punch at me. For a minute neither one of us didn't throw anything.

I could hear the voices in the background, some rooting for me while the others were against me. Then out of nowhere Karim swung a lazy hook and missed, and left his jaw clean open; but I didn't take the shot because the hook he threw was unexpected, even though I saw it coming from a mile away. I still didn't throw any punches. I was timing him, just like my father taught me. "Watch the shoulders," he would tell me.

I must've had my foot out too far because Karim tried to hit me with the old school and sweep my leg, hoping to knock me off balance, but he was too far back and I pulled it in just in time. I guessed he got tired of waiting for me because he launched an attack with a barrage of punches, hitting nothing but air because I slipped, ducked, and sidestepped everything he threw my way. And that was all I needed.

As I ducked and sidestepped his arsenal of undelivered blows, I caught him right in the gut. Karim bellied over, trying to protect his stomach area, causing him to leave me a clean shot to the head. I caught him straight in the temple. I could hear the crunching sound of my young knuckles as they connected with the side of his face. Like a *Rocky* movie, when Sylvester Stallone has delivered that final blow, the reaction of my punch seemed to be in slow motion. He made an attempt to grab hold of me as his legs gave, but I moved just in time. The next thing I knew, the kid Karim was laid out in the circle.

The projects went crazy like we had just won the Super Bowl or the NBA championship. I couldn't see nobody 'cause I was focused strictly on Karim, seeing if he was going to get back up; but he didn't, and right then I knew that I had knocked out somebody older than me on a one-on-one.

"Yeah! That's what the fuck I'm talking about!" I heard someone say.

"Yo! Mil! You got skills, kid," someone else said.

"That li'l nigga ain't nothing to fuck with," another said. I heard so many different things, but I didn't care about that. I just wanted to know why my hand felt funny.

When I looked at my right hand it had already begun to swell and my pinky knuckle was out of place. It was evident that I had hit Karim so hard I had broken my hand. I could see some of Karim's boys helping him up off the ground while the others from his hood got in their respective cars and began to roll out.

"Yo, I seen it in your eyes that you were going to take homeboy out," Mu said to me, putting his arm around my neck.

"Mu, I think I broke something, kid. It ain't feeling right," I told him.

Mu looked at my hand. I knew I had broken my knuckle. "Yeah, kid, your shit is broke. You gots to go to the hospital," he said.

"Man, my mom is gonna kill me when she finds out," I said as Mal and them walked toward me and Mu.

"Yo, you was just out here puttin' in work on some gangsta shit and you worried about what your moms is gonna do when she finds out?" Mu said to me. "Young buck, you shout out. Don't worry about all that; this is what we gonna do," he started saying.

"Mal, go home and tell your moms that your brother was playing on the monkey bars at Green Acres and fell off and sprained his hand, and somebody drove him to the hospital. By the time she gets up there, Mil will be getting checked out by the doctor," Mu said.

Kamal did as he was told. Mu drove me to the hospital. They admitted me, but they couldn't do anything until my parents or legal guardian was present, so we just sat in the lobby waiting until my moms got there.

"You did good today, kid," Mu said. "That's gonna be the talk of the town for a minute, and you gonna get a lot of props in the hood. You should be proud of yourself."

"I am," I said.

Just then, my moms walked in. "Are you all right?" she asked with a worried look on her face.

"Yeah, I'm okay, ma. I just messed one of my knuckles up playing on the bars at the park." It killed me to lie to my mother just then, but it was either that or be banned from going outside for the rest of my life.

"I know, your brother told me," she said. Noticing Mustafa, my mother said, "Thank you for bringing my son up here. Here, take this for your time," she said, reaching in her purse and pulling out a twenty dollar bill.

Mu smiled. "Oh, nah, I can't accept that. It was no bother, no problem at all. I was glad to be of help. Li'l man, you take it easy." He gave me the head nod.

"Well, thank you again," my mother said to Mu. "I really do appreciate it."

"You're welcome," Mu responded as he left the hospital.

Just as I figured, my pinky knuckle was out of place and they had to put a cast on my hand until it straightened back up. They had wanted to cut my hand open and reset the bones, but my mother wouldn't allow it because they told her it would leave a permanent scar. While examining my knuckle the doctor made a comment about my hand looking like I had hit something real hard in the head or something the way that it was swollen. I almost fell off the table when he said that, not trying to look at my moms.

"Nah." I laughed. "I fell off the monkey bars at the park," I told him.

They put a cast on my hand and then I was discharged from the hospital. The doctor told my mom that I would have to keep it on for at least three to four months. That was a long time, I thought.

As we were leaving, my moms asked the nurse at the desk for a marker. I didn't know what for until she began writing on my cast. She wrote in red letters, I LOVE YOU, MOM, and she colored in the heart.

That was the first out of many signings that I would get on my cast. Like Mu said, my fight with Karim was the talk of the town, and I had the cast on my hand to prove it. Luckily, my moms and grandmother didn't catch wind of it because that would've been my behind.

Right away, I had twenty-five to thirty names and signatures on my cast, from my boys to a lot of old heads in the hood, down to my immediate family. But besides my mom's and grandma's signatures, Lisa's was the one I read the most out of all of them. She wrote on the forearm part of the cast, LISA WITH LOVE FOREVER & ALWAYS! I'm not saying she was in love with me, but just seeing the word "love" told me that I meant a lot to her. The cast thing definitely had its benefits.

Chapter Fifteen

It was New Year's Eve, 1986, about to be 1987, and everybody was looking forward to the New Year coming in. Trevor was having a Ball Drop party at his crib because his mother had gone to New York with a friend to see it live and she left him the apartment for the evening. Mal and I had to damn near clean up the whole house from top to bottom just to convince our mom and grandmother to let us spend the night over at Trevor's crib. We would've cleaned four houses just to make it to the party because we knew that it was going to be more than worth it.

"Happy New Year!" everybody yelled when Mal and I stepped into the place. The music was pumping and the house was jam-packed. You could smell a combination of weed, alcohol, fried chicken, and sweaty teenagers from all the dancing. I saw Black and Shareef tag-teaming some shorties in a sandwich in the middle of the living room floor. There was nothing like a house party.

Trevor and Ant were approaching us with two cups in their hands. "Happy New Year, homies," Trevor said to Mal and me, as he passed me one of the cups that he had in his hand while Ant handed Kamal the other one that he had. "Let's toast!" Trevor said.

We all held our drinks together up in the air to honor the New Year's toast and then we drank. Lately it seemed like every time we got together on the weekends we were drinking to something, whether it was celebrating something good or some type of tragedy. Either way something that called for a drink was always happening in the hood. At least that was my excuse for all the drinking I had been doing.

Both Trevor and Ant had healed up from the bruises they had from the fight the day after the Christmas party. We even sat around drinking and talking about that day. When the fight is actually happening and you're getting your butt kicked or you're kicking someone's butt it doesn't seem funny; but after it's all over, you start remembering all types of stuff about it that's hilarious. Especially if you're drinking, or smoking weed, which my brother and I still hadn't graduated to.

"Yo, we thought y'all wasn't gonna make it," Ant yelled in my ear.

"Man! We had to clean up the whole dag-on projects just to get to this piece," I told him, exaggerating. He just laughed.

"We're trying to get a couple of these shorties to stay the night so we can really have some fun, know what I'm saying?" Trevor said with a lustful expression on his face.

"Yo, kid, Mil and me ain't trying to mess with none of these skeezers up in here. All the older heads already ran through all of them and ain't no telling what them dirty-dick niggas got. I ain't trying to get burnt or catch some crabs, know what I'm saying?" Mal mocked Trevor.

"Whatever, man, you two do what you want and Ant and me gonna do what we want. Ain't that right, Ant?"

"Yo, I'm with Mal and Mil on this one, kid. These shorties up in here trifling. They okay to dance with and bug out with, but not to be sticking my joint up in them," Ant told him.

"You scary-ass virgin muthafuckas! Y'all probably ain't had pussy since pussy had you," Trevor shouted back. "I'm gonna show you how to do ya thang tonight."

"Okay, show us how it's done, playboy," my brother said to Trevor.

"Happy New Year to the NPP," Black and Shareef said together while walking up on us.

"Yo, dancing with these shorties got my joint ready to explode," Black said.

"Word!" Shareef said. "My thang harder than a roll of quarters right now, kid."

We all started cracking up.

"Ay yo, Mil, you see that redbone shorty over there wit' homegirl I was just dancing with?" Shareef asked.

"What about her?"

"She asked me what was up with you and did I think you'd dance with her even though you got that cast on."

By now, I was feeling the alcohol in the punch that was in the cup Trevor had given me. I did want to dance, plus she was cute, so I told Shareef to tell her to meet me on the dance floor while I took off my coat.

As soon as I rolled up on shorty my cut came on: "Eric B. Is President" by Eric B. & Rakim. I broke right into the Whop with her. By the way she was dancing I knew she knew what she was doing. She turned around and put her butt on me while gently grabbing both of my hands and placing them on each side of her hips. She was working me, but I really couldn't rock the way I wanted because of the cast and so many people crowding the floor; so instead I just followed the motion of her hips and never lost a beat.

We danced for two more songs and then I was ready to chill.

"Yo, that's it for me," I told her in her ear.

"Okay," she said. "But do you even know my name?" she asked me.

"Nah," I said, shrugging my shoulders.

"It's Trina."

"Nice dancing wit' you. My name is Kamil."

"I know your name already," she yelled back to me. "Everybody knows your name."

"Nah." I laughed. "You got me mixed up. I ain't no baller or nothin'."

"You don't have to be a baller for everybody to know you." She laughed. "You crazy, Kamil."

I don't know if it was the alcohol or what, but Trina was looking like the flyest shorty at the party, so I didn't mind talking to her. She was around my height and had her hair cut in a style like Salt-N-Pepa. Her eyes were a light color and her complexion was more on the red side than yellow. Her face was perfectly round and her lips were full. Her body was developed in all the right places from her breasts down to her hips; and she smelled sweet. She looked familiar, but I just couldn't place where I had seen her before. The liquor in my system had me a little off balance so I figured that's why I couldn't remember. We talked for a little bit longer and then I told her I was stepping off. She told me to come find her when the ball started to drop. I said I would and then I left.

"Ten, nine, eight, seven . . ."

We were all counting down together as the ball started dropping in Times Square. It looked like there were a million people out there on the television screen and everyone looked to be enjoying themselves. I heard so many stories about how dangerous it was being out there, from being robbed to getting stabbed, but to me it looked fun. Speaking of a million people, it seemed like there were that many heads up in Trevor's crib. Guys and shorties were wall to wall, paired up like couples. I had found Trina, who was now sitting on my lap when the ball dropped. I didn't tell her to, though; she just took it upon herself to think that it was okay, and I didn't object.

"Six, five, four," we all continued the countdown. "Three, two, one, Happy New Year!" everyone shouted in unison. Everyone started blowing their horns, hugging, and giving those closest to them kisses. Out of nowhere, Trina turned around and kissed me and I kissed her back. She tried to slip her tongue into my mouth, but I stopped her. She smiled.

"Happy New Year, Kamil," she said. "I hope that it'll be good for the both of us."

"Yeah, me too," was all I could think to say. But after I kissed her, for some reason I felt guilty, and I knew why. It should've been Lisa I was kissing, but she couldn't make it just like I knew she wouldn't be able to; but, at that moment, I wished she were there. I asked Trina to lift up and I excused myself.

It was 12:03 a.m., January 1, 1987.

"Hello?" she answered. I could tell she was half asleep.

"Happy New Year, Ms. Matthews," I said to her.

"Hey! Happy New Year to you too." She became alive.

"What are you doing?" I asked.

"Lying in bed. I just got finished watching the ball drop and I was thinking about you."

"What do you have on?" I asked, but didn't know why.

"What?"

"Nah, I'm just messin' wit' you," I said, changing up.

"I'm serious, I was just thinking about you," she repeated.

"Yeah, right, you wasn't thinking about me."

"Yes, I was, for real."

"I believe you. I was thinking about you too; that's why I called."

"Thank you, you made my New Year complete."

"You too. All right, I'm gonna go ahead and let you go so you can get some rest. I'll see you in school," I said, about to hang up until she stopped me.

"Kamil? Before you hang up, since we didn't actually ring in the New Year together, do you think I could get a kiss over the phone?" she asked.

I was surprised that she had asked me that. "Happy New Year, Lisa," I said again after sending her a kiss through the phone.

"Muah! Happy New Year, Kamil," she returned.

The party turned out almost better than I thought. I was glad to find out that Trina wasn't from the projects. She wasn't even from Jersey. She was from New York like me but from the Bronx.

The reason she looked so familiar was that she was the little sister of Reecie, the girl Mu introduced us to the day we needed money to cop the Hawaiian suits. They looked almost like twins, only Reecie was a little taller and more developed, but you could tell that they were sisters because they both had hazel eyes and full lips.

Me and Trina talked for a while, while a lot of the other kids who were paired up were getting their groove on. I thought Trina wanted me to make a move, but I didn't press it because I didn't want her to think that was the only reason I was talking to her. Besides, I was too inexperienced to try to make any type of move. At the end of the day, we slept together, but we didn't do anything.

Chapter Sixteen

"'Happy birthday to you/Happy birthday to you!'" I woke up hearing my mom, grandmother, and sisters singing to me.

It was March 3, Sunday morning, and I was officially a teenager. Kamal's birthday was in January and they did the same thing to him, so I knew they'd be coming in the room again on mine.

"Boy, you think you old enough to lay up in here all day now?" my mom said jokingly.

"I know he better get his butt out that bed so I can give him a birthday hug," my grandmother said as she was pulling the covers off me.

"Grandma, go ahead!" I said.

"Chile, please! You ain't got nothing I ain't seen before. I know what your narrow behind and your little wee-wee look like. I put Pampers on you and bathed your yellow tail," she shouted, and everybody in the room fell to pieces. Even Kamal woke up out of his sleep, laughing. I couldn't help but join my family in laughter.

This was the first time since Christmas we had all sat down and eaten breakfast together. Lisa had called and wished me a happy birthday, like I knew she would, but what surprised me was when I heard her mother in the background telling her to say she wished me one too. For some reason, that really meant a lot to me. I told Lisa that I would see her later and would call before I came.

For my birthday, my mother gave me a card with fifty dollars in it, which I expected, because that's what she had given Kamal for his. My grandmother had knitted me a sweater and my sisters gave me hugs and kisses. Overall, I received all a thirteen-year-old could ask for from his family.

Mal and I dressed and made our way over the tracks.

"Yo! Happy birthday, kid," Ant hollered as Mal and I rolled up on him and Trevor at the court.

"Yeah, kid, happy born day, baby," Trevor followed up with.

Nobody was really out there except for kids our age shooting ball and a couple of crackheads and dopefiends looking to see if somebody was out hustling. Ant and Trevor had been out there smoking and drinking when we rolled up. Ever since Terrance was killed, Ant had been drinking and drugging heavy with Trevor.

"I saved this for you, kid," Trevor told me as he pulled out a bottle of blackberry brandy. "I've been saving this for a special occasion. You only turn a teenager once in your life, and this the shit that will put hair on your chest, my nigga!"

I took the bottle of brandy and hit it twice on the bottom with the palm of my cast like I had seen Trevor and them do all the time with their hands before they always cracked open a new bottle of liquor. I never knew what it meant, though, and I never asked. The taste of alcohol was sweet but burned my throat as I took a swig. I couldn't resist the cough. "This stuff is strong!"

"Yeah! That's what I'm talking about, kid," Trevor shouted. "You a man now, nigga." We all took turns drinking until it was all gone. It was kind of cold out but the brandy had me feeling warm inside. I had always heard the older heads talking about how blackberry brandy took the chill off when the hawk was out and they were out there getting that money in the freezing cold and snow. I thought they used to say it just to say it, but now I had found out firsthand that it was true. I was beginning to get so warm that I was ready to take off my jacket.

Ant and Trevor started smoking a joint. That's when I knew it was time to go, because no matter how many times Mal and I said no, they would always try to talk us into taking a pull; but we never did.

"Yo, good looking out on the drink," I told Trevor and Ant with a slight slur. The brandy had begun to take its effect on me. Ant and Trevor both let out knowing laughs as we all gave one another a pound, and then Mal and I stepped off.

"Bro, you a'ight?" Mal asked, seeing that I was staggering.

"Yeah, I'm cool," I replied, knowing I really wasn't.

"Man, you know we can't go in the house with you like that. You gonna get us in trouble," Mal protested. "I knew I shouldn't have let you take that last drink."

"Bro, I'm good." I didn't mean to, but I could feel myself smiling.

Just then, I heard my name called. The sound of Mustafa's voice was enough to quickly sober me up. He was coming out of Reecie's building. He must've just gotten around there because I didn't see any of his rides when I first came out, unless I just didn't notice.

"Happy born day, kid!" Mu said, slapping my cast five and then giving me a hug. "You growing up, huh, baby boy? How old are you now?" he asked.

"Thirteen," I managed to say without slurring.

"Damn! That's how old I was when I got in the game," Mu said as if he were looking back in time on his life. "Yo, I got something for you. I was just about to come looking for you after I left Reecie's crib," he told me. "And speakin' of Reecie, what's up with you and her li'l sister?"

He caught me off guard. "What do you mean?"

"What I mean is, every time I'm over there Trina's either askin' me questions about you or saying ya name a hundred times like you hit that or something."

"Nah, Mu, it ain't even like that. We just cool. I met her at Trevor's New Year's party and we just kicked it."

"Well, it seems like she wants to do more than just kick it," he said, smiling. "You know that she's three years older than you, right?"

"Yeah, I know, she told me."

"Oh! You into older women, huh? Ain't nothing wrong with that, kid, 'cause I am too. Although I like a li'l something young and tender up under me every now and again," he added with laughter. "Anyway, after I give you this you gonna have more shorties sweatin' you than you can handle." He pulled out one of the new link chains with a medallion on it that I had seen some of the older hustlers rocking.

"Oh, junk, Mu! Good looking out," I shouted, putting the chain over my head. To me, it was a perfect fit, even though I knew it hung kind of long. The link lay flat around my neck while the medallion lay flat on where I should have had a chest. "Yo, Mal, check me out."

After I said it, I could see the disappointment in my brother's face. Mu must've seen it too because he pulled out another one identical to mine and said, "I know you ain't think I was gonna leave you out like that. I know how you two roll. You like Siamese twins around this muthafucka, so I ain't never gonna give to one without giving to the other. And I knew your birthday was in January, but I wanted to wait until both of your birthdays passed before I gave you these."

"Mu, good lookin', man!" Mal said to him. "You be lookin' out like crazy for us and we appreciate that."

"Man, you li'l niggas is my family and if I have it and you need it then it's there," he said. "I gotta get up outta here but, before I go, you straight though, right? You don't need nothin'?"

"Nah, we straight. This enough right here," I said, pointing to my new chain.

"Well, here, take this anyway," he said, handing us twenty dollars apiece. "You might want to get some pizza or something later. Y'all be good, and don't let me catch your asses drinking." He grinned before stepping off, letting us know he had smelled the brandy.

All the kids our age were envious of my and Mal's chains, and for the first time I was glad to know a drug dealer. None of our boys were jealous, though, because they knew they could rock them anytime they wanted. When Lisa saw it, she liked it, but she thought it was too big for me. She was smaller than me so when I put it around her neck it hung to her stomach.

Lisa cooked me a birthday dinner, or at least tried to anyway, and then we watched a movie together on her VCR, *Krush Groove* to be exact, since she knew how much I enjoyed movies. I had gotten my cast off a few days prior so I was able to put my right arm around her as we watched the hip-hop–based movie.

Despite her mother coming downstairs every ten minutes to check on us, I enjoyed myself over at Lisa's. We had gotten so close that one would have considered us boyfriend and girlfriend even though we hadn't officially said we were. Teenagehood started off pretty good and I had a great birthday.

Chapter Seventeen

Summer had rolled around again, and Mal and I had made it to another grade. Shareef and Black did too, but we didn't know how much longer Black was going to last because he was still talking crazy and getting into unnecessary trouble in school.

As the days went by, he began to show less interest in school and more interest in the streets. We were trying to talk to him, but he had too much of his pops in him. His dad was considered to be a hardcore and violent street dude, who was said to have been skilled in martial arts and was notoriously known for the strong-arm game. It was said that when Black's dad came through an area you had to watch both his hands and feet with both eyes, because if he got behind you or too close to you it was a wrap. He was infamous for running up on hustlers and putting them in the sleeper chokehold or landing a punch or kick to the face that would send them to the canvas. Ant's brother had told him that whenever Black's dad left a scene it was guaranteed that somebody had been knocked out, and when they woke their pockets would be empty and their jaws or nose would be either broke or close to it.

Black's dad was killed by a young hustler who was tired of being repeatedly strong-armed and robbed by him. Lately Black had been getting into verbal confrontations with jokers from other areas and throwing his dad's name around like a form of intimidation. Some of the altercations were with young hustlers. Luckily we were always there to calm him, but we knew we couldn't be there twenty-four seven with him. I was afraid that Black's mouth was going to cause the projects to get into something and I didn't want to see a repeat of last summer's tragedy when Mark was killed and Shawn became paralyzed.

Shawn still didn't come out behind that day. '86 was a wild year for the projects.

Between guys getting smoked and going to jail, the faces were changing each month. There were only a handful of guys out there I knew. The rest of them were either guys Mu had brought around to hustle for him, or little project kids my age in the game. Like Mu said to me once, "The game doesn't change; only the players of it do!"

Lisa and I had been seeing a lot of each other over these past few months, but she still hadn't come to the projects, which was cool, though, because it was dangerous around there and I would have hated for something to happen to her accidentally while she was down there visiting me. I would never be able to forgive myself.

She spoke to my family on the phone all the time. I could tell they liked her just by the way they were talking to her. When you lived where we did, it was not that easy to get someone to come see you, especially if it was a known area for violence and drugs like my neighborhood. It seemed like every day someone was getting robbed, jumped on, or shot and you couldn't walk two feet without seeing drug paraphernalia scattered.

"Mal, you getting up or what?" I called over to my brother. "Yo, downtown opens at ten o' clock and we told Ant and them we were going with them today to get some new kicks."

"Yeah, I'm getting up. What time is it?"

"Almost nine thirty."

"All right, hold up. All I got to do is wash up and brush my teeth 'cause I took a shower last night. Gimme about ten to fifteen minutes." For him, that meant twenty to twenty-five minutes.

On our way to Ant's crib, I spotted Shareef but, from where he was positioned, he couldn't see me. He was up by the handball court with some other kid I didn't know. I was about to yell out to him until I saw him run up on a car that had stopped in the middle of the street. I didn't recognize the car from where I stood, but I was almost sure that it didn't belong to anyone around the projects. What I saw next only confirmed what I suspected. Shareef looked both ways before sticking his hand inside the vehicle on the passenger's side. As the car sped off, I saw Shareef shoving money in his pants pocket; and then he made his way back over to where the other kid stood posted up. When the green rusted Monte Carlo made its way down to where Mal and I were, the driver and I made eye contact. I noticed that it was some white man with brown bushy hair driving.

"Yo, Mal, you seen that?" I asked my brother, never taking my eyes off the car.

"Seen what?"

"I think I just seen Shareef serve that white man in that car that rode past," I told him.

"What? Get outta here. You buggin'," my brother said in disbelief.

"Yo, I ain't joking, kid. I just peeped it."

Seeing that I was not playing, Kamal became serious. By the time I went to point out where I had just seen Shareef, he and the other kid had vanished.

"He was just up there with some other kid," I stated.

"Let's go see what's up with Ant, and see if he knows what's going on," Mal said.

Everybody was at Ant's crib waiting for us, except Shareef. "Why we always got to wait on y'all all the time?" Trevor asked, trying to look serious.

"Nigga, shut the hell up," Mal spat back, not in the mood for Trevor's antics.

"Ay yo, check this out," my brother went on. "On our way over here Mil said he saw Shareef by the courts serving some white dude."

"What?" was everybody's reaction to what Mal had just said.

"You niggas buggin'. What the fuck y'all talkin' about?" Black asked, sticking up for Shareef, being as that was his best friend.

"Servin' what?" Trevor asked, dumbfounded.

"What do you think?" I replied.

"Nigga, if Shareef was clockin' I would know about it," Black said in his boy's defense.

"Yo, you sure?" was all Ant said.

"I know what I saw," I told them, repeating word for word everything I'd seen.

"The nigga ain't here," Trevor said. "The only way to find out is to go out there and see what's up."

"Yeah, let's do that," Black agreed.

Shareef saw us coming, and he tried to walk up to us like he was on his way to hook up with us already. "Yo, what up? Y'all ready?" he asked us.

"Yeah, nigga, we ready," Black spoke first. "Ready to find out what the fuck up with you."

"Yo, what the fuck's your problem, Black? Why you comin' at me like that? You better chill the fuck out, nigga," Shareef warned.

"Yo, Shareef, you out here clockin', kid?" Trevor asked him, hoping the answer was no.

Just then, everybody heard the sound of a beeper going off. All eyes zeroed in on Shareef.

"Look at this shit," Black chimed in disgust.

"Man," Shareef started out. "Yo, I knew you niggas was gonna find out sooner or later." Shareef stared at the ground. "I was gonna tell y'all, but I didn't know how to."

"That's bullshit," Black spat.

"Nah, what you talkin' is bullshit," Shareef challenged, now looking each of his friends in the eyes. "My moms lost her job last month and unemployment been bullshittin' her, and welfare is even worse. My moms ain't even have enough dough for Pampers and milk for my little sister, let alone to feed a growin' teenage boy and herself. Why you think I been eatin' shit up at your house every time I come over, nigga?" He directed his words to Black.

You could see in Black's face that he was sorry for coming at Shareef like that now that he knew the full story. "Damn, kid, I thought it was the weed that had you hungry like that. I ain't know, homie," Black said to him.

We all felt Shareef's pain because it could've been any one of us out there doing what we had to do to survive, and deep down inside we all knew we would have. I remembered when moms was going through a rough time when we were back in Brooklyn and my pops stopped sending home money. With something like that, if I were old enough back then there was no telling what me or Kamal would've done to help our moms. We weren't condoning Shareef's decision, but at least we knew what fueled it.

"Yo, we understand," Trevor said, and we all agreed with him.

"Who you out here slingin' for?" I asked him, hoping it wasn't Mustafa.

"I went to Clyde and explained what was going on at the crib and wit' my moms, and he took care of me with a fifty pack. If I don't take no shorts I make three hundred dollars. All he want is seven hundred dollars back off it, no short money. I can't complain about that," Shareef said.

"Yo, this Ice. He works for Clyde too, so we out here holdin' each other down; plus, Ice hustled before so he schoolin' me," Shareef added, seeing all of our attention turn to the kid none of us knew.

You could tell that Black didn't like the fact that somebody other than himself was holding Shareef down, but he kept it to himself out of respect for Shareef's situation.

"Yo, how old are you?" Mal asked him.

"I just turned fifteen last month on the sixth."

"Damn, you look like you twelve," Ant said.

"Yeah, I know. My moms said my pops used to look younger than he really was too before he got killed," Ice told us.

"Sorry to hear that," we all said.

"Nah, fuck that nigga. He never did shit for us anyway. He got stabbed trying to cheat some niggas in a craps game with loaded dice, right on the other side of the tracks, in the other projects as a matter of fact," Ice told us.

From the way he talked, we could tell why his name was Ice. He sounded like he was a cold-hearted li'l nigga. We all understood and gave Ice a pound, and then asked him if he wanted to roll with us downtown. He said no and he'd catch us when we came back. I could tell he was a good dude who, like all of us, was trying to make the best out of his situation.

Just as we were about to leave, he asked Shareef if he wanted him to hold his stash and sell it for him if he sold out and money started coming. Shareef left his package with Ice. None of us uttered another word about what we had just found out. Instead, we all gripped up and rolled out, making our way downtown.

Chapter Eighteen

"Ay yo, Lee, you got this in a size six and a half?" Mal asked the owner of Lee's shoe store. Lee's sat on the corner of East Front Street and Watchung Avenue. We had been going there forever, since we were rocking karate shoes, and Lee had always treated us with respect and gave us discounts on any footwear, because we normally came at least eight or nine deep.

Lee had the new low-top Delta Force Nikes in all colors and we were all copping a pair. We were guaranteed at least a five dollar discount on each pair because there were six of us.

"Why every time you come here yo' feet get bigga?" Lee said to Mal, not able to speak proper English. "All the time you say, 'Lee, you got size four and a half?' 'Lee, you got size five?' Now you say, 'Lee, you got size six and a half?'"

Everybody was on the floor in stitches cracking up at Lee's comment to Kamal. "Chinaman, just get my size before I rip your green card up,"

Mal joked back. Lee laughed and went into the back to retrieve my brother's size.

Just like I had thought, Lee knocked off five dollars on every pair. We wound up getting seven pair because Shareef brought Ice a pair.

"Yo, that kid Ice don't spend no money," Shareef told us as we crossed over to Park Avenue and headed to Ferraro's pizzeria. "I've known him for three weeks now and that's the same outfit and sneakers he's had on every day since I met him. He a cool nigga, and I want him to hang out with us, if that's all right wit' y'all," Shareef asked, respecting our opinions.

"If you cool wit' 'im, then we cool wit' 'im," Trevor spoke for all of us.

"Good lookin'. Yo, pizza on me."

There was no other pizza in town better than Ferraro's on Seventh and Park Avenue. Even when we visited from New York, Mal and I begged our moms to get us slices from the Italian establishment. We all went up to the counter and ordered the type of slices we wanted. Most of us ordered slices with extra cheese and ground beef, except for Ant. He ordered two slices with pepperoni and sausage. He was the only one out of all of us who ate pork. Shareef went into his pocket and pulled out a knot of money almost the size of the ones I had seen Mustafa pull out.

Only where Mu's knot consisted of hundreds, fifties, and twenties, Shareef's had twenties, tens, fives, and singles; but it was still a fat knot.

"Damn, nigga, why you walkin' around wit' all that dough in ya pocket?" Trevor said, beating me to the punch.

"You niggas was acting like y'all was rushin' me like y'all was in a hurry when we was at the court so I didn't have time to run in the crib. Besides, it just looks like a lot. It's only like three and some change."

"Nigga, fuck you mean it's only three and some change? Like that ain't a lot of money for a fourteen-year-old?" Black yelled at him.

"Nah, I'm sayin'," Shareef said, laughing, "I be havin' more than this sometime, so it ain't really a lot. Shit, you should see Ice. He be havin' like a G on him sometimes," Shareef told us.

He had no way of knowing how much everyone hung on every word he spoke and how his words would affect all of us. We all sat in Ferraro's enjoying our pizza and kicking it the way we were used to doing. As the day ended, we all made our way back to the projects. We eventually all took it in for the night. All of us except for Shareef. He stayed out on the block.

Chapter Nineteen

I had $275 put up and tomorrow was Lisa's birthday. I wanted to get her something real nice, but I just didn't know what and from where. I couldn't ask my mom or grandmother to help me pick something out because they'd want to know where I got the money from. Honestly, I didn't do anything wrong to get it, but they'd never believe that. Between what Mustafa had given me and saving my lunch money, that's how I really saved up. The only person I could ask was Mu.

Mu and the rest of the older heads were having a dice game up at the handball court when I rolled up. From the looks of things, Mu had the bank because he had a stack of money in his left hand and the dice in his right. As I got closer, I could hear him saying as he rolled the dice, "All down is a bet. Money on the wood makes the game go good; now open up the pussy so I can dick you niggas out ya paper."

"Yeah! Cee-lo, niggas! Nobody move, nobody get hurt," Mu said while collecting all the money that was on the ground in front of all the betters in the cipher. The same group of guys who had bet before dropped more stacks of money again, along with a few others who now wanted to get in the game. There were at least a couple thousand dollars scattered over the blacktop. I heard some of them say they were betting what they had placed under their foot while stepping on a stack of dough.

"Aw, you done fucked up now. My li'l peoples done came up in the spot," Mu said, referring to me as he noticed me off to the side. "If you don't want to lose ya shit better pick it up before I throw these babies," he warned them all, but nobody listened.

"Nigga, just roll that ace and let me see ya face," one kid said.

"A hundred four or better, slick talker," Mu said back to him.

"Fifty you don't," a next kid said.

"Bet! Mil, come here," Mu hollered. "Blow on these, baby boy, and if I hit, that fifty is yours." He put the dice in my face.

I blew on them, and made a wish too, because I really wanted to win that fifty dollars. Mu shook the dice, threw them in the air, and snapped his fingers.

"Get 'em, girls!" he exclaimed, as the three dice hit the wall. Two of them stopped on the number three as the third one kept spinning. All the betters moved in closely, anticipating the third die to fall on the number one, so that Mu would have to pay them back a portion of their losses he had won. Then, all of a sudden, it just stopped.

"You see it, niggas!" Mu yelled. "Head craps!" The die landed on the number six. "Mil, get ya money while I get mine."

"Man, I ain't payin' this li'l nigga," a disgruntle better exclaimed.

You could hear a pin drop when Mu paused from collecting his winnings and looked up. "You gonna pay one way or another," Mu stated coldly. His eyes went from light brown to charcoal black within seconds.

Before I had time to determine whether I should get out of the way or stay put, the angry better shoved a fifty dollar bill against my chest. "Man, fuck this wack-ass game," he then mumbled before storming off.

"Fuck you too, sore loser." Mu laughed as he finished collecting his earnings. No one else said anything or involved themselves. Their only concern was placing their next bet, hoping to get back what they had managed to lose so quickly.

I told Mu I needed to speak to him, so he played a little bit longer, rolled Cee-lo again, and just when I thought he was going to pass the bank, out of the blue he flung the dice in the field and said, "You niggas ain't gonna win with my rocks!"

Mu's action was the cause of a lot of angry expressions on hustler's faces. If looks could kill, Judkins Funeral Home around the corner would be holding Mu's funeral, but nobody said anything. This was not the first time I had seen someone do what Mu had. When someone had had a good roll, they usually tossed the dice. Sometimes the loser would even throw them if he got bucked with them.

"Today was a good day," Mu said, handing me a bunch of singles as he finished counting his winnings. "Damn, I struck 'em for forty-two hundred dollars, kid," he told me. "That ain't bad. That ain't bad at all," he repeated.

I had shown up at the right time, I had thought. With the fifty I had gotten at the game and the singles Mu gave me, I picked up a quick hundred-and-something bucks. There were at least seventy-five singles in the stack that Mu had given to me.

"Yo, what's up, Mil? What you wanna rap about?" He leaned up against his Benz.

"I got this female friend from the east end. She's like my girlfriend," I began to ramble. "And tomorrow's her birthday and I don't know what to get her or even where to go to get her something."

He just grinned at me. "Okay, playa! I see you turnin' into a real ladies' man."

"Nah!" I laughed back. "I ain't tryin' to be no playa. I'm just tryin' to show this girl that I really like her. Besides, every holiday or any special occasion she's always buying me something or doin' something for me, and I ain't been able to do nothin' for her, so I wanted to go all out now that I got a li'l something saved up," I said, letting him know how much Lisa meant to me.

"You never cease to amaze me, man," Mu said. "I respect you for that and I'm gonna help you get ya li'l shorty something nice. Let me go get this dough from these li'l niggas and we gonna be out."

If my mom knew that I was in New York right now she'd have a fit. I didn't even know we were coming out here until I saw Mu pay the toll for the Holland Tunnel, but by then it was too late so I just went with the flow. Mu found a parking spot on Canal Street. As many times as I had been on Canal Street, going back and forth from

Brooklyn to Jersey, before we had moved, I had never actually been on the street on foot to shop, or for anything else for that matter. As we walked, all you could see were stores filled with car and house stereo equipment, all the latest gold that the hustlers and rappers wore, and stores that had clothes by the bunches.

"What did we come out here for, Mu?" I asked.

"Yo, one thing you need to learn about females is that they all love jewelry." He smiled. "I don't care how old or how young. That's why we out here, to get your shorty something nice to wear."

It wasn't hard to tell Mu knew more than I did about females, and he never told me anything wrong since I'd known him, so I was going with his suggestion. "All right, but one thing I know is that she doesn't like big chains."

"You wouldn't get her no big chain anyway. That's tacky on a shorty. You gots to get her something that's nice and some earrings to match, you dig?"

"Mu, I don't got enough for all that. I like her, but I don't want to break myself."

"You think I'd bring you all the way out here if I didn't have your back, kid?"

"No," I replied. "I wasn't sayin' that. I know you got me, I just wanted to do this on my own," I said, hoping he would understand.

"Nigga, you is gonna do it on your own. You pick it out, spend what you willing to spend, and if it don't cover what you like then I got the rest." That sounded like a good deal to me so I rolled with it.

We went up in some Chinese jewelry store that Mu said he got some of his jewelry from and I started looking around. It was like Fort Knox up in there. Gold was everywhere, chains, earrings, bracelets, gold teeth, you name it, and it was there. There was so much to choose from, but I had finally seen something that I liked that I knew would look cute on Lisa.

There was an advertisement of a little rope chain with a female's name on it and a pair of medium-size earrings with the same name too.

"Excuse me, how much is that chain and those earrings?" I asked the Chinese man behind the counter. He opened up the glass slider, checked the back of the nameplate on the chain and the side of the earrings, and said in his best English possible, "Chain, hundred sixty dolla, earring eighty dolla, wit' name everyt'ing."

"Come on, man!" Mu jumped in. "I come in here all the time to buy my shit and you can't even cut my li'l brother a break?" Mu pulled out his knot. "Two hundred dollars right now and the name put on today," he told the Chinese man. I didn't even know it took two to three days for the names to be put on, until I noticed the sign off to the side, but the way Mu was handling it I knew the man was gonna have it done today.

"Okay! Okay! For you, two hundred dollar for name and everyt'ing, you buy today," the Chinese man told Mu. "Come back two hours." He wrote a receipt out while asking for the name that I wanted to put on them. Mu gave me the receipt and then we left.

"Yo, just give me a hundred a fifty dollars," Mu said as we were walking to get something to eat.

I had $135 from the dice game already. I just had to put fifteen dollars more with that from the money I had been saving, so that left me with $260. Things had definitely worked out for me that day. "Thanks, Mu." I was grateful for having someone like him in my life.

"Don't worry about it, kid." He gave me a pound and then we ordered something to eat from the shish kebab stand.

Mal and them were in the field when we pulled up. Mu said he wasn't staying so I got out and he left.

"Yo, nigga, where the fuck you been at?" they all wanted to know.

"Me and Mu went to NY."

"To pick up?" Mal asked.

I laughed. "Nah, stupid, to go shoppin'. I told you that I wanted to get Lisa something fly for her birthday, and I told Mu, so he took me to Canal Street to get her this," I said, pulling out the little bag with the jewelry box in it.

"What the . . . ! Nigga, you done went all out and tricked all ya dough on that shit for a shorty you ain't even fucking," Trevor said.

"Nigga, what?" I instantly became heated by Trevor's comment. "Yo, Trev, don't disrespect me like that unless you wanna get punched in the mouth."

"What the fuck you say?" Trevor snarled. I knew my words had caught him by surprise because it was the first time I had ever challenged him, or any of my boys for that matter. But when he made the comment about Lisa, something inside of me just snapped and I didn't feel like letting it go.

"You heard what I said," I barked, walking up on him.

My brother jumped in between us. "Both you niggas chill."

"Mil, that's your girl?" Ant asked.

"Yeah, that's my girl," I answered without hesitation. "And she do a lot of stuff for me, so I did something for her," I informed them.

"Yo, my bad, kid," Trevor apologized. "I ain't know that was your girl," he followed up with, extending his hand. "I didn't even know you had a girl." I took hold of his hand and embraced him.

"That's what I'm talkin' about," Ant said.

"Aw, look at the two lovebirds," my brother teased.

Trevor and I both turned on him and gave him middle fingers and then we all broke out into laughter.

"That shit is fly. How much you pay for that?" Mal asked.

From the looks on their faces, I knew they really wanted to know. "It only cost me fifteen dollars."

"Nigga, get the fuck out of here!" they all said at once.

"Yo, I'm telling you, that's what I paid," I said again, as I went off into the story about the dice game earlier and how Mustafa had talked the Chinese man down at the jewelry store.

"You a lucky muthafucka," Ant said. "That's how Terrance used to treat me." Ant's tone dropped. That was the first time he had mentioned his brother since his murder last summer. I didn't know what to say. None of us did. Ant picked up on the tension. "It's cool, I'm good. I just caught a li'l flashback, that's all."

We all walked over to Ant and gave him a group hug to let him know he still had us.

When I got to Lisa's house, I didn't see any cars in the driveway, so I knew that both her parents had already left for work. She had told me how they had jobs that required them to work on the weekends.

It was nine o'clock in the morning and I wanted to surprise her while she was still asleep. I rang the doorbell four times before she finally answered.

"Who is it?" I heard her say.

"It's Kamil."

"Boy, what are you doing here this early in the morning?" she asked as she opened the door wearing a T-shirt and a pair of shorts with a scarf wrapped around her head.

"I came to wish you a happy birthday in person."

"Aw! Thank you," she said as she let me in. "Give me a minute while I go wash my face and brush my teeth."

"Yeah, go do that," I said jokingly.

"Boy, shut up," she said back, laughing.

I watched TV as I waited for her to come back down so I could surprise her with her gift.

"You want something to drink?"

"Nah, I'm good. I just want you to come over here so I can give you something."

"Give me what?" she asked, curious.

"A birthday hug," I said, hiding my hands behind my back.

"Oh! That's so sweet," she said, approaching me with open arms. "Ummm!" was the sound she made as I wrapped my arms around her. Once I let her go, I revealed the box that I was hiding behind my back before I had hugged her.

"Happy birthday," I said, handing her the present.

"Kamil, ohmigod! What is this?" she asked with excitement.

"You won't know until you open it," I answered. She looked at me for a second, smiled, and then took the top off the box. When she saw what it was, I knew by the way her face lit up she liked what she saw.

"These are beautiful!" she said in awe. "I can't believe you spent this type of money on me." Her tone was appreciative.

"Don't worry about the money. I just wanna know if you like them."

"Like them? I loooovve them," she emphasized. "Thank you." Her reaction caught me off guard. Before I had a chance to counteract, she had already removed her lips from mine. It happened so fast I wasn't able to describe how her lips felt. "You wanna see how I look with everything on?" she asked, bringing me back to reality.

"Yeah, of course. Try 'em on," I told her.

One by one, she began putting the earrings in her ears. Then she turned around and asked me to put the chain on her. When she turned back around to face me, she looked like a million bucks. "Well, how do I look?"

"Like a model," I answered.

She stood there, smiling. She made her way over to the living room mirror to take a look for herself. "Ooh, this isss nice." She admired the accessories draping from her ears and neck.

"I told you."

She walked back over to me. "Kamil, can I ask you something without you getting offended or mad?"

"Yeah, you can ask me anything. What's up?" I replied, wondering what she wanted to ask me.

She took a deep breath. "You didn't do anything illegal to get this for me, did you?"

I burst out into laughter. "No. Why would you think that?"

"No particular reason," she said. I could tell she was embarrassed. I remember thinking how I should have been the one embarrassed.

"It's just that, I can tell that everything cost a lot of money, that's all, you know?"

"I'm a good saver and been saving all the money that I come across or earned," I said, cutting the topic short. "Anyways, you supposed to appreciate the gift, not worry about how much money it cost."

"You're right. I'm sorry. Thank you again." She moved in, wrapped her arms around my neck, and kissed me again. This time it was slower and I was able to savor the moment. "This is the best present anyone could have ever given me," she confessed after breaking our lip lock.

I knew that she really did love the gift, but I wasn't convinced that she believed my answer of how I had gotten it.

Even though I had laughed it off, it did bother me that she felt she had to ask me that question. That day, I wondered, if I were from the east end and not the projects, would she have been so concerned about the price of her gift, or questioned whether I had done anything illegal to pay for it?

Chapter Twenty

"Yo, where Black at?" I asked Shareef on our way to school.

"I don't know, kid. I went by his crib and ain't nobody answer," Shareef said. "With all the late-night pumpin' I been doin' for Clyde I didn't think I was gonna make it this morning my damn self."

"When's the last time you seen Black, Reef?" my brother asked.

"It's been a minute, 'cause I be tryin' to do my thang and he be off doin' his thang. You know he really ain't understanding my situation like he claims he does, so I had to break away from him. But between me and you I think he's clockin' somewhere on another block or something, 'cause he be having money out the blue too. Like knots of dough," Shareef told us.

"Nah, not Black."

"He probably got a job or something on the down low, and just didn't want to tell us," Mal said.

"He's just been acting real funny lately. He's been looking different lately, like I don't even know who he is," Shareef told us. "When's the last time y'all seen him?"

It had been a minute since we had last seen him, we told Shareef.

"Not since the time we all went downtown to cop the new Deltas together," Mal recalled.

"Damn, kid, that ain't like Black to not get at us for that long period of time. Something is definitely up."

"We'll check him out and see what's goin' on after school," Mal told Shareef.

"All right, yo. I'll get up after school," Shareef said, as we all went to our homerooms.

Ant and Trevor were playing Atari when me, Mal, and Shareef got to Ant's crib.

"Yo, how you niggas get in here?" Ant asked.

"The door was unlocked, that's how," I replied, heading to the kitchen to get something to drink.

"First you niggas just walk up in the crib like you pay rent up in here, then you go up in the kitchen like you buy groceries in this muthafucka," Ant said, half joking, half serious.

"Nigga, we been doing this for years; now ya punk ass wanna say something all of a sudden?"

Mal joked back, and everybody laughed.

"What's goin' on, Albert Einsteins of the ghetto?" Trevor asked.

"Chillin', that's all," Shareef said back. "Yo, Black been over here? 'Cause he didn't show up at school today."

"Nah, yo, we ain't seen him all day. As a matter of fact, I haven't seen him in a minute," Trevor told us.

"I saw him last night," Ant cut in. "But he act like he ain't hear me callin' him. I peeped him again comin' out his building like around ten thirty last night when I was goin' to the Dumpster. At first, I didn't know it was him 'cause he had on all black with some black beef gloves, but you know how Black walk all goofy and shit; that's how I knew it was him. When he didn't answer I just said fuck it and came back on in." Ant shrugged his shoulders.

"Shareef said that he think Black is clockin' on another block 'cause he had a fat knot on him the last time he seen him, but that doesn't sound like him," I said. "You know how much he hates drugs."

"Y'all went by his crib?" Trevor asked.

"Not since this mornin' before we went to school."

"Yo, he gotta be home because he watches his li'l brother until his moms get home at five, so let's shoot over there," Ant suggested. He and Trevor ended their game and hopped up.

"Yeah, what up?" Black answered the door with the safety latch on. He looked like he just woke up.

"Nigga, what you mean 'what's up'? Open the fuckin' door and let us in," Trevor said to him.

"Hold up a minute," Black said, closing the door on us.

"Yo, something funny with this nigga kid. You see how he lookin'?" Trevor asked us.

"Word!" Ant said.

"Yo, chill out until we get up in there and see what's up," I said.

"He ain't just start lookin' like that either," Shareef said. You could hear the chain sliding off the door.

When we walked in Black's little brother was sleeping on the couch. Black went and sat back in the chair he must've been occupying before we arrived. He had on a wife beater that should have been white but was now beige, and a pair of boxers with some house slippers. There was a slight foul odor in the air that I couldn't put my finger on but was vaguely familiar.

"Yo, why you ain't come to school today?" I asked him.

"Man, fuck school. I ain't wit' that shit no more," he dryly remarked.

"Come on, Black baby! I thought we went through this already," Mal said.

"Yo, that school shit ain't for everybody. It ain't even definite I get a job if I graduate. I could still wind up havin' to work at Mickey fuckin' D's," he spat.

"Black, I thought we agreed that we was gonna finish out school," Shareef said to him.

"Nigga, please." He laughed. "You out there slingin' and shit. Pretty soon you're gonna quit too," he said to Shareef. "If you don't get knocked off or smoked first!" he added.

"Fuck you, Black," Shareef said.

"Yo, that was some fucked-up shit to say to your man," Ant jumped in.

"Yo, I ain't speakin' nothing but the truth," Black stated. "Niggas play for keeps in the game, and if you don't deserve to be makin' it them muthafuckas is gonna take it by any means necessary. Sooner or later if the narcos don't catch your ass, the stick-up kids will."

"Yo! But ain't you out there somewhere pumpin' too?" Mal asked him.

"Hell no! Who the fuck told you that?" he wanted to know.

"Where you get that knot from I seen you with a couple of weeks ago then?" Shareef questioned.

"And what you doin' dressed in all black at ten o'clock at night for?" Ant asked.

"None of your muthafuckin' business," Black snapped back. "What is this? I ain't on no damn trial or nothing. I ain't gotta answer to you niggas."

"We the same niggas who care about your ass," Ant said, getting tight. "The same niggas you drink wit' and smoke wit', been playing football and all that shit wit', so don't try to front on us like you don't know who the fuck we be, Black."

"Yo, you know what?" Black said. "Get the fuck out of my crib." He waved us off in a dismissive manner.

"We ain't goin' nowhere 'til we find out what's up wit' you," Trevor spoke up for all of us.

"Oh! Y'all ain't goin' nowhere, huh?" Black repeated. Then all of a sudden, we saw it.

Black was brandishing a gun. Everyone froze.

"Now I'm gonna tell you niggas one more time: get the fuck outta my crib," he said, pointing the black .25 semiautomatic right in Trevor's face.

"You doin' it like that, kid?" Trevor said, staring Black in the face. "You pullin' out on your boys? You a killa now?"

Black cocked the weapon back. "Man! Just get up outta here."

"Yeah, all right, nigga, but you better keep that joint on you twenty-four seven," Trevor told him, neither impressed nor fazed by Black's actions.

"Come on, Trev," we said, pulling him toward the door.

"Yeah, get him outta here before I send him outta here," Black antagonized him.

We all left the way we had come in. A million and one questions went through all of our heads, trying to figure out what made Black flip.

"Yo, that nigga lost his fuckin' mind," Trevor was the first to say once we were safely out of Black's apartment.

"Damn, that nigga whipped out on us, yo," Ant said.

"I told y'all somethin' was up with him, but I think he must be getting high off that shit or something pullin' a stunt like that," Shareef said.

"I'm with Shareef on that one," I agreed. "Did you smell that? And where did he even get a burner from?" I asked.

"Fuck where he got it from; what's he doin' pullin' it out on us like dat?" Mal said.

"Like I told him, he better have that shit on him twenty-four seven, 'cause if I catch him sleepin' I'm gonna break his fuckin' jaw," Trevor said again.

"Yo, he's gonna come to his senses and apologize and explain, 'cause that ain't him," I said.

"Man! Fuck that nigga. He better not try to come around with that 'I'm sorry' shit."

"What if he accidentally pulled the trigger or even on purpose and shot one of us?" Ant asked. "That's it, I'm done wit' that nigga, kid," he ended.

I couldn't believe what had taken place with Black. That day I didn't recognize my boy. It was as if he were possessed. Either way, I knew after that incident, things would never be the same between us and him; I just didn't realize how different they would be.

Almost three months had gone by and none of us heard from or about Black, until one day Mustafa called us up to the courts while we were playing football in the snow out in the field. A few guys from another block were standing with Mu when we got there.

"What up, Mu?" we all said.

"Yo, where your other boy at?" Mu asked us. Seeing the puzzled looks on our face Mu rephrased his question. "Where's Black at?"

When he asked that question, my alarm went off in my head and I knew something was wrong. "We don't know, Mu. He doesn't hang with us anymore," I told him.

"Why not?" he wanted to know.

"He just doesn't," I said back.

"Man! Fuck that; if you ain't gonna tell 'im then I will," Trevor said as he began to recap the day we were at Black's.

"Mu, I told you!" one of the kids from the other block said as soon as Trevor was done.

"Yo, did you know your boy turned into a stick-up kid?" Mu asked us.

We all looked at each other like Mu was speaking another language and we didn't understand what he had said. I remember thinking, *Black? A stick-up kid?* It made sense. It explained the money, the dressed in all black with beef gloves, the gun, and it was definitely in his blood. His father was an old-school stick-up man and small-time bank robber.

We all shook our heads no.

"We knew shit wasn't right with him, but we wouldn't have never suspected that," Ant said.

"We thought he was pumpin' on the next block," Shareef said.

"Are you sure, Mu?" I asked.

"Yeah, li'l nigga, we sure," one of the kids from the other block said to me.

"Hold up, yo, this my family right here, Jeff," Mu stepped in. "You can't be doin' it like that around here."

"My bad, Mu. My bad, li'l man," the kid named Jeff said. "But I'm sayin' though this nigga done came around the way and robbed five of my workers all together for a least six Gs, and I heard another block got hit by somebody who fits this nigga description. I ain't even tell nobody else that the kid is from the projects on the strength of you, Mu, and I ain't wanna start no fuckin' wars over some shit that could be deaded, but something gotta give with this nigga," Jeff stated.

"Yo, you got my word that I'm gonna get at him and try to get that dough for you, but if I don't then anything outside of here is fair game. This ain't no project beef because the nigga don't clock around here. That's a bet?"

"Yeah, Mu, you got dat," Jeff said, and he and the guys he was with got in a Jeep and left.

Mu had a facial expression that I had never seen before, but I knew it meant that he was mad about the situation with Black. "Yo, what's that nigga's apartment number again?" Mu asked me.

Hating that I had to tell him I said, "Three B."

"All right, if any of y'all see his ass don't mention nothing about this, you hear me?" Mu demanded. We all just nodded in agreement.

We all knew that as soon as we left Mu was going to Black's crib. We just hoped Black would listen to him and Mu would give him a chance, because he had a look on his face that could kill.

We went back to Ant's crib and Trevor was the first to say something. "Yo, Black done flipped his fuckin' wig. He out there robbin' niggas, kid. You heard what that kid Jeff said?"

"Yeah, he said Black got him for about six grand and hit other blocks," Ant said.

"This shit don't even surprise me, kid," Shareef joined in. "He used to always be talking to me about how if he can't make it, he's gonna take it. Remember that day we was coming from school and he was sayin' all that shit?" Shareef said to me and Mal.

"Yeah, I remember," I said. "I didn't think he'd actually get on it like that. I thought he was just talking."

"Well, whatever he's into he got to handle that 'cause that shit is deeper than us or the projects," Mal said. "He wanna act like a gangster then he got to live like a gangster; that's on him. I don't feel sorry for that nigga at all," my brother finished saying.

The next day I saw Mu and asked him what was up.

"Mil, listen to what I'm about to tell you and take heed. Stay away from that kid Black. He ain't right. Nobody gonna stay the same all their life, some people change for the better; other people change for the worse. Ya man took a turn for the worse and it's gonna cost him in the long run. Always remember that anybody who doesn't mean you any good only means you harm, and when you can't trust them as far as you can throw 'em then you don't fuck wit' 'em. That goes for anybody!" he emphasized.

"What happened when you went to his crib?" I asked, wanting to know.

"Bottom line is the li'l nigga denied everything, but I knew he was lyin' by the way he was actin'; and then when I told him he better watch his back 'cause niggas is gonna try to see him, he started talking about if anybody step to him they better come correct 'cause he got something for 'em."

I took what Mu told me and I relayed it to my brother and them.

A week later, we had heard that Black was in a shoot-out with some kids from Hasely Street up at the diner, and he popped two of them. It was rumored that he had gotten shot, but we didn't get any confirmation where he was hit or how bad it was. Since then, we hadn't heard of or seen him.

Chapter Twenty-one

"Monique, you better tell those little pissy-tail boys to stop calling this house some one and two o'clock in the morning playing on the phone like they ain't got no home training," my grandmother yelled.

"Grandma, I don't know who that be callin' because I don't be giving the number out like that," my sister said, lying through her teeth.

"Well, whoever they callin' for, y'all better tell them to stop before none of y'all be able to use the phone."

Lately there had been a lot of guys calling for my sister. A few times, I had answered the phone and had gotten into it with them calling and acting all tough, demanding to speak to her like they owned her. My brother said he went through the same thing. Not only had she been getting a lot of calls, but she had been staying out and hanging out late, too.

Trevor had told us that he saw her all the time, when he went to the clubs or parties that we couldn't get into, dancing with other hustlers from other areas. He said he always stayed later than usual just to make sure nothing happened to her, because he knew that if the shoe were on the other foot we'd do the same, if he had a sister. When we'd ask him what she had on he'd tell us something totally different from what we'd seen her leave the house in, so we knew that she was changing her clothes somewhere else. Mal and I figured she was changing over at the house of one of the projects chicks Trevor said she'd been hanging out with when she was up in one of those spots.

I would hear my moms and grandmother questioning her about whether she was still a virgin, and of course her answer was always yes, after throwing a tantrum, claiming they were overreacting. But from what Trevor was telling us, Mal and I didn't believe her. It made me mad that we couldn't do anything about it because we weren't old enough to get up in the places where she went. We told Trevor that if he saw her leaving with some guy, to snatch her up like he was one of us. He gave us his word that he would and we knew he would keep it.

***

"Wake up!" A booming voice broke my sleep. When I looked up my sister was hovering over both Mal and me.

"What do you want, girl?" Mal beat me to it.

"You know what the hell I want," she shot back.

"Yo, why you come up in here yellin' and stuff, Nique?" I asked.

"Because I don't appreciate one of your fuckin' friends putting his hand on me, that's why!" she shouted.

Immediately we jumped up. "Who?" we both asked.

"That nigga Trev," she bellowed. "He lucky I didn't scratch his muthafuckin' eyes out, but I bet you he won't grab me ever again."

Now it all made sense. "You must have been doing something you ain't had no business doin' last night then," Mal said.

"Mal, you ain't my damn father," she reminded my brother. "The last time I heard he was in prison, so stop tryin' to act like him," she threw back.

While my brother and sister were going back and forth with each other, I tried to be the calm one out of the three. "Nique, what Mal means is Trevor was probably only tryin' to protect you or stop you from doin' something that wasn't cool."

"Kamil, what I do is my business," she snapped. "I keep telling y'all, I don't need no damn body-guard. I'm the oldest and y'all are my little fuckin' brothers," Monique spat.

"We not tryin' to hear that shit." Mal got more aggressive. "You're not gonna be satisfied until you get somebody really hurt. And you know if Dad were here you wouldn't be doin' none of this shit."

"Well, he's not and you're not him. And y'all the ones who got somebody hurt. I know y'all told him to do that shit because I don't even know him like that, and because of y'all your boy is nursing his wounds."

"What happened?" Mal asked

"I told y'all he put his hands on me, and when he did I made sure he thought twice the next time."

Me and Mal jumped up and started getting dressed. "Nique, keep doin' whatever it is you're doin' and watch what happens," Mal said to her.

"Kamal, don't threaten me, boy," she spat back.

"Whatever. You heard what I said."

"What's all this noise and fussin' about?" My grandmother burst into the room. Luckily, everything was over.

We all turned and sang at the same time as if we were angels, "Nothing, Grandma."

"Um-hm, I bet," she grumbled. "Y'all better not be in here fighting. Don't make me come up in here with one of your grandfather's old belts," she ended before closing the room door.

Mal and I both shook our heads at our sister. We hurried and dressed and then we were out the door.

"Yo, kid, I'm gonna tell y'all straight up, on the strength of the love I got for y'all I'm gonna wear these scratches." Trevor met us at the door. He had already applied Vaseline to the scars my sister was the cause of. The scratches were deep and nasty looking. I could tell she had really dug her nails into my friend's face. I felt bad that we had put Trevor in that type of position. "Ya sister flipped out on me, kid."

"What went down?" I asked him.

"Man, we were at Rocco's and your sister and her hooker friends were up in there. Everything was cool until your sister started drinkin' and shit and then she started dancing with this nigga from Monroe. Yo, she was dancing all nasty and shit and the nigga did what any nigga would do in a situation like that: he started feeling her all up and shit. She was so fuckin' drunk she wasn't even trying to stop him. I was gonna go over there and snatch her up, but her girls grabbed her up and sat her down. Normally, I would have been in the bathroom puffin'; but I chilled and was just sippin' on something light 'cause I had a funny feelin' that some nigga was gonna try to roll out with her, and my instincts were right.

"When the party was ending and everybody was leavin', another kid stepped to her and started kickin' to her. He must've gamed her 'cause they was walkin' over to this Volvo, and instead of the bitches she was wit' stopping her they just let her go, so that's when I stepped up and called her name. She really didn't know who I was, but she stopped just in time for me to get close up on her. I could tell the kid wanted to know who I was by the way he was looking at me, so I told him she was my sister. That's when she went crazy, talkin' about she ain't my goddamn sister, soundin' all drunk.

"So that's when I grabbed her arm and started sayin' that I was takin' her home. Then out of the blue she swung at me and caught me in the face, but I still didn't let her go. She started clawing the shit outta her. When homeboy seen what was goin' on he must've been like fuck it, 'cause he hopped in the car and murked out. After that, I let her go and her so-called friends came while she was callin' me every curse word she probably knew. I screamed on them skeezer bitches and told them if they were her friends they wouldn't have let her go like that, and if I find out they didn't take her home, the next time I see them I would kick their asses. And that was basically it."

"Yo, that was love, kid." Mal gave Trevor a pound and a hug. "I ain't never gonna forget that, and my bad for you havin' to get all scarred up like that."

"Yeah, Trevor, we appreciate the love," I said, following up. Although I felt bad for Trevor after hearing the story, I was grateful that he was there. I could only imagine what would have or could have happened to my sister had he not been.

"Like I told y'all before, I know y'all would do the same for me," Trevor said back.

I could see in Mal's eyes how heated he was and I didn't know what to do about it. All we really could do was watch Monique more carefully when we were at the same parties so she wouldn't do anything dumb, and tell every dude who called the crib not to be calling anymore.

We loved our sister but, no matter what, she was going to do whatever she wanted to do regardless of what we said, just like me and

Mal. I believed that was one of the traits we had all gotten from our father. It was hard for our grandmother to keep an eye on all of us at all times and we all knew that it was next to impossible for my moms to because she was never at home. After hearing how Monique was acting in the streets, that day I realized just how much our family was falling apart despite us being together.

Chapter Twenty-two

Once again, Mal, Shareef, and I, minus Black, had made it through another grade. Three weeks from now, we'd be chillin' for the whole summer and after our summer vacation was over, we'd be headed to high school, something we were all looking forward to.

The eighth grade graduation dance was coming up a week and a half before school ended and me, Mal, and Shareef were stepping out in style, 'cause Mu volunteered to take us in his Benz. We had already discussed chipping in for graduation to rent a limo. We were definitely trying to end our junior high careers with a bang.

As the bell rang, I bolted out of class, headed out the school's door. I had seen Lisa earlier and she told me she wanted to ask me something very important after school. It didn't matter to me what it was; I was just looking forward to hooking up with her. It had been a minute since she and I chilled together.

"Hey." I smiled and waved.

She was leaning up against my bike with her legs crossed, waiting for me. "Hey." She gave me a hug.

"So, what's up? Is everything okay?" I asked, trying to read her face.

"Yes, everything is fine." She sounded kind of nervous.

"You sure?" I asked.

"Yes, I'm sure." She smiled. She took a deep breath. "I wanted to know who you were going to the dance with."

"My brother and Shareef," I said without giving it a second thought.

"I don't mean like that, silly. I mean, who's your date?" she asked.

"My date? I don't have a date," I replied. "I didn't know I had to have a date to go to the dance."

"No, you don't have to." Lisa laughed. "But I wanted to go with you."

I couldn't believe how silly I was at that moment. I tried to play it off. "I figured you were goin' with Felicia and 'em?"

"They're going with their boyfriends, and I'm gonna meet them there."

I had no idea Lisa wanted me to take her to the dance because she never mentioned it before. Honestly, if she would've asked me, then I would've been more prepared, but me, Mal, and Shareef had been planning this for months. I was caught between a rock and a hard place.

"Lisa, I didn't know you wanted us to go to the dance together, 'cause if I did I would've gotten wit' you ahead of time and we would've worn the same color or something. What color are you wearing, anyway?" I asked her.

"Lavender, but if you don't want to take me, don't worry about it," she said to me. I could hear the disappointment in her tone.

I was wearing a white suit with a red bow tie and cummerbund, which definitely didn't match what she was wearing, but the look on her face and the sound of her voice made me feel messed up.

"Lisa, you know it's not even like that. I'm wearing red and white to the dance, but here's what I'm gonna do. I'm gonna go downtown and see if I can get a lavender bow tie and cummerbund or something close to that color. If I don't then I'll meet you at the dance and we'll hook up there, all right?"

"Yeah, Kamil, if you say so," she responded, not sounding too enthused.

***

I knew I wasn't going to find that color or anything close to it because it was one of those funny colors you had to order. They didn't even have any more purple in stock. I called Lisa to tell her. It almost sounded like she was crying when she told me she changed her mind about going. When I asked her why she said she didn't feel like going out anymore. I told her that I'd call her later and she hung up. Something was wrong, and I was too caught up with getting ready for the dance to pay attention or figure out what it was.

Chapter Twenty-three

"Yo, you three niggas lookin' real sharp tonight," Mu told us. "Y'all looking like some real young men. I'm proud of y'all for guttin' it out 'cause not many niggas from the projects make it through school or out the hood, but you three are gonna make it and don't let nobody tell you different."

We just listened as Mu spoke.

"All right, I'm done rappin'. Now go in there and get y'all groove on; and you got my beeper number so page me before it ends so I can come get y'all. Enjoy yourselves," Mu said as we got out of the Benz.

All the kids who were pulling up with their parents and walking up were checking out Mu's ride as we stepped out. You would have never thought they'd seen a Mercedes that looked like his before. It was calypso red with a pea-nut-butter color leather ragtop. The inside was customized in leather with the same colors, and he had deep-dished gold hammer rims. All the other kids were jocking us as we made our way to the cafeteria door.

Tonight was our night and we came to have a good time. This was a celebration of our last days of junior high school. It was better than elementary, but I knew it was going to be even better in high school. Milk and Giz's "Top Billin'" was pumpin' when we walked in. The middle of the floor was flooded with kids jamming.

"This that cut right here," Shareef said.

"Yeah, this a dope cut," my brother followed with.

Most of the guys there had on tuxes like us and some just had on dress pants and button-ups, with ties. All the girls had on dresses, though, and it looked like they outnumbered us three to one. Mal and Shareef scanned the dance floor to see what girls they were going to get up on. Within seconds, they spotted two they wanted to step to; they went to the middle and started dancing. To tell the truth there was only one girl I wanted to dance with and that was Lisa, but she wasn't there.

I was just standing there kind of dancing by myself when I heard a familiar voice from behind ask me if I want to dance. I knew it wasn't Lisa even before I turned around, but it was someone I knew.

"Trina, what are you doing here?" I asked, surprised to see her. She had on a black fitted dress with high heels and her hair was styled in a Chinese bun. I didn't think anybody looked as good as she did up in there.

"Mu came to the house and I asked him where you were. He told me here, so I threw something on right quick and told him to bring me up here. He said you didn't come with a girl so I came to hang out with you." She smiled. I could feel all eyes on me. I knew everyone wanted to know who Trina was.

"You crazy," I said to her as I took her hand and led her to the dance floor and started dancing.

We danced so much I had to take off my suit jacket 'cause the alcohol we had been drinking before Mu had picked us up began to kick in, and it was making me hot. I even took off my bow tie and unbuttoned a few buttons on my shirt.

After a couple of rap songs, the deejay stopped and made an announcement. "This next cut is for all the couples who made it through the school year!"

All you saw were brothers exiting the dance floor trying to find seats or a place to stand. There were no more than twenty couples paired up on the floor by the time the song came on. I didn't know why or how, but I found myself amid the group of couples with Trina.

Outside of with my moms I had no real experience in slow dancing, but I could tell Trina did. She stepped in closer and wrapped her arms around my neck. In spite of all the dancing, she still smelled good. Out of instinct, I put my hands around her waist; but she moved them to her butt then laid her head on my shoulder. It felt good dancing with her like this and I thought I was doing pretty good for it to be my first time.

That night, you would have thought I had slow danced with plenty of girls many times. I could feel myself rising from the way Trina was grinding me, and she knew what she was doing, too. With my hardness pressed up against her, she focused solely on gyrating and grinding that specific area with her body. My head was spinning between the music, the alcohol, and Trina's grinds. I felt like I was floating.

I was caught up in the mood but, out of nowhere, something brought me back to my senses. When I opened my eyes and looked to my left, I regretted opening them. I could see Lisa and her girlfriends on the side watching me and Trina. My heart instantly skipped a beat and a sense of embarrassment swept through my entire body.

Trina must've sensed something too because she stopped dancing. "What's wrong?" she looked up and asked.

I told her to excuse me for a minute, and I began approaching Lisa. By then Lisa and her girls were all walking toward the door. I caught up with them outside.

"What, Kamil?" she asked. "Go back and finish your dance," she quickly snapped. I'd never seen her like this.

"Nah, it's not how it looks," I began to say. "That was just a harmless dance. You the one I really wanted to dance wit', but you weren't here."

She let out a light chuckle. "Kamil, don't give me that," she said, as tears began to roll down her face. "It didn't look like she had on matching colors to me," she pointed out. "The only thing I seen matching were your two hands on her ass."

For some reason I felt like my father when he was explaining himself when my mother caught him in the visiting room with another woman. Just standing there seeing Lisa crying made me know that I was wrong and I had hurt her the way my dad had hurt my moms. All I could say was that I was sorry, because I had never been in a situation like that before and no one ever warned me.

I just stood there as Lisa and her friends walked off. I was speechless. When I turned around to head back into the party, Trina was standing in the doorway. From where she stood, I knew she had heard everything that had just taken place. The devilish grin stretched across her face was enough to confirm she had. I followed her back in and enjoyed myself as best I could under the circumstances.

Chapter Twenty-four

Graduation was over and my family all wanted to meet Lisa, which really made me feel like crap. I didn't even have the heart to tell them that we hadn't spoken in a week and a half, and I didn't think we'd ever speak again. I saw Lisa standing on the other side of the auditorium with her parents and I pointed in the direction as I described to them which one she was. They told me to get her so they could meet her and take a picture of us. Just when I was about to work up the nerve to go over there, I saw Lisa coming toward us.

"Hello, Kamil," she spoke softly. "I came to meet your family."

"Hey," I said back to her. "Ma, Grandma, Nique, Jasmine, this is Lisa Matthews. Lisa this is my moms, my grandmother, my oldest sister Monique, and my little sister Jasmine. You know Kamal already."

"Hello, Kamal." She smiled at my brother. "Nice to meet you all," she then said politely.

"It's nice to finally meet you too, sugar," my grandmother said.

"Yes, it's a pleasure to meet you, Lisa. My son has nothing but good things to say about you," my moms chimed in.

"Kamil, she's pretty," my little sister said.

"Let me know if my brother gets out of line. I'll straighten him out for you," Monique said.

Each time one of my family members spoke, it was like someone was sticking me with pins and needles, because I knew that I messed up. Lisa just stood there smiling and saying thank you as my family gave her one compliment after the other.

"Kamil, put your arm around her so we can take your picture," my grandmother said.

"Actin' like he all scared of girls," Nique joked.

"Is it all right?" I asked.

"Aw, look at my baby, he's a gentleman. Asking can he put his arm around her," my moms teased.

"Come on, Ma!" I said, feeling both embarrassed and guilty from a week and a half ago.

Kamal was standing next to my mother laughing to himself, because besides me and Lisa he was the only one there who knew what was going on since I'd told him about it when we got home.

"Again, it was nice meeting you," Lisa said. "Kamil, enjoy your summer," she told me in a way that let me know we wouldn't be seeing each other.

"You too," I replied dryly.

And then she left.

Chapter Twenty-five

It had been a month since I had spoken to Lisa. I tried to give her a call on her birthday, but her moms said she wasn't home. After that, I just stopped calling.

Ever since the night of the dance, I had been seeing more and more of Trina. While Kamal would be over at Ant's or Trevor's crib, I was over at Trina and Reecie's with Mustafa. A few times we all went out to eat or to the movies. Mu would give me like a hundred dollars so it would look like I was paying my and Trina's way all the time. No matter where we were, Trina was always all over me kissing and hugging me, or just up under me period. I didn't know if Reecie was Mu's girl, but I knew I had never seen her with anybody else. She was always up under him like Trina was with me, only more, but it seem like Mu didn't mind so neither did I. I was going to ask Mu if Reecie his girl, but I figured if he wanted me to know, he would've told me, so

I left it alone. Every time I got around Mal and them, they always asked me if I was having sex with Trina. No matter how many times I told them no they never believed me.

One particular day I went over to Trina's and she took awhile before she let me in. At first, I thought she had some other guy in there until she opened the door and told me Mu was in the back room with Reecie. I knew Mu wouldn't allow any other guy up in there to see Trina knowing that she talked to me. She was acting kind of weird and said she'd be back in a minute after she finished doing something, so I just sat in the living room, flicking through the channels on the TV. About an hour and a half had gone by and she still was in the back. So, I got up and went back there, not really to check on her, but to say what's up to Mu.

The door was slightly cracked, so I pushed it opened. I started to say, "What's up," to Mu until I saw what he, Reecie, and Trina were doing. I didn't know what to do or say. I was frozen in my tracks. I drew everyone's attention to me seeing that the door had opened.

"Yo, my bad, Mu. I ain't mean to—"

He cut me off. "Nah, kid, you a'ight, it's cool. Come on in," he said. "You were bound to find out anyway, being over here all the time."

In the middle of the room was a table. Reecie was on one side with a plate in front of her and a razor in her hand, while Trina was on the other side bottling up what Reecie was cutting up. Mu was by the bed counting the bottles and wrapping a rubber band around them. I noticed he had a white mask around his face, which covered his nose and mouth like the ones doctors and nurses used in the hospital. They all did. If I had to take a guess, I would have had to say that there were at least 3,000 bottles lying on the bed, and another few hundred by Trina on the table. Plus there were chunks of white rocks on the side of the plate Reecie was cutting up on, while she dug into a nice chunk on the plate.

"Yo, I know I don't gotta tell you this is between us, 'cause I know you already know that," Mu said to me.

"Mu, you know I'd never tell anybody your business or anything that we talk about," I said back. "I don't see nothing, I don't know nothing,"

"I know that, kid." Mu smiled at me. "That's why I fucks wit' you. Reecie, you and Trina can handle this, right? 'Cause I need to kick it to my man for a minute and then I'm gonna shoot this shit out to them li'l niggas outside waitin' on me."

"Yeah, we got this, Mu," she said, speaking for both her and Trina.

"Mil, you stayin' when Mu leave, right?" Trina asked me.

"Yeah."

"Okay, I won't be too much longer," she said, and then Mu and I stepped out of the room.

"Now you know why I be over here so much, Mil," he started out saying. "Those two are some good chicks and they know the game. That's why I dig you fuckin' wit' Trina, 'cause I know she ain't gonna shit on you like some of these other chicks will. She a ridah and she diggin' you and you ain't even out there getting paper. When you ain't here all she do is talk about you, kid. If I ain't know no better, I would've thought you were hittin' that, but she already told Reecie you ain't. Why? I don't know, but that's on you, kid. All I know is that you can hit that any time you want, it's up to you." He paused and then asked me, "You ain't no virgin, are you?"

I had been waiting for him to ask me that for the longest. "I been wit' girls before," I said. "But I never go all the way and stick my joint in something."

"Well, that means you're a virgin then, nigga," he said with a grin on his face. "I should've known that already, but don't even worry about that 'cause, check, I know how we gonna change that. Trina's birthday is next weekend and me and Reecie had already planned to take her out, but this is what I'ma do. I'm gonna cop two rooms at the Loop Inn. We gonna go to New York for a little bit and get something to eat, chill, and then come back to Jersey and have a couple of drinks up in my room. When I kick you two out and tell you I want some privacy, that's when the ball is gonna be in your court, and you just gonna have to take it from there, 'cause I can't put it in for you. You gots to do that part on your own," he said, smiling. "You should be all right, though, 'cause Trina ain't no virgin anyway, but she ain't no ho, either, so she gonna know what she doin'. Just go with the flow, a'ight?"

I nodded in agreement. Mu shook his head as he continued to grin. "A'ight, I'll catch you later." He hugged me before he glided out the door.

It seemed like the weekend had come around so quick. I told Mal where I was going and he helped me convince our moms to let us spend the night over at Ant's crib as an excuse to get out of the house. It was times like this I loved having a brother who had my back. Mal wasn't a virgin, but he still wanted me to give him full details whenever I got back. Like Reecie, when it came to beauty and body, Trina was bad, and everybody either fantasized about her or wanted a piece of her.

This was my first time ever going to Sylvia's to eat in Harlem, but I heard about how good the food was supposed to be, and how a lot of actors, entertainers, rappers, and celebrities would be up in there, so not only was I looking forward to the food, but also seeing someone famous.

Mu already had reservations for us, so we were seated as soon as we got there. There were pictures all over the walls of famous African Americans, and when I looked around I noticed a few celebrities, but I wasn't all excited like I thought I would be, because they looked like ordinary people out having dinner. In fact, the way Mu was dressed he actually stood out more than they did, and some people probably thought he was some type of rapper or something.

I had to give it to Ms. Sylvia, she ran a classy place and the food was excellent. It was almost as good as my grandmother's.

I knew Trina was enjoying herself, because it was written all over her face. When I looked over at Mu, he just gave me a wink.

After we finished eating, we walked to 125th, down by the legendary Apollo, to take pictures. 125th Street was like another world within itself. Everywhere you looked or turned there was some type of hustle going on, from selling clothes to music. It was a street that was real busy and loud. At that moment, I understood why they called the borough the city that never sleeps.

There were different picture backdrops to choose from. We all took one together in front of the black background, then Trina and I took one in front of Mickey and Minnie Mouse hugging. So did Mu and Reecie. Mu and I took one with the background that had two aces of spades that read, Two of a Kind, and then one in front of the one that had a Benz with a guy and three girls leaning on it. Trina and I took another one with me sitting in a straw chair, and her on my lap.

From there, we crossed over to the other side and went inside of the 125 Mart. We walked around for a little bit. The whole time Trina had her arm hooked around mine. While she was enjoying being with me I was enjoying the New York scenery. The night was winding down so we made our way back to the parking garage and headed back to Jersey.

Chapter Twenty-six

The sign read LOOP INN as we pulled into the hotel. Mu stopped in front of the door where you check in and told me to come with him. I slid up from under Trina and followed him.

"Yeah, I called you earlier about two honeymoon suites," Mu said to the man behind the Plexiglas.

"What's your name?" he asked.

"Ali. Mustafa Ali."

"Oh, yeah, I got you set up right here," the man said.

"Let me get four bubble baths and two logs with that," Mu told him, pulling out his money.

"With the logs, the bubble bath, and the rooms, that'll be $266.60," the man said back.

Mu peeled off three hundred-dollar bills and paid him. As we pulled to the back on the left side, I was wondering what made these rooms so special that it almost cost $300, because from the outside it didn't look like much; but when we stepped in Mu's room, my question was answered.

"Ooh, this is nice!" Trina was the first to say as Mu turned on the dimmer lights a little more than halfway. Her reaction led me to believe she had never been there before, unless she was trying to play it off. The room was fly, though. It was apparent that Reecie had been there before because like Mu, she had no reaction.

Right in the middle of the room there was a heart-shaped Jacuzzi with mirrors on the ceiling. There was a leather sofa to the right, with a marble table in front of it. To the left of that was a fireplace built inside the wall. You had to step down some steps to get to the bed, which was also shaped like a heart, with mirrors over it. To top it off, it was a waterbed. In front of the bed was a big-screen TV. I had never seen one that big before in person so I didn't know what size it was.

Mu picked up the remote and turned on the TV, or so I thought; but, instead, the radio came on. "Reecie, did you bring my tapes out the car like I asked you?" Mu asked her.

"I got 'em right here."

"Gimme them and go put some ice in that white bucket right there," he instructed. Reecie snatched up the bucket as Mu popped in a cassette tape. "Y'all too young to know about this. This is a classic right here," he said as he sang with the song.

"Who's that, Mu?" I asked.

"That's the Stylistics, the shit ya moms and pops made you off of," he told me, turning it up louder. I remembered my dad playing music like that in the house and in the car when I was little. But it bugged me out to hear Mu listening to it, even though it sounded good.

Reecie came back with the ice. "Mil, put that bottle up in there," Mu said, pointing to the bottle of Dom P.

Reecie was over at the Jacuzzi running water and putting bubble bath in. Mu went and lit the log in the fireplace while the champagne chilled. Trina and I were on the leather sofa just kicking it.

"Thank you for showing me a good time for my birthday, Kamil." Trina leaned in and kissed me on the cheek. "No other guy ever spent time with me the way you do. They just try to get what they can get and be out, but you're different," she said smoothly.

I just sat there and listened. "I'm just glad that you're enjoyin' your birthday, 'cause you deserve to have a nice time. I like being around you and spending time with you too. You're fun to be around."

She leaned over and kissed me again, only this time it was on the lips. She pushed her tongue into my mouth. I had kissed her plenty of times, but never like this. This kiss was different. It made me a little warm on the inside.

"Okay, birthday girl, you and Mil come over here and take these glasses so we can toast your born day," Mu said to us.

We all held our flute glasses in the air as we wished Trina a happy birthday and then we toasted. The champagne was smooth. There was a big difference from what I had ever tasted before. I knew it was expensive by the look of the bottle. Besides, knowing Mu, I knew he wouldn't buy anything cheap.

Once the bottle was empty, Mu popped open another one that he had put on ice earlier. What happened next took me by surprise. Out of nowhere, Reecie started taking off her clothes. She stripped down to her bra and panties. At first, I thought I was seeing things, until Trina started covering my eyes just as Reecie took off her top and was pulling her panties off.

"Reecie, don't be doing that shit in front of Kamil," Trina yelled.

"Girl, please!" she said with a slur. "Ain't nobody thinking about no Kamil looking at me. He's like family," she said as she stepped in the

Jacuzzi. I could tell the champagne had her tipsy. "Besides, do you see Mustafa complaining?" Reecie pointed out.

When I looked over at Mu, he was just sitting there by the bed sipping on a glass of champagne with a grin on his face. By now, Trina had lowered her hand. All she could do was suck her teeth and roll her eyes. "You play too much," she said to her sister. Her words were also slurred.

"If you don't want him to see me then go to your own room," Reecie told her.

"We will." Trina hopped up in a staggering manner. "Come on, Kamil, let's get out of here." She turned to me.

"All right, playboy, I'll catch you later." Mu held up his flute.

I just pumped my fist in the air.

"Come give me a hug before y'all leave, Mil." Reecie stood up with open arms and a huge smile plastered across her face. I was able to get an eyeful. Even with the bubbles partially covering portions of her body I could see her perfectly round breasts, flat midriff, and neatly shaved patch of hair between her legs.

Before Trina was able to protest, Mu intervened. "That's enough," his voice boomed. "Sit your drunk ass down and show your sister some respect."

Reecie's smile instantly turned into a frown as she sat back in the Jacuzzi. I knew that was our cue to exit. I snatched up one of Mu's cassette tapes and then helped Trina out the door.

Our room was identical to Mu's. As soon as we entered the room, I went over to the Jacuzzi and turned on the water; then I put the log in the fireplace.

"Look at you." Trina smiled.

Although I was winging it, everything just felt natural. I turned off the water in the Jacuzzi and popped in the tape. The sticker on it read KEN STOKES. Trina started dancing sexy as I walked over to her. She grabbed the front of my shirt and began kissing me. I could taste the champagne on her tongue. Trina started lifting my shirt up and over my head as we kissed. I could feel myself getting aroused.

I began to unbutton her shirt and unfasten her jeans. My heart was pounding like a warrior's drum and I could feel the perspiration building up under my armpits. I took a deep breath and tried to relax as I let her shirt fall to the floor while I slowly pulled her jeans down. They were so tight I wondered how she had gotten into them. She lifted each foot as I took her pants off and then I stood up. I had an idea that she had a nice body, but nice was an understatement.

She looked like a model standing there with a matching bra and panty set similar to the one her sister had on. Her body was better shaped than Reecie's. Where her sister's breasts were round but full sized, Trina's were medium in size and erect. Her breasts fit perfectly in the material while her nipples protruded through the bra. Her hips were not as wide as her sister's but they had more curve.

For a moment, I just stood there admiring her body, until she reached for my pants to unbutton and unzip them. I stepped out of my pants as Trina unhooked her bra, tossing it to the side and doing the same with her panties. The way her breasts sat up it looked like she still had her bra on. The silky patch of hair that started just under her waist leading between her legs was neatly trimmed. I took my wife beater off but left my boxers on, while she caressed my chest.

"Let's get in the water," she suggested, walking toward the Jacuzzi.

From behind, you could see the firmness in her butt. I was mesmerized as I watched her sashay to the Jacuzzi.

"Come on in, what you are waiting for?" she said to me. Her words were soft.

I pulled off my shorts and stepped in the water behind her. It was hot.

Trina slid over to me and began kissing me all over my face; then she started sucking on my neck. My manhood started to grow as she took me in her hand and began stroking me underwater.

Between the softness of her hand and the lubrication of the water, it felt as if I was about to explode. I just leaned my head back, looking up at the mirrors on the ceiling, while she licked me all over my chest, biting me on my nipples. Then I lifted up and pressed up against her, making her lean back as I began kissing all on her and then sucking her breast while I slid my middle finger inside of her. Her sex gripped my finger. She cooed as she gyrated her hips to meet my pace with my hand. I was still sucking on her nipples while I massaged her. As I finger popped her she began to moisten. Her body began to shutter as she moaned.

"Mil, you make me feel so good," she whispered. She was now breathing heavily. I slipped my finger out of her.

She cupped my face with her hand and kissed me gently on the lips then stood up and grabbed a towel and began drying herself off. "Dry off," she told me, and then she walked over to the bed.

I was so caught up in the mood that I didn't even hear the music stop. I flipped the tape and went to the bed. Trina grabbed my arms and pulled me to the bed. I lay on my back and just looked into her eyes; they glowed in the dimly lit room. I assumed they were glassy from the champagne. At that moment, she had the sexiest grin I had ever seen on her face.

"Don't worry," she whispered to me as she leaned in and licked around the outer part of my ear. "I'm not going to hurt you."

I just laughed to myself for her thinking that I was scared. I was a virgin, not a punk, but I didn't say anything.

Trina went from my ear, to my lips, to my neck, down my chest, and then to my navel, biting me lightly here and there. She was driving my young body crazy.

She was sucking and kissing my left side, moving her tongue around in a circular motion. I flinched each time she bit into my skin. She glided her tongue between my legs and began running it along the inner part of my thighs. Her hair brushed lightly past my stiffness as she positioned herself up under me. I looked down at her only to find her staring up at me. She wrapped her petite hand around my dick and licked around the helmet with her tongue while never breaking her gaze. Her lips were juicy. I felt like a human lollipop the way she licked me.

She then took me into her mouth. It was warm. I squirmed from the feeling. It was one thing to hear about it or think about it but it was another thing to experience it. I had never felt anything in comparison in my life. She had my toes curling and my ass cheeks tightening. Just when I felt like I couldn't take it anymore, she stopped. She started sucking between my thighs again then kissed her way back up until she found my lips. I wanted to move my head because I didn't want to kiss her after she had gone down on me, but I didn't want to offend her, either. I tried to block out what she had just done to me.

"That was for showing me a good time tonight," she said before kissing me, and I kissed her back.

I felt her hand grab hold of me. She lifted up then guided me inside of her. I started to resist because both Mu and Kamal had told me to make sure I used a condom. Mu had given me one earlier but it was way across the room in my pants pocket and everything was feeling too good to stop her. She was even warmer than her mouth as she started riding me. I held on to her hips and tried to keep up. She placed her hands on my chest and thrust her body into mine. I could hear the sounds of our bodies intertwining underneath us. By now, Trina was in a zone on top of me. She threw her head back and her pace quickened. "Yeah," I could hear her panting repeatedly. I could feel her getting wetter. Just then, I could feel something within myself. Then out of nowhere, like a bolt of lightning, it happened.

My entire body tensed up and then exploded.

"Agh!" I cried out. I tried to push Trina up off of me but she was still grinding her hips on me. My body had become limp.

"That was nice." Trina laid her head on my chest. We were both breathing heavily. I was winded and sweating bullets. "Round two in a minute," Trina said, biting me on my earlobe. I just smiled. At that moment, I felt like a man.

For the rest of the night Trina showed me how to sex her in different positions. First night out and I already had a favorite position: hitting it from the back doggie style.

"From the looks on your two faces I know y'all had a good time last night, and ain't no more virgins in the car," Mu said, messing with me.

"Mu, leave my baby alone," Trina defended me before I had a chance to say anything.

"Oh! That's your baby now, huh?" Mu said back. "My li'l partner must've put it on ya ass!" We all started laughing.

On the ride, I fell asleep. When I woke up, we were back in the projects.

"Are you coming over later?" Trina asked.

"Yeah, I'll be over after I check in, change my clothes, and get something to eat," I told her.

"Okay," she said, giving me a kiss.

"All right, Mu and Reecie, I'll see y'all."

"Yeah, I'll get up later, playboy," Mu said, still fucking with me.

"Bye, Kamil; and you better not try to play my sister now that you got some," Reecie said.

"Nah, I'm not like that," I assured Reecie.

"Reecie, shut up, girl," Trina jumped in. "Kamil, don't pay her no mind. I'll see you later."

I went over to Ant's house to get Kamal.

"Damn! This nigga hit, kid, I can see it in your face," my brother yelled as soon as I walked through the door.

"You even look different," Ant said.

"Get outta here."

"Nigga, what happened?" Mal asked.

"Yo! It was fly." I got excited just thinking about last night. "The whole night," I said as I went off into everything, detail for detail.

"Yo! You a lucky muthafucka," Ant said. "I knew shorty was a freak."

"Come on, yo, don't talk about her like that," I said.

"Ah, shit! Mal, your brother is one of those sucka for love–ass niggas. She got him pussy whipped already," Ant spat back.

Mal started laughing

"Nigga, you don't know what you talking about. Ain't nobody pussy whipped nothing," I hit him back with.

"Yeah, whatever. Take ya pussy-whipped ass home and take a shower 'cause you smell like sex, nigga. I get up wit' y'all later," Ant joked.

"Yeah, peace, we get up," Mal said as we were leaving.

"Yo, Mil, on some real shit, don't let shorty get ya nose open to where you lose focus, 'cause the pretty ones are the ones you'll have the most problems from," my brother warned me.

"Yo, it ain't like that, Mal. Me and shorty don't go together. We just cool, and I'll never get like that," I said.

"All right, kid. I'm just telling you 'cause you my brother and I love you. But you know you should've strapped up, though, right?" Mal got on me.

"I know," was all I could say.

"Mess around and be a daddy, kid," he joked.

I laughed, but I knew what my brother had said was nothing but the truth.

Chapter Twenty-seven

Ever since Trina's birthday, we had been sexing every day, and I had been using condoms ever since. The more we did it the better I got at it. For a fourteen-year-old, I was doing all right. A few times, I had Kamal cover for me again so that I could spend the night over at Trina's crib. It felt good to wake up with a naked body lying next to me.

One morning I woke up early and had to use the bathroom. When I walked down the hall I could see Mu sitting in the kitchen so I went to check him after I came out. As I entered the kitchen, all I saw were all types of utensils and materials on the table. He was running a playing card through what I thought was coke.

"Yo, what up, kid?" he greeted me.

"What's happening, Mu?"

"Sit down," he told me.

I had an idea what he was doing, but I never actually witnessed it with my own eyes. On the table there was a big box of Armors baking soda, a digital scale, a cake mixing bowl, a spoon, a strainer, some paper towels, little sandwich bags, and an empty mayonnaise jar. On the stove, Mu had a pot of hot water boiling and a bowl of ice water on the kitchen counter.

"You know what I'm doing?" he asked me.

"You cookin' up right?" I said back.

He smiled. "Yeah, I'm cookin' up, kid. You see this right here?" he said, pointing to the strainer. "You use this to strain the coke through after you shave the rocks down. Then you take a card and pile it all up after you strained all the rocks into powder. After that you take this baking soda and pour some in a sandwich bag and weigh it up on the scale to match the grams of powder." I watched as Mu studied the scale.

"You see this, right?" he said. "You take this card and spread the coke and start mixing the bake in like this, and when you finish doin' this, bend the card and scoop it up and put it in the jar. Then you take some water, pour it in the jar, and set the jar in the pot on the stove. While the hot water's cookin' the coke, all the good shit is gonna stay at the bottom and all the bullshit is gonna float to the top; that's how you'll know if the product is right," he explained as if he were my science teacher.

"Then you let that sit for a couple minutes and then take it out and set it in a bowl of ice water." While he was talking, he placed the jar into the big orange plastic bowl. "While it's coolin' off just take some cold water in your hand like this." He demonstrated. "And start throwing it in the jar and you'll see shit start to come together. Shake it around in the ice water a bit until it all comes together, then tilt it to the side and pour cold water in here. Once it looks like it's rocked up, drain the cold water out and dump it on the paper towels like this, and bam!"

When Mu poured the jar on the paper towels, I heard it hit the table like a real rock.

"You let this baby sit and air dry for a few 'cause it's still water up in here and after that you ready to chop it up," he told me. "But first, throw it on the scale and see how much coke you brought back, 'cause sometimes you lose grams when you cook up if the coke is bad or if you burned the shit up from letting it sit on the stove too long." I had taken it all in as he spoke even though I was sure I'd never need to remember.

"You think you'd be able to do everything I just showed you?" Mu asked me.

"I guess if I had to," I said.

"Either you can or you can't; there's no in between," he said back to me. "That's how you fuck up, from not being sure."

"Yeah, I could," I changed up. I didn't know why Mu made such a big deal about it, but I didn't want to disappoint him.

"I'ma show you how to cut some raw diesel, too, whenever I go cop, so you'll know the coke game and the dope game," Mu told me.

I didn't know why he was showing me all of this, but the more he talked the more I was kind of glad to be learning it, for some reason. As if reading my mind, Mu said, "Yo, I'm not teaching you this to get you in the game. I'm just showin' you how much work has to go into this shit. It's more than just goin' out there standing on the block clockin'. That's easy, but it's shit like this that's the hard part, and a lot of times shit gets aggravating and frustrating and even more stressful, but if you gonna play the game you gots to stay focused, 'cause one false move and it'll cost you."

Just like everything else Mu had told me in the past, I took what he said and stored it in my head. That day I learned more about the drug game than I ever thought I would.

Chapter Twenty-eight

The high school was bigger than my elemen-tary and junior high schools put together. Some of the students were driving to school. Most of them were juniors or seniors unless they were hustlers in the ninth and tenth grades. When we got up in the lunchroom, it was like one big fashion show. You could tell who was getting money and whose family just had money by the way everybody dressed.

The kids who came from good families had on new name-brand clothes but you could tell their gear came from the malls. The kids who were getting money had on all the new fly clothes that you get from Delancey and Orchard Streets, 125th Street, and spots like that. To enhance their wardrobe, they had on all the fat chains and rings with Gucci, Polo, and Louie Vuitton jackets, so you knew who was who, except for us. Anybody who looked at me and Mal would've thought that we hustled by the way we dressed.

The lunchroom was basically divided into two parts, east end and west end, except for the girls.

All the guys from both projects, our side and across the tracks, sat at tables in the same area. The rest of the west end heads from all the other blocks sat at tables on the left-hand side closest to the parking lot, while the right side consisted of the east end heads and the guys who lived borderline. The girls were able to sit on either side depending on what clique of guys they wanted to be around. Of course, the majority of them were on our side because our side was the liveliest.

High school was definitely the place to be if you had to be in school. I knew these next four years were going to be some of the best years of my teen life and also the turning point, but there was no way I could have looked into the future and foreseen the different directions it would go.

I hadn't seen Lisa all summer and to tell you the truth ever since I'd been messing with Trina, I hadn't given Lisa any thought, at least not until now.

"Hello, Mr. Benson," she said.

"Hey, Ms. Matthews," I returned, not able to read her mood.

"How was your summer?" she asked.

"Good, and yours?" I asked back.

"It was nice. I went away to visit my family in Barbados for a little bit and then for the rest I just hung out with my girls."

"I didn't know you were from there," I said.

"I'm from here, but my mother is from over there. I've been there a lot off and on," she said. "What did you do for the summer?" she asked.

"Same thing I do every summer, hang around the projects," I told her.

It was kind of awkward standing there having a conversation with her after all these months, but at the same time I wasn't trying to end it. I was glad Trina didn't go to the high school because if she'd seen me talking to Lisa she would have flipped. Lately she had been bugging out like she owned me, acting all jealous for nothing.

"My mother told me you called for my birthday, but I was already gone. Thank you for calling," she said.

"You would've done the same," I said, trying to act like it wasn't a big deal.

There was a long pause between us for a minute.

"Kamil, I missed you." Her statement caught me by surprise. "I mean, I miss talking to you," she quickly clarified. She was looking me dead in my eyes. All I could do was flash a half smile and match her stare as she continued.

"I thought about you while I was away and every time I see you in the lunchroom or hallways. You really hurt me the night of the dance, but I forgave you the next day. I just didn't know how to tell you after graduation and I regret that because it cost us a whole summer, time we could've spent together. If you're not mad at me I was wondering if we could at least start all over, if not pick up where we left off."

I was speechless at first. I shifted from side to side trying come up with the right words to say. "I was never mad at you, Lisa," I began. "I was mad at myself for making you feel like that. I wanted to kick it to you too, but I thought you kept telling your moms to tell me you weren't home whenever I called, so I figured you were done with me; and now that you tell me this I regret not speaking up that day at graduation, because I've missed you too."

Lisa stood there looking at me with those slanted eyes and cheesy little grin she always made when she was happy or in a good mood. "So where do we go from here?" she asked.

"I'm gonna call you later and we'll take it from there," I said to her. She gave me a quick hug before making her way to her next class.

Everything was back to normal with Lisa and me, but it got crazier with me and Trina. Somehow, I managed to maintain both situations.

Chapter Twenty-nine

We had all planned to meet at Ant's house to hang out. When we arrived, Ant and Trevor were engrossed in an intense video game battle.

"Why every time we come over you already over here?" my brother asked Trevor. "Are y'all fuckin' or somethin'?" he added while laughing.

"Fuck you, Mal," Trevor shot back.

I stepped over Trevor and gave Ant a hug and pound. Just as we were all saying what up to each other, Shareef rolled in.

"What it is, my niggas?"

"You tell us," Ant said.

"Yo, I want y'all to come check something out with me right quick outside." Shareef seemed excited.

"What?" we all asked.

"Just come with me for a minute."

Everybody got up and went outside with Shareef.

"It better not be no bullshit you about to show us," Trevor said as we were walking down the steps.

"So what's up, Shareef?" I asked him, but he didn't answer; he just started skipping toward the street, then he stopped. He stopped right next to a sky blue Oldsmobile '98 and said, "What'cha think?"

We all looked at each other.

"Think about what?" Mal asked.

"Man! About my new car," he said.

"Yeah, right, Shareef," I said.

"Nigga, stop playin' and tell us why you really got us out here," Ant said.

"Yo, I'm tellin' you this is my ride. I mean, it's in my mom's name, but I paid for it. We just got back from Langhorn, PA, a few hours ago."

"Nigga, you don't even know how to drive," Trevor said. "How you gonna have a car?"

"I know how to drive. Ice taught me in one of the rentals he be havin' from the fiends, and I go take my test for my permit this week so I'm gonna be rollin' legit."

"This really is your joint, huh?" Mal said.

"That's what I been tryin' to tell y'all."

"Well, let's roll up outta this muthafucka then!" Trevor exclaimed. "Take ya boys for a ride."

We rode through every known drug block in town like all the other dealers did when they copped a new ride or did something new to their whips. I had never toured the blocks like this before because I didn't have anybody to ride me through them except for Mu, but he wasn't with that. He didn't front the way most guys did in the game.

Guys and girls were flooded on every block we rode through. Every time we hit a different hood, they would be looking to see who was driving. They wanted to know who was pushing the '98 with the temp tag in the back window. I saw guys who I went to school with out there hustling on every block, and they must've noticed us too because they all waved or gave head nods each time we hit a certain spot. Shareef just beeped the horn.

"Yo, this weekend I'm going to Canal Street and cop me some beats," Shareef told us. "And then I'm gonna put some Trues and Vogues on my joint and smack a dark blue leather rag top on my shit." Shareef was amped when he spoke.

"Yo, kid, I'm not trying to tell you how to spend your money, but don't you think you need to be puttin' your paper up for a rainy day for you and your family? I mean, wasn't that the point of getting in the game in the first place?' my brother reminded Shareef.

"Word!" Me, Ant, and Trevor all agreed.

"Yo, I'm doing all of that," Shareef attempted to defend himself. "I got dough put up for me and moms and 'em. Coppin' this ride ain't even put a dent in my stash, and the shit I'm about to do to it, I'm gonna make that money on the grind," he enlightened us. "Y'all must think I'm still pumpin' packs for Clyde, but I ain't. I'm coppin' my own shit now from uptown. Ice found a connect up in Harlem on Broadway and turned me on to some of the *papis* so I be catchin' the train over there to pick up. Me and him got down fifty-fifty and be alternating on the pickup."

"Damn, kid, you moved up in the game like that?" Trevor was the first to say.

"Yo, that's the only way you gonna make money. And the cool part about it is that I be goin' over right when school be startin' and be comin' back when it be letting out or during their lunchtime over there, so I blend right in with my book bag and shit, and Five-O don't even fuck with me," Shareef told us.

"How much this joint cost?" I asked him.

"Only thirty-five hundred dollars," he said.

"Nigga, you act like you rich talking about 'only thirty-five hundred dollars.' You gettin' it like that?" Ant asked.

"Yo, I'm makin' money and I got money put up," he concluded.

We all sat there in deep thought as Shareef drove back to the projects. I didn't know what everybody else was thinking, but I knew that after hearing Shareef talk about how he was doing his thing in the drug game, once again, I had a different outlook on drug dealers.

Chapter Thirty

Only two and a half weeks had passed and Shareef had done everything he said he was going to do to his car. We were in the field chilling when we heard the bass and then the words as clear as day as Shareef turned the corner playing Biz Markie's cut "Vapors." When he pulled up on us, it sounded like we were in the club listening to it. Shareef had just gotten his whip out of the upholstery shop after having a dark blue leather ragtop with the three humps and lights on the side of the windows installed. You could tell he had it painted over because the light blue was now ice blue. His True rims were blinging and his Vogue tires were Armor-Alled up. To top it off, he added shocks in the back to lift the trunk up. The week before he had gone to Canal Street and thrown four ten-inch EV speakers in the back window and two fifteen-inch Red Line speakers behind the back seat, with a gooseneck equalizer and a Alpine radio, benzy box, along with a Zeus amplifier to push the woofers. The bullet tweeters he had had his music sounding crystal clear and made it ring off.

"What's the deal!" Shareef hopped out of his '98.

"Yo, this piece is phat as hell," Trevor said, giving Shareef a pound.

"No doubt! You hooked this joint up," Ant followed.

"It don't even look like that same ride."

"Yo, ya thang nice, Shareef," I said, admiring how he dressed it up.

"Shareef, you doin' ya thang, kid!" my brother said.

"Good lookin'. Y'all the only niggas I care about liking my joint; fuck everybody else," Shareef said to us.

"Who's that in the seat?" I asked.

"That's Ice," he said.

"Where y'all headed?" Mal asked.

"We about to hit the town, but we came to pick y'all up first so we can show 'em how NPP roll!" Shareef exclaimed.

There was definitely a difference the next time we rode through the blocks. Guys congratulated us and gave head nods of approval while girls were gawking. Whenever we got close to a different block, Shareef would hit rewind on the tape.

That day I learned the words to KRS-One's "The Bridge Is Over" cut from his *Criminal Minded* tape. I thought my eardrums were going to burst, Shareef's system was knocking so loud.

After touring the entire city Shareef dropped us all off back around the projects. I stood there and watched as Shareef and Ice drove up West Second Street. He had vanished up the block but still, a mile away, I could hear the bass of that song, "The Bridge Is Over."

Chapter Thirty-one

That night I was restless and couldn't sleep. For hours, I tossed and turned in and out of my sleep while images flashed through my mind. Visions of my dad's, Mustafa's, and Shareef's cars appeared back to back in my head, along with images of when I saw my dad counting all that money in our living room, Mustafa's money on his kitchen table, and the knot of money Shareef had pulled out that day at Ferraro's. My mother had told me that dreams meant something and that you just had to figure out what. I didn't know what my dreams meant or why I was even having them, but I wanted to know. The last vision I remembered having that night was of an image of my dad's, Mustafa's, and Shareef's cars all lined up next to one another, before my eyes shot open.

"Yo, Mal, you asleep?" I called over to my brother.

"Nah, what up?" he answered immediately.

"I can't believe Shareef got a car," I said.

"Yeah, I know. I was thinking the same thing," Mal agreed.

"Remember when we first found out he was out there hustling?"

"Yeah."

"He was out there moving fifty packs for Clyde and now all of a sudden he can afford to spend thirty-five hundred dollars on a ride and put another three to four thousand into it just hooking it up. He must be making a lot of money for him to be able to do it like that and still go to school," I pointed out to my brother.

"That's what I was saying to myself too," my brother said back to me.

"You know what we could do if we made that type of money," I said rhetorically.

"Yeah, we could get Moms and Grandma and 'em out of the hood." My brother had read my mind.

"Maybe get Moms another brownstone back in Brooklyn," I stated. So many thoughts were racing through my mind at that moment.

"Yeah, but Reef making it seem like it's too easy," Mal said, bringing me back to reality. "He's acting like it ain't nothing, but I know it gots to be more than that. We just don't see it," Mal added.

"Yeah, I know it's not that easy," I said in agreement. "It's a lot more to it than just going out there pumping. Shareef started out as a worker, but I learned it from seeing it from a boss's perspective. Mu been teaching everything he knows about the game to me," I told my brother.

"Like what?" he wanted to know.

"Everything!" I rose up and sat on the edge of the bed. "For starters, he taught me how to cook up coke and cut dope."

"What? Word?" Mal said, surprised.

"Yeah, kid; but not only that, I know how to chop up the coke and bottle it, and measure the dope and bag it from watching Reecie and Trina."

"Reecie and Trina?" I could tell by his facial expression my words had again surprised him.

"Yeah, that's who Mu got doing his stuff for him while he rubber bands all the work up," I began to explain. "He wraps the bottles up into twelve: two for the workers who get high and a straight hundred for him, and twelve bags, getting a straight two hundred off that. That's why he be standing out there, to watch them so they won't run off with his stuff. The packages he passes out to the kids who don't get high bring him back the same three hundred and fifty dollars that Clyde wants off his fifty packs.

He told me that the dope game and the coke game are totally different. He explained to me how the dopefiends will kill for a bag and sell out their own mother if they had to for a fix. He said you have to be on point at all times, especially in the dope game, 'cause it could cost you your life or your freedom."

"Damn! That's deep," was all Mal said.

For the rest of the night Mal and I stayed up and I told him about everything Mu ever told me about the drug game. We talked until the sun came up and, by the time it was daylight, a decision was made.

Chapter Thirty-two

"Now any other time we come over here, this nigga Trevor's ass is here; now all of a sudden the one day we got something important to talk about this muthafucka late," Mal said to Ant.

"The nigga said he was comin' right over," Ant said in defense of Trevor.

"What up? What up?" Trevor came in saying.

"What took you so long?" my brother asked him.

"Nigga, fuck all that. I'm here now, ain't I? What up?"

Normally Mal would have gone back and forth with Trevor, but instead he just looked at him, brushed it off, and then started talking. "Yo, me and Mil was doin' some heavy thinking last night and since y'all our boys we wanted to see if you'd be interested." My brother took a deep breath before continuing. "We're tryin' to get in the game," Mal said.

I tried to read the looks on their faces to see how they were taking in what he had just said, but I couldn't. They just stood there.

Trevor was the first to break the silence. "Yo, that shit is crazy, 'cause me and Ant was thinking the same thing," he confessed.

"Word up?" Mal replied.

"Yeah," Trevor said. "But besides what Ant remembers about Terrance and what Shareef told us, we really don't know shit about hustlin' except for serving patients and fiends."

"Yeah, the game changed since T was in it, and Shareef didn't really tell us nothing besides how good the dough was," Ant said.

"Yo, don't worry about that," I stepped in. "I basically know all we need to know to get started."

"How you know what to do and how to go about it?" Trevor questioned.

"That's beside the point; the point is he knows, trust me," Mal spoke for me. "The important thing we need to know is do y'all have any money saved up? 'Cause we not tryin' to hustle for nobody but ourselves," Mal added.

"I got a buck fifty put up, and could probably scrape up another fifty," Trevor said.

"I think I got like two and some change stashed," Ant said.

I was thinking, *Man, I got more than both of them put together and they're older than me.* I wondered what had they been doing with their money all these years.

"That's a start," I told them. "If the two of you get down together you should have at least four hundred dollars."

"How much y'all got?" Ant wanted to know.

"Put it this way, we've been saving," I offered as an answer.

"That shit still don't tell us how much y'all workin' with," Trevor chimed in.

"Between me and Mil, we got over a G," Mal answered.

"Daaaaammmn!" they both exclaimed. "How the fuck y'all niggas save up a G?"

"We were just puttin' up, that's all," I replied. "But we're not starting out with this much."

"I think we should all get down and split everything four ways," Trevor suggested.

"Nah, it'll be better if you and Ant got down and Mal and I get down together 'cause y'all be together all the time, and Mal's my brother and we live together."

Before they had a chance to respond, Mal intervened. "Besides, y'all could do your thing while we at school and we can do ours when we come home."

"That makes sense," Ant agreed.

"So, how much we gonna make if we flip four hundred?" Trevor asked.

"It all depends," I answered. "It's a lot of things I have to break down to you the way I think we should do it. I just need y'all to have your money ready in a couple of days while I try to set everything up. If things go right then it's gonna be on and next year this time all of our families will be up out of here!" I said with confidence.

"We'll be ready," both Ant and Trevor stated.

When Mal and I left, I knew I had motivated Ant and Trevor; but, what was more, I hated that I motivated myself.

Chapter Thirty-three

"What's up, stranger?" Trina greeted me at the door. "I thought you forgot about me."

"I didn't forget about you. I just had to play the crib for a while 'cause my moms been riffin' about me and my brother being out late all the time. She and my grandmother think we be hangin' in the streets. You know how that goes," I told her.

"Yeah, I know." She kissed me. "But I missed you still. I miss being with you." Her words almost made me forget why I really stopped by.

"I missed you too," I said. "I'ma start comin' back through; just give me a minute. But is Mu here?" I asked.

"Yeah, he's in the back," Trina replied dryly. "That's why you came here, to see Mu?" she asked, disappointed.

"No, I came to see you," I tried to clean it up. "But I need to see Mu, too."

"Yeah, right, Kamil."

I felt kind of bad because Trina didn't deserve how I had been treating her. It wasn't on purpose; I just needed some space so I started going over to see her less than she was used to.

"I did come over here for you," I repeated. I grabbed her by the hand and pulled her closer to me. I kissed her on the side of the neck just the way she liked.

"Stop," she cooed. "You know that's my spot. Don't start nothin' you can't finish."

I smiled. "I won't." In that instant, she got me aroused.

"Don't try to leave without giving me some."

"I got you." I really meant it. Not just sexually, though. I knew based on what I had planned, I needed her, just like Mu had told me. And, in return, I was going to make sure she was good also.

"Who is it?" Mu's voice boomed from the other side of the door. I told him it was me and he invited me in. "What's up, li'l bro?"

I saw that he was in the bed. "I didn't mean to wake you," I apologized. "But I really needed to talk to you about something important."

My words got his attention. "Is something wrong? Run your mouth. Somebody fuckin' with you?" Mu bombarded me with questions.

"No, nothin' like that," I assured him.

"So what's up? Talk to me."

Before I got to the apartment I had rehearsed how I was going to present everything to Mu, but now that I stood before him I didn't know where to begin or how to come out and say it. I inhaled. "Mal and I wanna get put on." As soon as I said the words I regretted them, but there was no turning back now; they had spilled out into the air.

For a minute Mu just stared at me. I could tell it hadn't really registered with him yet. "What?" I could tell by his facial expression he was not happy at what I had said.

"Mal and I—"

Before I could finish Mu cut me off. "What the hell are you talking about?"

I didn't know what to say.

"I knew this shit was gonna happen." Mu shook his head. Silence lingered in the air for a moment and then Mu broke it. "Are you sure?" he asked.

I nodded my head.

"No, I wanna hear you say it," he stated.

I cleared my throat. "Yeah, I'm sure."

"Tell me why," Mu said.

I wasted no time answering. "Man, it's rough. For my family, everything. Me and Mal can't do nothing about it. We supposed to be the men of the house, but we're not acting like it. We just wanted to do something to help our moms and grandmother out and try to get them out of these projects," I said all in one breath. "Besides, we can't depend on you forever; we gotta do for ourselves," I added.

Mu shook his head again. "I knew it," he repeated. "The shit is in ya blood." He paused. "A'ight yo. If that's what y'all want."

"Yeah, this is what we want to do," I told Mu.

"Okay, as long as you're sure. You remember everything I been schoolin' you on all these years? 'Cause I told you shit ain't no joke out in them streets."

"Yeah, I know. I never forget anything you tell me, Mu," I said to him.

"That's good, kid. That's good. So you and Mal have been talking about how y'all gonna do shit, huh?" he asked. "What do you need me to do, front y'all some work or something?"

"Nah, nah. Nothing like that," I told him. "We got our own money saved up and we wanted to spend with you," I cleared up as I went off telling him about the conversation Mal, Ant, Trevor, and I had previously.

"That's good that you told them that it was only going to be you and Mal and they should get down with each other, 'cause when you get money shit change and so do niggas. At least you know that your brother will always be your brother no matter what; but, in the game, your best friend can easily turn into your worst enemy. Remember what I told you about having somebody's back and they havin' yours?" Mu reminded me. "Only one you can depend on is your brother and vice versa. Damn, kid, you 'bout to fuck with the major leagues now; no more minor leagues, baby. It's a man's world in the streets. Ain't no room for no little boys," Mu said. I just listened.

"Check what I'ma do for you, though," Mu went on to say. "The last thing I want to see is you and Mal go out there and fall on ya face or get knocked off, so for the first month I'm gonna be out there holdin' you down and pointing out your mistakes; but Ant and Trevor on their own except for their connect. I know I taught you how to cook up and all that but it's still easier said than done, so I'm gonna do that for you and you gonna be there every time watchin' until you perfect it and then you teach Mal. It's up to you whether you gonna show Ant and Trevor, but the less you expose your hand the better it is for you, 'cause niggas will always have to depend on you until they catch on. You can get Trina to cut and bottle your shit up but you gotta learn that, too, just in case you don't have Trina around no more to do it for you. You never know what might happen. The more you spend, the more extra grams you get, so if you put their money with yours all the extras will come to you and Mal. That's free money," he pointed out. "I've been schoolin' you. But I'm gonna be schoolin' you even more now, and by the time I'm done with you, you're gonna be a ghetto genius out this muthafucka."

Mu laughed and then went on. "I'ma tell you straight up, though, you got some competition on ya hands out there. Between my boys I got, and Clyde's runners, you're gonna have to get your clientele up to G off. Then you got your boy Buff and his man Ice puttin' work in. They be out there grindin' hard makin' that paper; but I got a plan for you and Mal to bust out with so y'all can get some customers. One of the things you need to know about getting into the game is you gots to be in it to win it. Ain't no half stepping, Mil, and that's on the real," Mu finished saying.

"I'm ready to do whatever it takes to get money!" I told him.

"All right, kid!" Mu said, smiling. "I know you are, and you about to start gettin' it, too." Mu put his hand on my shoulder. "How much you got to flip?" he asked.

"Twelve hundred," I said. Ant and Trevor gave us $200 apiece and Mal and I had matched it with $400 apiece of our own.

"Damn! Y'all li'l niggas holding like that already?" he asked, impressed.

"Well, most of it is my and Mal's, eight hundred anyway," I told him.

"You two dudes never cease to amaze me. Y'all about to blow. Trust me. Make sure you get that paper to me by this Thursday. You got two days. If you ain't ready then you gonna have to wait until my next flip a couple days after," Mu said.

"I'll have it for you by then," I promised.

"Cool! Now go out there and make sure your shit is straight wit' Trina 'cause she has been walking around all week with her lips poked out 'cause you ain't been over here. No matter what, you have to keep the shorties happy, regardless how many you jugglin'," he said.

"I got you, Mu. I'ma get on top of that right now."

"Damn!" I rolled off top of Trina and onto my back trying to catch my breath. I didn't realize how backed up I was until just then. Trina made sure she made up for lost time as well. She was going wild underneath me. I felt her cum four times. She had me sweating like crazy. "Yo! I needed that," I said while catching my breath.

"Me too, nigga," she said back. "You've been acting all stingy with the dick lately."

"Nah! I told you what was up." I laughed. "But it's cool now 'cause I'm gonna start being back over here like before," I told her.

"Is everything all right?" she asked. "I know you said you had to talk to Mu about something important."

"Yeah. Everything's good. I was just about to kick it to you about that," I told her. "I'm about to start hustlin' around here and I need you," I said, looking her in the eyes. "I need someone like you to keep it real wit' me. When I get on my feet you not gonna want for nothing. I just need to know I can count on you," I expressed to her.

"Baby, you should already know that you can depend on me. I'll do anything for you, 'cause I love you."

She caught me off guard saying she loved me, but I didn't have any reaction because I didn't want to mess nothing up, so I just listened to her.

"Whatever you need me to do consider it done; and I'm not doin' it for what I can get out of you, I'm doin' it 'cause I wanna see you doin' good, that's all," she said.

I had to admit, I really felt what Trina said to me. She was a trooper and I respected her for that. Even though she said she wasn't looking for nothing, I had already made up my mind that once I blew I was still going to take care of her. With Mu as my mentor, Mal as my right hand, and Trina as my rider, I knew the only way I could go was up.

Chapter Thirty-four

Everything was set. I got the money from Ant and Trevor, and put it with mine, and Mal's, then took it to Mu before we went to school. Today was a half day, so I figured by the time I got home and went over to Reecie's crib Mu would be waiting for me. Things with Lisa and me were still good, but I had to concentrate on handling my business and putting in time with Trina.

Just like I had thought, Mu was sitting in the kitchen waiting for me, with all the necessities on the kitchen table, and everything set up like when I first saw him at work. He had two separate Ziploc bags of coke, and automatically I knew the smaller was ours.

"Listen," he started saying, "for the twelve hundred I got you two and a half Os. You only suppose to get two ounces and ten grams but my man looked out, so the extra four grams goes to you and Mal. For future references, just so you know, right now ounces go for five hundred, and it's twenty-eight grams in an ounce. Sometimes ounces cost less, sometimes they cost more, depending on the *papi*s in NY and how much their supplier charges them. You know how many grams in a whole pie?" he asked, referring to a kilo of coke.

I learned all of that in science class so I knew the answer. "One thousand, right?"

"How you know that?"

"I learned it in school."

"Well, you ain't gonna learn this shit I'm about to break down to you right here in school," he said, laughing. "Like I said, it's twenty-eight grams in an ounce, a hundred twenty-five grams in an eighth, which is four and a half ounces; two hundred fifty grams in a quarter key, which is nine ounces; five hundred grams in a half, which is eighteen ounces; and you already know it's a thousand grams in a whole pie, and it's thirty-six ounces in that. You need to know that if you in the game," Mu told me as he started to strain the coke.

I sat there and watched him do everything to a T the way he did before, and I picked up a few more things this time that I missed while he was cooking up. After he was done, he let it dry and then he put it on the digital scale. "You see this?"

he asked. "The scale read 69.8. That means that this shit is bangin' and the crackheads are gonna be open off your shit. We got us a good batch here, kid!" he said proudly.

"Trina is gonna be cutting your product up and bottling it for you, but today I'm gonna chop it up for you 'cause I can cut better than her and Reecie put together. She can still bottle your shit up, though." I just nodded.

Mu chopped my whole package up with finesse within an hour, and when he gave me the plate, it had hundreds of little rocks on it.

"Looking at this I say Trina will probably bottle up thirty-eight to forty clips," Mu told me.

"I appreciate that, Mu, I really do," I thanked him.

"Don't thank me, kid. I really don't have no business turning you on to this shit like this, but . . ." Mu paused. "Never mind. Just go take the plate to Trina."

I wondered what Mu was about to say, but I didn't press the issue. Instead I just made my way to the back room.

Each time Trina finished with fifty bottles I would rubber band them. Mu told me to clip them in tens because I wasn't passing any packages out, only hand-to-hand sales, so it would be easier to manage how much I made off of every

clip. I had banded thirty-five clips so far and
Trina still had a nice amount of rocks left on the
plate. Each time I banded a clip my adrenaline
increased. I knew it was nearing crunch time.
The total amount was thirty-nine clips and four
extra bottles. Mu was right: almost forty clips.

"Be careful," Trina said, giving me a kiss before
I left the room.

"Thanks, I will."

"How many did she make?" Mu asked when I
reentered the front room. I told him how many.
"Yeah, that's good," he said. "Now, check, this
is what you do. Give Trevor and Ant twelve
clips for their four hundred dollars, and that'll
leave you and Mal with twenty-seven and some
change."

"You sure twelve clips is good?" I asked.

"That's more than good, kid. You only supposed to double and then some. Twelve clips is
twelve hundred dollars. That's triple. You ain't
jerkin' nobody; you bein' smart. You the master-
mind behind them gettin' on, so of course you
benefit the most. All this shit here I used cost
money: the bottles, the bake, the scale, and all of
that. They ain't give no extra dough to help out
on none of that; this is all on the strength of you.
You can't be soft in this game, Mil," Mu snapped.

"I understand."

"Now, like I was sayin', you and Mal got twenty-seven clips and four extras, so that's $2,740, but all you wanna see back now in this trip is $2,400, which is triple what y'all put up in the first place. The other thirty-four bottles is gonna be for you to get ya clientele up. That means you gonna be able to take three hundred forty dollars worth of shorts. You gonna get all the paper that the niggas who been out there for a while won't take. The one for seven, or one for eight, the two for fifteen or the two for sixteen, the three for twenty-five, or the six for forty, and the seven for fifty, and the fourteen for one hundred, 'cause niggas only given up twelve, maybe thirteen, and that's how y'all gonna get known.

"Never get greedy, either. If you hit 'em for a couple of hundred for the day, cool out and catch a next day. You ain't gotta sell out in one night; let them other niggas take a risk of getting knocked doin' that. Besides, you still have to go to school so you can't be pullin' all nighters either, anyway, unless it's on the weekends, but even with that I'll let you know if it's cool. A couple more things I want to tell you." He paused.

"Don't be out there fuckin' with ya boys while they smoking weed and drinking and all that other dumb shit on the block. Stay up outta them dice games; you out there to make money not lose it. And, most importantly, always look around before you make a sale to see if it's safe. Always stay on point for the jakes," he told me, referring to the police.

"Yo, go take them clips to them niggas and come back, but before you do take out six clips: three for you and three for Mal, and tell Trina to hold the rest. You only need enough out there to keep you from havin' to run back and forth out of this spot, 'cause you don't wanna get the crib hot. You know I keep my shit stashed here, too, sometimes, so you know you gots to be on point, 'cause niggas gonna be clockin' your every move and I don't want to have to have to kill a nigga over no bullshit," Mu said with a straight face.

"I got you, Mu."

"A'ight, be safe."

I gave Mu a pound and hug; then I was out the door.

Chapter Thirty-five

Hustlers were everywhere, running up on customers and to cars. It looked like a war zone. I heard one kid tell a patient to get the hell outta here and that's when I stepped to him remembering what Mu had said to see what he wanted.

"What up?" I said as I approached.

"Yo, you'll do me a favor and let me get two for fifteen? That's all I got right now, but I'll bring you the other five back later, I promise."

"All right, I got you," I told him, knowing he wasn't going to bring me no five dollars back.

"I appreciate it, li'l man. What's ya name so I know who to ask for if I don't see you when I bring ya five dollars back?"

I didn't want to give him my real name so without thinking I just said K.B.

"All right, good lookin' out, K.B. And this weekend I'ma hook up wit' my white boy and look for you 'cause he be spending all day, nothing under fifty dollars a whop," he told me.

Mu had warned me about guys like him so I just agreed. "I'll be here," I told him. That was my first sale in the game as a hustler. After the crackhead left, a sense of power swept through me. For some reason I felt superior, like I was in control. That was the icebreaker I had needed to turn my nervousness and fear into confidence.

I was giving somebody one for eighteen when Shareef's car pulled up. He and Ice hopped out. I was already up to a clip in sales and was working on my second one.

"Say it ain't so," Shareef yelled, walking up on me and giving me a pound.

"What'chu mean, kid? We can't be chillin' in the back seat of your ride for the rest of our lives," I said to him jokingly.

"What up, Mil," Ice said.

"What's happening, Ice," I returned.

"Just another day in the hood, that's all," he replied. "And another dollar, too. No offense, but I hope y'all did ya thing earlier, 'cause we about to come out here and shut the block down," he then said to me.

I just laughed.

"Damn! Look at us now," Shareef pointed out. "All my boys out here hustlin'." He shook his head in disbelief. "Who y'all pumpin' for, Mu or Clyde?" Shareef asked, thinking it had to be one of the two.

"Neither one; we all out here on our own."

"Yeah, all right." They thought I was lying.

"I'm telling you, we hustlin' for ourselves."

"Word? Okay! That's what I'm talking about; get that paper for yourself. Fuck that workin' for a muthafucka shit. All right, Mil, we get up, I'm gonna go get at Ant and 'em, but watch ya'self out here, kid," Shareef said.

"Yeah, no doubt watch ya'self, kid," Ice followed up with as they both gave me dap.

It was almost ten o'clock at night, and I only had six bottles left from the three clips I brought out, and Mal had nine. Combined we had sold about five clips, which I thought was decent, considering we came out at like 5:00 p.m. Today was our first day and most of the regular hustlers were out, especially Shareef and Ice. They wasn't playing when they said they were coming to shut the block down. I know they'd G off like crazy.

Ant and Trevor got rid of another clip and a half, and Mal and I had six more left between the two of us. He had four and I had two, but just as we were about to leave, a crack patient came up to me and said, "Yo, what you'll give me for forty dollars?"

I was so glad to be getting a forty dollar sale, after getting ones and twos all day. I told him six and on one day in as hustlers Mal and I had sold out what we brought out for the day.

Once we got back to Ant's crib, everybody counted up what they had made. Off of my three clips, I made $265, taking thirty-five dollars' worth of shorts, and Mal made $280, so we made $545 off of six clips, which wasn't bad. Ant said he made $242 off of two and a half clips, and Trevor made $189 off of two clips; they only took nineteen dollars in shorts between the two of them.

"Damn! That was sweet," Trevor was the first to admit.

"Yeah. If only Terrence were here to see me, he'd be proud," Ant stated.

We all shook our heads in agreement.

"Yo, why y'all take all them shorts like that?" Trevor asked.

"That's all that was comin' to us," I said.

"I'm tryin' to get dollar for dollar off our shit," Ant said.

"Money be comin' out there, it's just that niggas had regular customers. Long as me and Mil profit somethin' that's all that counts with us," my brother said.

"Yo, we about to roll out," I told them. "We'll catch you tomorrow after school."

"All right, yo, we get up," they both said. "We'll probably go back out a little later and try to rock some more," Trevor said.

"Mal, I'll be there in a minute. I'm goin' over Trina's crib right quick to get at Mu."

"All right. Tell him what's up and good looking for holdin' us down today."

When I walked in, Mu, Reecie, and Trina were eating pizza. Reecie waved while Trina jumped up as soon as she saw me. "Hey, baby! Want some pizza?"

"Yeah, I'll take a slice, but I can't stay long 'cause I got to take it down so I can get up for school in the mornin'."

"What up, big time!" Mu shouted.

"Nah, you the big timer. If I had your hands I'd trade mine in," I said jokingly, as we pounded each other up.

"Mu said when you get some time in on the block ain't nobody gonna be able to stop you out there," Trina said to me.

"That's what he said?" I asked, eating my slice of pizza.

"Yep! And I told him I knew that already."

"All right, that's enough blowin' his head up," he told Trina. "Mil, let me rap to you in the back for a minute. Excuse us, ladies, while us men talk." Mu smiled at Reecie and Trina. I followed him to the back.

"So what did you think?" he asked me.

"It was decent. Me and Mal did all right for our first day."

"That's not what I asked you. I know how y'all did out there because I watched every sale you two made. By the looks of things y'all probably moved the whole six clips. What I want to know is what did you think about out there and what did you learn?" he asked again.

I thought for a moment before I spoke. "I noticed what you were sayin' about how the patients are going to say any- and everything to get that blast, especially if they got a short. I seen how certain hustlers got their own steady customers and other just be runnin' up to sales tryin' to cut throat."

"What else?"

"I peeped how when Shareef and Ice came out nobody couldn't really get no money, and I caught how guys be turnin' down a lot of shorts 'cause that's all Mal and I really been takin' all night."

"Don't worry about takin' the shorts," he reminded me. "Like I told you before. But all the shit you said you picked up on was what you was supposed to. You did good," Mu told me.

"The only thing you did that you should have shortened was kickin it with the patients and with Shareef and Ice when they came up. While you talkin', niggas is makin' sales. Shareef and Ice got dough so they can afford to talk. The patients are gonna talk you to death until you sell 'em those rocks. The name of the game is cop and go, 'cause time is money and money is time, but like I said, you did good and you'll do better. Tell Mal that I was diggin' his hustle. He's a smooth nigga," Mu said. "What you make off them six clips?" he then asked.

"Almost five hundred fifty dollars," I said. "We made five hundred forty-five, fifty-five dollars in shorts."

"That ain't bad, considerin' what y'all tryin to accomplish, but make sure you keep track of that because when you movin' a lot of clips it's easy to take over three hundred dollars' worth of shorts. If y'all get to three hundred forty dollars' worth of shorts before you sell out, then you gonna have to pump the rest of ya product for straight dough. Never go under what you said you wanted to bring back," Mu ended.

After our conversation was over, I went and ate another slice of pizza, chilled with Trina for a little bit, then went home. I replayed my conversation I had with Mu to my brother while we were in our beds, and then we took it down for the night.

Chapter Thirty-six

The hood was out today and the hustlers had definitely brought their hustle game with them. It seemed like there were more people out today than yesterday. Both Ant and Trevor were in the midst of all that was going on out there and they had their running shoes tied tight. Mu was supervising his workers, but when he saw us he waved me over.

"How was school?"

"Same ol', same ol'," I said.

"Yo, money is comin' out here, so go snatch some work up for you and Mal and come back out. The same amount as before."

Yeah, money was coming because as soon as Mal and I got out there we pumped a couple bottles. Some of the same people who copped from me yesterday looked for me today saying that my product was good, and this time they had correct money. Some of them told me that my product was better than what Clyde's workers had. They had said Clyde's workers were selling B-12. I didn't know what that was, but I knew it wasn't anything good. Mu told me later that it meant the product was garbage.

"Li'l man, you workin'?" a short, dark-skinned crackhead asked me.

"Yeah, how many?"

"Let me get six for fifty dollars."

Before I pulled out the clip that I was working out of, I look around like Mu had told me. The clip only had three left in the rubber band, so I pulled out a second one. The crackhead seemed to be acting kind of strange to me, but when he paid me for the six bottles, I brushed it off.

"Good lookin'," he said and then took off running. The money was partially balled up when he gave it to me. Something told me to check the money as soon as he handed it to me. When I did, I saw that the fifty dollar bill was a fake.

"Yo, Mal, grab that nigga right there!" I yelled to my brother as I took off running in the direction of the crackhead who just beat me. He was just darting past my brother when Mal tripped him up. Mal had him on the ground by the time I caught up to them.

"I didn't do nothing," I heard the slim crackhead scream.

"Shut the fuck up!" Mal said. "What this nigga do?" he asked me.

"He just beat me for six bottles with a fake fifty dollar bill," I chimed.

"Nigga, where my brother shit at?" Kamal punched him in the face. "You think we sweet, muthafucka? Mil, check his pockets," Mal told me while he held the crackhead man around the neck. After I checked him, I found the bottles in his right pants pocket. I pulled them out and then stood up and kicked him right in the stomach. As soon as Mal released his neck he bent over and grabbed his gut.

"Nigga, if you ever come around here again and try that shit I'm gonna stomp the shit out of you. You hear me?" I said. My adrenaline was pumping.

"Yeah, I got you, yo," the crackhead bellowed.

"Now get the fuck outta here." For good measure, I kicked him in his ass as he hopped up and fled.

Mal and I started laughing about how the little crackhead took off running down the street when we let him go, holding his stomach with one hand and his jaw with the other one.

"Bet he won't try that shit around here again," Mal said to me.

"Word," I said, still laughing. Even though I was laughing and found humor in the incident, on the inside I was surprised by my actions. I couldn't believe I had just handled the situation the way I had, but all I kept thinking about was that Mu was watching and he had told me that there was no room to be soft in this game.

"I'm goin' back up the block," I told my brother.

"All right. Hold it down up there and start checkin' that money from now on before you give ya shit up."

Mu must've had an idea of what happened because when I got back up there he was shaking his head and laughing. A couple of guys out there saw me and Mal on the other end and asked me what happened and I told them. They had told me how the crackhead always came around trying the same thing.

With the exception of the patient trying to beat me, things were going smooth for us. Mal and I sold out our normal six clips and Ant and Trevor had almost finished their whole twelve, which made sense because while we were in school they were out on the block.

It was only a little after nine o'clock and we were shutting down for the night. Mal wanted to rock some more while I went to cool out with Trina, but I told him we didn't have to rush anything and that we were just going to stick to six clips a day for now. Besides, I wouldn't have felt right knowing that he was out there and I wasn't out there to watch his back.

Before I went to Trina's crib Mal and I tallied up. We had did better than yesterday at taking shorts. That day we only took thirty-three dollars in shorts, which meant we had made $567 for the day. We were doing good. In two days we had made our $800 back, plus $200 and some change more. From there on out everything would be a profit.

Chapter Thirty-seven

"Yo, what made you want to get in the game?" Shareef asked us riding home from school in his ride.

"Man, we're not tryin' to live in the projects for the rest of our lives," Mal started out with. "We're used to having, not wanting. When our dad was here, our family didn't want for anything. Now it's up to us to get it back like that and until we graduate high and finish college we're not gonna be able to do that. We the only men in their lives they got to depend on, so we gots to get this money so they don't have to struggle for the rest of their lives, either," Mal said. He almost quoted verbatim what I had told Mu.

"I'm with you on that, kid," Shareef said. "I'm tryin' to help my mom get a house right now 'cause she's ready to get up outta those projects too. She's been up in there going on twenty-one years now, before I was even born."

"Word. Our grandmother was one of the first to move in them raggedy muthafuckas when they finished building them twenty-three years ago," Mal told Shareef.

"That's crazy," Shareef said back.

"Yo, if y'all need my help or anything just get at me and let me know. Y'all my boys and I love y'all like we came out of the same womb. We got to stick together."

"That's good looking," Mal and I said.

It was time to re-up and we were ready. Off the twenty-seven clips and four bottles Mal and I wound up making $2,500, instead of the $2,400 we thought we would. We only took $240 worth of shorts out of our whole package. With the $350 we still had after our first flip we had $2,580.

We took the fifty dollars, spilt it, decided to flip another $800, and put two Gs up. Ant and Trevor were flipping $600 this time but they didn't tell us how much they brought back, and we didn't ask.

After Mu finished cooking up, this time Trina cut and bottled my work up, and I helped. Mu cooked his own work up while Reecie cut and bottled his. Mu got us more extras than before so I figured we'd get more clips than the last time if Trina could chop up like him, or close to it.

When Trina was done, I banded forty-eight clips and two loose ones. Mu said he could've gotten me fifty, but what she got was still good. Like before, I gave Ant and Trevor enough clips to triple what they had flipped, and Mal and I kept the rest, leaving us with a little over three Gs worth of product.

Mu tested me by asking how many I was going to give Ant and Trevor. I told him eighteen clips. Then he asked me how much shorts I was willing to take, and I told him no more than $320, which would have let us make at least $2,700, but he said no.

He told me we had been out there a whole week, so customers knew our faces now, so this time around we could still take shorts but to try to bring back as close to three Gs as we possibly could.

Since we had more product than last time, Mal and I started bringing out four clips apiece instead of the three we brought out before. I couldn't believe that after only one week, patients were asking for me. I even had some ask me if they could run me some sales, which worked out good for me because they brought to me people I would normally see copping from one of the other guys out there. It didn't matter how many a person wanted; I was giving the runner one bottle for every five sales he brought me. That wasn't bad at all, considering he moved almost two clips for me. I gave him an extra one just on the strength. He told me that he'd be out there tomorrow to help me again if I needed him, but I knew he was lying. They all did.

"Five-O!" I heard somebody yell as the narcs rolled up on the court and jumped out.

I was standing there between the field and the basketball court when they jumped out. I just froze. You could tell by who ran who had drugs on them or had warrants. The narcs knew who was out there clocking because they chased certain guys and hemmed them up. Ant and Trevor were walking toward me as I saw Mal stepping toward the crib. When we looked, they had both Shareef and Ice posted up on the wall along with some of the other hustlers. I didn't see Mu anywhere in sight, which I was glad about. We didn't want to move or anything to look suspicious, so we just acted like we were playing in the field. We looked so young and were so small that the narcs overlooked us.

After they finished searching everybody who was on the wall, they started putting the hand-cuffs on Shareef and Ice, and let the rest of the guys go. We went to let Shareef's moms know what happened, and then we called it a night.

Mal went home and I made my way over to Trina's.

Mu was in the back with Reecie when I got there, so I didn't bother him. I chilled with Trina for a few hours sexing and just bugging out with her. She was happy for the little quality time that I was able to put in here and there. We had grown closer in the short period I had been a hustler. At ten thirty I went home.

Chapter Thirty-eight

"Kamil? Is that you?" I heard my mother yelling as I came through the door.

"Yeah, Ma, it's me," I said.

"Get your butt in here right now!" she shouted. It had been years since I heard my mother's tone sound like that. My spider senses immediately went off. I knew something was wrong.

"What did I do, Ma?" I asked, trying to sound innocent as I reached my room door.

When I walked in the bedroom, I saw Kamal sitting on the bed with his arms crossed with a odd look on his face. I instantly drew my attention to my moms. My heart nearly dropped out of my chest at what I saw.

"What the hell is this?" my mother asked, holding up what looked like a fresh clip of bottles.

"I don't know," I said, shrugging my shoulders. I tried to cut my eyes over at Mal in search for some type of answer, but my mother shut me down.

"Don't look at him," my mother yelled. "So you mean to tell me that this junk isn't yours?" she asked.

"No! That ain't mine," I shouted back.

"Don't you lie to me, Kamil." Before I knew what had hit me, my mother had smacked me across my face with all of her might. The blow nearly dazed me. "I swear to God I will kill you in here," my mother shouted.

I refused to cry but the tears began to come out on their own. I no longer felt like a man. I was a kid again and my mother had the upper hand.

"So it's not yours and it's not yours?" my mother said, looking back and forth between me and Kamal. "And neither one of you know where it came from? That's what you're trying to tell me?" she asked.

We both remained silent.

"All I do for you two and as hard as I bust my butt so that I can make sure you have clothes on your back, food in your mouth, and a roof over your head, and this is how you repay me? By going out there in the streets, like your father, selling this garbage? Well, I won't tolerate it, not in my house and not in my mother's house. You will not live under this roof running the damn streets. I don't care how old you are. If you think you're grown then I'll treat you like you're grown. Since you want to be running them then that's where you'll be!"

The tears were coming down hard from my mother's eyes as she breathed uncontrollably. I hadn't seen her cry like that since my dad had betrayed her. Now here my brother and I had inflicted a similar pain.

"Get out!" she yelled. "I want you and your brother out of here tonight. Pack your things and get out!" she yelled again.

We couldn't believe what we were hearing. We just looked at each other dumbfounded.

"You heard what I said, pack your stuff and get out before I call the cops and give them this junk and let them take you out of here."

Just then my grandmother walked in. "Sister, please! You're not thinking straight right now. Those are your babies," my grandmother came to our aid.

"Mommy, stay out of this. These are my kids and I raised them, and before I let them disrespect me I'll disown them. They are no longer welcome in this house," she said.

"Sister, I helped raise them too and I think you're wrong," my grandmother said to my moms.

"You think I'm wrong?" my moms screamed back at my grandmother. "Well, wait until I put their asses in jail tonight then," she said, picking up the phone next to my bed. She began dialing. "Hello?"

"All right, Ma!" Mal shouted, pressing down the phone. "We're leaving. You ain't gotta call no police on us."

Everything was happening so fast. It was like one big nightmare. I couldn't believe this was happening, but it was and it was real. My grandmother went and got Mal and me some black garbage bags. By now tears were streaming down her face. We began putting all of our belongings in them. When we were done, my grandmother gave us a kiss and hug, and told us not to worry, that she would straighten everything out; but somehow I didn't see that happening.

Monique and Jasmine were both standing in their nightgowns crying as well as we dragged our bags out. Jasmine waved bye, and Monique asked where would we go. I told her that we'd be at Trina's crib until we got situated; and then we left.

Chapter Thirty-nine

It took awhile for someone to answer the door, but then Reecie came. "What's up, Kamil?" she asked, half asleep.

"Yo, Reecie, me and Mal need a favor. My moms found some stuff in our room and she flipped out and kicked us out. We ain't got anywhere to go. I was wondering if we could crash here until we talked to Mu."

"Oh, shit! Yeah, you know y'all welcome here," she said.

"Thanks," we both said.

Trina must've heard my voice because she came out of her room. "Hey, baby, what's up?"

"My moms put us out," I told her.

"What? For what?" she asked.

"She found a clip in our room and flipped out. Reecie, what time is it?" I asked.

"Almost twelve o'clock."

"Yo, I don't even want to talk about this right now; I just need to get some rest so we can go to school in the morning. You think you can get Mal some covers or something so he can hit the couch, Reecie?"

"Yeah, sure."

"Yo, kid, that was my bad," Mal said.

"Don't sweat it," I told Mal. "It could've been either one of us who slipped like that," I said, knowing that he was referring to him being careless leaving the clip in the drawer.

I went in the room with Trina and fell out.

The next morning, before we went to school, we went to check with Ms. Richards because Shareef's car was gone so we thought they might've released him last night into her custody, being that he was still a minor. Shareef's mom answered the door.

"Good morning, Ms. Richards," I said. "Did Shareef get released last night? 'Cause I see his car ain't out here."

"Come on in, you two," she told us. When we stepped inside the apartment was a wreck. That was unusual, I thought, because Shareef's mom always kept a neat home.

"I don't think they gonna let my baby go." She sighed. "The police came back with a search warrant, and tore this house apart. They ain't find no drugs in here, but they found a whole lot of money in Brian's room. They confiscated his stereo, TV, VCR, video games, and said they had a warrant saying they could take the car. They asked me did I have the keys to it and I told them no, so they called for a flatbed and towed it away. Brian called me this morning right before you two got here, and said that his friend Ice was in the county jail with a seventy-five thousand dollar bail, ten percent with a bondsman, and for me to call one and bail this boy out.

"I told him how they came in here and found all that money, and he starts yelling at me about why I let them in the house and how it was over twenty-five thousand dollars he had in there. My heart can't take it. I tried to tell Shareef to stop before, but he wouldn't listen. Now, look. I still got the eight thousand dollars he gave me to put in the bank for our house, but I ain't using that to bail nobody out of no jail when me and my baby struggling, and I ain't got no job. Now that Brian's locked up, I got to rely on that money in the bank. I'm going up there in a bit. Y'all stop by later and I'll let you know what happened then."

I noticed how tired Ms. Richards looked. "All right, ma, we'll stop in to check on you and the baby to make sure you good." *When it rains it pours*. First, we got put out and now Shareef got hit hard and him and Ice were both knocked off.

"Tell Shareef we said what's up and we here for him if he needs us," I told her, and then we went to school.

School just wasn't the same that morning. Too much had happened in one night and I couldn't concentrate in none of my classes at all. All I kept thinking about was the words that my mother had said to us, and how hurt she looked. It was the same look she had when I was eight years old and saw my father with another woman the time we went to visit him on his birthday.

I still couldn't believe that she had put us out, though. That was the last thing I would have ever imagined.

I felt bad for Ice, but I knew there was nothing that we could do to help him or Shareef, because Mal and I had just got in the game, and we didn't have that type of money to be bailing Ice out. If we did, we would've definitely helped out because we knew that he was good for it.

As for Shareef, he couldn't get bail. It was up to the judge whether he'd be released. I didn't want to be in school today, so at lunchtime I decided to leave early once I found Kamal.

"Hey, stranger, where you speedin' off to?" I heard Lisa's voice say.

"What up, Lisa? I'm lookin' for my brother so we can get up outta here."

"Why? What's wrong?" she asked, concerned.

"Nothin', I just don't want to be here today. I feel cluttered. Today's not a good day for me," I lied.

"You sure you're not sick or something? Because you don't look like yourself today."

"Nah, I ain't sick or nothin' like that, I told you I feel crowded. I just need to get up outta here," I said to her in an almost nasty way.

"Excuse me!" she shouted sarcastically. "I didn't mean to be nosey." She began walking off.

"Lisa, wait!" I yelled, reaching out for her arm. "I didn't mean to talk to you like that. I apologize. Things are just crazy for me right now at home and I think I'm kinda stressed out, that's all."

"Aw, I knew something was wrong because I can see it all over your face," she said. "I understand, though. Is there anything you want to talk about?"

"Nah, not right now," I said back to her, but wishing that I had the nerve to tell her.

"Well, I'll call you later to see how you're doing and see if you wanna talk then."

"Nah, let me call you 'cause I don't know when I'll be in the house tonight, all right?"

"All right," she said. "I'll talk to you later." She waved good-bye and went her way.

Meanwhile, I was preoccupied with the many thoughts running through my mind. I didn't know what to do, but I knew I had to do something.

Chapter Forty

Mu had an angry expression on his face when he saw us walk through the door of Reecie's crib. "Yo, what the hell happened, kid?" he asked.

I began explaining everything that took place the night prior, while he listened. The only thing I left out was the fact that it was Kamal who had put the clip in the drawer, and not me. But it really didn't matter which one of us had actually left it there, because it had belonged to both of us and either way the end result would have been the same.

"You didn't even have to take the shit in the crib with you," he said. "It don't take but a hot minute to run that shit over here and give it to Trina. I told you before, Mil, never lay ya head where you shit at, didn't I?" Mu stated, not really looking for an answer because he knew that I knew better. He shook his head and began to calm down.

"Yo, the damage is already done now, so ain't no need in dwelling on that no more. Our next thing we need to worry about is findin' you two a crib of ya own, somewhere close around. How much paper y'all got put up?"

Between what we made yesterday before the narcs came, and the two grand we had stashed, we had about $2,400, plus a nice amount of product left. It would've been more, if my mom hadn't flushed the clip that she found down the toilet before she kicked us out.

"Like twenty-four hundred dollars," I told Mu, "and another twenty-four hundred dollars in work."

He hesitated for a second and then he said, "Right now that ain't enough but, listen, this is what I'm gonna do. I'm gonna try to find a li'l studio apartment or something in the area, and put up whatever it cost to move in for y'all. Whenever y'all stack up enough dough you can hit me back then. As for the necessities, you gots to cop that yourselves, like beds and shit like that. By the end of the week I should have a spot for you, so try to make as much paper as you can and have ya re-up money ready to flip so you can make back what you gotta spend on this crib. It's time to step your game up 'cause you out on your own now, and it cost money to survive and maintain out here," Mu pointed out. "You ain't got Moms and Grandma to clothe and feed you no more, and keep a roof over ya head. You gots to do all that shit for yourselves now, kid. This is what the game is really all about. It's a dog-eat-dog world and only the strong survive; the weak get stepped on and over."

Mu was staring us straight in the eyes while he talked to let us know that what he was saying was real. Mal and I both knew that what he was saying was no joke. It was real.

"We understand, Mu, and we appreciate what you're doin' for us, 'cause we'd probably be somewhere living on the streets if it weren't for you," I told him.

"Never that," he said. "As long as I'm alive y'all ain't never gonna ever be fucked up like that, and that's on the real. We're family now." Mu had officially taken us under his wing as a mentor and a father figure.

"Since y'all home early from school you might as well go out there and put some work in 'cause you know tomorrow's Thursday and I'm goin' over. Tonight might be one of those nights when you can pull an all-nighter, know what I'm saying?" Mu said to us. He was right; we definitely had to step our game up.

Mal and I wasted no time hitting the block. "Yo, what y'all doin home so early?" Ant asked, as we rolled up on him and Trevor.

"We need to make some money," my brother said.

"Y'all heard about Shareef and Ice?" Trevor asked. "That's fucked up and they took Shareef's ride."

"We know. We spoke to his mom this morning and she told us," I said. "Ice's bail is seventy-five Gs with a bondsman, and they found over twenty-five Gs in Shareef's room. I don't know if that was theirs together or all Shareef's, but Shareef wanted his moms to bail Ice out before he knew they raided the crib."

"Damn! Them niggas had twenty-five Gs in the stash?" Trevor asked. "Them muthafuckas was puttin' that work in, kid. I ain't think they was holdin' like that," Trevor finished saying.

"What's up with you two niggas, though?" Ant asked.

"Nothin', just chillin'," I said back.

"Something's up." He wouldn't let it go. "Don't bullshit me," Ant said, insisting something was wrong. Ant had been around me and Mal long enough to know how we acted when something was not right. I was glad to have a friend like him who could pick up on stuff like that. Mal stepped in and told him what went down.

"Get the fuck outta here," Ant and Trevor both said at the same time.

"I can't believe ya moms went out like that," Ant said.

"You think your grams gonna be able to fix shit up?" Trevor asked.

"We don't know, but it don't even matter 'cause we can't hustle and live there anyway, so we can't go back there," I told them.

"That's crazy!" Trevor exclaimed. "Especially since they're the reason why y'all started hustlin' in the first place, to help them." Trevor was right. It was a crazy situation. What started out as a way to help our family ended up being a way to hurt it and break it up. Now we had no choice but to hustle if we wanted to survive ourselves.

"Yo, you know one of you can stay at my crib and the other can stay with Ant's," Trevor offered.

"Nah, we cool but we appreciate that though," I said.

"So what are y'all gonna do then?" Ant asked.

I told them what Mu was going to do for us and I could see the admiration in their faces as I spoke.

"Mu is a good muthafucka," Trevor said first.

"Yeah, that's why he probably last this long in the game, 'cause he got his shit together," Ant said.

"Yo, it's money comin' out here, too," Trevor told us. "We been doin' our thing all day so we'll help y'all move some of y'all shit so you can get ya paper right for the crib."

"You don't have to do that," I told them. "We know y'all got ya own shit to pump."

"Man, that shit ain't nothing. Y'all shit is more important, and y'all our boys so we here for you," Trevor said back.

"Yeah, yo, if y'all out here all night, then we out here all night too," Ant joined in.

Mal and I didn't know what to say. If it didn't make me seem like I was weak, at that moment I would've shed some tears from the love Ant and Trevor had offered us. That day, our bond had strengthened more than ever.

It was four in the morning before we all decided to shut shop down for the day. We originally planned to hustle until at least 8:00 a.m. to catch the early morning smokers who needed a blast before they got to work, but this was the first time for any of us pulling an all-nighter, and we were practically asleep on our feet. With the four of us moving my and Mal's work, we got rid of fourteen clips, the most me and Mal had ever made in one night, thanks to our boys.

Ant made $285 off the three clips I gave him, and Trevor made $290 off the three he had. I thought that if I wouldn't have told them they could take shorts they wouldn't have, because they always took straight money. Mal said he took fifty dollars in shorts on his four clips and I had taken thirty-five dollars on mine, which wasn't bad since Ant and Trevor took twenty-five dollars total in their shorts. We made almost $1,300 off fourteen clips.

Trina gave me her keys so we could get in without waking her and Reecie. She was a trooper for real and I was starting to care about her more and more. She even told me that I could stay with her and Reecie for as long as I wanted to. I told her how much I had appreciated it, but I wouldn't feel right because I was supposed to be able to take care of myself, and not have to depend on a woman. Besides that, Mu had always told me never to move into a chick's crib, because when she got tired of you, she could easily throw you out because it was her place, even if you were paying all the bills; and I didn't want to end up in that type of situation. She said she understood, but even if she wouldn't have, I would have never moved in. Now that we were basically homeless, it was time to make a bad situation better.

Chapter Forty-one

Me and Mal never missed a day of school that whole semester. We figured taking the day off wouldn't hurt so we could try to knock the rest of the clips off and be able to flip more by the time Mu came to pick up the dough. Knowing he'd be on time, as tired as we were, Mal and I went back out at nine, with only four hours worth of rest, giving us four more hours to scrape up a couple of extra dollars.

Ant and Trevor said they had gone back out at eight and caught the early morning paper before the patients went to work, like we wanted to do. They said they sold three out of their last five clips within forty-five minutes because they were the only two who had base. Everybody else who had been out since six a.m. had dope.

By the time Mu pulled up, we had pumped four and a half clips. We would've moved more but, by eleven o' clock, the block was packed. There were mad heads out, so money was going everywhere. We made $435 off the four and a half clips, because a lot of straight money was coming through. We only had five and a half clips left, and Ant and Trevor sold out, so we went to Ant's crib to get their flip money and then I shot over to Reecie's to get with Mu.

Trina was holding all of my and Mal's dough, so when I got there I went in the room to count up. Everything came to $4,320 when I finished counting. My heart was pounding just to know that all that money belonged to my brother and me, and that we had made it with our own hands on the grind. I took $120 out of the singles, put $1,200 to the side, and gave Trina the three Gs back. Ant and Trevor were flipping a G, so with all that together was $2,200. We were sure to get some nice extras with that, at least ten to fifteen, I was thinking.

"What up, Mil?" Mu greeted me.

"Nothin' much, just tired than a mug. We didn't really get in until four in the morning and then went right back out at nine. It was rough last night, but we did our thing. Ant and Trevor stayed out there with us and helped. Between yesterday and now we moved almost twenty out of the twenty-four clips we had left," I told him.

"Yeah, that's what I'm talking about," Mu said, giving me a pound. "Step ya game up, kid.

That's how I used to be when I was out there hand to handing it. How much you flippin'?" he asked.

"Me and Mal flippin' twelve hundred, and Trevor and Ant flippin' a G."

"I see them li'l niggas tryin' to come up too, huh? That's good. Y'all got more so you should flip more 'cause you gonna need all the shit you can get. Product is money; that's what you and Mal need. Go get another five hundred dollars to flip 'cause the first is almost here and that's 'Mother's Day,' when everybody gets their checks and shit, so money's definitely gonna be coming."

I went and did as Mu said. This was the biggest flip we had ever made so I was hoping that everything would go right. When Mu left I went back over to Ant's crib to let Mal know how much we had flipped and to split the $120 in singles with him; then we went back out to try to get rid of the rest of the work. By the time Mu got back we had sold out, making an even $500 off of them, taking the count back up to three grand. I tried to catch up on some sleep before he got there, but Trina was horny so I had to give her some because she had been more than patient and understanding.

"Yo, y'all should see a nice profit off this flip right here," Mu told me, "'cause I got a extra half ounce. When you and Trina chop this up, chop an ounce at a time so you can see how many clips you're getting off each one."

He set the Ziploc on the scale and it weighed 173.6. Take away four and a half grams for the bag and it would come to 168 grams, which is six ounces to a T. Mu rocked it up as usual and me and Trina went to work. I had gotten better at both cutting and bottling, but still not close to Trina or nowhere near Mu. The first ounce I bottled up I made thirteen and a half clips, which wasn't bad because I was supposed to make a little over fourteen or more like Trina was. I only chopped up two and let her do the other four.

It came to ninety-three clips at the end. I remember thinking that was a lot of bottles. When I told Kamal how many we had he was just as amped as I was.

"Yo, if we make at least six grand off these sixty-three clips we'll be close to double digits on the G tip," he said.

"Yeah, but we still gotta spend money on the stuff we need for the crib when Mu gets it, so we really won't be there until our next flip," I reminded him. But still, he was right; we were definitely off to a good start.

Chapter Forty-two

December 1 was going to be an important day for Mal and me. Not only would it be a day where we would make a lot of dough, but it would also be the day we could move into our one-bedroom apartment Mu had gotten for us. He took us by there so he could show us the spot. The landlord lived across the street from it, so she was there to let us in to look around.

The crib was over what used to be a little candy store and arcade up the street and around the corner from the projects we were from on Liberty Street. The store was abandoned but there were two apartments upstairs for rent. We remembered when it was open because we used to buy penny candies and play video games; but we never noticed it had an apartment on top. The good thing was that it was up around the corner from the block, so we were within walking distance.

When we climbed up the steps there was another door. Ms. Rodriquez unlocked it and there was another set of steps at the top. As soon as she turned to the left there was a bathroom and when you walked past that and turn to the right there was a little kitchen. There was a little living room area and a bedroom in the back. It was just what we needed. Mal and I both liked it instantly.

"So what do you think?" Mu asked us.

"Yeah, it's cool. We like it," I said for both of us.

"Mal, do what you think?" Mu asked.

Mal looked at him and said, "Yeah, this'll work right here."

"Good enough then," Mu said.

By the time the first of the month came, Mal and I had accomplished a lot. We had copped two full-sized beds with nightstands and dressers along with a stereo system for the bedroom. We had a pullout couch and a coffee table for the living room, and a kitchen table with chairs since it already came with a refrigerator. Just for all that alone we spent $1,100, which was nothing because we already sold thirty-something clips.

Trina and Reecie went shopping for us to get us things we needed for the place that men wouldn't think about like sheets, blankets, pillows, kitchen products, and bathroom products, stuff like that. The deliveries were scheduled to be there at eleven in the morning. Trina and Reecie agreed to meet them there and hook everything up for us and have it set by the time we got there, so we could get that "Mother's Day" money.

It was one o'clock in the morning when Mal and I decided to call it a day. Both he and I broke another record for the night, and it was a good feeling. The first was definitely a good day. Reecie had stopped by earlier and told us how nice the place looked, and how Trina said she was going to stay there and wait for me to come in.

We didn't check the crib out until morning because Trina was asleep when we came in. To say they had hooked the spot up would be an understatement, because they worked a miracle. It didn't even look like the same place. They organized everything to a T. They had made the beds and put our clothes away. They put little paintings they had bought up in the living room. They had a tablecloth on the table with napkins, and salt and pepper along with other kitchen accessories. The fridge was stocked with all types of foods Trina knew I ate. The bathroom was piped out in dark blue and light blue. I knew Trina did the bathroom because, first, she knew my favorite color was blue and, secondly, I saw her favorite color toothbrush in there.

I remember thinking, *This must be what it feels like to be a man out on your own.*

Me and Mal were in the kitchen eating cereal and counting up when Trina walked in with just a T-shirt and panties on. She kissed me on the cheek.

"Girl! Go put some clothes on," I told her.

"What? Why? Ain't nobody here but you, me, and Kamal," she protested.

I didn't know why it bothered me because Kamal was my brother, but it did. "You heard what I said," I told her again, shooting her a look of stone. She must've caught it because she stormed out of the kitchen.

"Yeah, that's wifey right there," Mal said.

"Get outta here," I denied.

"Nigga, that's your girl, that's why you actin' like that. I don't even hear you talk about Lisa no more like you used to."

"It ain't about being my girl; it's about respect," I said. "And I still be talking to Lisa, but you know a lot of stuff been goin' on and she wouldn't understand right now. She doesn't come from our world, you know that," I retorted.

"Yo, kid, you been up under Mu too long, because you startin' to sound like him," Mal laughed. I laughed with him.

"Is this better?" Trina asked, coming back in with a pair of my sweatpants on and one of my Dallas Cowboys jerseys on.

Mal and I started laughing even harder. After all, it was much needed.

Chapter Forty-three

"Trina, where that money at?" I asked her, getting the last seven clips we had. Mal and I had counted up $2,120 back at the house, so like usual we took the $120, split it, and put the two Gs up.

"Oh, you don't trust me with your money now that you got your own place?" she spat.

"What the hell are you talking about?" I asked, wondering where the statement had come from.

"You heard me," she snapped back with attitude.

"First of all, I don't owe you no explanation about mine," I started out saying. I was in no mood for the drama. "If I tell you to give me something that belongs to me, don't question me. But since you made that dumb statement that just came out ya mouth, I'm gonna tell you why I'm really takin' the money: 'cause I don't want my dough where my damn product is at, that's why! If they run up in here and raid, how the hell am I gonna be of any help if they find my paper, huh!" I stated rather than asked.

"You right, baby," she said, half crying. "I didn't mean to question you like that. It's just that now that you got ya own place and making money, these tricks are gonna be sweatin' you and Mal," she confessed.

"That's what this is all about?" I asked. I shook my head. "I don't care about none of those chicks out there, and can't no chick play me like that. I'm tryin' to get my dough up, and keep a roof over my head. I ain't got time for all of that. Besides that, I know who was there when I didn't have nothin', and I'm not gonna ever forget that, so stop worrying about nothin'."

She burst into tears then threw her arms around me. "I love you, Kamil."

"I love you too," I said, surprisingly.

Chapter Forty-four

It was funny how things could change in a matter of months in the game. Here it was, June of '89, about to be summer, and Mal and I were talking about going to cop whips. Just six months ago, we had gotten thrown out of our grandma's crib and had to move out on our own. Now here we had thirty Gs put up and a nice two-bedroom apartment decked out.

We were doing our thing for a fifteen- and sixteen-year-old. Ice had gotten out about two months ago on bail by working something out with Clyde, while Shareef had nine more months to do in a program. Ice told us that was all the money he and Shareef had when the crib had gotten raided.

Ant and Trevor were still getting it. They now had matching Jettas hooked up. Ant's was white with a burgundy top and Trevor's was white with a blue top. They spent a lot of money on cars and jewelry. They told us they had paid $5,500 apiece for the cars, but spent six Gs apiece just hooking them up, and that their gold combined cost four Gs.

Mal and I were still the same. We weren't really into spending as freely as Ant and Trevor were. Despite not hearing from or seeing our moms, we were still hopeful that she'd change her mind, speak to us again, and then let us move her, our grandmother, and sisters out of the hood. Because we had the money and it didn't hurt our pockets, Mal and I did cop matching Big Daddy Kane flat links with the Nefertiti heads on them, which ran us $1,300 apiece, but other than that we spent our money on gear and the crib.

As promised, I made sure Trina always had dough to get her hair and nails done and to shop. Joyce Leslie and the mall became her second homes. She had been putting that money to good use because she stayed super fly. Lisa still didn't know what I did. I told her that Mal and I moved in with another relative. I had been trying to find the right time to tell her but there never seemed to be one.

Me, Mal, Ant, and Trevor all hung out where all the other dealers hung from all over. We were hitting spots like the Amboy movie theatre, the skating rink out in Teaneck, Echo Lanes bowling alley, the Jamaican club out our way, and all the rap shows. Normally we shot up to the diner back in town after the out-of-town spots closed. I couldn't help but remember how we used to walk up there when we were younger after a party at the Neighborhood House and see all the fly whips, the phattest clothes, and the prettiest chicks, and be amazed; but now to be amid the crowd and a part of the game was a totally different experience.

Out of all the places I liked going, the Jamaican club was my favorite. Even though it was run by a West Indian woman and her son, and was supposed to be full of West Indians, the projects were always the deepest. It was like our own private hangout on the weekend. From watching the Jamaican kids up in there I learned how to whine and I would add my own moves to it when I was out on the dance floor with a chick. I got turned out on drinking Heinekens and Canei; I liked how they made me feel.

You would've thought Ant and Trevor were Rastas by how much weed they smoked and Guinness they drank. I remember taking pictures was one of our highlights in the club.

"Ay yo, Pop, let me get these flicks right quick," Mal said to the old cameraman everybody referred to as Pop. They said he had been taking pictures at clubs and events for over twenty years.

Mal and I had just finished taking a few flicks with some project heads and females with sexy outfits on and then just us, when a voice echoed out of the crowd of people waiting for their turn.

Me and Mal both looked to see who the voice belonged to. Standing there were two nice-looking chicks with sexy grins plastered on their faces. One was brown-skinned with big breasts and thick hips; the other one was light-skinned and a little shorter with nice breasts and a butt to match. They both had on tight jeans, button-up designer shirts, and Reebok classics. What stood out the most though were the big earrings they sported and the long chains they rocked around their necks.

"Yeah, y'all can get in," Mal said, answering their request from the sidelines.

I was into redbones and Mal always said light-skinned girls were problems, but somehow he wound up with the light-skinned one and I was with the tall, brown-skinned one. Good thing I had my 40 Below Timberland boots on, or else she would've made me look like a midget. We wound up taking two more flicks, gave them one with us, and kept one.

"Y'all from the projects, right?" the brown-skinned one said as we moved out of the way so the rest of onlookers could take their flicks.

"Yeah. How you know that?" I asked.

"'Cause we be seeing y'all out there when we be ridin' through, wondering who were them two cute guys who be dressin' alike all the time?" she said.

Me and Mal just started smiling. "I'm Kamil." I extended my hand. Kamal followed up with his name.

"I'm Ke Ke, and this is my cousin Shanda," the brown-skinned one told us. "Y'all twins?" they asked.

"Nah, we're just brothers, a year apart," Mal answered.

"How old are you?" she asked me.

I knew she was older than me, I just didn't know by how much, so I boosted my age up by two years and said that I was seventeen, making Mal automatically eighteen. "How old are you?" I asked her.

"I'm twenty and my cousin is eighteen," she said. "Y'all goin' to the diner after this?" she asked us.

"Yeah," we said in unison.

"All right, then we'll see y'all up there." Then they walked off, waving.

Mal and I just looked at each other. We didn't have to say it to know what the other was thinking because we both thought the same. People were starting to notice us.

Chapter Forty-five

The diner was packed. Some of the flyest whips around were there. Hustlers and chicks were everywhere. Guys were blasting their car systems either battling or trying to impress the chicks. Other guys were playing dice, something I had become interested in, and the rest of them were either trying to push up on females to take them home or to the hotel or just straight fronting hard because they had a phat ride, a phat chain, and a pocket full of dough. We were just chilling.

When we got out of Ant and Trevor's car, we saw Shanda and Ke Ke kicking it with some kids from Third, so we just went over to Red Tower and ordered something to eat. Somehow, in the midst of their talking they must've seen us because Shanda came in and spoke before I peeped her handing Mal a piece of paper and telling him to make sure we called. We got our food and went and leaned on Ant's car, eating.

Out of nowhere, people began to scatter. The sound of gunshots invaded the air.

Someone started shooting. Everybody started jumping in their whips peeling out. We were all used to that, so gunshots didn't even faze us anymore; it was just another part of the game. I hopped in Shareef's ride while Mal hopped in Trevor's, and we called it a night.

Chapter Forty-six

"Kamil, your sister Monique came by here today looking for y'all," Trina told me when I walked through the door.

I immediately became alarmed. "What did she say?" I asked.

"She told me to tell you as soon as I see you to call your grandmother house before your mother gets in."

"Did she say something happened?" I asked, thinking she was hiding something from me.

"She didn't tell me anything besides to tell you or Mal to call, and I gave her the number to y'all place. She didn't even know you weren't staying here anymore."

I took the number from Trina and wasted no time dialing it.

"Hello?" I heard my grandmother's voice.

"Grandma, it's me," I said. It had been almost eight months since I'd seen or heard from any of them.

"Thank you, Jesus, it's my baby! Kamil, how's everything, suga'? Are you all right? Are you eating? Where are you?" my grams bombarded me.

"I'm all right, Grandma, everything's good. How about you?" I replied with a smile.

"I'm blessed. I been praying that the Lord watch over you and your brother in them streets. I miss y'all so much."

"I miss you too, Grandma." My chest began to ache. Talking to my grandmother took me back to the night my mother had put us out. I could still see the hurt in my grandmother's eyes.

"Where's Kamal?" she asked.

"He's at the house," I told her.

"What house?" she wanted to know.

"Mal and I got our own place now, Grandma," I said.

"Your own place? Y'all ain't old enough to be taking care of yourselves, let alone have your own place," she said back. "What, y'all living with some little fast-tail girls?"

I laughed. "Nah, Grandma, just me and Mal. We've been taking care of ourselves going on nine months now," I said proudly.

"Lord! Help me, Jesus, please deliver my babies from evil!" she shouted, quoting a scripture from the Bible.

"Grandma, go 'head with all that. I told you we're all right. How's my moms doing?"

"Sister is still Sister. She don't even want to bring up that night, and she don't even mention y'all anymore, but I know she's hurting and regret what she done. I know my child."

It hurt me just listening to my grandmother speak about it. "Me and Mal still love her, though," I told my grandmother. "How's everything with Jasmine?"

"Oh, she's getting so big and grown, you should see her."

"What's going on with Monique?"

My grandmother paused and took a deep breath. Right then and there, I knew something up.

"Grandma, you heard me? What's going on with Nique?" I repeated.

"Kamil, baby, I'ma tell you, ever since you and your brother been gone, your sister been out of control. Most of the time she's staying out all night, and we don't even know where she is because she don't call. Your mother wanted to put her out too, but I talked her out of it. Boys are still calling here in the wee hours of the night hanging up and being disrespectful. One time I picked up the phone while she was on there and heard her talking to some boy about what they were gonna do when they hook up and all that mess. I didn't tell your mother because I knew she'd kill, but I know she ain't no virgin like she's been saying. To make matters worse I think she done dropped out of school, too, because sometimes she strolls up out of here around the time school's about to start, before the summer came. I don't know where she was going, but it wasn't school."

"Is she there, Grandma?"

"Yeah, her trifling, lazy butt back there in the room. She don't do nothing but lie back there and eat and get fat."

"Let me speak to her."

"Hold on. Monique!" I heard my grandmother shout. "Pick up the phone."

She must've asked who it was because my grandma shouted my name.

"Hey, bro, what's up?" she answered the phone.

"You tell me," I said.

"Grandma, hang up the phone, please," she said, knowing that my grandmother hadn't hung up yet.

"Chile, please, nobody wants to hear what you got to say," my grandmother spat. "Kamil, baby, you take care and stay in touch, you hear?"

"I will, Grandma. I'm gonna have Nique give you our new phone number so you can call us anytime if you need anything or whatever. If you can, tell my mom we said we love her."

"I will, suga'," my grandmother said before hanging up.

"What's goin' on?" I asked my sister as soon as I heard the receiver hang up. "Grandma telling me all this junk about you, how you might've dropped out of school and just a whole bunch of other stuff."

I could hear her sniffling as if she were crying. "Mil, I'm in trouble," she said.

"What?" My heart started racing. So many thoughts flashed through my mind and none of them were good. "What do you mean you're in trouble? What kind of trouble?" I asked.

"I'm pregnant."

As soon as she said the words my heart dropped to my stomach and my blood began to boil. "What? By who? How the fuck did you let that happen?" I was not a big fan of cursing and it took a lot for me to get that upset, but Monique's situation was too much not to be angry.

"Mil, don't start. I can't deal with all these questions right now. I came to y'all 'cause the guy I was messing with is acting all funny and talking about the baby isn't his, he used a condom, and he's not taking care of no baby or paying for any abortion for a kid that's not his."

With every word I became sick to my stomach just hearing my sister talk like that. But what burned me up most was how some guy had treated my big sister. "Who's the nigga?" I questioned.

"You know Tone from Arlington Avenue?"

"That nigga? Yeah, I know who you're talkin' about. Don't even worry about it." By now I was fuming.

"Mil, leave that alone, please. I just want to take care of this and be done with it," my sister cried.

"Yeah, all right," I dryly replied. "Anyway, how much you need?" I asked.

"Before I only needed four hundred seventy-five dollars, but now I need six hundred because I waited too long."

"Damn, Nique, we used to try to tell you all the time to watch ya'self and cool out, but you didn't wanna listen. And how you gonna drop out your senior year? You know when moms find out she's putting you out, right?"

"School was just too much for me right now, Mil, being pregnant and all, and I can't find no job. I think about coming out there with y'all sometimes. I be seeing girls out there hustling and I'm more thorough than them."

"You talking crazy. We ain't trying to hear that. If you need anything let us know, but all that you hustlin' junk is out the window. It's not what it seems. Just concentrate on going back to school when it opens back up. We got you, I promise," I assured her.

"I'ma go back to school, Mil, but just not this year. Probably next year," she said.

"All right." In my mind I knew she would never go back. "I'm gonna leave the six hundred dollars wit' Trina, and another one hundred fifty for you and Jasmine. Tell her we love her, and we love you too."

"I know. I love y'all too."

I told Kamal everything I found out about the family. I knew he was going to take the stuff about Monique hard because he always tried to prevent something like this from happening. I had to calm him down because he wanted to go to the kid Tone's block and hurt him. I told him to chill. Plainfield wasn't but so big and I knew eventually we would cross the kid Tone's path.

Chapter Forty-seven

"Hello, can I speak to Ke Ke?"

"Who's calling?" a female's voice asked.

"Kamil."

"Hey, li'l man, this is she."

"Nah, I'm not little," I corrected her.

"Oh, okay, excuse me," she said, laughing. "But I was only talking about your height."

"My bad, but I got a thing about that little stuff."

"I see." She laughed again. "What's up, though?"

"I was just callin' to see if this was the right number, that's all," I said jokingly.

"Now that you see it is, what are you gonna do?"

"I'ma see if we can get together or somethin'."

"That's cool, what y'all wanna do?"

"Whatever, it doesn't matter."

"Y'all drivin'?"

"Not yet, but we will be," I told her. Mal and I had been discussing copping rides lately.

"That's all right, because we are. Call us on Friday or Saturday and we'll hook up or something," she suggested.

"All right, cool, talk to you then," I said, and then we hung up.

Chapter Forty-eight

"Mu, what up?"

"Nothin', just came to cool out and shoot the shit with my dawgs, that's all. You two niggas done got so large now, you can take days off, huh?" he said, playing. We both laughed.

"Nah, it's not like that. We just tryin' to get this money together so we can go drop on whips," I told him.

"Word, y'all ready for that?" he asked, impressed.

"Yeah, we think it's about time we show people we been puttin' that work in," Mal said. "Besides, it's getting played out ridin' shotgun," Mal added.

"Nah, worrying about what people think is the wrong reason. Do it 'cause you're tired of muthafuckas takin' you here and there, but fuck what people say or think," Mu said.

"You right," Mal agreed.

"Speaking of askin' niggas to take us here and there, you think you could take us out to St. George's Avenue?" I asked. We all burst out laughing.

St. George's Avenue in Linden had everything from Benzes to Beemers, Jaguars to Jeeps. All the phattest whips, you name it they had it. They even had whips already hooked up that the dealers sold, or they brought from police auctions. We didn't want to cop anything too flashy; that would draw heat on us from the cops. The narcs still didn't really mess with us, probably because of how little we were, so we didn't want to mess that up.

"Yo, Mil, look at these joints right here," Mal yelled over to me, as Mu and I were checking out this fly convertible BMW.

"This is us right here, kid," he said, pointing to two Audi 4000s.

They did look like they fit us. They were both in good condition on the outside and on the inside. There weren't any price tags on them, just the year. One of them was an '84 and the other was an '85.

"Excuse me, sir, how much are these two Audis right here?" Mal asked the gray-haired white man.

"This white one is fifty-two hundred dollars and the red one is fifty-seven hundred dollars," he said.

"What's the difference?" I asked.

"The year, mileage, and the condition of them. The red one has fewer miles and runs better."

"Can we check them out?" Mu asked. Mu had four cars and knew about mechanic stuff, so he was an expert at shopping for whips. "Pop the hoods for me," he told the salesman. Both engines looked identical to me. They were both clean and fairly new. Mu touched something on the white one under the hood.

"Vroom! Vroom! Vroom!" was the sound of the engine when he revved it, and then he did the same to the red one. It sounded the same.

"The white one sounds like it idled too high and the red one sounds like the timing is off," Mu said to the white car salesman.

Mal and I looked at each other. We didn't know what Mu was talking about.

"I knew that already, and I was gonna fix that whenever I sold them. I give all my cars a tune-up before they leave the lot," the man said.

"What about the warranty?" Mu asked.

"Ninety days."

"Yo, what up?" Mu turned to us. "What y'all wanna do?"

"Yeah, we want 'em," we told Mu.

"All right. Ay yo, we'll give you ten Gs cash right now, tax included, for the both of them," Mu told the man.

"Nah, I can't do that. Even if I wanted to," he said back.

"All right, we appreciate ya time though, thank you," Mu said and then told us to go. Although we liked the cars and wanted them, we didn't question Mu's decision.

"Hold on a minute," we heard the man say just before we exited the lot. "Step into my office and maybe we can work out something."

It was apparent Mu knew what he was doing. He was good.

"This is the lowest that I can go with taxes and everything combined," he said, showing Mu a number on a pocket calculator. It read $10,500.

Mu showed us, and we shook our heads in agreement. Even though we had all the money on us, Mu told him we'd give him $5,500 now and the other $5,000 when we came to pick them up in a few days.

"Who will the vehicles be registered to?" he asked.

Mu looked at us.

"Put down Zella Benson," I said. That was my grandmother's name. I wasn't 100 percent sure, but I knew if anyone would let us put our whips in their name, it would be her.

Against her better judgment, my grandmother agreed to do it. We offered her $1,000 just because, but she refused to take it. Thursday we picked them up. Mu dropped us and our grandmother off before he went to New York. We had flipped more this trip to make the money back from the whips. Ounces had gone up to $625. We usually copped twelve, and Ant and Trevor would cop twelve too for $14,700 plus the extras Mal and I still got. This time we had to put out for a half a key.

We had both cars registered and insured the same day. To show our appreciation we took our grandmother out to lunch, and then dropped her back around the projects. We drove the cars home and then parked them.

"Yo, we gonna hustle hard as hell for three weeks straight and then throw our shit in the shop and get them hooked up," Mal said to me all hyped.

"Yeah, I'm with that, but I want some beats this week," I said. After riding in Mu's and Ant's and 'em rides I had fallen in love with loud music.

"Oh, no question, we're gonna hit Canal first thing in the morning, kid," he said back to me. "We gonna get Ant and Trevor to roll out there with us since they got licenses, and know the people who be hookin' them up out there. Let's hit the projects and put this work in."

I was right behind Mal as he made his way out the door.

Chapter Forty-nine

Ant and Trevor pulled up a couple of hours later.

"Where y'all been all mornin'? We came by the house but you weren't there," Ant said.

"We had to go take care of some important business," Mal said to them.

"Like what?" Trevor asked.

"Like coppin' our own whips so we ain't gotta sweat y'all no more for a ride," I said with a smile on my face.

"Oh, shit! Get the fuck outta here," Trevor yelled. "Where they at?"

"At the crib," Mal answered.

"Well, let's go see 'em," he said to us.

"Man, we tryin' to get that money back, and besides we already know what they look like," Mal said, joking.

"How much you pay for 'em?"

"Almost eleven Gs," I said.

"What, you got Beemers?" Ant asked.

"Nah, Audi 4000s."

"Okay, them joints is phat. I seen a couple of them hooked up."

"I know you gonna hook them shits up, too," Trevor said.

"We ain't with that," Mal said, not wanting them to know. "We gonna go check them out right quick. We'll be back."

"Yo, we gonna put some music in them though and we want y'all to take us over to Canal in the morning," I said before we forgot.

"Yeah we got you."

Mal and I got the same hookup: four tens, top-of-the-line EVs, in the window, a pullout radio, Blaupunkt EQ, bullet tweeters, and a Zeus amp. Due to the build of our whips our joints was loud. We had the Holland Tunnel rumbling when we came through. We both spent a hundred dollars on Ron G's, Kid Capri's, Doo Whop's, S & S's, and Jersey's DJ Juice's mixed tapes before we left Canal. Like everybody else, when we got back in town we hit every block in town, pumping our systems. I was playing "The Bridge" and Mal was pumping "Project Ho," both off the MC Shan *Down by Law* album.

When we bucked the corner to ride through Arlington, the first face I spotted was the kid Tone.

Our eyes met. He shot me a stupid grin when I drove by, and I knew what it was for. He knew Monique was my sister. It took everything in me not to jump out and punch him in the face, but they were too deep out there so I let it ride. Our last stop was the projects. All the project chicks and hustlers were out when we came bucking around the corner. We all hopped out and left the music blasting. When they all saw who it was, you could see all the different types of reactions on everyone's faces.

Trina was at the gate talking to one of the new guys on the block when I pulled up. I could see it in her face she was trying play it off when she saw me like she wasn't really talking to him. She started walking over to me. "What's up, boo?" she said, wrapping her arms around me. "Y'all cars are fly."

"Thanks," was all I said.

"What's wrong?"

"What you doin' over there talkin' to that nigga while he's out here tryin' to get money, huh?"

"Who Steve? He ain't nobody," she answered, nixing my question. "I know you don't think I was letting him push up. I don't get down like that, Mil. I fuck with you and only you," she said, making me feel like I had overreacted.

"Anyway," I said. "Me and Mal goin' out tonight so I'ma be in late. You can either stay at the house or I'll see you tomorrow," I told her, knowing she wouldn't want to stay at my place by herself.

"I ain't stayin' over there by myself. I'll just see you tomorrow. I need some more money, though, 'cause me and Reecie goin' to the mall later."

I pulled out my dough and peeled her off three hundred-dollar bills.

"Where you goin' tonight?" she asked.

"Out, I told you."

"It better not be with no other bitch," she snapped. "Don't make me fuck somebody up."

"Go ahead with that," I said. "You always accusing me of something and be wrong," I shouted at her, trying to use reverse psychology.

"Nigga, you heard what I said."

Mal, Ant, and Trevor started dying laughing.

"I'll see you later. Take your ass in the house," I told her.

I watched as she spun around and sashayed her way to Reecie's.

I just shook my head because I knew the more time that passed, the more of a problem Trina would become.

Chapter Fifty

For the next three weeks, we hustled liked crazy as planned. That following week we put our cars in the shop and were back on foot. When asked, we told everyone that they had gotten repo'ed, but Ant and Trevor knew better because they knew that our whips were paid for, so we told them that the cops impounded them for thirty days, for driving without a license. We had made the dough back that we put out for the cars and systems, plus another twenty-something on top of that, not including the fifteen grand we put to the side to hook our rides up.

We went all out. Paint jobs, ragtops, sheepskin interior, rims, wings, kits, fender trim, rocket panels, and chrome double tailpipes, coming to $7,500 apiece. Mal was getting his painted super white with a blue rag, and I was changing from red to light blue with the blue rag too. We both were getting Maxima kits cut and fitted on them, and writing on our rocket panels. Mal's was going to say ANOTHER ONE TO GET JEALOUS OF, a saying he got from MC Shan's tape, which was his favorite, and mine was going to say STOP, LOOK & LISTEN, something that I got from an MC Lyte cut. The people who were doing it hooked up all of Mu's cars, so we knew that they were going to be dope.

"Yo, Mal, get up," I yelled to my brother. "Mu is gonna be here any minute."

"I'm up, I'm up," he yelled back.

"Well, get ready then so we can go pick our pieces up."

Beep. Beep. Mu was already here.

"Mal, you ready?"

"Yeah, let me just put on my sneakers."

"Don't forget to snatch your radio up."

When we stepped outside, Mu was sitting in a charcoal gray Benz 300E with a temp tag in the window.

"Damn! This shit is dope," Mal said behind me as we were walking over to it to get in.

"I picked it up last night. I gave up the Volvo and sixteen Gs for it."

"Yo, it was worth it, kid, this piece is dope," Mal said from the back.

"I can't have my li'l mans out doin' me, so I had to turn it up on y'all to show you who your mentor is," he said jokingly. "Let's go pick up y'all whips, though, so y'all can be shinin' too."

When we pulled up, they were sitting behind the gate facing each other like they were on display for a car show. Words could not define how they looked. To me we had the hottest whips in the world.

"Goddamn," Mal said. "Look at our joints, kid."

I was speechless. I just smiled. Even Mu was impressed.

"Them shits are pretty as hell," he said. "Y'all niggas got some straight-up Pussy Machines!"

We started laughing.

"Ay yo, Sal, why you don't put that much time into my joints when you hook 'em up?" Mu asked the short Italian man.

"Come on, Mu, you know I do my best work on all your cars," Sal said.

"I'm just fuckin' with you, Sal," Mu said back.

"So, what do you think?" he asked.

I reached out my hand to shake his and said, "Sal, you hooked us up."

Mal followed up by saying, "No doubt."

Mu was leading the pack in the 300E, and we followed, riding through downtown and then down to Third Street. We saved the projects for last. I had my Slick Rick tape ready. When we got close, I put on "Children's Story" and Mal played "Young World," off the same tape. People were stopping in their tracks when we came through. I could see guys putting their fists to their mouths with the "oh, shit" expressions on their faces.

Chicks were dancing to the different songs we pumped. This was the projects' year to shine and this time we were a part of it. The projects were where we really got our props at when we rolled up. Mal, Mu, and I pulled up on the grass side by side.

"You niggas went all out," Trevor was the first to say.

"I knew y'all was frontin' about that impound shit. Yo, I'm going to cop something new tomorrow," Ant joked. "You niggas ain't gonna be shittin' on me like this."

"Yo, they look all right?" I asked them.

"Nigga, stop frontin', you know y'all got the hottest shit in town right now," Trevor said.

They didn't even say anything about Mu's Benz and his was worth more than both of ours put together. All the other hustlers from the hood who were out came over to check our whips out. Everybody started talking about how they were going to cop this and that, or do this and that to the whips they already had after seeing ours. We had definitely amped the hood up around the way.

Later that evening, we all pulled up in the diner parking lot one by one: Ant, Trevor, Mal, and then me. Mu was sitting on top of the hood of his 300E talking to some girl I didn't know when we got there. It was perfect, because we pulled right over by him and a few other whips from the projects. Guys and chicks were checking out our whips telling us how phat they were. Some were checking us on the low because they didn't like us, but they liked our rides. We all said what's up to Mu, and then Mal and them went inside to get something to eat, while I headed over to the dice game on the side of the Kentucky Fried Chicken spot.

"Ay yo, Mal, get me a breast and three wings with two extra rolls, and a Pepsi. I'll be over here at this Cee-lo game," I told my brother.

"Leave them dice alone, kid."

"Could you just get me the number four like I asked?"

"I got you."

I could tell that they were having a big game tonight because there was a lot of known money-getters in the circle of betters. Most of them I knew, but a few of them I didn't. One face that stuck out above all, though, was the kid Tone's. He was rolling the dice and had the bank. My first reaction was to run up on him and hook off, but I wasn't sure who was with him. Besides that, I knew how gamblers got if they losing their dough and the game gets broken up, so I didn't want to chance it.

He was so busy rolling that he didn't even see me. I just stood there in the crowd watching the game and listening to see if I could pick up on who was with him. The more I looked at him the more I wanted to knock him out. Just knowing this joker had violated my sister got me mad all over again. As he looked up to see who all was betting, he spotted me. I knew he knew who I was because he looked me straight in my face and said some slick shit that only I caught.

"You niggas put ya bets down so I can get this money. I gotta pay for an abortion," he said. Some of the betters laughed.

That was all she wrote. I couldn't take it anymore. As soon as he rolled the dice, went to pick them up, and came back up, I caught him on the jaw. I saw him buckle as he tried to grab hold of me. I pulled away. Out of the blue, I heard somebody say, "What the fuck!" and he caught me on the side of the head. He didn't daze me or drop me. I just turned in the direction and ducked out of reflex in case something was following it, and then I grabbed the kid who hit me. I felt punches to my ribs and on my back from a different fist and I knew I was being jumped. The next thing I knew, I didn't feel hits anymore as I leaned forward and pushed the kid who snuck me to the ground. When I lifted up, I punched him in the eye, and kept punching him until somebody pulled me off of him. It was Kamal. When I looked around every hustler from the projects was fighting somebody, including Mu.

The shots that rang out caused everybody to stop fighting and take cover. Once I saw Mu and them jump in their whips, Mal and I jumped in ours and peeled out too. There was officially a beef again between the projects and Arlington Avenue. The last time the projects had beef with them was in 1986 when Terrance and Mark got killed, Shawn got paralyzed, and a couple of dudes from their block got hit up.

A meeting was called to meet in the field the next day by Mustafa.

"Yo, the block's gonna be hot for a minute, so it might be best to shut down until we handle this shit. Everybody who clocked around here is in this beef. If muthafuckas don't fight or do something, then they can't clock around here no more. I don't care where you catch one of them niggas at; you better jump out and fuck them up, and whoever wit' 'em. Everybody should have a ratchet so start bringin ya shit out 'cause if they drive through here they ain't gonna be sightseein', they gonna be bustin', so you better bust back. If I find out anybody was on some sucka shit while we beefin' I'm gonna step to you myself, so if you ain't wit' it you better say somethin' now." Mu had the attention of every hustler from the projects in attendance.

Nobody said a word.

"All right, then, let's handle this shit," Mu said.

Everywhere we went, we went deep, clubs, movies, skating, bowling, wherever, and something always kicked off because they were always there. It was like we were going out just to beef instead of to have a good time. This was the longest beef the projects had ever had and it lasted all the way until school started back up.

Besides me and Mal there were only three other kids from the projects who still went to "The High," so we knew it was going to be rough going to school. Arlington had more than double our amount who attended and their block was right down there street from the school, but there was no way we weren't going to go. Our reputations were on the line. Mu got us ratchets from New York and told us to take them to school with us. They were still in the boxes, brand new with an extra clip, two 9 mms.

Throughout all the beefing, I wound up with a cut over my eye, a doughnut under the eye, and a couple of bumps, scrapes, and bruises, so technically I was doing all right. On the first day back only one out of the other three projects kids came to school besides me and Mal. He was a kid named Kev. He was a sophomore too, but nothing about him was soft. He stood about five foot ten, and was built like a linebacker. He was with whatever.

"I didn't think y'all was gonna show up, but I should've known better 'cause y'all be fuckin' with Mu," Kev said. "Chris and punk-ass Phil ain't comin', so I guess it's just us three homies. What y'all workin' with?" he asked.

"We brought our nines with us but they're in the car," I said.

"Nah, go get them, 'cause unless they got a reason to they don't be searchin' you up in here. Either you put it in ya waist or tote it in your book bags. You never know how these niggas actin' up in here. I'm bringin' it to them wherever," Kev said, and we knew he meant that.

We toted our guns around all day and showed face in the lunchroom to let everybody know that we weren't no punks even in small numbers. It was no secret; everybody knew we were beefing. There were about nine guys in the cafeteria from

Arlington, but none of them made a move when they saw us, I didn't know why, but either they didn't want to set it off in there or they knew we weren't sitting up in there three deep without backup on us.

Lisa came over to where we sat while I was picking over a piece of cake. "Kamil, can I speak to you for a minute?" she asked.

I slid over so we could have a little privacy. "What's up?"

"Why didn't you tell me you were a drug dealer?" she said.

I almost choked on my cake. "What?"

"Don't try to deny it, Kamil. I already know. Everybody's been talking about how nice your and Kamal's cars are. Y'all don't even have jobs or licenses. Then I hear y'all have been beefing with Arlington Avenue since the summer. I thought I knew you better than that," she said. "That's why I really haven't heard from you or seen you all summer, because you were too busy selling drugs and fighting."

Now wasn't a good time for me to be hit with all of what Lisa was confronting me with, but I did want to clear the air because it had been bothering me that I couldn't tell her.

"Everything you said is true. I'm not going to deny nothing, but what you don't know is the reason behind everything you heard or have been hearing. Yeah, I hustle, but how could I tell you my moms threw my brother and me out in the street, and we had nowhere to go and didn't know what to do? How could I tell you that if it weren't for a friend of mine who hustles too, I would've had to drop out of school because I wouldn't have been able to feed or clothe myself, or have nowhere to lay my head? How can someone just come out and say it? And what am I supposed to do if I have a sister who runs the street and sleeps with niggas who don't give a fuck about her, and just knock her up leaving her all pregnant, and then brags as if he did something? What am I supposed to do if she comes to me for help, telling me she needs six hundred dollars for an abortion, and she had to drop out of school her senior year and shit? This is what drove me to selling drugs and this is why I'm beefing with them niggas from that block, but how am I supposed to explain all that to you, and make you understand, huh?"

Her eyes began to moisten and the tears began to drop as I summed up all that happened in the past eleven months or so in my life in a matter of a minute's worth of words.

"I didn't know," she said with a shameful look on her face.

"It's not your fault." I put my hand on her shoulder.

"If you would've just told me, or tried to tell me, I would've tried to understand."

"They weren't your problems; they were mine."

She dropped her head and I lifted it back up. "You're actin' like they're your problems now."

"I feel like it, because I care about you, Kamil," she said back to me, looking me straight in my eyes.

"Wipe ya face, Lisa. I'm all right and I'm going to be all right."

"Kamil, if you have problems with these guys why did you come to school?" she asked, concerned.

"Because I need an education," I said with a smile.

"You always think everything is so funny," she said back, smiling too.

"Nah, seriously, I can't let this stop me from finishing school. I need this."

"You sure it's not your pride or ego that has you here today?"

"A little bit of that, too," I said, laughing.

"Kamil, please be careful," she said.

"I will. I always am."

After school, we headed to the parking lot and, sure enough, the dudes from Arlington was out there squatting on us.

"Yo, we just gonna walk up and whip out on these muthafuckas, that's all," Kev said.

"Hold up, they look like they standing out there waiting to talk. They don't look like they in fighting mode, so let's see what's up," I said.

"How the hell can you tell they ain't in fighting mode?" Mal said.

"Look at 'em. They outnumber us, but they look more scared than we do."

The parking lot was crowded, as everyone waited to see what happened. We walked over to our cars. I hit my alarm on my car as I was approaching it. They all just stepped away from the cars a little.

"Yeah, what's goin' on? What's up?" Kev asked, spreading his arms out.

"Yo, we wanna talk to y'all so we can dead this bullshit," the kid named Keyshawn said.

Mal cut him off. "Nigga, it ain't over no bullshit. It's over my muthafuckin' sister, kid. That nigga Tone violated and my li'l brother stepped to him. You niggas know how the game goes."

A few of them didn't like what Mal said and acted like they wanted to move out on us. Kev sensed it and pulled out.

Clack! Clack! "Yeah! What's up?"

Everybody froze.

"Yo, Kev, chill. Niggas just wanna talk, kid," I intervened. "Ay yo, Keyshawn, listen, if niggas wanna dead it we can dead it, or it's whatever," I said, lifting up my shirt to show that I was packing too. "All it's goin' to do is boil down to some of your mans getting killed or goin' to jail, and the same happening to some of our mans or maybe even some of us. So if we gonna squash it we can do it now; you just tell ya boys and we'll tell ours."

"Yo, I'm with that, Mil," he said.

We didn't shake hands, but we gave our words, which was as good as anything in the streets.

The block was getting back to normal now that the beefing was over. Mu was right when he said beef and cash didn't mix, because while we were beefing we were spending a lot of dough and wasn't really bringing none back in. I stopped messing with Trina because she was snaking me by creeping with a dude from Third on the low. Mu found out and put me on. I really didn't care because between Lisa and Ke Ke I had my hands full anyway. Mu made Reecie put Trina out, and she did it, too. Even though Mu was my peoples I thought it was messed up Reecie chose him over her own flesh and blood, but I guessed Mu was more beneficial for her than Trina was.

Seven months had gone by since me and Ke Ke had started messing around. She was way more experienced than Trina was, both sex-wise and streetwise. I remember the first time I had sexed her she wouldn't let me unless I went down on her. I wouldn't at first, but I wanted her so bad that I agreed to. She tried to dress it up for me by squirting strawberry whipped cream between her legs, trying to convince me that it would make it taste better. She was a freak and she was trying to turn me into one. She was always bringing some type of flavor to the bed-room like melted caramel, honey, or chocolate, pouring it over my joint and then licking it all off of me. One time she opened up my jeans while I was driving back from the movies and started giving me head. It took a lot for me not to crash and kill us both.

Lisa and I hadn't slept together as of yet. Our relationship wasn't about that. I got from her what I couldn't get from Ke Ke, like normal and personal conversation, nothing about the streets, because she wasn't from the streets. I guess you could say that I had two girlfriends: a street girl and a homebody one. I felt like I was getting the best of both worlds.

Chapter Fifty-one

"Welcome home, kid," I said to Shareef, as I gave him a hug. Shareef came home exactly ten days after my birthday, on March 13. "Damn, what they was feeding you in there? You got ya weight all the way up. You're lookin' good, baby boy," I said.

"Word! What was you doin', hittin' iron up in there?" Mal joined in.

"Nah, just pull-ups, push-ups, and dips, and eating like a mutha."

"Either you ain't have no fights or you won 'em all, nigga, 'cause I don't see no marks or bruises on ya ass," Trevor said.

"You know I'm from the projects, nigga. I ain't takin' no Ls," Shareef said with a serious face.

"Yo, back together again like the old days," Ant said.

"Nigga, you actin' like I just did a ten-year bid or somethin'. I only did eighteen months," Shareef said back. "Yo, while I was biddin' you niggas' names been ringin' bells up in the youth house and the programs like crazy when I went down, especially y'all." He directed his words to Mal and me.

"I heard you niggas been gettin' it and puttin' that work in on the beef tip. That Arlington Avenue shit was all over. I even had to knuckle one of them niggas up in detention for runnin' his mouth in there, even though Plainfield be tryin' to stick together to go to war with them Elizabeth heads. When we get to the programs we click up with Elizabeth to beef with them Newark cats, 'cause they always think they run shit 'cause they be the deepest, but they be the softest. Even in the prisons it's like that, but worse," Shareef told us. "That shit used to have me feelin' good whenever I heard about y'all, and I couldn't wait to come home."

"Well, you're here now, kid, and we gonna make sure you all right, know what I'm sayin'?" I said to him.

"I know if I need anything I can ask, but Ice is suppose to have a few dollars for me, so I'ma see what he got."

Lately, from what we'd been seeing, the kid Ice wasn't doing too good out there. It seemed like ever since he and Shareef took that fall, he hadn't been able to bounce back. A few times

he came to me and Mal for work because he
had messed up Clyde's dough and needed to
make up for it. He always came correct with us,
though, so we never had a problem with hitting
him, plus it was on the strength of Shareef.

"Yo, we ain't tryin' to hear that shit, nigga,"
Mal said to him. "If the shoe were on the other
foot you'd be blessin' us." I knew Mal had said
that so Shareef wouldn't have to depend on Ice
and set himself up for an upset.

"Whatever Ice hits you with that's cool, but
we're your family and family sticks together, so
take this paper before we change our minds," I
told him as we all started digging in our pockets.
I had about three Gs on me and I peeled off the
first fifteen hundred-dollar bills that I had in
my knot. Mal gave him a G. Together Ant and
Trevor gave him $1,700.

"Look at you niggas, actin' like you Scarfaces
out this muthafucka," Shareef said smiling.

We all laughed. "That ain't nothing, yo,"
Trevor said. "That's just something to put in ya
pocket. Me and Ant gonna take you shoppin'
tomorrow 'cause that shit you got in your closet
ain't fittin' you no more, and we can't have our
mans walkin' around with tight shirts and high
waters on."

Shareef laughed.

"Yo, you decided what you wanna do now that you home, like go back to school and shit?" I asked him.

"Nah, I ain't going back to school. I got my GED while I was in there, so that's good enough. Bottom line is I'm tryin' to get money and move up out these projects like I was tryin' to do before wit' my family. I ain't do no eighteen months to come home and get a nine to five. That li'l bid just turned me into a smarter criminal. Like Michael Jackson said, a smooth criminal, know what I'm sayin'?"

"Yeah, we hear you, and we're here for you whenever you ready to get back in the game. We got you, so don't sweat that," Trevor announced. "You ain't gotta be clockin' for no muthafuckin' Clyde, 'cause you wasn't clockin' for him when you left. We got ya back. These our projects now on the low and it's more paper out here than when you was out here before. They call these shits the Crack Capital of the city, kid, and that's because of us," Mal told him.

"Yeah, no doubt," Shareef said. "I know y'all got me but I'm gonna get at Ice and see what he talking about."

"Yo, kid, Ice fucked up in the game right about now," Trevor blurted out. I guessed he couldn't hold it any longer. "We didn't wanna get all into that because we know that the two of you was a team, but shit ain't the same no more, fam. Look how long he been out, and he still pumpin' for Clyde. Mil and Mal hit him with work a few times because he fucked Clyde shit up. The boy still on foot; he ain't even got a hooptie. Come on, Reef, we know that's ya mans, but he ain't been able to maintain since you two took that hit. I ain't telling you all this to shit on him. I'm telling you 'cause you my dawg and I love you, and I don't want to see you get caught up in that like that."

Shareef just listened, and then spoke when Trevor was done. "Yo, I know where you comin' from and I appreciate all of that, but when I was struggling that nigga took me under his wing and schooled me, so I'd be a fucked-up nigga if I didn't see what I could do to help him, dig where I'm comin' from? Mil, you and Mal out of all people should know what I'm talking about. If it was Mu who was fucked, would you shit on him?" he asked us.

"Come on, yo, you know the answer to that already, and nobody telling you to shit on kid; we just telling you not to think that niggas are still the same, that's all," I replied.

"I know, and I love you niggas for that. It's good to be home. It's good to be back with my dawgs."

***

It only took Shareef five months to turn it back up on the block. It was as though he had never left. He copped himself a Nissan Pathfinder and a bike for when the summer came around; and he told us that by the New Year he'd have his moms and li'l sister up out of the projects.

He tried to bring Ice back, but he was unsuccessful. Ice had messed up so much of Clyde's money that he struck him for one big package and bounced somewhere, and nobody had seen him since. Mal got his license and I had it duplicated with my picture but his name on it because I couldn't apply for mine until next year. I needed the proper credentials so I could travel legit with my gun. Lately, it had become apart of my dress attire. Even though I didn't have any problems with anyone or didn't think I'd have to use it any time soon, there was just something about having it in my possession. It gave me a new sense of power and control, like when I had first gotten in the game and made my first sale. I think just knowing that the six metal bullets in the clip and the one in the chamber gave me the ability to play God, and gave me a rush.

I got rid of my Audi and Kamal crashed and totaled his coming from the Echo Lanes bowling alley. He cried like a baby that day because he loved that car. We both copped Honda Accords and hooked them up just as we did the Audis, only better. Mal painted his pearl green and white, and piped it out the same color; mine was white with a blue top, piped out the same. I threw Autoform rims on my piece and he went with deep-dish Hammers. Our music was ridiculous. We both had four tens in the window, with two twelves and the fifteens in the seat. We had an amp to push the joints in the window and the ones in the seat. We had a Zeus for the tens and a Kenwood 1020 for the twelve and fifteens. Instead of one EQ, we went with two Blaupunkts this time. What made them so loud was the fact that the seats in the Hondas dropped in the back, so when we pumped out our shits it sounded like a disco when we came through.

A couple of months later Mal brought a Jeep Wrangler, painted it the same as his Accord, dropped it, and threw some low profiles and rims on it. I didn't get a Jeep, though. I copped a bike instead, a CBR600. The game had been good to us, but like they say, "all good things must come to an end." But you never knew when.

Chapter Fifty-two

1991: my junior year, and one more year to go before I graduated. Mal and I had been talking about getting out of the game and paying our way through college. Mal wanted to go somewhere local like Rutgers or Seton Hall, but I wanted to go away to somewhere like Virginia Union in Richmond or Hampton U, to get away from everything. Plus I'd be able to cool out with Mustafa because that's where he spent most of his time now that he had his businesses operating down there.

He had opened up a beauty salon and barbershop with his son's mom and a Laundromat identical to the one he had opened in Plainfield. He popped in and out of town to come check us and to collect his dough from the little niggas he still had pumping for him out here, but it still wasn't the same as when he was there and I could kick it to him whenever I wanted to. He had been trying to get Mal and me to come down for the longest to cool out, but we had been try-ing to put mad work in and stack so much paper that we hadn't had time for any type of vacation; but we planned to slow down once summer hit.

As usual, the block was jumping. I noticed lines of drug buyers and heavy traffic flow when Mal and I came out. We were in search of Ant and Trevor. Me and Mal and 'em were supposed to go out to the Bronx to meet up with four chicks we had met while we were shopping on Delancey Street last week.

"Yo, Shareef, you seen Ant and Trevor today?" I asked.

"Nah, I ain't seen them niggas since last night."

"Their cars are parked in the back so they gotta be around somewhere," Mal said.

"They probably over at some chick's crib in one of these buildings. You know they be tryin' to fuck every shorty with a fat butt around here," I said.

"You went to their crib?" Shareef said.

"Last night we did, but we didn't get no answer," I said. "And their cars were still parked in the back."

"Yo, let's go over there and check the crib again, 'cause they told me that they'd be out in the a.m.," Shareef told us.

"Yo, Ant! Trevor! Wake the fuck up, niggas," Shareef yelled, banging on the door, but there was no answer.

Something told me to try the doorknob and when I did, it was open. As we walked in, a foul stench smacked us dead in the face.

"What the . . . ? What's that smell?" I asked.

"It smells like shit," Shareef said.

Mal covered his face and made his way to the back. The smell was unbearable and I felt like I was about to vomit. The smell was coming from the back room.

"Aw, man! No!" we heard Mal yell.

When we turned around in the direction Kamal was facing, where the odor was coming from, we saw what made him react the way he had. Between the smell and the sight, I couldn't hold my breakfast down any longer. I sprayed the floor with vomit like in *The Exorcist*.

"Aah, shit!" Shareef cried. "Nah! Not my muthafuckin' boys."

"What the fuck happened? How this shit happen?" Mal asked.

We were all in tears but they were tears of anger. Even now, that day haunts me and is the cause of some of my many sleepless nights, and why I wake from my sleep in cold sweats.

Sitting there, tied and gagged, facing backward, were Ant and Trevor, with what we knew were bullet holes in the back of their heads. Somebody had killed our friends execution style.

"I can't believe this shit." Shareef punched a hole in the wall.

"Who could've done this shit?" Mal wanted to know.

"We can't worry about that right now," I said. "We gotta make sure it's clean for when Five-O gets here."

"You right," Shareef said. "You two search the house; I'll take care of this."

Nothing out of the ordinary had been touched in the kitchen or the living room, but when we got to the back the rooms were destroyed. On the bed lay an open safe. Right then and there we knew Trevor and Ant had been robbed and killed for whatever was in there. We knew they didn't keep their guns and drugs in the safe with their dough, so we kept searching.

Not too long after, we found a brown paper bag with a plastic bag inside of it full of clips, along with two Tech 9s, a Mac 10, two regular nines, and a pump. We gathered up everything wrapped it up in a blanket, and took it with us. When we came out of the room, Shareef told us that he reported everything to 911, so we left before they sent the police.

Within the next twenty minutes, the projects were flooded with cops and medics. All we could do was stand there and watch while they took our boys out in body bags. Nobody besides us knew what happened, or who was in the bags. We knew who was in the bags, but not what actually happened; but we were determined to find out.

The next day everybody had heard of Ant's and Trevor's murders, either from the newspapers or gossip. It had spread all over town. The police made a statement saying that the incident was drug related, possibly a robbery gone bad, but there were no leads as of yet.

Meanwhile, we were doing our own investigation around the way. We questioned chicks Ant and Trevor messed with, which was damn near the whole projects, we asked niggas when was the last they seen them, either together or separate, and we even got at the fiends and patients who were usually out there all night whether they seen or heard anything. We told everybody on the low that if they came up with something solid we would take care of them for their help. It was easier to solve a crime on the streets if you were from the streets than if you were the police, because things had a way of getting out in the hood. Some stupid muthafucka always slipped up and started running his mouth at the wrong time, in the wrong place, around the wrong people, and that's what we were waiting for.

Ms. Smalls was hysterical when she found out what happened, but Trevor's mom couldn't be located. This was the second child Ms. Smalls had lost to the streets by the gun, and she looked as if she were going to die right then and there herself. We tried to console her, but the pain was just too much for her to bear, as she cried out torturously.

"Why? Why, Lord? Why both my babies? Why'd you have to take both of them?" she kept saying.

I found myself in the same position from five years ago when Ms. Smalls cried in my arms over Terrance's death. I couldn't possibly imagine or begin to know what she was feeling right then. That was between her and God.

As I held her I saw a familiar face in my presence, and she too had tears in her eyes. It was my mother. Mal stood there just staring at her, not saying a word. I turned Ms. Smalls over to Shareef and approached my moms.

"Ma, what's wrong?" I asked her.

She reached for both Mal and me. She just stepped in, flung her arms around us, and began to cry out loud. This was the first time in almost three years we had been this close to our moms since she had put us out, let alone felt her hugs. Almost simultaneously, Mal and I began to shed tears with our mother.

"I heard about little Anthony and little Trevor," my mother began saying, while wiping her face. "I don't want to go through that with you two. I feel responsible for you being out here already because if I hadn't put you out, you wouldn't have had to grow up so fast in the streets. Maybe you would've stopped selling that junk back then, but now it's too late because too much time has passed and the both of you are in too deep out here. Look at you, you don't even look the same anymore," she pointed out. "You have that same look your father had when he was your age. You look like grown men who have lived hard lives, but you're still kids acting grown.

"I haven't had a peaceful night's rest since that day. How can I sleep knowing that my children are out there in the streets, being subjected to what goes on out here? Every time I hear gunshots, my heart jumps and I get on my knees and pray to God that none of them bullets have neither one of your names on it. I don't want to get a phone call telling me to come identify your bodies, and go through what Philyss and Joan have to right now. I don't want to lose you and I don't want you ending up like your father. Please listen to what I'm saying, and learn from your friend's tragedy, because it can happen to either one of you too."

We both hugged our moms again.

"Ma, ain't nothing gonna happened to us," I said. "We smarter than that."

"Ma, stop cryin'. We all right," Mal said. "We ain't gonna put you through nothing like this, ever!"

We tried to reassure her. That day was a memorable one as well as the turning point of our lives. That day we had lost two loved ones but had regained a connection with someone we loved and longed for.

Chapter Fifty-three

Two months had gone by and still we weren't any closer to the truth, and neither were the cops. We had sold all of the work we had found that day up in Ant and Trevor's crib and split the money between both of their moms. Trevor's mom had taken the news just as hard as Ant's mom when she found out. There wasn't enough dough in the world to take the place of their sons and our friends. They were missed dearly.

Their wakes were unforgettable. That was the first time I had ever seen so many hustlers from different hoods in the same area all at one time. Everybody came out to pay their respects and at least one brother from every block came up to us and told us how they had their ears to the ground, and if they found out anything they'd slip it to us. Even brothers we had once gone to war against and really didn't like came through. It was funny how tragedies and celebrations brought our people together, but outside of that there was total chaos and confusion among us in the street. They say that something good always comes out of something bad, but I couldn't see it that way right then. The only thing that really did happen that was a good thing was the fact that what happened to Ant and Trevor brought Mal and me back closer to our family.

It was New Year's, going into 1992, and we were going to be stepping out to Times Square to see the ball drop. Mal was taking his girl so I wanted Lisa to go but her parents still had a tight hold on her. She told me how her mother tried to threaten her to stop dealing with me, but it only pushed her closer to me. Lately we had been touching lightly on the subject of sex because she was a little shy and uncomfortable since she was still a virgin. I never pressed the issue or applied any pressure. I was cool with how things were going with Ke Ke, so I wasn't too bothered.

I had called and invited Ke Ke to New York but she had a boyfriend now so she was ringing it in with him. We had a funny relationship. We could mess with anybody we wanted as long as we made time for the other. Mal had changed since he found a girlfriend. She was cool, but because of her, we chilled together less. I felt like he was putting her before me some times, something I had never done, even when I was dealing with Trina. But I understood that's how it went when you were in a serious relationship. I guessed that's why I was single, because I didn't want anything to come in between me and the streets.

While I was sitting in my car in deep thought waiting for it to warm up, somebody tapped on my window and scared the hell out of me. Luckily my gun was under my seat and not in my lap because out of reflex that would have been a dead ass. When I looked, it was Baseball Betty. We called her that because her hands were so big from shooting dope that they looked like baseball catchers' gloves.

"Mil, roll down the window." She gestured with one of her mittens.

"What, Betty?" I asked, irritated by her presence. "What's up?"

"I'm not tryin' to buy nothin'," she said. "I have to talk to you. Let me get in." She looked around nervously as she wiped her running nose. She had on a filthy tee with a filthy jacket to match. I could smell her through the cold. She smelled as if she hadn't bathed in months.

"Are you crazy?" I asked. There was no way she was getting in my ride.

She looked around again before she spoke. "It's about your boys."

My heart skipped a beat. "Get in." I unlocked my doors.

I flicked my high beams at Mal like a maniac, who was sitting in his Jeep. He got out and started walking back toward me and Betty.

"Yo, what up?" he asked, approaching the car. When he leaned in he saw Betty. "What the fuck she doin' in there? You couldn't find no better date than that, kid?" He laughed at his own joke. When he saw that I wasn't laughing with him he knew something was up. "What's goin' on, bro?"

"Yo, Betty knows something about Ant and Trevor."

"Oh, shit!" He climbed into the back of my whip.

"Pull off, Mil. I don't want nobody seeing me in here with y'all, especially them niggas." We didn't know what niggas she was referring to, but we were more than eager to find out. I pulled up into the park and killed my lights.

"So, what you know about Ant and Trevor?" I asked Betty.

"Hold up! I ain't sayin' nothin' until I know how much you gonna hit me off wit' for what I'm about to tell you," she said all tough.

In a blink of an eye I had my 9 mm in my hand pointing it right to her head. "Bitch! Ain't nobody got time to be playin' no muthafuckin' games. Now either you run ya mouth or I'ma be cleanin' ya blood outta my shit tonight," I told her.

"Mil, chill, kid. Betty tryin' to help us out; she just wanna know what she getting for helping us, right, Betty?"

"Yeah, that's all. I'm gonna tell y'all what I know. I just want mine 'cause I could get killed for this shit if them li'l crazy niggas find out it was me who told y'all."

"Betty, listen, if what you feel you about to tell us makes sense and had any truth to it, then we gonna take care of you on the lookout tip and make sure don't nobody fuck wit' you," Mal told her. "We just makin' sure you ain't bullshittin' us cause you wanna get high."

"Nah! I ain't bullshittin' y'all. See, I got some shit already," she said, showing us a couple bags of dope and a few crack vials.

Mal went into his pocket and pulled out his knot. I saw Betty's eyes light up. "Look, I'll give you three hundred dollars in cash and three hundred dollars in product when we get back to the projects. Now tell us what you know," he said, handing her the three hundred-dollar bills.

"Make it four hundred dollars in cash and four hundred dollars in product," she said.

I cocked my burner. "Betty, this ain't *Let's Make a Deal* and we ain't Monty Hall, so what you gonna do? You gonna take door number one or door number two?" I said, putting the steel against her head so she could feel that shit was real.

"Mal, tell him to get this gun out of my face." Despite the threats, she was not afraid. She spoke calmly.

"Mil, come on, man, cool out."

I hesitated for a minute and then put my gun in my lap.

"I'll take door number one, as you put it," she said sarcastically. "Mal, your li'l brother is crazy," she added.

Mal ignored her remark. "Betty, what do you know?"

We sat there as she began talking. "You know my daughter Belinda? Well, she messin' with this boy, well, at least I think so, 'cause he always comin' around getting high with her, shootin' up and smoking weed, and she ain't got no job so I know he supplying her. At first I thought he was a drug dealer and just used on the side 'cause one day I came home and seen him counting lots of money about two months ago. He noticed that I saw him and he gave me a hundred dollars and told me to keep my mouth shut, which was kind of strange 'cause who would I tell? But I still didn't think nothing of it."

She paused, sniffled, and wiped her nose. "Not until tonight did it dawn on me that he could've had something to do with your friend's death. Tonight when I came in, him and my daughter were in the living room. They didn't hear me when I came in 'cause they was too high. Belinda was lying across his lap nodded out, while he was stroking her hair talking to her. I couldn't really hear what he was sayin', but just out of being nosey I got close enough so I could really hear him. He was sayin' something to her about not being worried 'cause after him and his boy do another job like before, he was gonna take her away with him. Then I heard him say this time he ain't gonna let his man shit on him again like he did last time, and only give him thirty Gs while he kept sixty, especially when he did most of the work. I knew that them boys was getting a lot of money around here so I figured he had to be talking about them. I wouldn't have thought that they was holding like that though if I didn't hear it wit' my own ears. I know a lot of people who would kill for less," she finished saying. We knew that they were holding like that because we had twice as much.

"Betty, what's the kid's name who mess with your daughter?" I asked her.

"Let me think. She calls him something like Ka or Qua, something like that."

"Qua!" It instantly came to us as soon as she said the name, and it all made sense to us now. It was Quadir, the same Quadir we grew up with, who moved up out of the projects about five or six months after his moms met some man with a little bit of money back in the day.

The last we heard he was getting high, but we didn't know for sure because we never saw him, and he never came around our way to cop anything if he was. I began to get a headache just thinking about the fact that some niggas we came up with did this shit and not some strangers. All types of thoughts were racing through my head, and I knew that the same thoughts were going through Kamal's mind, but we couldn't let Betty know what we were thinking or how we were feeling right now.

"Did he ever mention his boy's name?" I asked.

"No," she answered.

"All right, Betty, we gonna look into it," Mal said, as calmly as he could.

I kept my composure as best I could too, but on the inside I was on fire.

"He didn't say who his boy was, but I saw them together once and I recognized him," Betty said out of nowhere.

"Who was it?" Mal asked.

"It was one of them boys y'all used to run around here with when y'all was kids." Mal and I looked at each other. Before we could figure it out she answered for us. "It was Black!" she spat.

"Muthafucka!" Mal exclaimed.

"Bitch-ass nigga!" I followed up with. "Yeah, Betty, we appreciate that," I told her as I started the car. "And pardon me for treatin' you like that before." I was thankful for the information and felt bad that I had treated her the way I had. I went into my pocket and gave her the extra hundred dollars that she wanted earlier because it was well deserved, and then some.

After we gave Betty the clips, we paged Shareef. As far as we were concerned our New Year's had been cancelled. We didn't have partying on our minds, only revenge. Either Shareef didn't have his beeper with him or he just wasn't answering, because we called him over twenty times, and even put in our code, 505, to let him know that it was important. Mal and I stayed up drinking all night, both deep in our own thoughts.

Chapter Fifty-four

"Hello?"

"Yo, what up?" I heard Shareef's voice on the phone saying.

"Where you at?"

"I'm at the Loop."

"You didn't get our beeps? We been trying to get at you all last night."

"I heard my shit goin' off, but I was in some guts and shit was too good to be comin' up out of. I was tryin' to cum in it," he said, laughing at himself. "I seen the five-oh-five this morning though. What's going on?"

"We found out who's behind the shit that went down wit' Ant and Trevor."

"Oh, shit, yo! My bad, kid, that's my bad for not answerin' my shit last night. Who the fuck was it? Anybody we know?" he asked, upset.

"Yo, we'll talk when you get here."

"I'm on my way. Trina, get dressed," I heard him say as he was hanging up the phone.

I just laughed.

***

"Them crab-ass muthafuckas," Shareef barked when we relayed to him what was told to us by Betty. "Yo, I'm gonna murda them niggas. Nah, fuck that, I'm gonna torture them niggas' punk asses when I catch them. I should've known it was somebody we knew, 'cause Ant and Trevor don't be slippin like that, 'cause they always got heat on 'em. Damn, we broke bread together wit' these niggas, and slept under the same roof."

"We know, kid," I said. "We just as mad as you about this shit and we ready to hunt these niggas down."

"Yeah, but we gotta do this shit right, 'cause that bitch Betty can tie us into shit if it comes out something happened to these chumps. The way she sold them out is the same way she'll sell us out, so we gotta be smart about this," Mal said.

The way I was feeling right then and there, I was capable of doing anything. But I couldn't believe that we were plotting to commit murder, especially of somebody we were once friends with; but like Mu told me a long time ago, when you in the game some friends become foes, so what we were planning had to be done because that was one of the rules of the game: an eye for an eye.

What we came up with sounded like it would work. It was just a matter of following through with it. Finding Quadir and snatching him up would be easy, but Black was a different story, because he'd been sticking up niggas left and right for so long now that he had eyes in the back of his head, and he kept at least two burners on him at all times, so timing had to be everything when it came to him.

A few days had gone by before we finally saw Qua. At first we didn't recognize him because he had gotten a lot taller and much skinner since the last time we had seen him. He used to be the biggest out of all of us when we were growing up, but now it was obvious that the drugs and the streets had taken a toll on him, because his jaws were sunken in; you could see his jawbone line. We knew he was high now because his eyes were all wide and he kept looking around like he was paranoid, as he stepped out of Betty's crib. Had he been sober he might have spotted us sitting across the street in the old Buick, but it was to our advantage that he wasn't. Not that it would've mattered anyway because either way we weren't going to let him get away, even if it meant gunning him down right then and there. We wanted to get him while he was still on Sycamore Avenue, before he hit Front Street, to avoid anyone seeing something.

"Yo, you ready?" Shareef asked us.

"We ready," Mal answered.

"Well, let's get this nigga then."

We all pulled our masks down and jumped out.

"Yo, Qua!" Shareef yelled.

Quadir stopped in his tracks and turned around. Shareef caught him right in the mouth with the butt of his nine and knocked him out. He never knew what hit him. I leaned over him, put a rag in his mouth, and then blindfolded him. His face was bleeding; Shareef had split him open from the blow. Mal secured his hands behind his back with duct tape while Shareef did his legs.

After that, Shareef snatched him up and threw him over his shoulder. Mal went to go pop the trunk and I ran to start the car. *One down, one to go.*

"Yo, what the fuck is this?" Qua said, regaining consciousness, seeing that he had been taped and tied to a chair the same way he and Black had done to Ant and Trevor. I took the rag out of his mouth and the blindfold from off his eyes once we got him to the abandoned building.

"Shut the fuck up!" Shareef said, throwing gasoline in his face.

"Aah!" Qua yelled. The gas stung the open gash he had on his mouth and lip. "Yo, what I do?" he asked.

"Nigga, you know what the fuck you did," Mal shouted, spitting on him.

"Nah, word up. I don't. I don't even know who you niggas are."

Qua must've done so much stuff to niggas that he couldn't think of who could be holding him like this, but we wanted him to know.

"Muthafucka, you know us," I said as I pulled my mask off. By the look on his face I knew that he knew why he was there now, but the nigga still tried the best he could to play it off like he didn't.

"Mil, what's up? What the hell is this shit?" he nervously asked.

I walked over to him and smacked fire out of him. "Qua, come on, man, don't play on my intelligence. You know why you're here," I said, as Mal and Shareef pulled their mask off too.

"Man! Mil, I swear to God I don't know what the fuck is goin' on or what you talking about, kid," Qua said in an almost convincing manner. If he were a nominee for an Oscar that night, he would have won an award for best actor, but this wasn't the Oscars; this was the streets, and we weren't trying to hear that shit. I smacked him with an open right hook.

We knew that he was lying to try to score some points and protect himself, because Betty had already told us about how he was talking about his and Black's next job. He probably was talking about us.

"What he did to them I didn't agree with, and I tried to stop him before he did it, but he threatened to kill me. I'm telling you, the nigga is crazy. He even crossed me up on the dough they had up in there, givin' me only thirty Gs and keepin' sixty."

Just hearing him talk about it made me want to blow his muthafuckin' brains out the back of his head, but we needed him alive for now, until we found Black.

"Where's Black staying at?" I asked him.

"I don't know."

Shareef flicked his lighter and put it to Qua's face. "What the fuck you mean you don't know? That's your partner in crime, nigga."

"I'm telling the truth," Qua said, trying to move his head away from Shareef's lighter. "I usually beep him and he calls me back; then he meets me wherever I tell him to pick me up at."

Mal pulled out his cell phone. "What's his pager number?"

Qua gave him the number "555-9276. It's a 201 area code."

"Is there any type of code you put in to let him know it's you?"

"We still use the old code we had when we were kids: five-oh-five."

I wanted to snap his neck when he said that. "Nigga, you better hope you telling the truth, 'cause if this some funny shit, you gonna be in the dirt."

He must've thought we were going to let him live, like he had some chance in hell of making it up out of this in one piece. Little did he know that today was the day he would be taking his last breath.

"When this nigga call back, you better be real convincing to make him meet you somewhere," Shareef said. "Tell him to pick you up on South Second, across from the Motor Vehicle, just before Rockland Avenue. Tell him to blow the horn when he gets there and you'll come right out."

"What he drivin'?" I asked.

"A gold Legend, the old body style, four door."

We discussed our plan while waiting for Black to call back, to make sure we were all clear on how it was going to go down once he called back. It only took five minutes before Mal's phone rang.

"Yo, what up? Where you at?" we heard Black asked, while Mal held the phone up to Qua's ear.

Qua spat everything verbatim like we had told him to, and Black said he'd be there in about twenty minutes, which was more than enough time for us to get situated. He had brought it and it was about to go down.

"What about me? I did my part," Qua said.

"Go to sleep," Shareef said back, punching him in the jaw, knocking him out again.

We saw the Acura pull up, just the way Qua described it. Black blew the horn and then waited. I snuck up on the passenger's side and smashed the front door window with the biggest rock that I could find. I saw Black look in my the direction as he reached for his guns, not seeing Shareef come up on his driver's side and put the nine to his dome.

"Put ya muthafuckin' hands on the steerin' wheel, nigga."

By then I had opened the door and grabbed the .357 that he had reached for lying on the seat. I knew he always kept at least two guns on him, so I patted his waist to make sure he didn't have another one and there wouldn't be any surprises along the way; and sure enough he had a .38 tucked in his belt. I snatched it out and took it, as I got in and closed the passenger's door.

"Move over, nigga," Shareef said, disguising his voice while opening the driver's door.

"You niggas trying to rob me? I'm in the same game as you. We ain't got to go through all of this. I'll give you the dough I got in my pocket," he said, calm, cool, and collected.

"Nigga, shut the fuck up. It ain't ya money we want, it's ya muthafuckin' life," I told him, pointing my burner with the silencer at his eye.

He laughed. "What, you tryin' to sound hard or somethin'? 'Cause you ain't scarin' me. It sound like you tryin' to disguise your voice, so I must know you niggas up under them masks."

"Didn't I tell you to shut the fuck up?" I said, smacking him in the eye with the barrel.

"Aah, shit!" he yelled, grabbing his eye.

"Nigga, put ya fuckin' hand down," I said, poking him in the side with the .357 I took off of him.

"You niggas better kill me, 'cause if I make it out of this you're dead."

"You won't," Shareef told him. "Come on, nigga; get the fuck out the car."

We all had our joints ready to gun Black's ass down if he tried to get on some superhero shit, but he just walked in the building peacefully. It wasn't until he saw Quadir sitting there tied up that he began to act up.

"You bitch-ass nigga!" he shouted at Qua. "I knew you was a weak link. I should've smoked ya punk ass like I started to."

I caught him in the back of the head. "Sit the fuck down."

He started to laugh again, as he sat in the chair next to Qua.

"Put your hands behind your back, nigga," Mal said.

He started putting his hands behind his back as Mal walked behind him; then all of a sudden he grabbed for Mal's mask. Just as it came off, I pulled the trigger.

"Aah! You muthafucka, you shot me," Black screamed, holding his right shoulder with his left hand with Kamal's mask in it.

Black took a look to the side and saw who had been wearing the mask, and began to laugh out loud. "I had a feelin' it was you niggas 'cause it would take a bunch of stupid muthafuckas to try to pull this off."

Shareef and I took off our masks off. "Nah, nigga, you the stupid one for thinking you was gonna get away wit' that punk shit you did," Shareef said to him.

"Muthafucka, gimme ya hands," Mal yelled, snatching both of Black's arms behind the back of the chair.

"Take it easy, killa, you see ya scary-ass brother shot me in the arm."

"You lucky I ain't shoot ya ass in the mouth for all the tough shit you talking."

"You niggas is a bunch of jokers and, Qua, you a coward. You ain't got no backbone, nigga. How you gonna let these three chumps creep you?"

"The same way you did, bitch!" Shareef said.

"Nah, if this nigga ain't set me up you niggas wouldn't have never got this close to me without getting bodied, 'cause you niggas ain't no killas. You probably didn't even figure this shit out on ya own as slow as you niggas is. Somebody had to tip you off that knew this dopefiend-ass nigga."

"Fuck all the talking. We ain't bring you here for no fuckin' family reunion," I said, getting heated because he thought he was so smart, like he had it all figured out.

The whole time Qua remained quiet, still thinking that he may have a chance up out of this and get cut loose, especially with Black running his mouth like he was, taking all the weight for everything.

Mal finished taping Black to the chair and came over by us.

"So now what? You gonna shoot us like we shot them two screamin'-ass niggas."

"Yo, Black, how'd it get to this, man?" Mal asked. "Them was ya boys, ya family, and you just took their lives without any remorse."

"Nigga, save the speeches for when you become president. What happened was all a part of the game. You gotta get yours by any means. They had it and I needed it, so I had to get it, cut and dried."

Shareef ran over to him and started pouring gasoline all over his body. "Well, now you all wet, muthafucka, and this is all a part of the game too, just like your soul. You gonna burn in hell tonight, nigga."

Black must've thought he was going to get a quick and easy death, because when Shareef said what he said about burning, his whole facial expression changed. "Oh, that's how it's going down?" Black said.

We all just looked at him as Shareef flicked his lighter. "Yeah, that's how it's going down, chump."

Whoosh! The fire took to the gas instantly. You could hear Black's cries all over the city, as the flames went ablaze. I tried to stand there and watch, but as his skin began to melt, I had to turn away before I vomited. The look on Qua's face was indescribable, as Shareef walked over to him.

"Please, Shareef, don't do me like that, baby boy. I'm sorry. I didn't mean it," he cried.

"Confess ya sins in hell, nigga!"

Whoosh!

The flames caught just as quick as Black did. We left them there to burn, and now our dawgs could rest in peace.

Chapter Fifty-five

I woke up in a cold sweat from the nightmares that had been haunting me for the past few months. They were the same ones every night. Pictures of Black and Quadir burning, standing in my room door. Images of Ant and Trevor slumped over in the chairs, gunshots going off. I hadn't had a good night sleep since then.

"Mal, let's bounce to VA and cool out down there for a little bit," I suggested.

"Man, we can't just breeze like that right now. Too much stuff going on and we been spending a lot of paper lately anyway. Between that loss we took on that last brick and me copping another whip, that's over forty Gs we put out just this last month alone, not including the fifteen you lost down in Atlantic City and the miscellaneous Gs we've been spendin' just partyin' and shit without doin' any hustlin'. We been takin' out but ain't been puttin' back in for the last three months or so."

"Mal, you actin' like we ain't got paper or somethin'."

"That's not the point; the point is we hustlin' backward. We ain't got nobody on the block right now. You be with Lisa most of the time and I be with Keya, and you know we be spending when we with them. We both been on some lazy shit and we gots to tighten up."

I felt where Mal was coming from, because we had been spending excessively lately. Honestly, I was getting tired of all of it, the partying, the hustling, the chicks, just everything and it was beginning to take a toll on me. I didn't have the same energy in me that I had three years ago. Everything Mu warned me about the game was coming to pass.

"Yo, I know what you sayin' and I agree, but it ain't nothin' to go out there and hit 'em hard for the next couple of months. Let's go out there and hug the block until summer hit, and then take a trip to check Mu out. You know next week is my born day. Lisa wants to go to New York to some Broadway show and out to eat. After that, we can rock out until school lets out, because I really wanted to go away for graduation, like Cancun or somewhere. Speaking of New York, who turn is it to pick up, mine or yours?"

"Nigga, you know it's on you. I went last week."

"Oh, yeah, all right. I'll go after my birthday. By then we should be done with everything we got left."

"Bet."

Chapter Fifty-six

This was my first time going to a show on Broadway, or any play for that matter, but it was all right. Lisa told me her parents took her to shows all the time. I had seen the commercial for the musical *Cats* a million times on television and I thought that it would be fly to check it out, but I never actually thought that I would get to see it.

Lisa made the reservations at Tavern on the Green in Central Park for us to eat at, which was cool because they had decent food. I had been there a few times before. Lisa was looking exceptionally good tonight with her Toni Braxton hairstyle, a turtleneck sweater, a long denim skirt, and some high leather boots. Although you could tell that she had matured over the years, she still looked like she did when we were in the sixth grade. After dinner we took a carriage ride through the park. Now that shit was really nice. That's one of the things I liked about Lisa. She always turned me on to new things, just like things that I might've overlooked or neglected.

"Thank you for a nice birthday evening."

"You don't have to thank me, Kamil. You're welcome anyway, but it's not over yet."

"What you mean it ain't over yet? It's past twelve a.m. already, so technically I'm eighteen and one day old now," I said, smiling.

"Shut up, boy. I'm not talking about that. I'm talking about we're not done celebrating your birthday," she said.

Something in my heart and in my mind gave me an idea what she was about to say.

"My parents went away for the weekend and I want to be with you."

I didn't know what to say.

"Did you hear me, Kamil?"

"Yeah, I heard you, but are you sure?"

"What do you mean am I sure? I've never been more sure of anything in my life."

"Wow, that's deep."

"That's how you make me feel. I can't describe it, but I know how I feel about you."

Again I didn't know what to say. Our carriage ride ended and we were on our way back to Jersey. The whole ride back home Lisa slept. I thought the Long Island Iced Tea she had put her out because she wasn't a drinker. She only drank it because it was my birthday and she wanted to toast with a real drink.

So many thoughts were going through my mind as I drove. This was a long time coming and I wanted it to be as perfect as it could be.

"Lisa, wake up, we're at your house."

"Huh? Oh, okay. Sorry for going to sleep on you, but that drink had me feeling a li'l funny."

"That's all right, long as I made it home without dozing off and killin' us." We went inside. "Where's the light switch at?" I asked.

"What for? We're not staying down here anyway, we going upstairs; just give me your hand."

She flicked the TV on with her remote and her room lit up. This was my first time ever being in her room. It was nice and neat, and very feminine. She had stuffed animals all around with posters and pictures on the walls. When I looked on her mirror she had the picture that we took in eighth grade at graduation; and there were a few club flicks that I had taken throughout the years and had forgotten about that I had either given to her or she stole from me.

"Damn! You still got this graduation picture?"

"Yeah! I love that picture."

"Nah, I look crazy, and you looking cheesy."

"Ha! Ha! Ha! Very funny." She pulled the sweater over her head and began to unzip her skirt. "I'm going to take a shower. I'll be back."

Her body looked firm from the back, with her milk chocolate complexion. I smiled as she walked off, covering herself. "Don't be looking at my butt, either."

I hit the radio on as I turned the television down. She had it on WBLS but nothing was on. She really didn't have any tapes, either, besides Keith Sweat's first one, which was a classic, so I popped it in and hit rewind. I could hear the shower running from her room. Instead of pushing play on the tape player, I stripped down and went into the bathroom.

"Boy!" she said.

"What?"

"You scared me." She was standing there all soapy, covering her breasts.

"Let me see that rag," I said as I stepped in the tub. I began washing her body. Even through the washcloth her skin felt smooth. I lathered her up from head to toe and then she rinsed off. She took the rag from me and rinsed it out, then began washing me. I had never had a woman bathe me before, and it felt good.

After I rinsed, I pulled her closer to me, pressing her body against mine; then I started kissing her. I had one arm around her waist and the other between her thighs as I tried to put a finger inside of her. She flinched at the touch of my hand as her body refused to let my finger penetrate her. I removed my hand and cupped her left breast as I kissed, licked, and sucked the right one. She moaned, reaching down between my legs and grabbing hold of me. Between the water and the softness of her hand I felt like I was going to explode right then and there, but that wasn't how I wanted things to go.

"Let's dry off," I told her.

We stepped out and began to dry one another off. My heart was pounding and I was trying to calm down. I could feel hers through the towel, too.

I popped the tape on as soon we entered the room. "You may be young but you ready." Keith Sweat's voice filled the air.

Lisa was standing there with her towel on. I slid the towel from her body, and let mine fall to the floor, while kissing her on the forehead, nose, and on both of her cheeks. Then I began sucking on her ear.

"Ooh, Kamil," she said as I blew into her ear gently with my warm breath, and then inhaled so she could feel the cool air. Her body began to squirm each time my lips touched a part of her. I put my hand between her thighs again and pressed my finger inside of her. This time she felt moist and hot as my middle finger slid inside of her. "Um!" she cooed as she tensed up.

"I got you," I told her, slowly moving my finger in and out.

I started sucking on her breasts, her stomach, and her sides, and then I parted her legs and sucked her there, too. I couldn't hear what she was saying, but I think she was calling out my name. She dug her fingers into my hair and clamped on. I kept sucking and licking until I felt her legs begin to shake, and I knew she had an orgasm. I came back up and kissed her, and then I entered her.

"Ssss!" She arched her back, trying to ease the pain. The moistness between her legs made it a little more bearable. I widened her legs, and started stroking as lightly as I could, but it was no use because she was a virgin, so either way it was going to be painful, but pleasurable. With the exception of how wet she became, she was so tight that it felt like a suction cup gripped me. I tried speeding up my rhythm to loosen her up and I felt her reach another orgasm. I couldn't hold on any longer as I sped up my pace. Then as if on cue, we both climaxed together. I just lay there and I could feel her muscles squeezing me.

"Oh, my God!"

"What? You all right?"

"Yeah, but I just saw stars." She exhaled.

I didn't know what she was talking about. "What?" I asked.

"I seen stars just now when we were making love."

I started laughing. "You crazy. You ain't seen no stars."

"How you gonna tell me? I know what I saw."

I lay beside her. "You're right."

She started laughing too. "I never felt like that before." She slid up under me and laid her head on my chest, then looked up at me and said, "I love you."

I kissed her on her forehead and told her that I loved her too, only this time I really meant it. She fell asleep on me.

When I got in Mal was already up. "Damn, nigga, 'bout time you brought ya ass home. You must've had a good-ass birthday."

"Word! I did. What you do last night?" I asked him. "Probably had one of them stankin'-ass chicks up in here."

"Chill!" he said, whispering. "Keya in the back, nigga."

"Oh, my bad, yo," I said, laughing, "You talk all that shit though like you got it on lock."

"Fuck you, Mil. Yo, you ready? 'Cause I got this dough all counted out for you."

"Yeah, that's why I came here anyway. I'm going just like this dirty dick and all."

"Oh, word, it popped off with you and wifey?"

"Yo, that's my heart forever, kid. That shit wasn't like no other experience I ever had with a girl. That was definitely my first time making love, no frontin', know what I'm sayin'?"

"Yeah, I'm with you, bro. That's how I feel about Keya."

"Yo, how much we flippin'?"

"You know we ain't got nothin' and this the week we gonna be grindin' hard. We should be able to get a brick and a half with that. You got money on you to get the bottles and shit?"

"Yeah, I'm good."

"Here, take the Jeep 'cause that car is too flashy and it's too cold for the bike."

"All right, gimme a minute to use the bath-room."

I hit the alarm on the Jeep, got in, and threw the book bag with the dough in it on the passen-ger's side floor. "I should go snatch up one of the shorties from the projects to take this ride with me," I said to myself.

Just as I was about to put the key in the ignition I saw a big van behind me through the rearview mirror, and then I heard those unforgettable words: "Freeze! Don't move! Put your hands where I can see them!"

I knew who it was. I was trying to figure out which one they wanted me to do: freeze don't move, or put my hands where they could see them.

The Jeep door opened and when I looked I saw the black officer with his DEA hat on and badge around his neck. They had the Jeep surrounded.

"Step out of the truck slowly with your hands on top of your head."

I complied, as he spun me around telling me to put my hands on the Jeep while kicking my legs apart. I almost did a spilt.

"You got any weapons on you?" he asked me.

"No, I don't carry a weapon, Officer."

"Sure you don't, Mr. Benson," he said dryly. After frisking me he grabbed my hands and cuffed me behind my back all rough, and then put me to the ground on my stomach.

"What the hell is this?" I yelled.

"Be quiet," I heard one of the other officers say.

I thought they had raided our house, but when I looked over I saw Kamal at the window peeking out the curtain, so I was confused. One of the officers said, "He had a bag in his hand when he came out. It was a black book bag with the New York money."

"What am I under arrest for?" I asked.

"A lot of things," he said. "You'll find out when you get to the station."

"Whoa! Would you look at this!" the other officer said. "I wonder where you were going with all this."

"Shopping," I said.

"Yeah! I bet. For what?" he asked sarcastically.

I didn't say anything.

I had been charged with three secret indictments, which meant I had served an undercover cop at least three different times, or I served three different officers three times. On top of that, they were threatening to charge me with four murders: Ant's, Trevor's, Black's, and Qua's. I knew they were fishing and didn't have nothing, because if they did they wouldn't have ever brought Ant's and Trevor's names up to me, knowing that they were my boys. And if they knew something I wouldn't be the only one down at the station right now.

"Excuse me, can you tell me what my bail is so I can make a phone call?"

"As of now you have no bail," the female booking officer said. "They haven't sent down the additional charges yet."

"For what?"

"For the currency found in your possession."

"What?" I jumped up. "Man, they buggin' the fuck out."

"Sir, I'm going to have to ask you to have a seat in there."

I sat in the bullpen and waited.

"Mil, what up?" someone lying in the corner said.

"Who dat?" I turned around.

"It's me, Charlie." He was one of the customers who came around the way running a lot of sales.

"Oh, what up, Charlie?"

"Man, you think you can help me out? My bail is only a hundred dollars for an old warrant. You know I'm good for it. I'll come around the projects and work it off as soon as I get it."

He got me mad. "Nigga, what the fuck is you talking about? I don't be around no projects; don't be talking no stupid shit to me."

He looked confused, and then it must've dawned on him. "My bad, man. I thought you was somebody else."

"Yeah, no problem," I said.

"Mr. Benson. Kamil Benson."

"Yes?"

"Your family just called asking about your charges and your bail, and I explained to them what I told you. I was just told that you won't

be getting bail tonight, and that you'd be trans-
ported to the county jail."

"Oh, shit!" I laughed. They waited until I
turned eighteen before they came and arrested
me, so they could get more money up out of me.

The booking officer looked at me like she felt
sorry for me. I had never been locked up before.
The closest I ever came to the county jail was
riding past it, but now here it was I was actually
about to visit the inside of it. I wasn't scared or
anything because I probably knew more than
half the guys in there or they knew me; besides
that it wasn't no different from the streets, and I
held my own out there so I knew I could hold my
own in there.

When I got to county, I had to go through
the whole process and procedure thing all over
again with the million questions and all of that
'cause I had never been in before. They gave me
some more bullpen therapy and sent me up to
4B, the reception block. When they cracked the
cell, there was an old white man on the top bunk
and a black kid on the bottom.

"Where am I supposed to sleep?" I asked the
officer.

"There should be three mattresses."

I knew how niggas were, so I was prepared for
whatever.

The kid on the bottom was still lying in the bed when the cell locked, like he didn't hear anybody come in.

"Yo, my man!"

No answer.

"Yo, my man!" I yelled again, tapping him on the back.

"Yo, what?" he said, rolling over. When he turned over I recognized him and he recognized me too.

"Nigga, fuck you mean what?" I said.

"Yo, I ain't know who you was, Mil. What's happenin', baby?" he said, trying to clean it up. It was the kid Karim I had broke my knuckle on back in the day. Over the years he had fallen off and started getting high, sniffing dope. "I thought it was one of them Elizabeth or Newark heads tryin' to come up in here running shit."

I just kept grilling him.

"What you in here for, traffic warrant or something?" he asked.

"Nah."

"You got knocked around the projects?"

"Nah, yo. Don't feel like talking about that shit. When we come out."

He laughed. "Oh, shit, this must be ya first time in here. You just missed when we come out. That's it for the night. We in this muthafucka twenty three and a half hours a day. The other half is to shower or make a phone call. I know you getting bailed out tonight though, right?"

"I ain't got no bail."

"Damn! Fuck you got knocked wit', a ton? Or killed a couple niggas?"

"I'm here on some bullshit, that's all."

"Me too, kid. They tryin' to charge me wit' selling dummy bags. I told them niggas they was fake, but they talking about they sending shit to the lab. I've been sittin' here for two days waiting for that shit to come back. Yo, they probably give you bail tomorrow."

"Yeah, probably."

"Yo, I'll hit the floor, don't even worry about it," he told me, like he really had a choice, because I wasn't trying to sleep on that filthy-ass floor.

Between Karim vomiting from withdrawal and the old white man farting and snoring all night stinking up the spot and keeping me awake, I was ready to strangle these two bastards. I tossed and turned all night, and by the time I closed my eyes it was time for breakfast.

The shit they were serving didn't even look edible, so I gave my tray to Karim and lay back down. I heard somebody outside my cell asking, "Where Benson locked at?" and I got up to look out the door. It was my cousin on my father's side, Marlon. He had been in county for three years fighting a murder charge. You could see that he was living good in here because the nigga looked like the hulk with his wig corn rolled to the back. He was big as hell.

"Li'l cuz, what's goin' on?"

"What up, yo!"

"Somebody working downstairs last night told me you came in. I was fucked up. I called my shorty to get the word on what was going down out there and she told me they ran down on you. That shit is all over the streets she said, and that shit is in today's paper, too. Damn, kid, they caught you with about thirty grand on you plus three secret indictments. You niggas came up out there, huh?"

I hit him with half a smile.

"Yo, you know they can bring the feds in 'cause of that dough. It's over ten thousand U.S. currency," Marlon told me. "I don't think they will, though. I'm just letting you know. If they said you being held without bail, that's probably because of the money. You just turned eighteen, huh? They said they was squattin' on ya ass. You all right in there?"

"Yeah, I'm cool. Hungry as hell, though."

"Don't worry about that. I got you. I'ma send some cakes and shit down for you. If you ain't out in two days, I'ma see if my man can get you on the tier with me. I'm on the workers' tier, so you'll have to get a job. You need me to call anybody for you? 'Cause you don't come out until tonight."

"Yeah, call Mal for me and ask him what he found out."

"All right, what's the number?"

"555-7672." I gave it to him.

"I'll be back this afternoon; I'll let you know what he said."

"Good looking, yo."

"No doubt. Hold ya head, kid."

"Yeah."

"Ay yo, Malik, this my li'l cousin up in here. Look out for him," Marlon said as he was leaving.

"I got you, yo!" I heard someone yell, but I couldn't see him.

"Mil, wake up," Karim yelled. "Your cousin is back."

"Ay yo, I spoke to Mal, and he said he got a lawyer Mu gave him the number to, and that the lawyer supposed to come check you out today, and get you in court for a bail hearing tomorrow, so just cool out until that happened. He said Lisa gonna be at the house tonight when you call, and a whole bunch of other chicks been calling to see what was up wit' you. You two niggas sound just alike. I told him I was holding you down. He said he was gonna send me a couple of dollars and some flicks of some shorties at the club and shit. Yo, here some honey buns and shit. I'ma bring you some more tomorrow."

"Yo, what's up with your case?" I asked him.

"I'm still going to trial unless they come wit' something like a twelve wit' a six or ten wit' a five. That ain't shit, seeing as how I been sitting for over three already."

"Yeah, I hear you, but I ain't trying to do no time."

"Oh, you gonna get somethin' for that shit they charging you wit'."

"But, yo! This my first offense. I ain't never been locked up for drugs before."

"It don't matter. You pose a threat and they need you off the streets for a little while. It's all politics, baby boy. The question is, is your paper long enough to get the lowest plea bargain possible? 'Cause money talks when it comes to the system."

"Man, I'm tryin to get probation or somethin', fuck that."

"Yeah, a'ight, keep thinkin' that. Yo, I'll talk to you tomorrow when I get off work. Let me know what your lawyer tell you."

"Kamil Benson," the CO shouted. "Get ready, attorney visit."

"Mr. Benson, My name is Muhammad Bashir. You can call me Mr. Bashir. A friend of yours and a brother of mine, Mustafa Ali, along with your brother, contacted me earlier yesterday. Since then I've been trying to find out all that I can about what exactly you're being charged with. I have copies of the charges and I'm going to give you a copy of them. I need to ask you a few questions just to clarify what prevented you from being granted bail. Based on what you can remember about the arrest, tell me word for word what happened, just how it happened."

I explained it to him word for word from the time they put the cuffs on me until now.

"So you're telling me that while you were cuffed on the ground the officer searched the vehicle without asking permission, and didn't show you a search warrant of any sort?"

"Nope. I mean, yep, that's what I'm telling you."

"Very good. Don't worry. I'll have you out on bond tomorrow.'

"Thank you," I said. "Have you spoken to my brother or Mustafa today?" I asked him.

"Yes, they're downstairs in the car waiting for me," he said, smiling.

"Oh, all right. Thank you again."

"You have a collect call from Kamil, will you accept the charges?"

"Yeah. Yo, what up, kid?" Mal said, happy to be hearing from me.

"I'm good."

"You sure? Ain't nobody take ya ass or nothing, did they?"

"Nigga, shut the fuck up?" He made me laugh, something I needed right now 'cause this twenty-three and a half hours of lockup with three niggas in the cell was killing me. I heard Lisa in the background saying, "Kamal, don't say that."

"He know I'm playing, girl, cool out! Yo, bro, Bashir told us that he should be able to get you bail tomorrow 'cause they did some bullshit taking the money like that. He was sayin' somethin' about illegal search or something. Mu know more about it than I do."

"When Mu get up here?"

"I called him as soon as they knocked you and he flew up on the next flight and got in touch wit' Bashir. Yo, we'll be there tomorrow in court, so I'ma let your wife talk to you. Look at her cheezin' and shit."

"Kamal, shut up! Hey, mookie, how you doin'?" Lisa asked. "I miss you," she said as if I had been locked up for years already. "I wish I had never let you leave my house that day, and then you wouldn't be in there."

"Nah, don't say that. It ain't ya fault. They was gonna—"

"Time up! Everybody lock in!" the officer yelled.

"Damn! Lisa, I gotta lock in."

"Okay! I love you."

"I love you too."

"Benson, time's up I said."

"Yeah, I heard you."

"Baby, go ahead. Don't get in no trouble," Lisa told me, picking up on the irritation in my tone of voice.

"I ain't. I'll talk to you."

"Bye."

Still, I couldn't sleep, especially with having court on my mind, so I stayed up until the morning came. By the time the lawyer had stated the obvious, and requested this and requested that, filing this and filing that, the judge had granted me bail: $100,000 with 10 percent, meaning I could use a bondsman. I felt like I just beat a murder rap, and by the sound of everybody in the back you would've thought I did too. My moms, my grandmother, Nique, Jasmine, Lisa, Mal, his girl, Mu, and Shareef were all there.

"Depending on how long the paperwork takes, you should be out sometime this evening. Call me tomorrow so we can discuss your options," Bashir said as he was leaving.

I saw him and Mu exchange handshakes and hugs before he left. I could see Lisa wiping tears from her eyes as they were escorting me out of the courtroom.

"What happened in court?" my cousin asked.

"They gave me a hundred thousand dollars bail."

"Word! They tryin' to make an example out of you, probably 'cause of all that money you had. Can you make it?"

I just laughed. "Yeah, I should be out before the night's out."

"Damn, you niggas is livin' it up out there. Mal must've overnighted that shit 'cause I got the money and the flicks today. He sent me two hundred dollars. That was good lookin'. You niggas chillin' in the flicks, too."

"What flicks he sent you?"

"The ones when y'all at some club in New York with all these Spanish chicks and shit up in there."

"Oh, I know what you talking about. Yo, you still got the number, right?"

"Yeah, I got it back at my cell."

"If you need anything get at us, all right?"

"That's peace."

"Yo, I hope you beat that body or get something light."

"Appreciate that, yo. Let me get out of here, one!"

When I got outside, Mu and Mal were leaning against a green Land Cruiser. "What was you eatin' in there, kid? You look like you put on some weight," Mal joked.

"Yeah, all right. What's up, Mu?"

"What up, baby?"

"I'm all right. Appreciate the lawyer."

"All I did was call him. Y'all paying him," he said.

As I looked up I could see niggas from county up in the windows. Somebody was waving. I thought it was Marlon, but I wasn't sure. I still waved back, because those two days I felt their pain and shit was rough.

"Damn, kid, how the hell you catch three secret indictments?" Mu asked.

"I don't know, yo. Probably fuckin' wit' all them white guys."

"Not necessarily. It be black muthafuckas, too, so you ain't gonna be able to figure out who you served. You niggas making too much paper to not have niggas out there for you anyway. I know y'all ain't so stingy and cheap that you can't pay niggas proper to move that shit for you. You know you ain't getting that money back, right?" he said. "I spoke to Muhammad and he told me that you definitely gonna have to do some time but it ain't gonna be a lot if ya paper right. I told him to discuss that wit' y'all. Make sure you call or go see him tomorrow, 'cause I'm leaving tomorrow morning. I just wanted to make sure you got up outta there 'cause that county jail shit ain't no joke. You only sit if you have to, not if you don't."

"Yo, Lisa's at the house waitin' on you, and Mommy and them said make sure you come by tomorrow," Mal told me.

"I will."

Lisa jumped on me as soon as I came through the door, kissing all on me with her arms around my neck and legs around my waist. "Welcome home, baby!"

"Lisa, you act like I been gone for years. I seen you in the courtroom crying."

"I couldn't help it. It feels like years."

"What you gonna do when I gotta do years?"

"Don't talk like that. You ain't gonna have to do no time."

"I wish you were right, girl."

"Hey, Kamil, welcome home," Keya said.

"Thanks, it's good to be home."

"Yo, Mil, I'm gonna get up outta here and take this truck back to Reecie. I'll call you when I'm back in VA."

"All right, Mu. I'll talk to you."

"Lisa, it was nice meeting you. Take care of my li'l brother while I'm gone."

"I will. Nice meeting you too."

That night, after I took a long, hot bath to get the jail stench off of me, Lisa and I made love all night long. It was as though we belonged together, like we were made for each other.

Chapter Fifty-seven

I had missed a total of five days from school and this was going to be my sixth because I had to go see my lawyer. I took off the first one, for my birthday on the third, and I was locked up on the fourth and the fifth and got out on the sixth. School wasn't a priority now for me. I had to focus on this case and what I might be looking at. I wasn't ready to go to prison, but I knew that it was one of the options in the game, and like everything else you do there are always consequences and repercussions behind it.

When I called Bashir I told him that I'd be there by 11:00 a.m., but I was a little early.

"Yes, may I help you?" the receptionist asked.

"Yes, I have a scheduled appointment with Mr. Bashir at eleven o'clock."

"And your name is, sir?"

"Kamil Benson."

"Oh, yes, Mr. Benson. Mr. Bashir is expecting you. Please have a seat while I inform him of your arrival."

"Thank you."

"Kamil, come in please. How are you this morning?" he asked.

"I'm fine and yourself?"

"Each day Allah allows me to wake up to see another day I'm blessed," he replied. "Did Mustafa fill you in on what I said in reference to this matter?"

"Basically he told me that you said I'd be looking at some time."

"That's correct, but let me explain how it works. I've been talking to the prosecutor who will be handling your case and he feels strongly about what he has against you so he won't hesitate to take this to trial if you don't agree to plead out, and he will push for the maximum sentence; but you don't have to worry because I'm advising you to plead out. That is what I feel is in your best interest, because I've dealt with this prosecutor before and if he says he has something on someone then he has it. He offered you a seven with a three-and-a-half stipulation."

"What?"

"Calm down," he said, smiling. "I said he offered it. I didn't say we'd take it. We negotiated and negotiated and I got him down to a three with an eighteen-month stip, and that right there, my young brother, is a gift. If you agree to this they will not pursue the charges on the money; however, you will have to forfeit the right to fight for it back."

"I don't care about that money," I told him.

"That's what I was hoping you'd say. Now, like I said, he's willing to offer you three years with a mandatory minimum of eighteen months. Automatically that makes you eligible for a half-way house and work release, but you will probably do about six months before your paperwork goes through, which isn't bad considering your charges. So you'd basically do six months in a youth correctional facility and the other twelve months in a halfway house going home on the weekends on furlough. What do you think?"

I thought for a minute. The way he broke it down didn't sound too bad, and it seemed like I didn't have any other choice. "Yeah, that sounds decent if that's the best you can do."

"This is the best anybody can do in your case, no matter how much you're paying them. I have to call him back by five thirty and let him know so he can draw up the papers, and this thing will probably take place next month and you'll be sentenced by May."

"May? Of this year?"

"Yes."

424 J. M. Benjamin

"Why so quick? I thought cases be getting dragged out for months and months, sometimes years."

"Not everyone's situation is the same. If you were sitting in the county jail that would probably happen, but instead you're out. The prosecutor has so many cases that he's trying to get the cut-and-dried ones out of the way first. He has trial dates coming up and other people to negotiate with. He's set on your case and he's trying to get done with it and get it out of the way."

"Man, that's right around the corner, and I'm supposed to graduate in June."

"I'm sorry, brother, but this is how it is, we either take it or leave it. They provide you with an education in those institutions, though; you could probably work something out with the education department up in there to allow you to finish your twelfth grade in there. So, what do you want me to tell the prosecutor?"

"Tell him I'll take the three wit' eighteen months."

"Good choice. I'll notify you of the court date either by mail or by phone. Call me next week, or if you have any questions or change your mind."

"All right. Thank you, Mr. Bashir."

I filled Mal in on everything my lawyer told me when I got home.

"That ain't nothing. Shit, it could've been worse," Mal said.

"Oh, yeah, no doubt, I'ma take it. It's just that May will be here in a minute and that ain't really no time to do shit."

"What you gotta do?"

"Spend time with Lisa, for one; go places and do shit. And I ain't even gonna be able to graduate. That was my main reason for staying in school this long, to get that diploma for Mommy and Grandma. They gonna be hurt."

"Yo, you still have time to finish school. Like Bashir told you, they got an education department in there, or you can go when you get to the halfway house."

"Yeah, you right. I'ma shoot to Mom's for a few and then pick up Lisa and I'll be back. I know Lisa is a good shorty, but she might not be able to handle this. It might be best if I just dead things with us until I come home."

"Yo, before you do anything see what she says and how she feels. You never know. I know none of them other chicks you be fuckin' wit' ain't gonna troop no bid wit' you. They may be good for a phone call, visit, or letter here and there, but not on no consistency-type shit."

"Word! I know how it goes. Shit don't stop 'cause I got knocked," I agreed.

"Like I said, Lisa's a good girl. She'll probably be there for you."

"Yeah, you probably right. I'ma see what she says."

Chapter Fifty-eight

It killed my moms when I told her. She started blaming herself again, and how she tried to prevent us from turning out and ending up like our dad. Every tear she shed was like a needle sticking me in my heart. I couldn't bear to see her cry; I had to leave because it was too much for me. I knew that I was going to go through the same thing with Lisa as I did with my moms once I told her, only worse because she was a very emotional female. She cried all night and told me how she'd be there throughout the whole bid, and I believed her.

I was sentenced on May 5 and taken into custody. I had to go through the whole 4B process all over again for a couple of days before they put me on a sentencing tier. Between the twenty-eight grand I got knocked with, ten grand it cost to be bailed out, and the fifteen Gs the lawyer charged me, not to mention over fifty Gs we spent a few months ago, we had blown through over a hundred grand. It's funny how one minute you can be living ghetto fabulous and the next minute you're stripped down to nothing. If it weren't for Kamal holding it down out there I'd probably be assed out or having to depend on my moms and grandmother; but if anything happened to him then I'd be in jail struggling. I knew that Lisa would do all she could for me if things went wrong with Kamal, but I knew my pride would get in the way of asking because I'd been on my own for the past four years and never had to ask nobody for nothing.

I'd been in the county jail for two months now and I was ready to get up out of here. I was tired of these fifteen-minute visits with Lisa and my moms through the window. Kamal didn't even come to check me 'cause he said he wasn't coming to see me through some glass, so he just sent money and flicks that were stressing me out 'cause I wished I could be there.

If it weren't for the little cakes and shit they sold I'd have been messed up 'cause they starved you in there with the little portions of meals they served, from the honey bun sandwiches, to banana sandwiches, to other cakes. And trying to work out on the universal weights I looked like I put on a little size. My moms and Lisa said my face was getting fat and I was getting yellow from being out in the sun. My hair even started growing so I got it plaited up in box braids. Niggas do the same ol' shit in county, trying to get their weight up and talk about how they was doing when they was out and what they had, how many chicks they had, and who was messing with the same chicks.

It seemed like everybody messed with everybody in every town. Niggas and chicks tricked locally and out of town. I didn't join the conversations, but I listened. Trina's and Ke Ke's names came up a few times. I just laughed because it wasn't surprising. A few chicks Mal messed with came up too, and some of the names niggas were saying was wifey, me and Mal had messed with and Mal was still messin with some of them, while niggas was sitting up in here putting their word on how they knew their girl wasn't cheatin' on them.

That's one thing I didn't get all into with Lisa. She was her own woman and whatever she was going to do she was going to do whether I was out or in, but I trusted her. Besides, what I didn't know couldn't hurt me. I would hear guys on the phones questioning their girls about where they had been, who they were with, and all of that, stressed out talking about how they were going to kill them when they get out. Mu had told me a long time ago not to ask a question that you really didn't want answers to or couldn't handle, so I had no intention of asking.

Guys would be fighting all the time over bullshit like the TV, the card games, who worked out first, or some old shit that happened on the streets. Sometimes they started out joking and it led into a fight because somebody couldn't take a joke or somebody crossed the line by inviting them to their private parts.

I messed with a few guys from out of town, not all of them, some. Even though Plainfield stuck together like Shareef had told us before, I realized just because they came from the area didn't mean they were cool. You had snakes from all over that came in all different shapes, forms, and colors, and there were definitely some from my town in there. I met a few guys who were cool from other towns and we kicked it here and there on some regular.

The one thing I noticed the most though was that jokers could come to jail and be whatever they wanted. There were guys I knew from the town who were straight-up soft, but in there they were acting like they were killers or something. Then there were guys in there I thought were stand-up cats but were in there messing with guys who were gay. You had dudes who were living like kings on the streets who were living like crackheads and dopefiends, and crackheads and dopefiends living like kings. Jail was crazy, but the way I was out in the streets was the same way I was in here.

They finally shipped me out of county after four months. My lawyer had told me that there was a backlog in the system—that's why it took so long to get out of county—so I still had to do six months at whatever prison they were going to send me to.

I went to reception in Yardsville to get classified. When the nurse examined me I weighed 155 pounds. I was 143 pounds when I first got knocked, so I gained twelve pounds.

When I went to the rec yard guys were yelling through their windows who knew me. They were trying to tell me to stay there and who was there from the town and from the projects, but when I went before the class comm. I didn't get a chance to talk. They just told me where I was going: a youth correction center in Annandale.

The Dale, as it was called, was as sweet as it got for your first time being in prison. It was structured like a college campus, but you knew it was a jail by the COs who worked there. They had dorms called cottages, and I was in one with the most guys who were either from the town or the county. I got a job in the kitchen, the first real job I ever had. Here I wouldn't work a nine to five at Micky D's if my life depended on it, but I come to jail, bust my ass, and let them slave me for ninety dollars a month.

"Benson, visit," the officer yelled.

That was the highlight of my week, seeing my girl or my moms, even though they both cried each time they came to see me. I always felt bad when my moms came up because her tears reminded me of the ones my dad had caused. I also felt ashamed that I was putting my own girl through the same thing my dad had put my moms through.

Mal came up once with Shareef and brought me some KFC and pizza, and we just polled about what was going on out on the streets. Mal said it was hot out and he ain't been doing nothing but chilling. He told me his shorty was pregnant and due in July so he played the house mostly. He told me a lot of chicks were asking for my address and he had been giving it to them, but I told him that ain't none of them chicks got at me and to stop giving my information out. I was only focused on hearing from Lisa. Shareef pointed out all the girls he was creeping with who were up here visiting dudes.

"Hey, mookie," Lisa said, giving me a hug and a kiss. "You get bigger every time I come up to see you. What are you eating?"

I smiled. "That's all that bread and poultry I be eating, plus what you be bringing me and hittin' that iron."

Four and a half months down the Dale and I was up to 180 pounds. They made sure you had plenty to eat. Some guys preferred prison over the real world they lived so good, which seemed crazy to me. I wanted nothing more than to be free.

"Have you heard about the halfway house yet?"

"Nah, not yet. I'm still waitin'. It's been almost five months now, so my name's got to be coming up soon."

"I miss you; I'm ready for you to come home."

"I know. I'm ready to come home too, but it's up to these people. It's whatever they say. They callin' the shots."

Lisa began to cry. "I can't wait until you come home because my mother and father be bugging out now about you calling the house collect and how you writing me from jail. I'm ready to get out of there."

"Mal don't be giving you the money for the phone bill like I told him to?"

"Yeah, he does, but I got to call him 'cause he's always doing something so he forgets, and I don't like calling like I'm begging him."

"Nah, it ain't about beggin'. That's my paper too. He's giving you what belongs to me. But don't worry about it. I'm going to call tonight and tell him to just hit you off."

"Kamil, it's not about that; it's not about the money at all. I still got the money that you gave me before you left, so money isn't the problem. The problem is I want you home and you can't be there."

I didn't know whether she was saying she didn't know how much longer she could take this like she missed me, or didn't know how much longer she could take this like she wanted to end it. I wiped her face.

"Stop crying. I know it's been rough for you out there, and it's been rough for me too, but these places are designed to tear relationships apart, and put a strain on them. I know that one day seems like a lifetime to be apart when you miss and love someone, but I already have half my time in, and within a month I should be getting furloughs so I can come home on the weekends. I need you stay strong and stay focused for the both of us, 'cause I don't want to lose you over no bullshit."

As I listened to myself talk, I wondered if this was what my father tried to say to my mother just before she told him she couldn't take it anymore.

"You're not going to lose me. I'm not going anywhere. I was just saying how it was hurting me not having you there with me. Do you know what it feels like to love someone so bad you're not able to eat or sleep because you miss them so much? That's what I'm going through out here."

Just to hear her say that she wasn't going anywhere was a relief because I thought for sure that I was about to lose her, which would've hurt me because throughout the past eight and a half months I had become so vulnerable and dependent on her. It would've felt like I lost a body part. I had said and shared things with her about myself that I had never told no one before, not even my brother. Things only me and God knew about.

"Let's go take some pictures," I said.

"We take pictures every week."

"And we gonna keep taking them until I get out 'cause you looking different every time you come up here."

"Yeah, right. Anyway, have you tried to finish school yet?"

"Nah, too much shit be goin' on so I ain't even look into it. I'll do that when I get in the halfway house."

"Visits will terminate in fifteen minutes. I repeat, visits will terminate in fifteen minutes," the speaker announced.

"Damn! That was a quick-ass two hours."

"I'll be back up next week, so just call me tonight." I could see the sadness in her eyes and I knew I was the cause and could do nothing about it.

Right before the final call I said, "All right, gimme a kiss so I can let you go. I don't want you to have to wait at the back of the line because it's a lot of people here today."

"Visits are now terminated. Please start exiting the visiting area."

Chapter Fifty-nine

Dear Mr. Benson,
We have reviewed your request for our halfway house program and we have agreed to consider you for the program. Your approval date is March 17, 1993.

That was the news I had been waiting for. That was less than a month away and fourteen days after my birthday. All I could think about was how I was out of that hellhole. I really hit the weight pile hard and got my weight up before I was released. I called everybody and told them the good news; I mean, everybody like Mal, Lisa, moms, and them. They all were happy for me, especially Lisa.

For the rest of the month I just chilled. I counted the days down until my day was to arrive. By now I only had a week remaining.

"Ay yo, Mil, you wanna rock with me in spades?" a kid named Sneeze from my projects asked.

"Yeah, I'll rock. You know I'm the best in the building anyways."

"Yo, we playin' for cigarettes, you good?"

"Yeah, I got smokes. How many a game?"

"Five packs a man."

"That's cool. I got like six cartons, even though we ain't gonna lose. Who we playin'?"

"Some Newark kids; they bums."

"All right, I'm comin'."

The cards just weren't falling our way. These bum-ass niggas beat us out of ten cartons, and they couldn't even play. I didn't really care 'cause I was leaving next week anyway, and I still would've had a carton left after I paid my five. Sneeze put his five in a brown paper bag with mine and we paid them. Sneeze and I were kicking it in the dayroom when they came up.

"Yo! What the fuck y'all niggas think, we soft or something?" the tall, skinny one said.

We both stood up. "What? Fuck you talking about?" Sneeze retorted.

"Nigga, you know what we talkin' about. Five of them cartons was dummies. Them shits was stuffed with newspaper."

I didn't say anything. I just looked at Sneeze.

"Nigga, them shits was legit. Get the fuck out of here."

"Yo, Sneeze, stop playin wit' me, kid, and get mine to me."

"Nigga, you paid already," Sneeze told him.

The kid caught Sneeze in the face and they started banging out. His partner tried to hook off and I caught him. He grabbed me and we started wrestling. I kneed him in the face while I had him in the headlock. He was punching me in the back and ribs.

"Break it up! Break it up! Code thirty-three. Code thirty-three. Cottage ten."

Unbelievable. Six days to go and I get into a fight and go to lockup for ninety days. On top of that, I lost my status and my date to go to the halfway house. It looked like I would be doing the rest of my months in jail.

Mal understood because he was from the streets, but my moms and Lisa didn't. They took turns: one chastised me while the other expressed her disappointment and hurt. There wasn't anything I could do or say. The damage had been done.

I got out of the box seventy-five days later, fifteen days early 'cause they needed the cell, and I was scheduled to see parole in two weeks. I was glad I wasn't seeing them from the box because they would've definitely given me a hit. When I got out, Lisa's phone had a block on it. She said her parents put it on there, but then I got a letter from her saying she wasn't coming up this week because she couldn't deal with seeing me right now. I didn't even write her back. I decided not to until I got my fate from the parole board.

The fight had cost me in more ways than one. Not only did they deny me community release, but they also gave me a twelve-month hit, which would damn near max me out, and I still had three months left on my stip to do. I called my brother and told him, but I didn't call anyone else. Lisa had written me a few more times asking that I please respond and let her know what was going on, but I never did. She stopped writing and stopped coming to visit me.

Six months later, my brother came to visit me. "Yo, what up, kid? You looking good. I ain't know ya shit was knotted up like that."

"Yeah, I be getting it in."

"What you putting up."

"I can hit four and some change."

"Word? How much you weigh?"

"Like one-ninety something."

"Damn! I weigh one eighty-seven, but my shit come from drinkin' and shit."

"How my niece doin'?"

"She all right. She's getting big."

"How you?"

"I'm good."

"You heard from Lisa?"

"Nah. I ain't seen her nowhere out there, either."

"It don't matter. I'll be home in about six more months. What made you come up here today?"

He hesitated. "Yo, I had to tell you something that I couldn't tell you over the phone."

"What up?"

"Yo, Mu got knocked by the feds down in VA."

"What?"

"Yeah, yo. His baby moms called me a couple of days ago and told me. She said they took the businesses and seized all the whips and the crib. They found a hundred Gs in the crib and froze all his shit in the bank. Then the other day I heard they shut his stores up here, too. She said that he told her to call me and ask me could I hit her wit' some paper until he finds out what the deal is. I'm supposed to drive down there tomorrow to hit her wit' some dough, and stay a few days to holla at a lawyer for him while I'm down there. His shorty in a motel right now so I'ma hit her wit' enough paper to get a place to stay for her and his son."

"Oh, shit, not Mu. I thought he was down there chillin'."

"I thought so too, but he told me that he'd been selling to a fed for the past four months."

"Damn, that's fucked up. That shit got me fucked up right now. Yo, when will you be back?"

"Probably Thursday, so call me Thursday night."

"All right. If you speak to him tell him I said one love and to hold his head."

That night I couldn't sleep. I couldn't believe that Mu had got knocked. He was the one who taught me everything I knew about the game. He was the one who put Mal and me on when we didn't know how to get on. He was the one who used to stress the importance of hitting 'em and quitting 'em in the game.

Thursday night came and Mal filled me in on all he knew. Mu had been serving the fed for the past four months like he said, but the worst part was that it totaled up to over one hundred kilos in the four-month span, which made him eligible for life in prison. One of his son's mom's cousins who was working for him got caught and he agreed to cooperate by introducing Mu to the agent in exchange for immunity.

The lawyer wanted fifty grand just to take the case as a retainer fee to fight to get the life off his back, 'cause he was a career criminal. We didn't even know he had been to jail before. Mal said he gave the lawyer half and gave Mu's son's moms another twenty to get a place. Mu was scheduled to go to court next Monday so Mal had to hit the lawyer with the rest by then. He said he had it and it wasn't nothing 'cause things had been poppin' for him lately. I wasn't worried about the money though 'cause I know Mu would've done the same in a heartbeat. What I was worried about was Mu getting life in prison. I just couldn't see it. All anybody could do now was just wait and hope for the best.

Chapter Sixty

On June 17, 1994, I was released on parole with only a few more months left to max out.

Everybody was telling me that I should've maxed out so I wouldn't have the paper trail when I went home, but after serving over two years you aren't trying to turn no type of freedom down. I was 220 pounds when I walked out of jail. I had put on fifty-seven pounds and it was my time to shine. Nobody knew I was coming home and that was the way I wanted it. I just caught a cab to the new address that Mal had sent me to where he had moved to on the east end. Mal brought a nice home, with a two-car garage.

I walked up the steps and rang the bell.

"Who is it?"

"It's me."

I could hear the safety latch being taken off the door.

"Ah, man, my dawg is home!" Mal shouted, wrapping his arms around me, and I hugged him back. It was an emotional scene. The tag-team partners were reunited once again. We sat in the living room for a while and talked, while I bounced my niece Nafisa on my knee. She looked like a combination of Mal and me put together. You knew she was a Benson.

I took a shower and dressed in the outfit Mal ran downtown and got me until we could go shopping. It felt good to be in some new clothes. After we left the barbershop, Mal drove me around the projects. He told me how he had a team of young guys out there getting it for us. Three of them I knew from when they were little, but they looked different. It's amazing how someone grows in two years, but then again I was living proof.

"Yo, niggas is gonna flip when they see you, kid."

"Man, I don't care about none of that. I'm just coming through 'cause you wanted to. Muthafuckas ain't give a fuck about me when I was gone. Most of them niggas was probably glad I got knocked so they could start making dough."

Mal looked at me. "Cool out, yo. You home now. You ain't got to be all militant no more like you still locked up."

"This ain't no act, Mal. I'm for real. Outside of you and Shareef and a couple of other project heads who was down the Dale with me, I've got no love for none of these niggas around here." Prison had made me bitter. It had also opened my eyes to a lot of things about the game and the players.

"All right, yo, but be easy 'cause that's a part of the game. You know how that goes."

"Yeah, I know."

"Oh, shit, my nigga home," one kid yelled.

"Damn, kid, you shinin'," another said.

"What's the deal, Mil?" another said.

Everybody was acting like they missed me and we was partners before I left. The new niggas on the block and the younger heads were wondering who I was. Some of the li'l jokers were trying to look hard and grill me. It made me laugh. I shook a few hands and took a few hugs on some fake shit because on the real I didn't feel anything from none of these niggas out here. I was paying more attention to the little honeys in the field who were checking me out. They looked sixteen or seventeen, tops, but they were stacked.

"Yo, Mil, these our little troopers right here: Nut, Lou, Mart, and this is Rob. You know li'l Nut and 'em. Rob from BK though over in Albany projects."

They all said what's up. I just nodded. They looked bigger than we did when we first started hustling, but I knew they were around the same age, maybe younger, like thirteen or fourteen. One of the li'l honeys in the field was steady clockin' me, and she looked familiar.

"Yo, Mal, who that li'l light-skinned chick right there lookin' over here? She looks familiar."

"You know who that is. That's Roger li'l sister, Tonya. Remember we used to always say she was gonna be bad when she got older?"

"Word! That's her. Damn! Shorty grew up. What's she like, about fifteen now?"

"Nah, she's a senior in high school so she gotta be at least seventeen. You want me to call her over here?"

"Nah, nigga, ain't nothing changed. I still got my push-up skills. I ain't never gonna lose that."

"Shorty don't fuck wit' nobody around here 'cause she said she ain't fuckin' wit' no project niggas, so I don't know, kid, but let me see you work."

"Bet a hundred," I said to my brother.

"Bet." He smiled.

"How you doin', ladies?"

"Fine," they all said.

"Damn! You lookin' real nice." I directed my attention to Tonya. "The last time I seen you, you didn't look like that. I mean, you were still gorgeous, but now you're more beautiful."

"Thank you," she said, trying to look all shy and innocent.

"Do you remember me?"

"Yeah, you're Kamil. I used to watch you out my apartment window when you used to be around the New, but you look different too. You got big. You look good, though."

Now it was my turn to smile trying to be all modest. "Nah, I still look the same."

All the girls spoke at once, "No, you don't!"

I started laughing. "Where y'all from?" I asked her friends.

"The same place you are, the New Projects," they all sang. They all named their older brothers or sisters and instantly I remembered them.

They were all cute, but Tonya stuck out above all. "Listen, I'm about to go, but I wanna see you later, that cool?"

"Yeah." She smiled.

"All right, then. I'ma come back through. You gonna be over here or in the New?"

"Here," she replied.

"Bet, see you later. Ladies, y'all be good."

They all smiled. When I turned around, I ran straight into Shareef.

"Nigga, what's good?" He hugged me. "You ain't been out a whole day and already tryin' to snatch up the baddest li'l thing in the hood," he said, laughing. "Damn, it's good to see you, kid."

"You too, bro," I replied. And it was the truth. Shareef was more than my boy now. He was like a brother to me. We had been through a lot together since we had been in the game. Especially the murders of Ant and Trevor. What touched me the most was he wrote me letters even when Mal wouldn't.

"You know where we goin' right?" he stated.

"Where?" I was clueless.

"Shoppin', nigga, that's where. You think I forgot how y'all set me out when I came home?"

"Nah, I know you didn't. But for real we gonna have to put that off 'til tomorrow 'cause by the time I go see my moms and 'em I'ma be ready to hook up with shorty," I told him.

"Man, she a dick teaser. You ain't getting none of that on the first night."

"We'll see," was all I said.

My moms and grandmother were looking good and my sisters had gotten big. Jasmine was home on school break. She was in college now. The only one out of the four of us to go. I wound up getting my diploma after the parole board hit me, which my moms was proud of. Kamal stopped going after I got locked up and Monique never went back. My grandmother still refused to move out of the projects even though my moms had gotten back on her feet and brought a little house on the east end. While I was at my moms, out of respect for the time Lisa did with me and the love I knew she still had for me, I gave her a call.

She sounded half asleep when she answered.

"Go brush your teeth," I said to her. When we were younger, I used to always say that to her when she sounded like she had just woken up.

"Hey, mookie," she said, suddenly awake.

"What's goin' on, Ms. Mathews?"

"Nothing much. How are you?" She sounded kind of strange.

"I'm good."

"Tha . . . that's good," she stuttered. "Can you please hold for a minute?" she asked me. I guessed at that moment it had dawned on her. "How come you're not calling collect?" Before I could answer, she answered for me. "Oh my God, you're home!" she exclaimed.

"Yeah." I started laughing.

"I can't believe it. I can't believe it," she repeated. She started crying. I could hear her mother in the background asking her what was wrong. "Mommy, he's home," she yelled.

"Lisa, calm down." I tried to calm her but it was no use. Then suddenly the phone dropped.

"Hello?"

"Hello, Kamil?" The voice belonged to Lisa's mother.

"Yes. How are you doing, Mrs. Matthews?"

"Fine, and yourself?"

"I'm just happy to be free."

"Welcome home."

"Thank you."

"Kamil, Lisa can't talk right now. Can you call her back maybe tomorrow?"

"Is everything okay?" I asked.

"Yes, she'll be all right, just needs some time."

I didn't understand, but I agreed. "All right, I'll call back tomorrow then."

"Okay, you take care."

"I will."

"Bye."

Something was wrong, I just didn't know what. But I'd have to deal with that another day.

***

Mal had brought me a Lexus SC 400 coupe as a welcome home present. I went to go scoop Tonya up. I copped some Heinekens and a pint of Hennessy 'cause she liked to drink. We went to Red Lobster to get something to eat and then straight to the Marriot. I asked her if she had a problem with me getting a room. She said no, so I was confident how the night was going to turn out.

We started sipping on the Henny and chased it with the Heinekens; I was starting to feel the cognac. Tonya damn near quoted my whole rap sheet from back in the day about how I dressed, and what type of shines and whip I had. I could tell she studied me because some of the shit she said I didn't even remember I had.

By the time the drinks were done, I had sexed Tonya three times and put her to sleep. Between the two years and three months I did and her tightness, I was cumming every five minutes. I knew after that night Tonya was going to be my new little honey. My welcome home was just what the doctor had ordered.

Chapter Sixty-one

For the rest of the summer Mal, Shareef, and I went everywhere together, and did everything together. We went to all the Greek Fests, Freaknik, Belmar, Philly, Jones Beach, Myrtle Beach, Virginia Beach, and Mardi Gras in New Orleans, Bike and Black College Week in Daytona and Miami, even the jazz fest in Cancun. I was off parole so I could go wherever. I went crazy when we shot out to Vegas. It was like five Atlantic Cities in one, but I still loved AC because after I gambled I could dip back up to Wildwood and cool out. I was an amusement park junkie so we hit all of them like Great Adventures, Kings Dominion, Action Park, Dorney Park, Coney Island, and even Disney World. Sometimes we took chicks, so I would take Tonya.

I had called Lisa back that next day and we talked for a while. She told me the reason she acted like that was because she was seeing somebody and she felt guilty when she heard my voice on the phone because all the love she had for me resurfaced. If any other female would've said that to me I would've been like yeah whatever, but Lisa was different. She was the realest shorty I knew. That's why I believed her. And even though I wanted more, I agreed to still be friends.

Chapter Sixty-two

The summer was ending and I was ready to turn it up around the way. Even though we had four little dudes out there pumping for us, there was still just something about being in the projects, in the midst of everything. Mal didn't like the idea of me being out there like that especially since it bought him back out, being that we still followed the same rules of the game that Mu had taught us, about holding each other down and watching one another's back at all times. Even Shareef started coming back around. It felt like the projects used to, back in the day.

One day it started raining right in the middle of an intense dice game we had going on, so we took it inside of one of the buildings. I had the bank, and my arm was on fire. I was up like four or five Gs when we got in the hall, and I was ready to roll again. It was so noisy in the hall we couldn't even hear ourselves think. I knew people in their apartments wanted to complain, but nobody dared to since there were so many of us in there; but they wouldn't hesitate to call the police on us.

Once I saw joker's money down on the ground, I rolled the dice again. I didn't roll a point, so I went to pick the dice back up, and as I did, all of a sudden, it got dead quiet in the hall. When I looked up, everybody was looking at me and then behind me, so that put me on point. I had my burner tucked in my waist, and I knew that if it was the police behind me I was going straight to jail with a fresh charge.

At first I thought it was the stick-up boys, but I knew it couldn't have been them because niggas would've been acting different, so I knew it had to be Five-O. I cupped the dice and turned around. It took me a minute to figure out exactly who the person was standing there in front of me. I knew he wasn't a cop. I stared at him for a second, and then it registered. Standing there just a little taller than me, and about twenty pounds more, was someone I hadn't see since I was a kid. It was my father.

"What's up, boy?" he said.

I was speechless.

"Oh, you don't know who I am now, looking just like me?"

I grinned because he was right; it was almost like looking in the mirror. "I know who you are."

"Can I get a hug then?"

I opened my arms and he embraced me. It was an unfamiliar feeling.

"I missed you, man," he said just before I broke away.

"Yeah, me too," I said back to him. "When did you get home?" I asked.

"Today."

It had been twelve years since I had seen my dad, and if it weren't for the strong resemblance, he would've looked like a stranger to me. "How you been?"

"Good, good, it's good to be out."

Those were the same words that I used to describe my release.

"Where's your brother?"

"He went to get something to eat, but he'll be right back."

"Man, you big. You put all that weight on while you were locked up?" he asked me.

I was surprised. "What?"

"You heard me. Oh, what, you think I don't hear things 'cause I was locked up? Sometimes you find things out quicker in the joint than you do on the streets. You should know that. I've been hearin' about my son in the penitentiary for the last six years."

"Don't believe everything you hear."

"Ha! You sound like your ol' man with that line."

"Nah, I sound like me."

He looked at me funny. "Listen, I gotta go, but I'll be back through later. Where can I find you two at?"

"If we're not here, we at home."

"Where's home?"

"We'll be here."

He chuckled. I figured he laughed because I refused to tell him where we lived. "All right, it was good seein' you, Mil-Mil."

I hadn't heard that name since I was a kid. A name only he called me. "Yeah, me too."

"Tell your brother that I was here."

"I will."

The whole time we were talking everybody who was in the dice game was just listening and looking. Each was in their own thoughts of their childhoods, and about the last time they had seen or heard from their fathers. It was as if as though that was all of their fathers who had just left, because we were all raised without Dad, hoping for the day he'd return.

Mal thought I was joking at first when I told him, until everybody who was there confirmed it. He had the same facial expression I had when I turned around and saw my father standing there.

"Damn, he home, huh?" Mal shook his head.

"Yup," I replied.

"Where he said he was staying?"

"He didn't."

"I hope that muthafucka don't try to get in touch with moms," Mal spat.

I was thinking the same thing. "You know she's not messin' with him like that," I assured my brother. "She has too much going on for herself to be goin' backward."

"Yeah, no doubt. Moms got her shit together. The last thing she needs is his ass in her life. I wonder if she knows he's home," Mal said.

"I don't know."

"Well, we gonna wait here until he comes back and hear what he's gotta say. If he said he heard about us while he was locked up then he knows we getting money. He might wanna get hit off on the strength that he's our pops, but we don't owe him shit," Mal barked. "Everything we got we got it on our own."

I could tell my brother was angry. Out of all of us, he had taken the situation with our parents the hardest. I would always say how he had hated my dad for breaking our mother's heart.

"Let's just see what's up with him and see what he wants." I tried to calm my brother.

"Yeah, let's just see," Mal repeated.

Chapter Sixty-three

"I see you got good taste like your momma. Who all lives here?"

"Me, Mil, my girl, and my daughter."

"Daughter? You mean to tell me that I'm a grandfather?"

"Yeah, I guess so," Mal said.

"You got a daughter, don't you?"

"Yeah."

"Last time I checked I was still your father, ain't I?"

"Yeah."

"Well, that makes me a granddad, wise guy, how old is she?"

"She just turned one this past July."

"What's her name?"

"Kafisa."

"Where'd that come from?"

"Her moms and her family are Muslim."

"Oh. What about you? You got any kids running around?"

"Nah, not me."

"What, you shootin' blanks or something?"

Mal chuckled at the joke.

"Yeah, okay, keep thinking that."

For some reason it seemed natural to be bugging out with our father. I wasn't mad at him anymore.

When we got inside, Keya and Kafisa were asleep.

"You want something to drink?"

"What you got?"

"Heineken, gin, vodka, Hennessy, orange juice, cranberry juice, soda, spring water."

He smiled. "Man, where's your bar at?"

"Mil, you want a beer?"

"Yeah."

"You two guys are something else, I tell ya," he said as he looked at the pictures we had in the living room of us and the family. "Man, your mother and them are looking good. Your sisters are all grown up now, huh? I know you two had to crack a lot of heads over the years."

We both laughed. "We stopped counting," I said.

"You tell them I'm home yet?"

"Nah. Nique's in Florida visiting somebody, and Jasmine's off at college."

"College? Wow, my baby girl made it to college, huh?"

"Yeah, my moms and grandmother stayed on her the whole time," Mal said, not wanting my dad to take any credit for it.

My dad picked right up on it. "Absolutely," he said. "What about you two?"

"Nah, I got my high school diploma down the Dale," I told him.

"I stopped going my senior year, and so did Nique," Mal said.

"At least you got some type of education, no thanks to me."

I was surprised to hear him take the blame for our limited education.

"Anyways, I wanted to talk to you two about something."

"What's that?" we both asked.

"About what y'all into. I been hearin' this and that and how y'all got it going on and all this mess, and I blame myself for leaving you out here like that, but I'm home now and I know y'all been out there for a while, but this junk has got to stop."

We looked at each other, making sure we both heard what we thought we did. Mal spoke before I could. "What?"

"Y'all been out here long enough to have put up enough money to where you can just walk away from the game before it's too late. It's time to stop the nonsense now."

"Hold up! You been gone for fourteen years and my moms had to struggle with four kids, and we been on our own since '88, and you gonna try to come home and lay some law down? Nah, don't try to come home and be no father now. It's too late for all of that!"

I stood there listening as Mal screamed on my pops, and then I looked at my dad. I could see the hurt in his face, like my brother had just slapped him as hard as he could with a dose of reality. I almost felt sorry for him, but then I didn't because Kamal was right. It was too late to try to come home and play the daddy role. We were not babies anymore. We were grown, and we called our own shots.

For a while, he said nothing, and then he looked at me for some type of confirmation to see whether I felt the same way as Kamal did. My look confirmed it all. He turned around and began to walk toward the door.

"Damn, kid, you ain't have to rip him like that," I said to my brother as my dad made his exit.

"Man, fuck that. This nigga think he gonna just come up in our shit and start calling some shots. It ain't happenin'. I don't feel guilty about nothing I said 'cause that shit is true and he knows it."

"Yo, I'm wit' you on all of that, I'm just sayin' you could've said the same thing but a different way, that's all."

"It came out like I meant it to come out."

"All right, Mal. I'm gonna go catch him and drop him off wherever he needs to go. I'll be back."

"Whatever, kid. I ain't beat for that bullshit."

"Yo, Dad, hold up."

He stopped.

"You ain't gotta walk. We said we'd make sure we dropped you off where you needed to go."

He got in the truck.

"Where you stayin'?"

"Out in Linden."

"With who?"

"Carol."

"That's your woman?"

He smiled. "That's my lady friend, like I told you before."

"Oh, I got you; I got a few lady friends myself."

"I'm sure you do," he said, laughing.

"Look, Dad, what Mal said back there at the house, how he said it was probably a little messed up, but he was right."

"You ain't gotta make no excuses for your brother; he's his own man."

"I ain't trying to make no excuses. I'm just tellin' you."

"I know, and I know he's right. If somebody would've rolled up on me and ya uncle Jerry like that, father, grandfather, whoever, it would've been a problem. I knew it would be hard because I knew the two of you were spitting images of me, and that's what kills me the most, 'cause I know how I am. I wasn't tryin' to change you; I was tryin' to save you. I just don't want y'all turning out like how I did. You been locked up before so you know what it feels like. But them little years you did ain't nothing compared to what you could be looking at if you don't slow your roll. Y'all gonna have to learn the hard way like I did," my father ended.

"I guess so."

"Turn right here. See where the Volvo is? Right there."

I took a pen out and wrote how he could get in touch with us if he wanted to. "This right here is our home number, this is my truck cell phone, and my regular cell number, and these are Mal's. Use 'em if you want, whenever."

"I will."

I reached in my pocket. "Here, take this." I handed him everything I had on me. It was about two grand.

He hesitated for a second and then he took it. "Thanks, son. Tell your brother that I still love him, and I love you too."

"I will and the same." I couldn't bring myself to say it because it just didn't sit right wit' me, but I knew that somewhere inside I still had love for him, and I wanted my dad in my life.

As he got out, he turned and said, "Let your sisters know that I'm home."

"I'll do that," I said, and then I peeled off.

Chapter Sixty-four

It had been almost eight months since we had last seen or heard from our father. A lot had gone on since that day when he first came home. Mu had gotten sentenced to twenty-five years in federal prison a week before his thirtieth birthday on February 4, 1995. Mal and I flew down on his sentencing date and hit his baby moms with enough dough to hold him, her, and their baby down for a few years.

Speaking of baby, I got Tonya pregnant. She was two months, and I got a next chick pregnant who I met at a party. She was a month. I wasn't ready to be a father, but neither one of them wanted to get an abortion, so there was nothing that I could do.

Keya and Mal broke up because she caught him cheating for the tenth and last time. He had a new girl and a new baby on the way as well, so Keya was beefing over that. She had been acting funny when it came to him seeing his daughter.

Shareef got cased up again, but not for drugs, for a shooting charge. He was at the club and got into a fight the one night Mal and I didn't go with him, and when he got outside, I heard they tried to jump him, but he made it to his car and reached his burner. Between the weed and the Henny in his system, they said that he was wilding out and shot niggas. Instead of them keepin' it gangsta, the niggas pressed charges on some punk shit, so he was facing three attempted murders. Mal and I had been trying to get at these niggas to keep them from going to court and testifying because the police never found the guns; they were only going by what they said.

Me and Mal basically controlled the projects. 80 percent of the cash flow coming through was coming to us, and the other 20 percent everybody else was fighting for. We had stepped it up and started pumping dope and weed with the coke and crack we were already moving. Our little team of niggas was twelve strong, but they were going in and out of the youth house, getting knocked from the projects being so hot this year.

"Hello? Which one of my sons am I speaking to?" I heard my father's voice say.

"Hey, what's up, Dad? This Kamil."

"Yeah, what's up, kiddo?"

"I'm all right. Where you at?"

"I'm just getting off the exit to come to town."

"Where you been?"

"I been down South. Me and Carol moved down there six months ago and brought a double-wide trailer down in South Carolina."

"South Carolina? What you doin' way down there?"

"I'll talk to you when I get there. Meet me at your house; I should be there within the next twenty minutes or so."

When we looked out the window to see who was blowing the horn, we saw our dad stepping out of a brand new pickup with a camper on the back.

"What the fuck Dad drivin'?" Mal said, as we both laughed. He was leaning on the truck when we got outside.

"What's up, knuckleheads?"

"What's going on, old man?" I said back.

"Ha, yeah, right. I bet this old man can take your young behind on any given Sunday."

I laughed back.

"What made you move all the way down South?" Mal asked him.

"A couple of reasons. For one, Carol has family down there; two, it's nice and quiet, and respectful, too, not like up this way. Third, 'cause the money's good down there."

"Oh, you got a job down there?" I asked.

"Yeah, I wish," he said in a funny sort of way. "They don't pay you nothing down there because the cost of living is cheaper than it is up here."

"So what you mean the money is good?"

"I'm talking about Southern street money."

Me and Mal couldn't believe our ears.

"Don't look surprised. Where you think you get it from?"

"You got back in the game, Dad?" I asked.

"I was never out of the game, son. Those fourteen years I pulled in the joint was all still a part of the game. How you think I got this truck and trailer? The brothers in the South are real hustlers and ballers. They get that big money down there. I'm just down there moving a few ounces here and there. I'm not even going hard like I know I could 'cause I'm too old for that. That's why I came to talk to you two."

"About what?"

"About leaving them hot-ass projects alone and coming down South with me and making yourselves some real money."

"We already makin' real money," Mal said.

"Man, that ain't no real money you makin'. That hundred to two hundred grand y'all putting up ain't nothing. The money y'all done made in seven years up here, you can make in seven months down there if you know what you doin'.

It's just a matter of time before they snatch your butts up for messin' with them projects, if they ain't already planning to run down on you now. I pay six hundred a ounce in New York and take it back to South Carolina and bust it down and make nothing under twenty-five hundred, and I'm buying four and five ounces a whop."

We had impressed looks on our faces.

"But that ain't what I want y'all to come down and do. I want y'all to come and sell weight."

"What?" Mal said.

"Yeah, sell weight. Bring New York to them; that's where the money's at. I mean you only gonna get double or something not even that, but the money is in the quick flip, you follow me?"

"We listening," we both said.

"Say you cop two bricks for twenty-one thousand dollars apiece and sell them for twenty-eight thousand dollars apiece right off the back, that's a fourteen thousand dollar profit right there; or say you come and sell ounces to the younger kids wholesale twelve hundred an ounce, or a thousand, if you sell thirty-six ounces a G a whop, that's thirty-six thousand dollars. If you sell them for eleven or twelve hundred, that's forty-three thousand dollars a key. That's what the quick flip is about."

The way my pops broke it down sounded good, but we had never hustled in the South or, for that matter, anywhere else other than the projects so we didn't know what to believe. Mal didn't sound like he was interested, but I was willing to check it out.

"Dad, that sounds cool and all, but we good where we at and how things are going, right, Mil?" Mal said.

"Yeah, you right, but what Dad was talking about sounds like somethin', and you know the PJ's are on fire right now."

"Yo, we don't know nothin' about no South, kid, and look what happened to Mu."

"Mu got set up, Mal; up until then he was killing 'em down there."

"Who's Mu?" my father asked.

"You may remember him. He's from around here. His name is Mustafa."

My father had a puzzled look on his face at the mention of Mustafa's real name. "Maybe by face." He shrugged his shoulders. "But, look, why don't one of you come back down with me and take somethin' with you and see what happens? The worst that can happen is that you don't sell nothin', right?"

Mal looked at me. "You gonna go?"

"I'll go see what's up."

"You sure?"

"Yeah, I'll go. I need to get away 'cause this baby shit got me a li'l stressed," I said.

"What baby stuff?" my pops interrupted.

"You jinxed him last time we saw you, 'cause he got two girls pregnant and they're a month apart."

"You still goin' up in them girls raw? You better be worried about catching the AIDS instead of who you got pregnant because that's the number one killer for our people right now."

"I do be strapping up, sometimes, but them things be bustin', and they take away from the sex."

"Yeah, well when sex takes you away you won't have anything to worry about."

"He don't be using condoms anyway. He probably don't even know what a condom looks like," Mal said, laughing.

"You don't either; that's why you don't know who burned you last week."

We all started laughing.

"Listen, enough of the joking. I'm leaving in two days, so do what you gotta do and I'll be back to you then."

"Dad?" Mal called out to my father right before he was about to leave. "I didn't mean everything the way it came out."

"I know, son."

***

The day Mal went to pick up, I had him cop an extra nine ounces for me to take down South. If I was going to be staying for five days, I figured that should hold me.

"Yo, watch yourself while you down there, and if things ain't looking right catch a flight back home, because we ain't got time to be playing no games. Dad might be exaggerating anyway."

My pops came to pick me up.

"Keep me posted on what's going on. I got things covered up here."

"All right, I'll hit you when we touch down."

WELCOME TO SOUTH OF THE BORDER, the sign read. We had been driving for over nine hours and still had about an hour and a half to go. I stayed in the back of the camper, drinking, eating, and sleeping the whole time. My pops tried to get me to drive some of the way, but I wasn't trying to hear it; besides, I started to feel the pint of Hennessy and it knocked me out.

"Wake up, sleepyhead, we're here."

I hopped out of the back of the camper, and sitting right there was a big trailer home.

"Welcome to my domain," my pops said.

It was laid out and real clean. I was properly introduced to Carol and then she cooked for my dad and me after we took showers. When we finished eating, we got in Carol's Volvo and hit the area. Either everyone knew my father or they were just extra friendly, because every time we rode past somebody, they waved.

My father said it was a little bit of both. We went to all these different houses and projects and he introduced me to all different old men and women. Even though I didn't talk business with anybody, I knew these people had to be the heavy hitters in the town. What I noticed was that my pops didn't talk to or introduce me to nobody around my age. After we hit the areas and spots, he told me that we should hear something by tonight. The South game was definitely different than up top.

"Ay yo, Dad, no young cats hustle out here?"

"Yeah, but I don't deal with them. That's where you come in at. You gonna cut them in too after the word is out that we got that raw and that cook up. I'm gonna stop at these projects, over at a house of a lady friend of mines, where the kids around your age get the most money at."

"Oh, you got another lady friend down here?"

"Just business," he said, laughing.

It reminded me of back in the day when I used to sell hand to hand, only smaller and slower; but you could tell this was where it was at. I thought most of the money came through all the projects around the world on the drug tip. While my pops ran inside, I got out the car and leaned on the trunk.

"Yo, you got some ready rock?" a man asked me.

"What?"

"Some cook up?"

"Nah, go check them cats over there."

"Where you from, the city? 'Cause you don't sound like you from down here."

"Yeah."

"You brought some of that New York dope with you? That butter?"

"Nah, yo, I'm just visiting my peoples."

"Oh, my bad, sorry about that."

I couldn't stop laughing from the way he talked and what he said. He was more country than a muthafucka.

"What's happenin', man?" one of four kids said, walking up to me. "You kin to Jay and dem?"

"Yeah, that's my pops."

"Oh, that's chill. Big Jay good peoples. You from New York then, ain't ya?"

"Yeah."

"Where at?"

"Brooklyn."

"I know peoples in Brooklyn. You know Travis?" he asked as if there were only one person named Travis in the whole borough.

"What part he from?" I asked, dying on the inside from his questions, trying to keep a straight face.

"I don't know what part he from."

"I know a lot of Travises, kid."

"Yeah, you right. That was a stupid question."

"Nah, it's cool. If you knew where he was from I might've known him," I said, trying to smooth things out.

"My name's Calvin. These my boys, Dre, Slick, and Wood."

"Yo, I'm Mil."

"How long you down here for?"

"A couple days."

"There's something going on at the BBQ's tonight. Ya daddy know where it is. We gonna all be up in there if you wanna come. We got you; ain't nothing gonna kick off up in there unless we do the kickin' off."

I liked Calvin and them already because they reminded me of the project niggas back home. That's how it was whenever we went out.

"Yeah, that sounds legit. I'ma come through and check it out. All of you live around here?"

"We all grew up around here. All of them there by the front, them our niggas too, but us four be together."

"What y'all be movin' out here?"

"We be slingin' that powder and that cook up mostly and some weed, but we all smoke too much. You drink?"

"Nah, I sip though."

"You what?"

"I drink."

"Oh, yeah, we do a lot of that too."

The whole time I was talking to them I saw a monster flow come through. People in cars, pickup trucks, vans, bikes, and on foot coming from all angles, just like the projects.

"You brought something down wit' you?" Calvin asked.

"A little something."

"Well, if you bring some to the club you can move at least three or four ounces of it if you got it like that."

I was thinking, *He's gots to be crazy if he thinks I'm taking drugs to a club.*

"All them rock stars be out in the parking lot at night and somebody from across town always lookin' for a double up to make some money off of."

I figured rock stars were no different from crackheads. I didn't know what he was talking about when he said "double up," but I wasn't going to let him know that. "I'll see what my pops talkin' about and I'll catch you at the spot later."

"All right, New York, we'll see you."

My father was coming out just as they were leaving. "I knew you was gonna make some kind of connection; that's why I left you out here," he said as we pulled off.

I told him about the conversation I had with Calvin and them and then asked what a rock star and double up were. He told me a rock star was just like a crackhead, and a double up was anything you sold somebody that they could double their money off of; and he said that BBQ was the place to be tonight, and that's where we going anyway.

The spot was like no other club I had ever been to. It was more like a juke joint and the users and dealers partied together. It was crazy because you really couldn't tell who was who. I hooked up with Calvin and the rest of the cats I met earlier and we had a few drinks together. My father was outside the majority of the time and only came in to check on me here and there.

I was feeling the drinks and started dancing a little. Niggas and chicks watched as I did shit that hadn't come down there yet. Calvin and his boys could dance, but they couldn't fuck with me.

This caramel shorty with a short-ass skirt and a fat butt to match was on me. Calvin peeped it and said, "You want that ho? I'll set that up for you tonight."

I said, "All right." By the time it was over it was official: shorty was leaving with me; and my pops said he moved four ounces; and I had only been there one day.

Just as we were about to leave Calvin hollered at me, "New York, let me kick it to you for a minute."

"What up, kid?"

"Ay, what you do for me for three hundred dollars?"

Off the top of my head, I couldn't remember what my father had said so I just used the lingo that I knew. "On the strength I'll hit you wit' something to make at least a G."

"All right, bet. I'll have three bills by the morning."

"I'll come check you; and good lookin' with shorty."

He laughed. "Man, that ho ain't nothing. Don't even worry about it."

***

Within two days, the nine ounces were gone. I hung out with Calvin for the next two days before I was going back a day early. He had hipped me to fifty slabs, a hundred slabs, eight balls, and quarters where you could wind up making $1,400 off an ounce; and he told me that if I fronted cats' ounces they could bring back $1,800 off an ounce. I wound up making almost ten Gs off the nine ounces I came down with.

Calvin introduced me to a female cousin of his named Tia, who had a little daughter; they lived up in the projects too. I stayed the night with her but didn't hit it, which was cool because she was schooled to the South game and I had other intentions, bigger plans than just sexing her.

Chapter Sixty-five

"Damn, nigga, you lookin real country," Mal said, joking, giving me a hug.

"I missed you, bro."

"I missed you too, kid."

"It was sweet just like Dad said. All I did was party, 'cause that shit was gone in two days and niggas still was askin' did I have that shit."

"Word!"

"Yeah, kid. Dad moved four ounces for me at a club for eleven hundred dollars a piece. Then two more the next day and I moved three up in these projects down there with come cool country cats, and I bagged a nice shorty who lives in the same projects."

"So now what's up?"

"Yo, I'm telling you this is where it's at for us. I think if I would've taken a whole pie I could've moved it in four days."

"Get the fuck out of here."

"I'm telling you, straight up."

"All right, we'll take a brick down there this weekend then."

Chapter Sixty-six

It only took two and a half days to move the brick we had taken down South. By the time we had sold out, we had met dudes from almost every part of South Carolina and some from North Carolina. We were moving ounces by the threes or more. I had wifed Tia up, Mal found him a shorty from the next projects, and Calvin and them were ready to be fronted ounces, so things were going good thanks to our dad. This was definitely our time to blow.

Our first year down there we had moved about fifteen to twenty keys. We could've moved more but the South was funny like that. It had its dry spells some weeks and months. Then there were times when we had to make examples out of cats who didn't believe that we were built like that. Without going into details, we had to put in work and, when we did, it slowed the flow down.

By 1998, our third year down there, we were bubbling hard. We had both copped double-wide trailers not too far from our father's, plus two houses in town. Mal had a Navigator and I had an Escalade, and we both had a 500SL coupe and a Range apiece, and 1100s back home. We had come up on some liquor licenses for cheap and opened up a club in Florence, South Carolina.

By 1999, back home we opened up a family grocery store on the west end in Jersey, not too far from the projects. Business was good both legal and illegally. Tonya wound up having a girl and so did Felicia. My daughter's names were Jamiyah and Kamiyah. I moved Tia up out of the projects and into a house because she was carrying my third child, but we still kept her apartment to pump out of. It was crazy how I went from not having or wanting any kids to having three back to back by three different women. I realized that's how it was when you were ballin' and you're sticking in moving. Overall, I had no complaints and neither did my brother.

"Yo, this is too much money in the crib," Mal said. We had just finished counting $430,000.

"Not really, 'cause when I go up top, three of that is goin' to the fifteen bricks I gotta get."

"Still, that'll be a hundred thirty Gs left down here; plus, we got mad work out right now, we don't need all of this in here."

"You're right. I'll just take a hundred of that with me, 'cause I gotta stop up there to check on your nieces anyway, so I'ma go through Jersey on the way."

"Yeah, you could do that. Stop and check on Dana and li'l Mal for me, and call and see if Fisa need anything."

"I got you."

"Put that hundred separate from the three hundred, so I ain't gotta be worryin' about that when I get up there. I'ma take five of that thirty to travel with, just in case something new came out that we ain't got."

"No doubt, and cop me a pair of white on white, and red and white Air Ones while you up there."

Ring! Ring!

"Yo, who this?"

"Kamil, this Christy, Tia's friend."

"Yeah, what's up?"

"Tia went into labor. They just took her to the hospital, and she told me to call you."

"Word! Oh, shit! A'ight, which hospital they take her to?"

"The one in Florence."

"Okay, thanks,"

"Who in the hospital?"

"Tia. She went into labor."

"Word?"

"Yeah, kid, I gots to shoot out there to Florence."

"Yeah, handle ya business, yo. Don't even worry about this. I'll go up and take care this. You go see ya newborn and you just double up on the next two trips."

"Word!"

"Congratulations, kid. I hope it's a boy."

"Me too."

"I'll hit you when I'm in the area."

"All right, one."

What me and Kamal had hoped for came true. It was a boy. On June 10, 1999, Tia gave birth to my third child, who was also my first son: seven pounds, eight ounces. She wanted to name him after me, but one of us was enough in the world, so instead I named him Khalif and, out of respect for Mustafa, I made his last name my son's middle name, which was Ali. Khalif Ali Benson was what the birth certificate said. I loved my daughters, but I was proud and happy to have a son.

I stayed at the hospital all night with Tia. Mal called me earlier and told me that Moms wasn't home when he went to drop the money off so he was going to drop it off on the way coming back. Since then I hadn't heard from him.

The next morning, I woke up to my cell phone ringing. I was stiff and sore from sleeping in the hospital chair. "Yeah, what's up, who this?"

"Hello, Mm . . . Mil?" I heard someone crying through the phone.

"Who this?"

"It's Dana." When she said her name, my stomach began to hurt.

"What's wrong?"

She started to cry even harder.

"Dana what's wrong? Where's Mal?"

"They killed him."

My heart skipped a beat and I felt like I couldn't breath. I thought I was hearing things. "What! Who? What the fuck you talking about?"

"The cops. They killed Kamal," she said again.

"Hold on, Dana, my moms on the other line. Hello?"

"Oh my God, Kamil!"

"Ma, what happened?"

"Your brother is dead," my mother cried through the phone.

"No! Ma! No! Say it ain't true! Say it ain't it true!"

"I'm sorry, baby, he's gone."

"Ah, man! Aah, man!"

"Kamil, what's wrong?" Tia asked, waking up to find me hysterical; but I couldn't speak. The pain was too unbearable. I felt like dying myself.

I jumped up, slammed my phone down, and stormed out of the room.

"Kamil, what's wrong?" Tia asked again.

I screamed as loud as I could, "They killed my brother!"

Chapter Sixty-seven

My father and I caught the next available flight to the Newark airport. Dana picked us up. I had regained my composure and calmed back down after a few drinks on the plane, but I still felt like I'd been run over by a bus or something.

"Tell me what happened," I said to Dana as soon as we got in the car. Just knowing that this was my brother's Benz made tears spill out of my eyes and run down my face, because I knew that I would never see him drive his car again, or see him do anything else for that matter. I not only lost my brother, but my best friend also.

"The news said that the state troopers pulled him over on 78, and when they asked him to step out of the truck, he pulled off. They chased him about four miles down the highway until he had spun out of control and hit the divider and flipped over six times. They said he died instantly." She paused. "They said they found fifteen kilos of cocaine and sixty-five thousand dollars in cash in the truck, which is why they believed he pulled off."

After hearing the story, I knew the police had taken $40,000 off of Kamal after he died because I knew for a fact that he had $100,000 on him to give to my moms, plus an extra $5,000 spending money. *Why didn't he take the ticket or whatever? He was driving legit.* So many thoughts, so many questions. I began to cry harder. These tears were guilt. I knew it was my turn to make the trip up to New York, but Tia had gone into labor.

Damn, why she have to go in labor then, of all times? That should've been me in the truck instead of Kamal. Why the fuck didn't I delay the trip? I cursed myself as I gazed out the passenger's window.

My mother, grandma, and two sisters were at the house when my dad and I got there. As soon as I walked through the door, my moms flew into my arms. You could see that they all had been crying, because everyone's eyes were bloodshot and puffy. As my mother sobbed, her tears melted through my shirt and went straight to my heart.

"Why y'all couldn't just listen to me? Why?" she cried out. "Why, Kamil?" she yelled again.

She pushed away from me and smacked me in the face then started beating on my chest. "Why?" she repeated. She was hysterical. I tried to grab her arms, but she was too out of control. "You promised me. You two promised me!"

"Ma! Ma!" I called out to calm her down, but she couldn't hear me. She just kept smacking and punching me.

"Sister, stop! Sister!" my grandmother yelled, but my mother continued until she was too tired to swing anymore. I wrapped my arms around her again and held her. My sisters came over and joined me. I rocked my moms back and forth while she cried out to God. I rubbed her back and tried to assure her that everything would be okay. A few more minutes went by before she regained her composure.

"I'm okay, let me go," she said to me.

I released her from my hold. "You sure?" I asked.

"Yes, I'm okay," she replied as she wiped her face. "What is he doing here?" my mother asked, spotting my dad.

"He flew up with me as soon as we heard what happened."

"He don't belong here. I want him out!"

"Jane, he was my son too," my father said.

"Your son? Jay, please! You gave up those rights a long time ago when you chose the streets over your family, so don't stand there talking about how he was your son too. I raised these kids, all of them. I was their mother and their father, not you. Me!"

"Ma, calm down."

"Kamil, stay out of this." She pointed at me. "You think if you would've been the man or at least half the man you claimed to be, my children wouldn't have had to be subjected to the type of environment I had to raise them in? Do you think if you would've cared about them like you cared about yourself and those damn streets back then, my sons would've had a man in their lives to teach them how to be men? It's because of you I lost my child. You're the one who gave us all up. It was you who wasn't there for them and it was you who even took them to the South and got them believing that it's all right to be out there. What type of man would condone his own children in the streets, living the life of crime and corruption? You're not a man, not at all! Get out of my house! Get the hell out!" my moms yelled.

I thought my father was going to say something that would trigger a bigger confrontation, forcing me to intervene, but he didn't. Instead, he turned around, and walked out the door.

I didn't follow him this time like I did when Kamal had verbally assaulted him, because this was between him and my mother. Her words had been a long time coming and I had no right to interfere.

Chapter Sixty-eight

My moms and grandmother made all the funeral arrangements. I told them to pick whatever type of burial they thought was best for Mal, regardless of the cost. Dana had shirts made up with his picture on the front and R.I.P. GONE BUT NOT FORGOTTEN on the back. Everywhere I drove throughout the town, some-body was wearing one of the shirts. They thought they were paying respect to my brother, but what they really were doing was hurting the people who truly loved and would miss him, because every time I saw the picture on the shirt it pained me more, and reminded me of the fact that my other half was gone.

The turnout at the wake alone was ridiculous. More people than Ant's and Trevor's wakes combined had shown up. People we knew from all over came out from New York, B-more, Philly, VA, NC, SC, Florida, ATL, Ohio, Indy, Detroit, and even Chicago. We had to schedule two viewings because there was so many. Flowers were everywhere, wall to wall, in the room. The casket they chose for Mal was marble green, with real gold trimming, which were his favorite colors. They dressed him in a solid green suit that almost looked black, with a beige shirt, and a green and beige tie, with the matching handkerchief.

My mother broke down when she went up to the casket. I had to go get her and escort her to her seat, while the usher aided me by fanning her. Monique wouldn't even go up there, and Jasmine passed out when she did. The whole while I fought back my own tears and stayed strong for the family. My grandmother kneeled down on her knees and said a prayer for him. When she got up, she began to praise dance and call on Jesus. My dad leaned into the casket, gave my brother a kiss on the forehead, and then walked out.

After Dana went up with Mal Jr., and Keya went up with Fisa, I went up. I didn't even recognize him at first. I knew it was him, but it didn't look like it. We no longer looked alike. I wondered if that was how I would look when my time came. I stared at my brother for a moment, studying his facial expression. He looked at peace. I could not remember the last time I'd seen him looking so peaceful. It had been a long time. Not since we were kids. I kneeled down like my grandmother had done, and I began to talk to my brother.

"What up, kid? How you doin' up there?" I began. I felt myself started to get choked up, but still I fought it off. "I know you're maintaining. I'm tryin' to hold it down on this end, but shit is crazy for me down here. I know you gotta be feelin' the way I do too right about now 'cause we not used to being separated like this for so long. Moms and them are going through it, but they'll be all right 'cause they strong. Hell, they gotta be strong if they raised us, right? I thought it was gonna get ugly between Moms and Pops, 'cause she let him have it." I smiled. "But Dad bowed down on some respectful shit.

"The kids are all right. Don't worry about Fisa and li'l Mal; you know they covered for life. I got you. Oh! I meant to tell you, you were right. It was a boy, so you ain't the only one with a son now to keep the legacy going. I can see the two of them together now, inseparable like we were." I wiped a tear from my face that had escaped my right eye. "But they ain't gonna be nothing like us, except good looking." I chuckled. "They gonna be better than us. I named my son Khalif Ali Benson. You know I got the Ali from Mu's name.

"Yo, let me ask you somethin'. Why did you pull off like that, kid? Damn! I know you used to always say how you wasn't never goin' to jail, but damn, dawg, you was more valuable alive than dead." I shook my head as four drops managed to release themselves from my barrier. "I don't know, maybe I would've done the same thing, 'cause you know great minds think alike. It don't even matter; you did what you did and it's over and done with.

"Moms and them went all out on the funeral. You would've approved. You're probably lookin' down at us right now checkin' out the whole scene. If you see Ant and Trevor tell them niggas I said one love and I ain't forget about them. Look at all these niggas and chicks up in this piece who came out to pay their respects like you were the last Don or something." I couldn't resist another chuckle.

"I know you smiling right about now, nigga." I could've sworn when I looked up he had a grin on his face. "Yo, anyway, I'm gonna put that work in twice as much as before now that you're gone, to make sure that the li'l ones don't ever have to go through the things we went through. We went through some wild shit when we were kids. Before I get out the game I'm gonna go to the Keys and cop that boat for you, too, and then after that it's over. The game is over for me. Believe that!" I promised my brother.

"All right, kid, I'm gonna talk to you later, but if you see me slippin' or something, get at me. Let me know. Show me a sign or something. I love you, Mal." I got up and, like my dad, I leaned in and gave my brother a kiss on the cheek. "One love, bro. Rest in peace."

I could no longer hold them back. The levy had been broken and my tears came pouring out like a tidal wave. They stained my brother's face. When I turned around, I could have sworn I saw my brother walking out of the church. I wiped my face with my handkerchief and tended to my family.

On June 15, 1999, there were just as many people at the funeral as there were at the wake. The chain of whips that followed the hearse and family car was well over a hundred. I rode in the limo with my moms, grandmother, and sisters while my father drove my car. He respected my mother's wishes and kept his distance. I admired him for that.

When Mal was laid to rest, I skipped the reception and me and my pops flew back to

South Carolina. I had grieved enough for a lifetime, and now it was time to tie up some loose ends. Now that my brother was gone, there was no need for me to continue playing the game that had plagued our family and friends for decades. I hated that it took for me to lose someone who meant the world to me to get me to see that what I was doing was never worth it.

Chapter Sixty-nine

Six months had passed, and I had sold most of the things that reminded me of Mal. I sold his house in the South, his Range, Lex, Navi, and bike. I let his wifey Deb keep the trailer for being a trooper, though. On top of that, I sold the club we had down there too because I didn't have the desire to party anymore now that my partner in crime was gone. It just wouldn't have been the same.

All the money I got from selling Mal's whips and other material things I put in trust funds for Fisa and Mal Jr. for their college educations and future. A shorty in Florida was pregnant by Mal. She told me she was going to surprise him with the news the day he was scheduled to come back from New York. I stayed in contact with her so I could make arrangements to set up my niece or nephew when they arrived into the world.

Everything Mal owned in Jersey I let Dana keep: the house, the whips; plus, I set up a bank account for her with fifty grand to start to take care of her and Mal Jr. I put another fifty grand in an account for whenever Fisa was old enough. It took me a year to get everything in order, but I had done it, and I was back on top of my game, as strong as ever.

June 10, 2000 was my son's first birthday and Tia and I decided to have it in Jersey at Chuck E. Cheese's so that his sister, cousins, and the rest of the family like Moms and them could be there. It was also better for me, because it was also the one-year anniversary of Kamal's death, so I would be able to visit his gravesite before we went back down South.

The birthday party turned out to be fun and tiring. All the cats from the projects brought their kids, and even chicks Mal and I had messed with in the past brought theirs. A few of the kids looked like they could be either mine or Mal's and I laughed to myself on the inside. Jamiyah and Kamiyah were playing with Khalif over in the bullpen. Both Fisa and Mal Jr. came too. Each time I looked at them, my heart ached because they were both spitting images of their father. Anyone with eyes could see how close they were by the way they stuck together at the party at all times.

I was sitting in the corner just watching everything, trying to digest the whole pan of pizza I had eaten earlier, when I saw Fisa and Mal Jr. coming toward me.

"Hey, Uncle Mil!"

"Hey there yourselves."

"Why you over here by yourself?"

"'Cause you kids wore me out, that's why."

"You miss our dad don't you?" Mal Jr. asked.

I smiled and picked him up, placing him on my lap. "I sure do, man."

"We do too," he said.

"Uncle Mil, you look just like our daddy," Fisa said.

"Oh, yeah, you think so?" I said, playing along with her.

"Yup!"

"Well, you and Mal Jr. look just like your dad too and your cousins Jamiyah, Kamiyah, and Khalif."

They laughed. "Were you and my daddy twins?" Mal Jr. asked.

"No, man, but we were just alike, and we used to be together all the time like I see you and your sister be."

"Can we come stay with you one summer down South, Uncle Mil?" Fisa asked.

"Sure, you can. It can be anytime you want; just call me and I'll be there. And if the two of you ever need anything don't hesitate to ask, you hear me?"

"Yes," they both said together.

Chapter Seventy

"What's the deal, bro? You missed a good party a couple of days ago. My li'l man turned a year old and we celebrated his birthday at Chuck E. Cheese's. Fisa and Mal Jr. was there. They told me I look just like you. That shit made me laugh 'cause they look more like you than I do. They wanna come down South with me for the summer so I'ma try to make that happen. You know Keya be buggin', but not too much since you been gone. If I don't get 'em this summer I'll definitely have 'em before the year ends.

"Yo! Guess where I'm going after I leave here? To the Keys, nigga! I'm goin' to cop a boat for you. Yeah, that's how I'm doing it for the new millennium! Shorty down there had a little girl. She named her Jasmyne Malika Benson. I told her that we had a sister named Jasmine so she spelled it different. The way she be talking, I know that girl really loved you. I sold damn near everything and put the dough in Fisa's and Mal Jr.'s names, plus laid out extra cash for whenever they need something.

"I took the coke game to another level since this German I was locked up with taught me the whip game. He showed me how to turn one into two or at least into an extra seven hundred and fifty grams. All that shit is free paper right there. I don't party no more since you been gone, but I be everywhere on some business shit. Niggas stay hittin' me on the hip for them thangs. On the cash tip alone I'm hood rich, a ghetto millionaire, but ssh! Don't tell nobody!" I joked.

"Like Mu told me back in the day, once he taught me all he knew I was gonna be a 'Ghetto Genius,' and that's what I've become, kid; but I ain't letting that shit get to my head 'cause none of this shit means nothing without you here, bro. I miss you like a muthafucka and I'd give it all up if it would bring you back.

"Speaking of Mu, I'm goin' to see him this weekend. He wrote me a letter and said he had to talk to me about something important. Yo! When I cop that boat I'm gonna pop the first bottle of Cristal and pour it out for the ones who ain't here; then the second bottle I'ma pour out strictly for you; and the third bottle I'm gonna toast to you and drink it to the head. I love you, big bro. Take care; see you next time I come through."

Chapter Seventy-one

When Mu appeared in front of the Plexiglas, I had to do a double take. He was big like my dad used to be when I was a kid, only he was scary big. He had muscles popping out in places I didn't know muscles existed. He was so huge he didn't even have a neck. To top it off, he had traded his beehive waves for shoulder-length dreadlocks, and his once chin-strapped beard for a long, fluffy full-sized one. He also sported a pair of what seemed to be reading glasses. I just stared at him like the first time I had when he had picked Mal and me up that day in his car. He sat down and grabbed the phone.

"Peace, *akhi*," he greeted me.

"What's goin' on, big bro?" My excitement showed in my voice. It was good to see him and I told him that. This was the first time in all those years he had been locked up that I had come to see him.

Mu smiled.

"How's everything?" I asked.

"As good as they can be under the circumstances," he replied.

"That's good to hear. I'm sorry for—" I didn't get a chance to finish. Mu held his hand up and stopped me.

"No need for apologies or regrets. The important thing is that you're here now," he told me.

"You're right," I agreed. Even after all those years, Mu was still schooling me.

"My condolences." His tone lowered.

I just nodded.

"He's with Allah now."

I didn't want to talk about my brother so I changed the subject. "So, is everything good? You said you had something important to talk to me about."

Mu ran his hand down his face then stroked his beard. I could tell he was collecting his thoughts. "Yeah, I do. I wanna tell you a story," he said.

I gave him a confused look.

"Just listen," he told me. "When I was eight years old, my mother introduced me to this man as her friend. He would come by every now and again and spend time with my mother and me. Every time he came around my mother would be on top of the world and whenever he didn't she was miserable. He would come by and take her out while a neighbor watched me or he would take the both of us somewhere nice. Every time a holiday came around, he never came through without bearing gifts. He would always ask me what I liked or what my favorite toy was and then a few days later he'd come back with it. My mother would always get on him about spoiling me and she would say that I was going to wind up being like him if he kept treating me the way he was.

"One day, after coming home from a half day of school, I accidentally walked in on my mother's friend mixing up some drugs in her bedroom, while my mother lay in bed asleep. When he saw me, he put his finger to his lips and stood up. He escorted me into the kitchen. There, he taught me what he was doing and everything else he knew. By the time I turned thirteen I knew everything about the drug game there was to know. Even though he taught me all of that, he always made me promise to stay in school and get an education.

"My senior year, I came home to find my mother in tears. When I asked her what was wrong, she told me that her friend had gotten arrested. Shortly thereafter, things began to get rough for my mother and me. So, one night

I caught the train over to New York, over on 145th Street in Harlem, where my mother's friend told me he went to get his product, and I posted up. I watched as jokers who looked like drug dealers approached Spanish dudes. Within minutes, I witnessed drugs and money transactions between the Black and Spanish hustlers. I waited until I thought I had found the right hustler and then I followed him. I followed him all the way to the subway station and then, right before he made it to the steps, I made my move. He never saw it coming.

"I crept up from behind, yoked him up, and put the knife I had hidden behind my back up to his throat. I told him to run his pocket or I would slit his throat, and I meant it. He reached into his pocket and gave me a small brown paper bag with a piece of tape on it to conceal it. I took the package with my left hand while holding the blade firmly up against his neck. Everything was going smooth until he made the fatal mistake of reacting. To this day, I don't know what he was trying to do, but he never got the chance to do it because, without hesitation, I slit his throat from ear to ear with the Rambo knife I had.

"I remember being scared to death, and I ran for my life. I ran nearly nonstop all the way down to 125th Street. I made my way to the

125th Street train station, headed back to New Jersey. I was paranoid the whole while. When I got home, I tore open the brown bag. Based on the color I knew it was coke. I went and got the scale I knew my mother's friend kept in the house. When I placed the package on there, it read fifty-six grams. That was the day I became a drug dealer.

"A year later, I moved my mother out of the projects and into a house. That following year she died. I went through her stuff, found letters from prison, and I knew they were letters from her friend. That night I sat down and wrote him a letter informing him of my mother's death. I also asked him a question, one that was always in the back of my mind: was he my father? He never wrote me back and answered, but as far as I was concerned, he was. Do you know why I'm telling you this story?" Mu asked me.

Honestly, I didn't have a clue, but I was glad he had shared that piece of his life with me. I answered no.

"The reason I told you that story is because the only father figure or male role model I ever had in my life, and the man I believe to be my real father, was my mother's friend. And"—he took a deep breath—"my mother's friend was your dad."

His statement caught me by surprise. I was positive I had heard wrong, but Mu's next statement let me know I had heard right.

"I felt it was important that you knew."

My first reaction was to get up and leave, but Mu told me to sit down before I had a chance to hang up the phone. I was fuming but didn't really know why. I didn't know whether I was mad at Mu for telling me the story or at my dad for not. I knew Mu wouldn't lie to me or make something up like that, so it had to be true.

I sat back down.

"Listen, I know what I laid on you is a hard pill to swallow, but with all that has happened, you needed to know," he started out saying. "At the end of the day, it doesn't matter how good he treated you, Mal, your sisters, and me; when it came to women, he was a rolling stone. It doesn't take away from how he felt about any of us."

As I listened to Mu, the more I stared at him the more I could see some of my dad's features in him. I didn't know how I hadn't seen it in all this time, all these years.

"Regardless of what is in my heart and in my mind you'll always be my family, blood or no blood, you understand?"

"We're family for life!" I looked Mu square in the eyes and said.

He put his fist up to the glass and I did the same. "I love you, li'l bro."

"I love you too, Mu." At that moment, I missed Mal more than ever.

Mu stood up. "One last thing," he said.

I waited for him to tell me.

"The game is officially dead. Get out of it!" And then he hung up and walked off.

Chapter Seventy-two

After visiting Mustafa so many things had invaded my mind. I called my father and played the story back to him that Mu had told me and then I asked him if Mu was my brother. He said he really didn't know, but he told me Mu's mother had said he wasn't. I took that as a yes, but he was too ashamed to admit it because it would have shown how he was cheating on my moms. I left it at that and moved on. I had too many other things on my plate to be worrying about my father's infidelities. As far as I was concerned, Mu was my brother long before he told me the story.

I flew down to Florida and Mal's baby moms April met me at the airport. We drove to the Florida Keys. The owner wanted $650,000 for the boat, but she knew him so I got it for $600,000. He was a rich cat from the streets who made it the legit way, so he didn't have a problem with me paying him in cash, which was cool with me because I had too much in the safe at my stash crib anyway that only I knew about. I knew it had to be close to a mil and a half 'cause I wasn't taking nothing under a hundred grand there each time and I knew since I had that spot I had been there over ten times.

I didn't even know how to sail a boat. I only got it because Mal wanted one so bad, so on the strength of that I was going to learn. The cat named Drew who sold me the boat was explaining the things I needed to know about owning a boat and then we sealed the deal. I had brought $750,000 with me anyway because I thought it was going to run me that much, so I was able to squash the whole amount right then and there. Drew was impressed. I could tell even if he didn't say so. He offered to take her out for a sail so I could get an idea of how it worked. I agreed.

After me, him, and April sailed back into the dock I asked them if I could get some time alone to myself. Drew said no problem, stepping off, not understanding, but April understood.

"Take as much time as you need."

"Thanks," I told her.

"Well, bro, here it is! This is for you, kid!" I looked up into the heavens. I popped the first of the three bottles of Cristal I had April pick up for me before I arrived in Florida, and then, one by one, I did just as I told Mal I was going to do.

Chapter Seventy-three

I went to bed early that night. All the ripping and running in the streets I had been doing finally caught up to me. I didn't think I had slept a good twenty-four hours combined in the past three weeks. Either I was on the highway driving to some other state, or I was on the plane flying somewhere. My peoples in Ohio and Indy were copping bricks like they were going out of style, and my other peeps in VA and NC were moving so many pies that they should've opened up a bakery, so I was constantly on the move.

The raw I had was definitely in demand. I was letting everybody I supplied know that I was about to close up shop and retire. It felt good to be able to lie in my own bed and get a good night's rest. I started dreaming about taking the boat and sailing it around the world, hitting some spots that I had always heard some of the rich people talk about on television.

As I was sailing the boat, all of a sudden my dream switched to a nightmare.

I was in the truck with Mal on the highway, being chased not only by the state troopers, but by the DEA, ATF, the county police, and the feds. They even had helicopters hovering overhead. Mal was driving and yelling at me at the same time. All I could hear him saying was, "We gotta get outta here!" over and over again.

I just sat there listening, trying to figure out what he was talking about. I tried to tell him to slow down, but he wouldn't listen. The more I demanded that he slow down the faster he drove. Then, out of nowhere, we hit the divider and the truck started flipping. When I looked at Mal, blood was dripping from his head on down to his face. He looked at me and said, "Mil, get out! You gotta get out!"

The truck stopped flipping and I tried to do as he said, but my seat belt was stuck, and I couldn't get out of the passenger's seat. Mal made it out somehow, though, and when I looked to my right he was on my side of the truck trying to help me get the seat belt off.

"Mil, you gotta get out!" he yelled again.

"Bro, I can't. I can't get out," I said, struggling to unfasten the belt.

"You have to. Get out now!" He was scaring me. I didn't know if the truck was on fire or what.

Then just like that, the seat belt came loose.

"Mil, hurry up. Get out now. They're comin'! Mil? Mil? You hear me?"

"Yeah, I hear you," I said aloud.

"Well, get up then. The police are at the door."

When I opened my eyes, Tia was standing over me.

"Huh?" I said, not having a clue what she said.

"I said the police are at the door," she repeated.

I had heard her, but I thought that she was Kamal. I jumped up once it dawned on me that I was no longer dreaming. I knew the house was clean because I never brought anything here, except for the gun I carried, and they'd never find that, so I wasn't worried about them coming up in here. "How many is it?"

"I only saw two white uniformed officers. They look local."

I could hear them pounding on the door as I made my way to the living room. "Yeah, just a minute," I yelled as I was walking to the door.

When I opened, it was just as Tia said: two local sheriffs from town. "Yes, can I help you?"

"Mr. Benson?"

"Yes?"

"You're under arrest," they announced. Then officers and agents came from out of nowhere.

"Get on the ground, now!" they all yelled as they entered the house with their weapons drawn.

"For what?"

"Sir, we have a state warrant and a federal warrant for your arrest. We also have a warrant to search the premises, and seize this home and any and all assets you may possess," a federal agent ran down. "You have the right to remain silent. Anything you say may be used against you in a court of law . . ." He finished reading my Miranda rights. "Do you understand these rights?"

"Yeah."

My son cries became louder as I heard Tia shouting. "What are you doin'?" she cried.

"Ma'am, you're under arrest," the female officer said to her.

"For what? I ain't done nothing."

"For aiding and abetting in a racketeering enterprise. You have the right . . ."

My ears went deaf. I couldn't believe this was happening. All I could think about was the dream I just had when Mal kept telling me to get out. It dawned on me that my brother was trying to warn me. He was trying to tell me that

I had slipped, and they were coming for me. All I could do was shake my head as they slapped the metal handcuffs on me.

Chapter Seventy-four

Child protective services had taken my son into custody until my moms was able to fly down and get him. They wouldn't release him to my father or to Tia's mom because they had both been convicted of felonies before. I had my pops call the same lawyer Mustafa used in his fed beef to represent Tia and me. The feds worked different from the state, so I didn't really know what I was actually being charged with until I went to my preliminary.

When Mr. Schmidt came to see me, he told me that my father had given him $100,000 to represent Tia and me. He also told me that he had good news and bad news, depending on how one would look at it, and he asked me which I wanted first. I wasn't in the mood for guessing games, but I told him to give me that good news first.

He started out by saying, "The good news is that the feds really didn't want your son's mother, a Ms. Katia Johnson, am I correct?"

"Yes."

"The bad news is that they really want you, and the hundred thousand dollars alone is just the beginning to cover your consultation."

I sat there just listening.

"Have you had a chance to look at this yet?" he asked, showing me some papers with my name versus the United States of America at the heading.

"Nah, I haven't."

"Well, take this copy; this is the copy of your indictment. I took the liberty of reading it this morning, and it doesn't look too good, it doesn't look good at all, but we're going to give them the best fight possible. It's basically saying that they've been investigating you and your deceased brother since the year 1998. They have photos, surveillance, wiretaps, and confidential informants against you. They're charging you with racketeering and trafficking, as well as possession with intent in nine different states plus other states that you've traveled to and from." He thumbed through some of the pages. "There are additional charges for murder, in South Carolina as well as in New Jersey. I can tell you now, Mr. Benson, whether you cop to this or take it trial, the DA is going to recommend life imprisonment unless you are willing to cooperate with the government."

"That's not an option, Mr. Schmidt."

"I know it's not, Mr. Benson. You and Mr. Ali have the same type of persona, but it's my job to advise you of your options. You will never hear me mention that to you again, though; my loyalty lies strictly with you and your best interest. One thing I'm sure of that is if you enter a guilty plea, they will release Ms. Johnson, but if you try to play hardball with them, they'll see to it that your son grows up without his mother and father. You seem like a family man, so that choice is entirely up to you."

"How were you able to get Mustafa twenty-five years and life is my only option?"

"Mr. Ali's case wasn't as severe as yours. His only involved drugs; yours includes murder. If somehow we could get the murder charges dropped then, yes, you would be eligible for a plea other than life, but that's not likely to happen."

"Why not?"

"Because to beat murder charges you must go to trial."

"Well, that's what I want, because I didn't kill nobody," I lied.

"Mr. Benson, are you sure?"

"Yeah, I'm sure. What do I have to lose?"

"You're right."

"Listen, tell the DA that I will plead guilty to all the drugs if he lets my son's mother go, but I am pleading not guilty to the murders of whoever they claiming I killed. Who is it, anyway?"

"I won't know until your preliminary Tuesday."

"All right, well, see what the DA says and I'll call you tomorrow."

I found out through my moms that they had frozen the bank account in my name, which was nothing because I only had like eighty grand in my savings and another twenty-five grand in my checking. Everything else was either in Tia's or the kid's name.

They shut my store down in Jersey and confiscated the house, the Benz, and the Range from Dana, and they froze the sixty grand she had left from the hundred I gave her for her and my nephew, only because she wasn't working. They took all my cars, trucks, bikes, and the one thing near and dear to me, Kamal's boat. They couldn't take anything from Mal's daughter mother in Florida because she was a real estate agent and had her stuff together.

I still had a lot of paper put up, scattered all around. I had stashed $750,000, trying to hit that mil mark, and I hit my sisters off with a hundred grand on the low. Tia's mom had $75,000, and I took Mu's shorty $150,000 to put up for me in case of an emergency, 'cause she was still riding with Mu hard. She even married him from jail. In cash alone I had at least a million and I knew the lawyer wasn't going to cost that much, so I was good. I just had to get these bodies off my back. Honestly, me, Mal, and Shareef, when he was home, put so much work in that I couldn't figure out what bodies they could be trying to charge me with.

"Hello, can I speak to Mr. Schmidt?"

"Who's calling?"

"Kamil Benson."

"Just a minute, Mr. Benson, I'll connect you. Mr. Schmidt had been expecting your call."

"Kamil?"

"Yes."

"How are you?"

"I'm all right, what's goin' on?"

"I had the opportunity to speak to the district attorney, and he's willing to release Ms. Johnson the moment you enter a guilty plea, but he wasn't happy to hear that you were taking the murders to trial. He even offered you a plea, which I doubt you'll agree to but it's better than life."

"What is it?"

"Four hundred and eighty months."

"What? What the hell does that add up to?"

"Forty years, Mr. Benson."

"Tell him I'll see him in trial," I said without hesitation.

"I already told him, sir."

They released Tia on April 10, 2002, the day I entered a guilty plea on the drug charges and not guilty plea on the murders. They were charging me with Travis Dempsey and Marlon Jones of Florence, South Carolina, and Black's and Quadir's murders, and conspiracy to murder. My stomach was doing somersaults and my heart was pounding so hard it felt like it was going to bust out of my chest, but my face remained stone. Even though I knew of the incident in Florence, I didn't know them two cats they named and I wasn't there so I wasn't worried about that. Mal had told me how some niggas from out there tried to do some ol' funny style shit and he had to handle them on the low. But the other two names I knew well, and the first person to come to mind as a confidential informant was Baseball Betty. *Damn! Mal said that bitch could trap us off if we wasn't careful.*

Knowing all of that, I was still going to trial to do everything I could in my power to weaken the DA's case on the bodies.

I called Tia at her mom's house.

"You have a pre-paid call from Kamil from a county jail, do you accept?"

"Yes. Hey, baby!"

"What's good, ba'y?"

"I'm all right. Missin' you like crazy."

"Yeah me, too."

"I spoke to your momma today and she supposed to bring Khalif down this weekend when she comes to see you."

"Come see me? Nah, tell her I don't want no visit."

"Why?"

"'Cause I don't, that's why. Check, I don't have that much time. I need you to click me into Shaheed right quick."

"What's the number?"

"908-555-1013."

"Hold on, baby. Here he go."

"Sha."

"Yo, what up, son?"

"Nothin', kid. They got me in a jam right now."

"I heard. That shit it all up here."

"Yeah, I figured that, but yo, listen; I need you to do me a favor."

"Anything, you know you my dawg. What's good?"

"You know how to play 'Baseball'?"

"Yeah, no doubt."

"I need you to play that game for me 'cause that's the only way I won't strike out. I mean, I really need you to play your best, and hit a homerun."

"Say no more, son; I got you on the strength."

"Good looking, baby!"

That was the only way I could talk to Shaheed without the feds picking up on what I was saying, and I knew he knew what I was talking about. I had basically told him to find Baseball Betty and kill her so she couldn't make it to court to testify.

"Yo, Mil, what you facin'?"

"That L, baby boy."

"Damn, kid!"

"Yeah, but if you play baseball for me, it might not be so bad."

"All right! One."

"Yeah. Tia, click me off."

"Mil, what were you talking about with baseball?" Tia asked.

"That's irrelevant. Listen, though; we might as well get this out the way now. No matter what happens with me I just want you to promise me that you'll raise Khalif properly and keep him out the streets, and most importantly make sure he knows his sisters and my brother's kids.

Don't worry about how you gonna survive 'cause I got you covered. You not obligated to ride out with me on this here 'cause I'm looking at a long ride, so I ain't gonna be mad at ya for doin' you."

"Mil, you talking crazy. I'm with you through thick and thin, better or worse, richer or poor, 'til death do us part, I love you."

I figured she'd hit me with something like that. They all did until it got too thick; then they flipped, because that was all a part of the game. I wanted to believe her but the rules wouldn't let me.

"All right, well, if that's how you feel then I love you for that. I'll talk to you later. I gotta go."

They indicted me on July 13, 2002 and I was scheduled to pick a jury August 20, 2002. The feds didn't play. They were known for ending cases and trials quick. Their conviction rate was 98 percent. Even knowing that, I still intended to go to war with them. The DA made a final offer to my lawyer for 332 months, which was thirty-six years, but Shaheed had told Tia to tell me that the baseball game was over in the first inning, so I was confident about going to trial and I rejected his offer.

The jury was selected and it was time to start my trial.

"Are you ready, Mr. Benson?" my lawyer asked.

I just smiled and said, "Yes."

I decided that I didn't want any of my family at my trial besides my father because he knew the game, and they respected my wishes. I didn't want my moms and the rest of them to hear what I was being accused of because it would've been shameful and embarrassing, whether I did it or not.

To my surprise, I spotted Lisa sitting all the way in the back. I didn't know how she even knew I would be in court that day, but it was good to see her.

By the time the government presented weak evidence that didn't implicate me whatsoever in the two bodies in South Carolina, I began to feel a little better, knowing that they had no evidence or witnesses for that matter to tie me to Black's and Qua's murders. My lawyer said there was no reason for me to take the stand on those matters because the DA was killing himself. Even my lawyer really began to believe in me. Once my lawyer said no comment at this time, the DA preceded with the murder charges from Jersey.

The description of those deaths was so accurate when he spoke I wondered how Betty knew all that. *She must've followed us to the abandoned building and watched.* "Sneaky bitch," I said under my breath.

When he spoke about how we had set Black up on South Second and snatched Quadir up on Sycamore, I knew Betty had to have seen us from her window and started following us then. As he finished his story, which he addressed to the jury, his next words almost caused me to choke. He told the judge that he wanted to call a witness. I looked at him, dumbfounded. He had this stupid grin on his face as to say, "Gotcha," as they called the witness's name.

"Your Honor, I'd like to call Mr."—when he said Mr. instead of Ms. or Mrs. I knew who it was—"Shareef Richards to the stand."

If there were ever a time I wanted to kill myself now would've been it. I couldn't believe my ears. I grilled Shareef as they brought him out handcuffed to the front with a suit on. He was serving forty with a twenty-year stip for blowing trial on those cases. His record made him eligible for an extended term. The same cases that I tried to get the dudes not to come to court on. Now here he was taking the stand on me. He couldn't even look at me while he was on the stand telling everything that happened verbatim. All I could wonder about was how much time they had offered to knock off his sentence for selling his soul and selling me out. It wasn't until the DA asked him if he saw the man in the courtroom who was with him the night of the murders that he looked in my direction and pointed at me. I began to perspire heavily.

"No further questions, Your Honor," the DA said.

My attorney did a hell of a job trying to shoot Shareef's credibility down and poke holes in his story, but one thing about the truth, it's always going to prevail, and that's what Shareef had in his favor. There was no more to be said.

Without the jurors' verdict I already knew I had lost the trial. I took one last look at my pops and by the look on his face I knew that if he had a gun in the courtroom right then and there he would have gunned Shareef down.

The jurors came back from deliberating.

"Has the jury reached a verdict?"

"Yes, Your Honor, we have," a white lady said. Eight Whites and four Blacks from ages twenty-five to about sixty-five held my fate in their hands. I looked back at Lisa and shot her my signature smirk. She had her hands up to her mouth with a napkin in her hand. It was apparent she had been crying.

"On the charge of murder in the first degree of Travis Dempsey, we find the defendant, Kamil Benson, not guilty!"

It was the verdict I'd anticipated.

"On the charge of murder in the first degree of Marlon Jones, we find the defendant not guilty!"

That one I also knew. Now was the moment I had been waiting for.

"On the charge of conspiracy to commit murder in the first degree against Quadir Davis, we find the defendant, Kamil Benson, not guilty!"

I thought I had misheard her, until I saw a smile slightly come across my lawyer's face.

"On the charge of conspiracy to commit murder in the first degree against Brian Taylor, we find the defendant not guilty!"

I didn't even smile or cheer; instead, I began to shed tears. They were tears of joy, because for some reason my life had been spared.

Shareef wasn't in the courtroom when the verdict was announced, but it didn't matter because I wasn't even mad at him anymore seeing as how his flipping on me didn't work. The judge said some things that I couldn't even hear and then he banged his gravel to dismiss the court. They escorted me out after I shook Mr. Schmidt's hand and thanked him.

As I was leaving I saw Lisa exiting the court-room. That day I thought that she was the angel God had sent down to oversee my trial and protect me. I heard my lawyer tell the DA that he'd be talking to him, as he and my father walked out together.

My lawyer told me the next day the DA offered me a plea of 264 months, providing that I handed over at least a million dollars they were sure I had tucked away somewhere. I consulted with my lawyer and he advised me to take it if I had the money because the offers wouldn't get any better than that, only worse, so I agreed. I gave them the address of where I had the bulk of my money stashed. I'd rather be broke and able to see light at the end of the tunnel than rich and sitting in prison for the rest of my life.

I was sentenced to twenty-two years in federal prison. I called my moms and told them how much time I had gotten, and they went crazy as if I had gotten life. They didn't understand that for 350 Gs to my lawyer, beating four bodies, handing over a million plus dollars, and only getting twenty-two years for drugs was a blessing in disguise. I'd be nearly fifty years old by the time I came home, just in time to see my grandkids grow up. That was better than a life bid any day.

When I called Tia to tell her she didn't take it so bad. I wondered how many years I'd get out of her before she flipped too; because that was all a part of this game we played in. Nothing in the game was guaranteed. You're loved for the moment.

Before the phone was about to hang up, Tia asked me what she was supposed to tell my son when he start asking for me. I told her to tell him the Bad People had me right now. . . .